PRAISE FOR THE NOVELS
OF JUDITH KINGHORN

"A gripping tale of family secrets, and a comedy of manners. . . . Historical fiction fans will not want to miss this gem!"

—Renée Rosen, author of *White Collar Girl*

"An absolutely delicious book . . . elegant and evocative to the last word."

—Elizabeth Cooke, author of *The Gates of Rutherford*

"Mysterious, evocative, and deeply sensual . . . this moving story is not to be missed."

—Simone St. James, RITA Award–winning author of
Lost Among the Living

"Lucinda Riley's readers will enjoy Kinghorn's manipulation of the story's timeline, fans of Sarah Jio will adore the novel's romantic backbone, and historical fiction readers will appreciate Kinghorn's eye for authentic period details."

—*Booklist*

"Kinghorn vividly depicts the turmoil of the postwar period. . . . Those who love the blockbuster show *Downton Abbey* will find much to enjoy."

—Historical Novel Society

"A touching, thought-provoking, and compelling read. Kinghorn evokes the years before the war as she skillfully envelops the reader in her imaginative, tragic tale."

—*RT Book Reviews* (4½ stars)

"Exquisite . . . a sensual and visual feast of a story."

—*Lancashire Evening Post* (UK)

"A glorious read, highly recommended."

—*The Bookseller* (UK)

"Judith Kinghorn has beautifully captured the thoughts and feelings of a particular group in a lost generation. . . . Above all a wonderful and heartbreaking love story . . . highly recommended!"   —One More Page (UK)

Also by Judith Kinghorn

The Last Summer
The Memory of Lost Senses
The Snow Globe

The
ECHO *of*
TWILIGHT

JUDITH KINGHORN

BERKLEY
NEW YORK

BERKLEY
An imprint of Penguin Random House LLC
375 Hudson Street, New York, New York 10014

Copyright © 2017 by Judith Kinghorn
Readers Guide copyright © 2017 by Penguin Random House LLC

BERKLEY is a registered trademark and the B colophon is a trademark of
Penguin Random House LLC.

Library of Congress Cataloging-in-Publication Data

Names: Kinghorn, Judith, author.
Title: The echo of twilight/Judith Kinghorn.
Description: First edition. | New York: Berkley Books, 2017. |
Identifiers: LCCN 2016019604 (print) | LCCN 2016027145 (ebook) |
ISBN 9780451472106 (paperback) | ISBN 9780698177864 (ebook)
Subjects: | BISAC: FICTION/Historical. | FICTION/Family Life. |
FICTION/War & Military.
Classification: LCC PR6111.I59 E28 2017 (print) | LCC PR6111.I59 (ebook) |
DDC 823/.92—dc23
LC record available at https://lccn.loc.gov/2016019604

First Edition: January 2017

Printed in the United States of America
1 3 5 7 9 10 8 6 4 2

Cover photographs: woman © Richard Jenkins Photography; sky by
John Lund/Getty Images
Cover design by Colleen Reinhart
Book design by Alissa Theodor

For my father, William

The
ECHO *of*
TWILIGHT

"Things will happen which will trample and pierce, but I shall go on, something that is here and there like the wind, something unconquerable, something not to be separated from the dark earth and the light sky, a strong citizen of infinity and eternity."

—Edward Thomas

PART ONE

Chapter One

Memory is a cruel thing. It lingers in dark trenches, whispering, or withholding, waiting to creep into the no-man's-land of our dreams. It knows what we long to remember, and what we hope to forget. And it knows Hearsay and Imagination will cover any gaps.

But I knew only what I had been told.

It was a golden evening in August when my mother came untethered. And the river must have shimmered as she walked into it, under it. And the water must have soothed and washed away her pain. And as her life ebbed, before her heart stopped and the high tide carried her upstream, she must have thought of me, surely? For it was the same golden evening I was born.

That my beginning coincided with my mother's end often made me wonder about a continuum, whether the passion that flooded her senses that day had leaked into me, whether my name, too, would one day be unutterable. But Kitty assured me that I was not like my mother, and it was not my birth that had unanchored her, she said; illicit love had been her undoing.

Kitty was my great-aunt, and the woman who brought me up, and in this and most other things she was right: I was not like my mother. By the time I was twenty-three, I had a respectable career and was almost engaged to be married. By the time I was twenty-three, I had lived in five different counties, and had at that time a vague notion to try all of them, every county in England. In fact, it was the mention of *travel* that drew me to the advertisement—and the timing was fortuitous.

Only a few days later, Mrs. Bart tearfully informed me that she was to move in with her sister. Naturally, I didn't tell her I'd already applied for a new position. I said how sorry I was, and she told me that she and Mister Darcy were very sad, too. This was a blatant lie. I knew the incontinent pug hated me as much as I hated it. But Mrs. Bart said she would make sure I was remunerated for the inconvenience and promised me an excellent letter of character.

My year with the old lady had served a purpose. A widow of straitened means, she had not minded "breaking me in," as she put it, and her penchant for elocution and French phrases had not been wasted. But in truth, I'd been more of a companion than a lady's maid to Mrs. Bart, or perhaps more of a *hearer*, because she liked me to listen. She would spill out her life without chronology or explanation until she went very still and quiet and there was nothing left, until the next day, when a dream or half-forgotten object triggered another great wave and she was returned to the Dorset of her childhood, her descriptions so rapturous that I was reminded about endings and beginnings, for Mrs. Bart, nearing her own end and closing the circle, had gone back to her beginning.

It was Mrs. Bart who gave me *The Private Shadow*, a sort of lady's maid's handbook in pamphlet form that she'd found in a secondhand bookshop. Aside from the old-fashioned jargon and some obsolete customs, a lot of what it said was common sense, for any position in service dictated honesty, tact and propriety of demeanor as requisite qualities. Common sense, too, that *A lady's maid must be neat in her person*, and that she should speak pleasantly and quietly, and be able to read and write well. And though at first I liked the title and the line from which it came—*A lady's maid is the private shadow of her mistress*—the bit that came after, *She is seldom seen or heard*, bothered me. A private shadow that was seldom seen or heard sounded more like a ghost than a maid.

I traveled up to London by train for my interview at the Empress Club on Dover Street. It was, I'd learned from Mrs. B., generally regarded as the most prestigious and luxurious of all the ladies' clubs in London. She had reminded me about my diaphragm, to stand up straight, look the person in the eye and breathe when I spoke—*in . . . and out . . . and in . . . and out . . .* And she had also told me to make sure not to lapse back into a London *F*. But she was exaggerating; I'd never had a London *F*—though Stanley did, and he got irritated whenever I pointed it out to him. "*Th*, Stanley," I'd say, pressing my tongue to my teeth as Mrs. B. had taught me. "It's *think . . .* not *fink*."

Lady Ottoline took only a moment to appear in the lobby once she was summoned. Smiling, she extended her hand. "Ottoline Campbell."

"Pearl Gibson, Your Ladyship."

I wasn't altogether sure of the correct etiquette, but I offered a slight curtsy. It seemed the right thing to do on introduction to a Lady. And she appeared to appreciate the gesture, for her smile softened and she said to me, "What a very pretty hat."

When I told her I'd made each one of the silk cherries myself, Lady Ottoline clasped her hands and opened her eyes wider: "Ah, so you're rather clever with a needle. That *is* reassuring to know."

She was a tall woman, and handsome, with fine pale skin and heavily lidded almond-shaped brown eyes. Her dark hair was only just beginning to fade at the temples, and she had the distracted air—a glance over my shoulder, a stifled yawn—of someone slightly bored by life.

"Please come this way," she said.

I followed the sweet scent of gardenia through a long lounge where a band was playing and footmen carrying tea trays moved hither and thither. And noting Her Ladyship's exemplary deportment, her long neck, her back as straight as Lord Nelson's Column, I extended my own self farther as we entered another room, not quite so palatial.

The rustle of silk chiffon came to a stop. "Do take a seat, Miss Gibson."

A number of women were scattered about the room, quietly reading or writing letters, and a low murmuring from the far side led my gaze to another girl like me being interviewed by a silver-haired woman wearing a pince-nez and bearing no resemblance to Lady Ottoline. The girl and I exchanged a quick glance, and I knew what she was thinking: *You got the nice one.*

"So, you've come from Bournemouth?"

"Yes, Your Ladyship, but I was actually born in London."

"Ah, you weren't a MABYS girl, were you?"

I knew this term and knew it didn't stand for *Mind and Behave Yourself* as some of the girls I'd worked with said. The abbreviation stood for the Metropolitan Association for Befriending Young Servants, an organization set up to train girls from workhouses, in order to discourage them from becoming prostitutes or alcoholics and turn them into good servants.

"No, I wasn't," I said, sitting up straighter in the large leather chair. "I went into service directly after school, Your Ladyship."

Lady Ottoline's smile faded and she lowered her eyes, and for a moment I thought she appeared disappointed. But then she went on, asking me about my experience to date, and I told her how I'd started out in Kent and had worked my way up. She asked me for my letters of character, and I handed them to her one by one, saving the best until last.

"Gracious," she said, raising her eyes from Mrs. B.'s elaborate hand. "I don't believe I've ever read such a . . . an effusive letter of recommendation."

Mrs. B. had kindly allowed me to read through her first draft of her letter, and to assist her with the penning of a second. I suggested only three changes: replacing the word *excellent* with *exemplary*, *valued* with *treasured*, and *regret* with *grief*.

Lady Ottoline folded the page and handed it back to me. She inquired about my personal circumstances. I told her I had no family to speak of. I knew better than to tell her about Stanley—and anyway, the somewhat unresolved issue of our engagement remained a private matter.

"I see," she said. "And no suitors?"

"None, Your Ladyship."

"*Quel dommage* . . . Though perhaps not for me," she added, twinkling and smiling. "You see, I require someone who is able to commit . . . and for at least two years . . ."

"That's not a problem. I'm looking for something long-term now."

Lady Ottoline smiled again. The position, she said, came with an annual salary of thirty-eight pounds and ten shillings, which could be paid either monthly or quarterly, and, of course, all accommodation and living expenses would be taken care of in the usual way. As well as every other Sunday off, I'd be allowed up to five days paid holiday a year, rising to ten days after two full years.

She recited all of this very quickly in a slightly breathless voice, and I was still computing the numbers, comparing them to my paltry wage and still-unknown terms of employment with Mrs. B., when she asked, "How does that sound to you, Miss Gibson?"

"Oh yes, that sounds fine, Your Ladyship."

"Forgive me for speaking plainly, but I do have one slight concern . . . and that is that you've moved about rather a lot."

"Only to get on . . . to see a bit of the world and move up the ranks, Your Ladyship."

"Understandable. Commendable, I suppose . . ."

She glanced around her in that distracted manner and then looked up to the ceiling. Scattered across the decorative moldings was a myriad of glinting lights reflected from the crystal drops of the vast chandelier. "Just like stars," I said, thinking aloud.

"Mm . . . aren't they?"

"You know, I saw a shooting star only three nights ago, and so I made a wish. Because you have to, don't you—when you see a shooting star? My great-aunt used to say, *If wishes were horses, beggars would ride,*" I added, laughing.

She fixed her eyes on me in a newly curious manner. Perhaps she thought me a bit simple, or perhaps she was waiting for me to tell her what I'd wished for, and I certainly wasn't about to do that.

"So," she said with sudden emphasis, "do you study the Fashions, Miss Gibson?"

"Oh yes, all of them."

She took in my hat once more as well as the flower corsage I'd copied from the *Lady's Pictorial* and had pinned to the lapel of my jacket. *"Et parlez-vous français, mademoiselle?"*

A *petty pear,* I thought. *"Oui, madame*—Your Ladyship. *Un peu . . . mais pas très bien."*

"Do you follow current events, read the newspapers?"

I thought for a moment. Kitty was the one who had told me not to believe anything printed in them. She said the people who worked for them were paid to make up bad news and that they had contributed in no small part to my poor mother's demise.

I said, "I prefer to read novels, Your Ladyship."

"Ah, and whom do you like to read?"

I'd been the best reader at my church school; it was the reason I'd gained a merit upon matriculation. And so I told Her Ladyship this, and was rattling off names when she interrupted me. "I believe you mean *Miss* Eliot."

"No . . . George."

"Yes, that was the name she wrote under. An identity she assumed to ensure her work would be taken seriously. Her name was actually Mary Ann Evans." She lowered her eyes, shook her head and sighed. "Though we're supposed to be living in more enlightened times, our fight is far from over . . . And yet, I can't help but feel our day is coming. Don't you, Miss Gibson?"

I nodded. I was flattered to be included in this *our day*.

"I must say, it could be frightfully useful for me to have a reader, because, you see, I happen to write." She waved a hand in the air dismissively. "Oh, nothing too serious or highbrow, you understand . . . a few serials for the ladies' magazines, that sort of thing. It's more of a hobby than anything else, but I have an idea for a novel." She paused, tilted her head and stared past me. "Yes, a love story."

For a moment she seemed transfixed by something beyond that room: an idea, a memory or perhaps nothing at all, a yet-to-be-written page. Then she came back to me, blinked her heavy eyelids a few times, lifted the small bejeweled watch pinned to her breast and glanced down at it.

"Do you have any questions, Miss Gibson?"

I did.

"The advertisement mentioned travel, Your Ladyship. And I was wondering . . . travel to where?"

"Our itinerary is always rather busy," she said, and went on to mention her husband, Lord Hector; a Foreign Office somewhere; a house in London and another in Northumberland; Paris, Biarritz, the French Riviera, Switzerland and St. Moritz; and she smiled as she said, "But we tend to spend our summers in Scotland." And when she said the name of a place, I envisioned a castle.

"I have two more girls from Mrs. Warren's registry to interview this afternoon," said Lady Ottoline, concluding the interview, "so if you'd like to go and do some sightseeing or shopping and come back here at . . . around five o'clock? I'll be able to tell you my decision then."

"I'm afraid I can't do that, Your Ladyship. I have another interview at five o'clock."

"I see," she said, eyeing me. She waited a moment. "Your interview, is it by chance with Lady Hanbury?"

"No, Your Ladyship."

"Lady Desborough?"

I shook my head.

"It's not with Mrs. Asquith, is it? I hear she's looking again."

"If you don't mind, Your Ladyship, I'd rather not say."

Lady Ottoline smiled. "I'm very pleased about that. Discretion is my first and foremost requirement."

Chapter Two

Stanley was waiting as arranged by the statue of Eros at five o'clock, reading the newspaper, in his good suit and cap.

"Hello, handsome."

He folded the crumpled sheets beneath his creased sleeve and stared at me as I looked about and allowed him time to take me in. I was used to this initial awkwardness; it happened every time we met, but after a few moments I turned to him. "Well?"

"You look nice."

"What's it say?" I asked, nodding to the paper under his arm.

"The usual doom and gloom . . . Some archduke's been assassinated."

The air was warm and his face was damp. Beneath the brim of his cap his pale skin shone with beads of sweat, and there was a scab at one side of his mustache where he'd cut himself shaving. I hadn't seen him in more than two months, not since he'd last come down to Bournemouth. It had been a Sunday, my usual day off, and despite the cold wind blowing in off the sea, we'd walked back and forth along the promenade and up and down the pier. Everything was closed and we had nowhere to go, but I kept myself warm imagining a time when we might.

It was a queer notion, a home of my own, because I'd never really had one. I'd spent the first few years of my life under my grandfather's tin roof; then, after he passed away, Kitty and I had moved into lodgings, and I shared a room and a bed with her until I went into service.

"*Veez-a-veez* the tea dance . . . ," Stanley began. He liked speaking in Latin—at least I think it was Latin; he'd told me it was. "I'm afraid they're a bit on the pricey side. And so is the Trocadero."

I'd met Stanley when I'd worked at a place on the outskirts of Winchester in Hampshire. I'd been a parlormaid and he'd been a footman, and—literally—on his way out. And I'm proud to say our romance didn't start until after he'd left the household and begun writing to me from London.

"So where shall we go?" I asked. "I've only got an hour or so before I need to head to the station."

"Well, there's always the A.B.C."

I sometimes wondered if I built Stanley Morton up into something more than he was, if it suited me to have an *absent* sweetheart. Because despite Kitty's *Absence makes the heart grow fonder,* and despite his good looks, there was often an element of disappointment in the reality of him. It wasn't that I wanted a poet, and I didn't really care about the Trocadero, but he might have thought to buy me some flowers—a bunch of violets, or a single rose, perhaps—from the flower seller a few yards away. And he might have planned where we could go, what we could do in place of his long-promised tea dance.

I said, "Fine, let's go to the A.B.C."

I'd once told Mrs. B. of my concern about Stanley's lack of imagination. It wasn't long after he'd mentioned marriage. Not that he proposed; he'd simply said, "Maybe we'll get married one day." I suppose it was more of a philosophical statement. Mrs. B. advised me not to set my expectations too high in that department. She told me that, in her experience, the masculine mind lacked the propensity for imagination. And bearing in mind she'd had five brothers, three sons and two husbands, I reckoned she probably knew more than most when it came to understanding *the masculine mind*.

In truth, I had a whole two hours before my train to Bournemouth, but I didn't want Stanley getting any ideas about going to the pictures. We'd done that the last time I'd come up to meet him, and it had been an ordeal: trying to concentrate on Mary Pickford's heartbreak with Stanley Morton's hands where they shouldn't have been and his tongue in my ear. Afterward, we'd had words. He'd told me that *it* was only *what any normal fellow expects*, and that there were plenty of girls who liked *it*. Fine, I said; go with one of them. I'd known plenty of them, too: girls who'd go with men for the price of a cheap dress, then ten months later give away a baby. Poor fallen creatures like my mother.

As we walked toward Shaftesbury Avenue, as I linked my arm through Stanley's, he said, "So, how'd it go with Lady Otterby?"

"*Ottoline*. Her name is Ottoline. And she's a lot younger than Mrs. B."

"How old?"

"Not sure . . . late thirties, maybe forty."

"Nice?"

I nodded.

"And you want it?"

"I wouldn't have come all the way up here if I didn't want it."

"Ha, and there's me thinking it was just an excuse to come and see me."

My little white lie about another interview had at first thrown Lady Ottoline. But it had also offered me an opportunity to pass a test—*her* test—on discretion. She didn't normally offer jobs on the spot, she said; she liked to "cogitate." I didn't say anything. Her *cogitation* sounded like a private matter to me. But my silence paid off, and after some shuffling and rustling, a glance about the room and then back at me, a queer little laugh and then a sigh, she said, "When would you be able to start?"

And so that was that. Seeing me to the lobby, Lady Ottoline shook my hand and told me she'd put everything in writing and send it out to me in that evening's post.

"I got it," I said to Stanley. "I got the job."

He stopped dead in his tracks: "She offered it to you there and then?"

I smiled. "She said she had no reason to look any further. I was perfect for the position."

The A.B.C. was packed and we were lucky to get a table. We had lamb chops, mashed potatoes, cabbage and peas, and bread and butter and tea, of course. I didn't have a pudding, but Stanley had the apple pie and custard. It has to be said, the A.B.C. did a decent high tea—and it suited Stanley's pocket. Working as a doorman at the Café Royal didn't pay a great deal. He'd been there for more than two years, standing about, watching people come and go. When he'd first started, he'd had ideas about moving up, becoming a concierge, even going into management. But now that didn't seem likely. Recently, he'd talked about looking for office work, a clerical position of some sort, but as far as I knew, he hadn't done anything about it.

"I have to hand it to you, Pearl," said Stanley, licking custard off the back of his spoon, "you're a one. I mean, coming up here and snapping up a position—just like that." He shook his head. "I bet there's hundreds of girls out there who've never been offered a job there and then from the likes of Otterby."

"*Ottoline*, Stanley. Her name is—"

"You're a bloody liar, Walter Giddings!" A woman at an adjacent table slammed down her cup and rose to her feet. She stood perfectly still for a moment as Walter Giddings continued to blow smoke rings up at the ceiling. Then she marched off across the packed room and toward the door, and Walter Giddings never so much as turned his head.

She was better off without him.

I looked back at Stanley. "As I was saying, her name is Ottoline. Lady Ottoline Campbell. She wants me to start as soon as possible . . . I'll be moving about, traveling quite a bit . . . France, Northumberland—"

"*Northumberland?*" Stanley interrupted. "That's Scotland."

I smiled. "Not quite—but I'll be going there, too. They have a place in Scotland as well."

It was better to get it all over with in one go, especially now he'd eaten. Men were always more docile once they had food inside them, Mrs. B. said. Stanley didn't say much at all after that, and I settled the bill. I knew he was a little short, had not yet been paid. As I rose from the table, I made a point of narrowing my eyes at Walter Giddings. And he smiled and winked at me.

"What a player *he* was."

"Who's that?"

"*Walter Giddings* . . . I just hope she doesn't take him back."

I slipped my arm through Stanley's, and we walked on beneath the dirty-leafed trees, retracing our steps toward Piccadilly Circus and the Underground station. We both stopped when we heard his name, both turned, and then Stanley quickly pulled away his arm.

"Is this your sister, then?" the girl asked, all breathless and pink cheeked.

"Oh no . . . No, this is Miss Gibson. We used to work together."

"Ah, like us," said the girl. She threw the stick of her ice lolly down on the pavement and wiped her hands on her skirt. "Pleased to meet you."

Her hand was sticky. I smiled.

"Eileen—Miss Poynter," said Stanley, "works over at the hotel."

"For my sins," said Eileen, affecting a grimace and rolling her eyes heavenward. Then she looked back at Stanley. "So, has your sister already gone, then, Stan?"

Stanley's eyelids fluttered. "We must get on," he said, taking hold of my arm. "Miss Gibson has a train to catch."

"Oh . . . I see. Well, nice to meet you . . . See you later, Stan."

"You and Eileen Poynter seem on very familiar terms," I said as we neared the steps down to the Underground.

He laughed. "Not jealous, are you?"

"No. But why did she think I was your sister?"

"Haven't the foggiest."

"Did you tell her you had a sister?"

We were right by the steps, and he stopped and turned to me: "Of course I didn't tell her I had a sister . . . To be honest, I think she's a bit touched."

"Oh?"

"They have endless problems with her at work . . . getting her to remember stuff. Hopeless. Hopeless, she is."

"But why did she say, 'See you later'? You said you weren't going into work tonight."

"It's a figure of speech, isn't it? *See you later?* Gawd blimey, Pearl, it's like the Spanish Inquisition with you." He pulled out his handkerchief, pushed back his cap and wiped his brow. He raised his eyes to the overcast sky. "Feels like *funder.*"

"*Th . . . th*under."

We stood for a few minutes, glancing about and not at each other, watching the pigeons pecking at litter-strewn flagstones, the flower seller packing up her stall, the newspaper boy as he called out about the murdered archduke.

"Well, I'd best get on," I said.

"Right you are."

"I'll drop you a line as soon as I know what's what."

"Yes, do that."

"And I'll send you the address . . . You will write to me, won't you?"

"Naturally."

"Good-bye, then."

He lowered his head and kissed my cheek. "Toodle-oo . . . Safe journey."

I wanted him to say something more. I wanted him to say, *Don't forget I'm very fond of you*—like he'd said last time—but he didn't. And though I turned to wave to him as I descended the steps, he'd already gone. And almost immediately I felt regret, and almost immediately I felt that familiar longing. I wished I'd told him the truth about my train, wished I'd allowed him to take me to a picture house and then accompany me to the station. If I had, perhaps he'd have told me he loved me. Because, you see, no one ever had, not even Kitty.

Chapter Three

And yet the whole kindly phase of my early life was due to her, my Kitty. And I can still see her, hear her and feel the warmth of her papery hand against my cheek.

Kitty. She was white haired and wise by the time I was born. And I was perhaps four and almost the same height as the range when she reordered my universe and explained to me that she was not in fact my mother, but that I had once, very briefly, been in possession of one. There was no mention of any father, not then. But a few years later, shortly after my grandfather—Kitty's brother—passed away, and at a stage in my life when I hungered for answers, she told me I had also had a father. I knew from her tone that he, too, was gone, and I asked her two simple questions: *Was he a nice man?* She couldn't say; she had never known him. *What was his name?* She couldn't recall; it was a long time ago.

Revelations can only be deemed such if they actually *reveal* something, and for me, the knowledge that I had had a mother *and* a father, and that I was, it seemed, just like everyone else, offered only a vague sense of disappointment. My parents were nothing more than nameless, featureless shapes floating in the dim and distant past, but I felt no sadness or grief, because I had never known them, and I had Kitty.

I'm not sure how old I was when I realized that my mother had not walked to the twilit Thames for a paddle after my birth, but had gone there to submerge herself and take her own life. I'm not sure how old I was when I realized my parents had not been married. But Kitty must have said something, or alluded to the fact, for I knew and understood the shame, and why it pained her to speak about my mother, her niece. I understood that the *things best not spoken of* were in fact only two people.

Thus, my mother's name was rarely if ever mentioned, and my father's never at all. My childhood and adolescence became concertinaed, its folds harboring the debris of unconcluded lives, lives I had no desire to emulate. Like Kitty, I tried not to dwell on the torment of my mother's final moments; like Kitty, I elected to spare my father from judgment by forgetting he'd ever existed.

Like Kitty . . .

Without a penny to her name, my Kitty was always neat and tidy. She was proud, dignified, abstemious and God-fearing. Old-fashioned, inherently superstitious, she appeared unconflicted by her pagan rituals and her devotion to God: watching the skies for signs and portents of doom or good fortune; habitually throwing salt over her shoulder, knocking on wood or saluting magpies; and rejoicing at the sight of a shooting star or four tiny leaves of a clover. She was the sweetest mass of contradictions with her pity for the poor and her awe of the gentry, her love of finery and her frugality, her mischievous humor and her priggishness. And in the absence of knowledge, she always fell back on a proverb.

In fact, Kitty was as good at proverbs as I was at upping sticks and moving county. Something better always lay in the next one, my destiny in *destination*. And so, like a small star in transit and at the mercy of the universe, I impaled myself on fate. And fate now had a name: Ottoline. Thus, ten days after my interview, I found myself back in London, but not to stay; I was, as they say, passing through.

And I was idling over a cup of tea in a far corner of the refreshment room at King's Cross station, watching people come and go and wondering where they were all headed and why. I was thinking about Stanley and the letter I'd written to him days before, and the half crown Mrs. B. had pushed into my hand along with an orange and her blessing, and wondering whether Northumberland would have any decent shops, and if Biarritz would be the place for a big hat. I was thinking about all of this when a shock of golden hair caught my eye.

And I don't for one moment imagine I was the only person struck by the light in the drab confines of the busy refreshment room that day. I don't for one moment imagine I was the only person drawn to an aura so bright, it was as though the sun itself had settled on *him* to do its work. For he shone, and around him emanated a warmth like nothing I had ever experienced.

He wore no hat, no tie, and was dressed in the pale colors of warmer climes, his clothes creased and disheveled from what had undoubtedly been a long journey, and had a dusty knapsack slung over one shoulder, a well-worn leather portmanteau in his hand. A colonial, I thought, watching him as he sat down, perhaps returned home from India for a while.

Bent over his paper, an elbow resting on the table, palm against his forehead, tanned fingers in his hair, he struck the pose of one of those ancient sculptures Stanley and I had seen at the British Museum. One of those sculptures cordoned off by a thick red rope. One of those sculptures I had longed to reach out and touch.

From time to time he glanced up and around, as though to check on who was there. Was he waiting for someone—a woman, perhaps? Was there to be a longed-for reconciliation, there, in the refreshment room? I longed for *her* to appear—to see what she looked like, witness their meeting; but in my distraction I had forgotten the time, and so reluctantly, hot and a little flustered, I rose to my feet and weaved my way through the scattered tables and chairs, and past him. But outside, as I stood staring upward, searching the board for my train, a deep male voice said, "Please allow me to be of assistance."

Standing under a shaft of sunlight, his hair brighter than ever, he smiled as he picked up my case. "I'm not surprised you were struggling with this . . . I hope there's not a body in here."

I tried to laugh. Inside my case were eleven novels, two volumes of poetry, my Bible and prayer book, the encyclopedia and *Guide to Wildflowers* Mrs. B. had given me, my two work skirts and blouses, a day gown and Sunday frock, an alarm clock, my wash bag, the brush and mirror Kitty had left to me, my nightdress, Kitty's shawl, my winter coat and boots, a pair of galoshes and an empty photograph frame I'd won in the League of Pity raffle. Inside my suitcase was everything I owned.

"Where to?" he asked.

"Platform one . . . Newcastle."

"Follow me."

And so I did: past the bookstall, porters and barrows, through the sea of caps and straw boaters, frothy gowns and foaming skirts, onto the hot, bustling platform.

"Carriage?"

"Second."

"Best take the one furthest away, don't you think? More chance of having a compartment to yourself."

I was a little disconcerted as he marched ahead of me down the platform with my suitcase, and I had to take small running steps in order to keep up, weaving my way through ticketed perambulators and bicycles, initialed trunks being loaded into the guard's carriage. We were almost at the opposite end of the train when he looked back at me over his shoulder: "This one?"

I nodded.

He gestured to the open carriage door, followed me on board and—sure enough—into an empty compartment. And after he had placed my suitcase on the luggage rack, I thanked him and he smiled. "Stedman," he said, extending a hand. "Ralph Stedman."

I gave him my white-gloved hand. "Ottoline Campbell."

His eyes widened. "*Ottoline Campbell*," he repeated. "And will you be traveling onward from Newcastle, Miss . . . Mrs. Campbell?"

"*Miss*," I said, and then I paused. "Yes, indeed—I'm on my way to visit my dear old aunt in Northumberland."

"Ah, a short visit, then."

"Unfortunately so . . . My itinerary is always rather busy."

His eyes had an almost fierce life in them. They were neither brown nor green nor blue nor hazel, but tawny, and framed by pale lashes and thick sun-bleached brows.

"And where to after Northumberland—back to London?"

I looked away from him, removed my gloves. "Yes, back to dreary old London, but only for a short while, and then to Biarritz."

"Biarritz? I was there only a week ago—on my way home from Spain. But when are you planning to travel? I only ask because . . . well, many of our compatriots are heading back to England."

"Really?"

"I think you might be well advised to delay your trip, wait a while . . . see how the current crisis plays out."

"Yes, possibly," I said, glancing away again, vague and unsure what else to say.

"You know, your name's very familiar. Have we perhaps met before—in Biarritz?"

I pondered this for only a very short time before shaking my head. "No. I don't believe so."

"Paris?"

I glanced up at the ceiling and blinked. "I think I'd remember if we'd met in Paris, Mr. Stedman."

"Quite so—how can one ever forget those encountered *there?*"

I laughed. He stared.

"You aren't by any chance related to Lord Hector Campbell, are you?" he asked.

I tapped a finger on my chin, shook my head again. "No . . . I'm afraid that name doesn't ring any bells at all."

Conflicted, panicking, I wondered if he intended to take a seat in that compartment, if I'd have to *be* Ottoline and make conversation with him about Biarritz, compatriots and crises all the way to Newcastle. I said, "Will you be traveling on this train, Mr. Stedman?"

He nodded: "All the way to Edinburgh. Third class."

My heart sank. For the first time in my life and thanks to the woman whose name I had borrowed, I was traveling in second. Now I wished I were plain Pearl Gibson and in third, with Ralph Stedman.

He picked up his bag. "I shall leave you in peace now, Miss Campbell, but it's been a pleasure . . . A *bientôt*."

I couldn't recall what this meant, but it sounded French and so I said, "*Bon voyage*, Mr. Stedman."

The light seemed to dim a little as the door slid closed, and exhausted from the encounter and yet strangely elated at the same time, I took my seat. My habit of assuming another identity when traveling had got me into scrapes before, and I'd vowed never to do it again after traveling to Dorset as Tess Durbeyfield. I'd not long finished reading the novel, was still thinking of it and *her*, and simply didn't imagine anyone—least of all the two old matrons I'd sat next to—would think anything. But whispered repetitions of that name had rippled through the warm carriage like a soft summer breeze. And amidst intermittent sniggering, I'd stepped down from the train long before we ever reached Bournemouth—then had to wait more than an hour for another.

It wasn't unusual for girls like me—girls in service—to put on airs and graces, to adopt the habits and mannerisms of those commonly known as their betters. I'd known quite a few who were breathtakingly good impersonators, able to mimic the style, accent

and subtle nuances of the ladies of the house so that if you didn't
know better, you'd never know it wasn't them. And Mrs. B.'s in-
struction had certainly paid off. Even she said my vowels were quite
perfect, that I could easily be mistaken for a real young lady. And
I was thinking on this, and halfheartedly practicing my A, *E, I, O,
U* sounds, when the train began to move and the door opened.
And I quickly lowered my feet.

"I say, don't mind if I join you?"

The gentleman sat down, removed his hat, placed a monocle up
against one eye and shook open his newspaper. There was a "Grand
Summer Sale" at Peter Robinson, and carpets were reduced at War-
ing and Gillow.

"News, eh? Damned worrying business, what?"

"Yes, indeed . . . I suppose we'll just have to see how the current
crisis plays out," I said, smiling at factories and chimneys, all sunlit
brick and corrugated metal.

"*Plays out?*" The man lowered his paper and leaned forward.
"My dear girl, we're not talking about a piano concerto . . . What
we're confronted with is a potential catastrophe!"

He shook his head and disappeared behind his newspaper once
more, and I wished he hadn't come into that—my—compartment
with his bad breath and talk of catastrophes. And as the train
picked up speed and line upon line of neat little houses drifted by,
and hoping I wouldn't have to engage in any further conversation
with the man, I settled back and closed my eyes . . .

*I am wearing rouge and my lips are painted. I see his face in the tall
glass opposite me, and I turn as he says, "Darling."*

"*Ralph!*"

He has walked all the way from Spain for our rendezvous in this bar at Biarritz, and his mouth is parched and dry when we kiss.

"I need to be with you alone," he murmurs . . .

I was still in Mr. Stedman's arms—and trying to be virtuous—when Mr. Catastrophe released a loud snort. His head fell forward; his monocle slipped; his newspaper slid to the floor. And outside, the tidy green squares of England flew by.

Chapter Four

What immediately struck me about Northumberland was the quality of the light, the vastness of the sky. It stretched all the way down to the earth—like a great canopy, pegged and anchored into the empty land. That peculiar luminosity left little room for shadows and Northumberland was, I decided there and then, the brightest county I had so far visited, though I had heard tell from Mrs. B. and others of the shimmering light and frequent rainbows to be witnessed in the Lake District, and of the long summer twilights in Scotland.

As instructed, I had taken a branch line train from Newcastle northward, catching intermittent glimpses of a steel gray sea as we rattled between dismal pit villages. But after an hour or so, the landscape became softer, more familiar, a patchwork of small fields amidst rolling moor and gorse, the sea bluer against those hues of green and gold. And I was thinking, *I have traveled the length of*

England; I am at the very top of it, when the little train began to slow and I saw the sunlit ruins of a castle and knew I had reached my destination: Warkworth.

I stepped down onto the platform of a grand little station in the middle of nowhere. And though Lady Ottoline had said someone would be waiting for me, the place was quite deserted but for an oily-haired young man in uniform. He looked me up and down, and up and down again, smiling. He asked me where I was headed, told me Birling Hall wasn't far, a twenty-minute walk at the most, and offered me directions. "You can leave that here," he said in a strange guttural accent, nodding to my suitcase. "I'll look after it till one of 'em comes to fetch it, eh?" he added, staring at my chest.

And so I set off into the dusty afternoon, serenaded by an incessant hum from hedgerows and squawks from seagulls circling above the adjacent fields. The roadside verges were thick with nettles and thistles, and wildflowers I was able to name: cow parsley, foxglove, daisy and bloody cranesbill. Above them, the air was filled with small orange-tipped butterflies. And stopping every few yards to put down my case, I cursed my books, for my arms ached from their weight.

I had been walking for longer than twenty minutes when I sat down on my case to empty my shoes of grit. Strands of hair stuck to my forehead and neck. My once white gloves were now gray, my blouse damp beneath my woolen jacket. And ahead of me the road stretched on and on, a line of molten silver. But in the distance, nestled among lambent trees and like a mirage, I saw the blurred shape of a building—part of a stone facade, rooftops and chimneys.

Each house I'd worked at had been different. Mrs. B.'s—a brick-built Victorian villa with far-reaching sea views—was without doubt the most modest, but also the warmest. Perhaps because, as Mrs. B. claimed, it caught *the tail end* of the Gulf Stream, or perhaps because of the contrast to the house I was at before. That place, the one in Hampshire, had been falling down about our ears—without any electricity or bathrooms, and riddled with damp. In winter, there was as much ice on the inside of the windows as on the outside. Birling Hall, I saw as I approached, was easily as big as the place I'd worked at in Kent, and grew bigger and bigger as I neared it.

The wrought-iron gates were open, and I stood for a moment beneath the tall beeches that lined the driveway. I was feeling light-headed and my mouth was parched. One of my heels was blistered and painful, and I longed to take off my shoes. Across the striped lawns, the pampas grass waved its plumes, and a horse-drawn delivery wagon moved in and out of shadows down another driveway. And beyond that, in the distance, and framed by two great Wellingtonia trees, I saw a thin steel line of sea.

I walked on toward the house. Its stone was weather-beaten and dark, and though many of the windows were open—some with blinds half drawn down—there were no signs of life within. But anyone might have been watching me, I knew, so I held myself tall and tried not to limp as I approached the carriage sweep, and then walked past a highly polished motorcar to the stone-pillared entrance. I stood firmly in the center of the large coconut mat and pulled on the bell. An inner door opened, and an austere-looking butler in the usual tailcoat and striped trousers appeared. I peeled my tongue from the roof of my mouth. *"Poll Gimsen,"* he said.

Then, happily, luckily, Lady Ottoline appeared. "Oh, my dear . . . We thought you were arriving on the four twenty-eight."

She took me by the hand, led me into the darkened hallway to a velvet-upholstered chair and asked me to take a seat. Someone handed me a glass of water, and Lady Ottoline stood back and watched as I gulped it down and the butler walked off with my suitcase. The house was entirely quiet apart from the loud ticking of a grandfather clock beneath the staircase where a bronze gong hung on a sturdy mahogany stand. On a circular table in front of me were carefully arranged copies of the *Times*, the *Morning Post*, the *Illustrated London News*, *Country Life* and the *Connoisseur*, and a *Bradshaw's Railway Timetable* and the *Postal Guide*.

"I'm so sorry, so terribly sorry you've had to walk from the station. It's not awfully far, but with a suitcase—and on a day like this . . . well, I can only apologize," said Lady Ottoline.

I can't rightly remember anyone having apologized to me before, about anything, ever, and I wasn't sure what to say. Then I heard the familiar clip-clap of paws on the marble-tiled floor and saw a little russet-colored dog with long floppy ears and bulging brown eyes. It growled at me, and I thought, *Here we go. Another one.*

"Lollipop! *Really* . . . We'll have none of that, thank you." Lady Ottoline scooped up the dog and kissed it. "This is my Lola, though I call her Lolly or Lollipop for short," she said, confusingly. "She's getting rather old—like her mummy," and she proceeded to talk to the dog as though it were a baby. "Lolly's very excited that you're here, aren't you, darling? Yes . . . yes, you are. And in a short while we're going to show Miss Gibson round the house, aren't we? Yes, we are." She glanced over at me. "Are you up to a little tour of the house?"

"Oh yes, I'm fine now, Your Ladyship." But as I rose to my feet, I winced with the pain from my heel—and she winced, too. "Just a blister," I said.

She gasped. "You must take off your shoes."

So in my stocking feet I followed that sweet scent of gardenia across cool marble and down endless carpeted corridors. And as Lady Ottoline opened the doors of big bright rooms, she gestured and turned to me. "The green drawing room, which we only ever use in winter . . . The library, of course . . . My sitting room, though I'm still not sure about this wallpaper . . . The morning room . . . The billiard room . . . The smoking room . . ." On and on it went.

I had never been in a house so opulently furnished, and it seemed to me almost too beautiful for anyone to actually live in. Each room had its own distinct character, and the whole—the gold and bronze patterned wallpapers, the sumptuous velvets and silk brocades, the polished mahogany and gilt, tasseled lamp shades, tapestries and rugs, glinting paperweights and crystal vases filled with fresh flowers—was like a work of art, a sensory feast of color and light, soft textures and scents.

"His Lordship's study . . . ," said Lady Ottoline, opening yet another door, this time onto a somber room with oak paneling, heavy dark gold curtains and a deep red and purple Turkey rug. Then, "Yes, dear, Miss Gibson has arrived—and a little earlier than we'd anticipated . . . We're doing the grand tour."

The gentleman removed his spectacles, rose to his feet and walked over to us. Distinguished-looking, he was tall and lean, with a prominent forehead, long nose and receding hairline; the tips of his mustache were beautifully waxed, and his thinning silver hair was brushed flat against his scalp and parted in a line down the center. He glanced down at my feet as he shook my hand.

"Blisters," said Ottoline, without offering any explanation as to how or why.

The gentleman grimaced. "Bad luck. Damned painful things."

Ottoline handed him the dog. "I'm afraid my husband's terribly caught up with events on the Continent," she whispered, closing the door behind us. "Isn't it all a horrendous worry?"

"A potential catastrophe, Your Ladyship."

Upstairs, on the main landing, a set of double doors led into Her Ladyship's suite of rooms: a bedroom of palatial proportion with tall south-facing windows overlooking the gardens, and draped in voluminous chintz, which matched the walls and bed-covers; a dressing room lined with bespoke cupboards and drawers; a large modern bathroom, its white china, glass and gray marble gleaming in the sunshine flooding in through yet another tall south-facing window.

"I shall talk you through my wardrobe, routine and all of that sort of thing tomorrow," said Lady Ottoline as we stepped back onto the landing and moved on.

We raced along more passageways. "Guest room, guest room . . . guest room . . . guest room . . . ," said Her Ladyship, waving a hand as we passed doors she did not bother to open. Then, up a familiar narrow staircase to an equally familiar long corridor, often called the Virgin's Wing, where the female servants' bedrooms were situated.

"You're here with the other girls, but you have the nicest room, I think. And, of course, you won't be sharing."

The room was unlike any I'd ever had, and at first I couldn't believe it was for me. Like Her Ladyship's room, it was south facing. The sun streamed in onto a gold and green patterned carpet—a fitted carpet, and one without any stains or holes. And there were curtains—proper curtains—hanging at the window, and a wash-basin with a looking glass above it in the corner, and an uphol-stered armchair, and a bookcase, a chest of drawers, a wardrobe and a big brass bed with a pile of starched white linen pillows. *All for me? All for me,* I kept thinking, and for a moment I thought I might cry.

"I do hope you like it," said Her Ladyship, moving over to the open window. "It's been freshened up, painted—and these curtains are new," she added, running the back of her hand down the fabric. "Not everyone's partial to yellow, but I thought it suited you."

"It's beautiful," I said. *Like you,* I thought.

I watched her as she stared out of the window, and it was then, I think, in her silent distraction, and as her smile fell away, that I first sensed some ineffable sadness about her. And because of that sadness and because no one had ever before chosen a color for me, I said, "In fact, yellow happens to be my favorite color, Your Lady-ship."

She turned to me. "Well, that is a good sign, isn't it?"

I nodded.

"I shall leave you to unpack now. Take what's left of today to settle in and find your bearings—and do bathe those feet. Mr. Watts will be along presently. He'll help you with anything you need and introduce you to the others. He's been with us a long time . . . is an exceptionally good butler, and, despite appearances, rather a dear man." She paused at the door. "Oh, I imagine you're in need of some refreshment. I'll have something brought up to you."

Minutes later, I sat down at the small table beneath my window. I unfolded the starched linen napkin, surveyed the silver cake stand in front of me piled high with dainty sandwiches, scones and cakes. I poured the fragrant Darjeeling into the porcelain china cup and stared out across the gardens to the cornfields. What would Kitty make of me now? I wondered.

My beloved Kitty had taught me more than prayers and proverbs. And my desire for betterment—to remove myself from the ignominy of my birth and have a place in the world—was no doubt due to her. She had encouraged me to go into domestic service. It was a life, she said; you got a bed to lie in, a good meal each day and a roof over your head. But it took a very superior sort of girl to be a lady's maid, she told me.

That evening, Mr. Watts introduced me to the others. They all lined up and shook my hand. He informed me of the monthly servants' dances, and of the "social evenings"—of cards, dominoes and general-knowledge quiz games, and of "Her Ladyship's raffle," which included such prizes as bath salts, handkerchiefs, chocolates, books, and, at Christmas, a hamper from Fortnum & Mason. It was, he said, a very happy household. Later, he took me aside and quietly reminded me that, as Her Ladyship's maid, I represented her to the other servants and must therefore be mindful of my conduct, and of gossip.

I learned from Mr. Watts that collieries in the north and returns on investments in mines as far away as the Argentine had added to Lord Hector Campbell's fortune, but that despite the name and Scottish ancestry, the estate in Scotland actually belonged to Lady Ottoline. It was where she had spent each long and happy summer of her childhood. And picturing the child Ottoline, and trying to picture the place, I asked him if the estate had a castle.

"I suppose it could be described as such . . . but it's really more of a fortified house."

I was disappointed. I didn't much like the notion of a fortified house, and though the name of the place—Delnasay—evoked an almost fairy-tale image, and I continued to see towers and turrets, I scaled it down, and removed the drawbridge and moat.

"However, if it's castles you're after, Miss Gibson, you've come to the right part of the world," said Mr. Watts. "We have more than our fair share, you know, including one at Warkworth. I imagine you know it from Mr. Turner's famous painting, or perhaps from Shakespeare?"

I didn't, but I smiled and nodded.

I ate a lot during those first days at Birling. Some of the food was different, new to me: black pudding, pease pudding, stottie cakes, kippers. And at breakfast, all sorts of eggs: large, small, colorful and speckled—from ducks, water hens, lapwings, and other birds on the estate and common to those parts. Every day there was a proper luncheon and dinner: steak and kidney with dumplings, pigeon pie, roast lamb with mint from the garden, and endless steamed puddings. Usually, at my other houses, it was roast beef and Yorkshire pudding on a Sunday, served cold on Monday and followed by cottage pie or rissoles on Tuesday, or sometimes liver and bacon; then, another joint midweek—invariably mutton—and, of course, fish on Friday. However, after my time with Mrs. B.—who'd survived on a diet of hard-boiled eggs and consommé, and had expected her handful of poorly paid servants to thrive on the same—it was like Christmas every day at Birling. I had never worked in a household where food was so plentiful or the servants so well fed, and I wondered if it would be the same in Scotland, because I enjoyed my food.

Stirring was the single word Lady Ottoline used to describe Scotland. She was standing in front of the long glass in her dressing room—where we were selecting woolens and tweeds—adjusting a deerstalker hat. "I imagine you'll find Scotland quite stirring," she said. I stood on my toes and pushed the amethyst and silver thistle hatpin into the cloth. "It's a wild, wild place . . . Possibly my spiritual home," she added. And as she surveyed her reflection, turning her head this way and that, the already scaled-down castle of my imagination changed location to a desolate, empty place and became shrouded in thick, swirling mists. She unpinned the hat and turned to me. "It's not like here . . . It's a little more primitive, I suppose, but all the same, terribly romantic."

I tried to smile, but I couldn't get excited about *primitive*. I had spent nearly ten years catching trains and omnibuses, trudging down muddy lanes to remove myself from any sort of primitive to take myself to comfort. And I couldn't picture Her Ladyship in any wild-wild place—or in any primitive *fortified* house. She was to me, even by then, a woman of infinite decorum and grace, a gentle woman of soft skin and temperament. And so I began to feel some trepidation about Scotland, particularly in view of the constant mutterings of an impending war, and I wrote to Stanley to tell him of my misgivings: *We're supposed to be leaving in a matter of days, at the end of the month at the latest, but I'm not altogether sure about it now. In fact, I'm secretly hoping fate might intervene and our trip north be canceled . . . Not that I want a war, of course . . .*

Though I had yet to receive any letter from Stanley, I was too busy to give his silence much thought, too busy learning Ottoline's routine; her likes, dislikes and preferences. She was eager for me to view Birling as my new home, and insisted on showing me about the grounds herself.

We stepped out from the drawing room to the flagged terrace, onto which the tall windows of all the rooms on the southern side of the house opened, and where Mr. Watts was busy lowering sunblinds with a hooked pole. Ottoline pointed to a shape in the distance: the tower at Warkworth Castle, she said.

"Is it haunted?" I asked.

"Of course. All the best places are haunted . . . Warkworth has the Gray Lady."

I wanted to know about the *Gray Lady*, but when I turned, Ottoline had moved on. With her parasol lowered, she stood beneath a wisteria-covered pergola. And as I walked toward her, I saw her close her eyes, move her cheek, nose and then her mouth back and forth over one of the dangling blooms, as though kissing it—and lost in some private reverie.

Quickly, I glanced over at Mr. Watts. Luckily, he had his back to us.

Ottoline opened her eyes and smiled at me. "Heavenly. Quite intoxicating."

She put up her parasol and we strolled on.

At the other end of the terrace was a stone construction with pillars and arches. The loggia, Ottoline called it. From there, steps led down to a sunken Italian garden with a large square pool, a bronze fountain with a sculpture of a boy with a dolphin at its center. Further on, across the immense lawns, beyond a huge deodar and monkey puzzle tree, was a gate to a wood, which, Ottoline said, a succession of snowdrops, primroses, daffodils and bluebells carpeted each spring.

We stood in silence watching the skylarks, singing in flight, over the meadow. "A nightingale once sang in Whittingham Wood," Ottoline whispered, abstracted. "It was the month I first came here, June 'ninety-three . . . Yes, that was the last time a nightingale sang in these parts."

We walked on, to the east of the house and the large, square stable yard, with its coach house and big black-painted sliding doors on one side, and loose boxes, tack room and chaff room on the other. Here, the familiar smells of horses and saddle soap, warm hay, oats and linseed infused the air, and as Ottoline chatted with one of the grooms about his mother—who, I gathered from their conversation, was the absent housekeeper, Mrs. Carney—I heard her say to him, "You must absolutely assure her, John, that her job will still be here for her when she gets out of hospital. What's important is that she get well."

Down a narrow lane, past weatherboarded cowsheds, pigsties and woodsheds, we entered the walled kitchen gardens: a peaceful, gently sloping expanse with row upon row of green vegetables and strawberries under low nets. Inside the long, interconnecting glasshouses were tomatoes, cucumbers, peaches, nectarines and melons, and vines heavy with grapes. Ottoline picked two and handed one to me. "No, not at all ripe yet," she said, rolling the small fruit between her fingers. She turned to me. "You've eaten it?" I had. I couldn't possibly spit it out in front of her. She said, "But you must never eat the pips of grapes, Pearl. They can bring on appendicitis."

Early on, Ottoline spoke to me about how to address her. She was *my lady*, and that was how I must address her, she said. We also decided that rather than use my surname, she would call me by my Christian name, "because it's such a pretty one." This, too, made me happy. I had loathed being *Gibson* at Mrs. B.'s and had always been *Pearl* before that.

Early on, I realized that Ottoline Campbell was different. I saw how she was with the other servants—her staff, as she preferred to call them—and I had barely been there two weeks when she gave me a silk blouse and a pair of real kid gloves she said she had no use for. I knew I'd been fortunate.

However, there were two things that made me uncomfortable—both in quite different ways. One was Ottoline's driving.

Only a few days after my arrival, she had taken delivery of a new motorcar. It was called a Lagonda and was a present from her husband. She was keen to take it out for "a spin" about the lanes and insisted I accompany her. I had been in a motorcar only once or twice and didn't much care for them, and it seemed to me—before we were even at the end of the driveway—that Ottoline drove very fast and very dangerously. Rather than stop at a junction, she simply honked the horn. Luckily, the roads around Birling were quiet and devoid of other motor vehicles that day, but we had a very narrow squeak when we came round a bend upon a slow-moving pony and trap, mounting the grass verge and whizzing past so close, I threw myself into my lady's lap.

The other thing that made me uncomfortable was Ottoline's lack of inhibition.

First, there were the Swedish exercises she did in her room each morning, in her underwear, and during which she sometimes spoke to me with her body folded over and her legs behind her head. Then there was the nudity.

I had been shocked the first time she'd walked into the bathroom—where I was filling the tub for her—completely naked. Naturally, I'd averted my eyes, but as I tried to leave the room, she'd gone on talking to me, so that I had to stand there, looking at the floor as she spoke about the impending war—as though it were perfectly normal to engage in conversation without a stitch of clothing covering one's body. The Swedish exercises were one thing, the brazen nakedness quite another. You see, I knew it wasn't usual for a maid to see her lady naked, for bathroom doors to be left wide-open, for chatter to continue. Certainly—and thank goodness—I had never seen Mrs. B. without clothing. In fact, I had never seen any other woman in that state before. Even when I shared a bedroom with other girls, we'd all managed to pull on our nightgowns before removing our underwear, and put our underwear back on beneath them the following morning. No one would have dreamed of walking about naked—not even in the height of summer when those attic bedrooms were often like a furnace.

And I should have known by this alone, perhaps, that there was more to come.

Like most married people of their kind, Lady Ottoline and Lord Hector slept in separate rooms. However, they appeared to me to have a happy and contented marriage. His Lordship was attentive and quite obviously filled with pride and admiration whenever he gazed upon his wife. He called her Lila, and each evening before dinner, when he stepped into her dressing room, he complimented her on how she looked and commented how very lucky he was. I saw for myself their exchange of smiles, witnessed him kissing her hand, her cheek, and heard him call her "my darling."

But late one evening, as I was unpinning Her Ladyship's hair—having curled and pinned it up earlier, before dinner—she said, "I shall have to brace myself, Pearl. Gigi will be with us in Scotland."

"Gigi?"

"Virginia Parker. She's my husband's *special friend* . . . if you understand."

"Ah yes," I said. Because I knew a lady's maid didn't ask questions. A lady's maid listened and acknowledged; that was all.

"Of course, her husband, Larry, will also be with us."

She smiled back at me in her looking glass, then picked up the glass bottle filled with rose water. "And Hugo and Billy have, as usual, invited a few of their friends, too," she went on, referring to her "almost grown-up" sons—both Honourables—both of whom were due to arrive home any day. She dabbed the fragrant water onto her forehead with her fingertips. "So there'll be any number of adorable young men to distract me." She leaned forward, peering at her reflection: "And Felix, I hope . . . at some stage," she added, though clearly more to herself than to me.

I picked up the hairbrush and began the one hundred strokes as Ottoline continued to reel off the names of our houseguests in Scotland. We were to be away for all of August and September, a whole two months, and I was thinking about Stanley and how he'd react to that, because I had already suggested that he come north and visit me, and I had completely lost track of what number I was up to when Ottoline swiveled round and said, "You probably know him better as Mr. Asquith?"

I shook my head. Unsure of the question, I said, "I'm afraid I've not met the gentleman, my lady."

Ottoline smiled. "Well, you will soon, Pearl . . . Unless this beastly situation escalates further, of course."

"Of course."

At every house I'd worked at there had been rules for servants to abide by. Some were a matter of common sense, others more specific to station, but in general they were the same: A servant should rarely, if ever, be heard beyond the servants' hall and kitchen, and should always make way for his betters, stand when being spoken to and look a person in the eye; a servant should never initiate conversation with the ladies and gentlemen of the house, offer an opinion—unless asked—and never talk to other servants in the presence of his employers; a servant should never be heard calling from one room to another; any maid found fraternizing with a member of the opposite sex was nearly always dismissed without any hearing. In most houses, including Birling, only the butler was allowed to answer the main doorbell. But unlike in other houses, the rule about not receiving visitors— friends or relations—into the house was not strictly applied. And as well as the staff dances—to which we were allowed to invite a partner, if we so wished—and the Christmas party, there was also a summer garden party, to which staff were encouraged to invite family. Without any family to invite, I was pleased I had missed this.

Birling was awash with servants: footmen, parlormaids, underparlormaids, housemaids, kitchen and scullery maids, gardeners and outdoor staff. There were also a number of old retainers living on and around the estate, and Harry, our thirteen-year-old hallboy.

In a dark gray suit, which had undoubtedly once belonged to his father, or even to his grandfather, Harry scurried about the servants' hall each evening, waiting on us and clearing our supper plates before Mr. Watts, Mrs. Lister, Charles—Lord Hector's valet—and I retired to take our dessert and coffee in the Pug's Parlor, a sitting room–cum–dining room reserved for the exclusive use of us upper servants. I was at the very top of a hierarchy I'd once pretended to sneer at; it was Harry and his ill-fitting suit that reminded me, and a camaraderie in our *no uniform* (top and bottom) status was sometimes shared in a quiet exchange of smiles.

One afternoon, as I stood in the laundry, pressing one of Ottoline's blouses, Harry appeared in the doorway. Sloppy in his suit, he leaned against the doorframe, picking at the peeling paint with his bitten fingernails.

"What is it, Harry? Is something the matter?"

I could see from where I stood that the stiff collar of his shirt, gaping about his pale neck, was gray with dirt, and I was wondering whether to offer to wash it for him when he said, "Do you think there's going to be a war, Mrs. Gibson?"

I put down the iron. "It's *Miss*, and I've told you before, you can call me Pearl . . . I really don't know about a war, but I don't think you need to worry. You're only thirteen."

"Fourteen next month, Miss Pearl."

"Fourteen," I repeated, as though it made all the difference. "Well, that's nice," I said. "We'll both celebrate our birthdays in Scotland."

He glanced up at me and shook his head. "They're not taking me . . . But Mollie says if there's a war, you'll all have to come back anyway . . . She says if there's a war, everything here will change."

"All this talk of war!" I said, lifting the iron.

"Best be prepared, Miss Pearl."

"It's Pearl, Harry . . . just Pearl . . . and do stop picking at the paint."

He stood up straight, pushed his hands into his oversize pockets. "It's not that I want there to be a war—it's not that, Miss . . . Pearl—

but I'm not sure about staying in service. And Mollie reckons it'll be years before I have enough money saved for a uniform. She says no one's going to take me seriously till then."

I said, "And does Mollie know *everything*? I don't think so. Between you and me, I think she has a few too many opinions for a kitchen maid." I looked down, pressed the iron onto the sleeve of Ottoline's blouse. "I'm sure your uniform will be taken care of when the time comes . . . and if you continue to work hard, there's no telling where you could end up. Who knows?" I said, glancing up again and smiling, about to say, *You may even be the butler here one day*—but he'd gone.

Heeding Mr. Watts's advice, I elected to keep to myself below stairs, and though I overheard one or two of the younger maids refer to me as "hoity-toity," and loud enough so that I knew I was meant to hear, I ignored them. And as I had yet to learn Her Ladyship's views on politics, and as I was not a political person myself, I elected not to enter any of the heated discussions and talk of impending war.

But I did listen. And from what I could gather, the King himself was now involved, which—and I imagine Kitty would've agreed—suggested the headlines were not all lies, and that *the current crisis* was perhaps more serious than I had thought. Certainly, this was the general consensus in the servants' hall, and though I quickly gathered that not all of those employed at Birling were of the same political persuasion, everyone appeared to be fervently patriotic. For "God Save the King!" resounded about the hall each evening—after grace.

When, one evening during dinner, Mr. Watts said, "I'm afraid

His Majesty's intervention signifies the gravity of the situation for England and all of Europe," I still had my doubts, still couldn't understand how events on the other side of the continent could affect us. But *there's no smoke without fire*, as Kitty would have no doubt said, and Mr. Watts's solemn pronouncement prompted me to remain in the servants' hall for longer than usual that particular evening, listening with the others as he read aloud from the previous day's newspaper.

Later that same evening, when I returned below stairs to check on Ottoline's breakfast tray and ask Cook if she would kindly ensure Her Ladyship's egg was soft-boiled, I heard Mr. Watts and Cook talking quietly in his pantry.

"I can't see how the prime minister will be able to join us at Delnasay," Mr. Watts said. "Not now."

Cook murmured something, and I thought I heard the word *warning*. Mr. Watts almost laughed. He said, "I wouldn't dream of it. It's not my place to tell her. Miss Gibson will make her own judgment. We all do." He sighed loudly. "But this war will certainly put a stop to that sort of thing. You mark my words."

There was a moment's silence, and then Mr. Watts said, "Oh, come, come, Mrs. Lister. We must be strong . . . and you must be brave for those fine young sons of yours."

I didn't wait for Mrs. Lister. I went to the empty drawing room. If I was going to read the newspaper, I wanted to read *new* news— not old news, because I'd done that once before. Not long after Kitty's passing, and while clearing the room I had once shared with her, I'd found two folded yellowing pages at the bottom of her sewing basket: the verdict on my mother's death circled in her violet

ink on one, the birth announcement of an "Arabella Godley" circled on the other.

The name had clearly meant something to Kitty, and instinc-
tively I knew it was a part of the jigsaw of my mother's life, and,
more specifically, her death. But it would be years before I'd fit the
name Godley into that puzzle and see the full picture emerge.

Chapter Five

I was awake at midnight. Awake at one, two, three o'clock and then four. It was the first day of a new month, and we had not long left Perth when the blackness faded and the stars disappeared. High up to the east, a silver blue sky flickered, then stretched itself farther, and as the dark contours of the mountains came into focus, my eyes followed their great sweep down to the tumbled rocks and boulders, and to the river.

No doubt tired from my lack of sleep on that overnight journey north, I found myself wiping away tears and couldn't help but think of Kitty and of all the things she had never seen. During those unfolding moments, I was acutely aware of the distance I'd traveled from her and my origins. I had crossed a border, entered a new country.

And yet I had so nearly not seen any of it.

Prior to our departure, the news had not been good. The situation on the Continent *had* escalated further, and there had been much discussion as to whether we should head north to Scotland, and whether there would even be a "Glorious Twelfth." Troops were being mobilized all over Europe, and Austria-Hungary had declared war on Serbia, where the recently unknown but already famous Archduke Franz Ferdinand had been brutally shot down weeks before.

But Ottoline was determined.

The morning before our departure, as Ottoline lay in her bath with rose-water-infused pads on her eyes and I sat nearby, packing items of her toilette as she'd asked, His Lordship's brown leather brogues creaked into the marble-walled bathroom.

"I've decided we should delay our departure for a week or so."

"We can't possibly do that. Watts and Cook have already gone . . . ," said Ottoline without moving. "And so have the trunks."

"Watts and Cook can come back."

"And the trunks?"

"They can stay up there until . . . until we know."

Ottoline removed the pads from her eyes and rose up from the scented bathwater. And though I quickly moved over to her with a towel, she didn't take it from me. She turned and stood facing His Lordship. She said, "Hector, whether we are here or in Scotland will make no difference to what's happening in Europe. We're heading north weeks later than planned as it is, and I'm afraid I'm not prepared to alter our arrangements again."

It has to be said, and particularly in view of her age, Ottoline had a magnificent body. Her breasts were still full and high, her waist slender, and her stomach betrayed no sign of having expanded itself to carry children. And I knew from touch that her skin was firm and unusually smooth, perhaps due to the precious oils she had shipped over to her from somewhere in the East.

"And anyway, what about Gigi?"

I saw His Lordship's eyes move down his wife's shape, his mouth twitch. "What about her?"

"Oh come, you know how she adores her trips north . . . and going for all those long walks with you."

He closed his eyes: "For God's sake, Lila, you know perfectly well this isn't about bloody Virginia!"

Ottoline took the towel from my still-outstretched hand, wrapped it round herself and stepped out from the bath. "I'm really not in the mood for a scene, Hector." She patted her arms with the towel as I quickly lifted another and placed it on her shoulders and dried off her back. "And I would've thought you had far better things to do with your time than march in here and be quite so aggressive."

Then, with newly measured calmness, and staring over at the window, His Lordship said, "I've just spoken to Winston. He says the city is in chaos, the world's credit system on the brink of collapse. Soon it will be impossible to cash a check . . . And meanwhile, there's a vast concourse of warships out there in the North Sea."

"All the more reason to go to Scotland," said Ottoline.

As the door closed, Ottoline dropped the towel to the floor. "Bloody Winston," she muttered.

I shivered as I stepped down from the train at the strangely named Boat of Garten. The air was a good deal cooler than in Northumberland, and the promising sky of earlier that morning had become ever more gray and low as we'd journeyed northward. It took some time for our luggage to be unloaded from the guard's carriage, and there was no sign of Mr. McNiven or the luggage van, or of any of the pony and traps to take us onward.

And I was thinking about Harry, because he'd been left behind, and because shortly before we left, I'd found him in a crumpled heap, sitting on the stone floor in the scullery. He was stifling tears and wiping his nose on the baggy sleeve of his old man's jacket, his stiff collar dirtier than ever against his scrawny pale neck. He said, "They're never going to take me nowhere, Pearl . . . not without a uniform." I tried to tell him that it wasn't the uniform; I tried to tell him that only a few of us were going north. And then, when he began his usual "Mollie says," I said, "Harry, I don't wish to hear another word about what that wretched girl thinks."

He looked up at me. "You don't like my sister, do you?"

I should have guessed, perhaps, but I hadn't. Nor had I managed to abate Harry's tears. I left him slumped on the cold floor, drowning in the heap of his suit.

Unlike the other servants, I had traveled first-class with the family. It was a privilege, of course, but the singularity of my position made me feel awkward. I belonged nowhere. I wasn't family. I was—no matter what Ottoline said—a servant, and yet I was unable to be with the other servants. And as I watched them, all together, smoking and laughing at the other end of the small platform, I felt newly envious. Meanwhile, His Lordship paced up and down, puffing on a cigar and pulling out his pocket watch every few seconds, while Ottoline held Lolly in her arms and chatted with her sons and their friends.

I surreptitiously watched the boys. It was hard not to—such a handsome group of young men, so confident and assured. They were not that much younger than me, or Stanley—who suddenly seemed middle-aged by comparison. Hugo Campbell was twenty-one years old and studying at Oxford. His younger brother and only sibling, Billy, had just turned nineteen and had recently finished at Eton. Both boys possessed their parents' good looks, and both had impeccable manners. In fact, I had never known any young men quite so polite. And whereas Hugo was clearly the more confident and ebullient of the two, I had quickly developed a soft spot for Billy.

Eventually McNiven appeared, uttering a long diatribe of unintelligible words; then he and another man set to work loading the van with our luggage—and hatboxes, fishing bags and fishing rods, picnic hampers marked *Fortnum & Mason*, and at least a half dozen new lamp shades. Minutes later, Hector, Ottoline, the dog and I climbed onto one trap while Hugo, Billy and their four friends crammed onto another, and the servants onto a third. And thus, in convoy, and with rugs over our knees, we headed out of Boat of Garten.

All around us were endless heather-covered hills, desolate and purple against the melancholy sky. And we climbed and climbed, zigzagging our way up the perilous road, and then down again, past a low cottage where scantily clad children waved to us, over an ancient humpback bridge and then up once more. And the clouds grew ever nearer until we were *in* them, and the landscape around us was blotted out by what Ottoline described as a "fine summer mist." I saw her close her eyes as she breathed in that damp air, and I saw her husband watch her and saw his mouth twitch.

I was beginning to feel sick, beginning to wonder why I'd ever

wished to see another country, when Ottoline pointed to something far below us and I saw silver gray stone and a single turret.
And though the mist seemed to follow us down into the valley, the
wilderness shrank back, and beyond the pillared gateway were the
vaguely reassuring contours of clipped shrubs and hedges, and a
manicured lawn with an herbaceous border. And then, finally, we
came to a stop.

It was not a castle, and not at all on the same scale as Birling.
It was simply a large gray-stoned house with a turret or two, and
castellated gables, and a round tower structure at the front where
the main door was situated.

I climbed down from the trap and followed Ottoline into a
lobby. It smelled familiarly damp. Worn-out galoshes and antique-
looking walking boots were lined up to one side of the stone floor
opposite a long coat stand, the lower compartments of which were
filled with canes and umbrellas, and above which hung multitudinous tweed cloaks and Mackintosh raincoats. A set of broad double
doors led into the main hallway, where a vast stone fireplace dom-
inated. Here, and hanging from every wall, were stuffed heads and
antlers, and lining the broad staircase that rose up from the hall
were weapons: shields, swords, spears and daggers—exhibited
where one would perhaps have normally seen ancestors' portraits,
or even quaint pastoral scenes. Primitive, I thought.

Although it was summer and still early afternoon, a fire burned
in the hallway. But the place felt horribly cold, and I wished we
hadn't gone there; I wished we'd stayed in Northumberland, with
its fitted carpets and new windows, and my lovely yellow room.
And then Ottoline said, "Isn't it magical?"

And I nodded and smiled. "Oh yes, my lady . . . Magical."

Though dead on my feet, I was busy all of that first afternoon and into the evening, unwrapping cashmere, silk, chiffon and, Ottoline's favorite, mousseline de soie, blouses from tissue paper; pressing garments; brushing off gowns and jackets; and hanging them all away. Much of Ottoline's underlinen came from Paris, beautifully appliquéd by French seamstresses. Her shoes were mainly from Pinet, with evening shoes of silk or velvet, many heavily embroidered; and her bespoke tweeds were made for her in London by Lord Hector's tailor.

She had told me that she'd take me with her to Paris—to the fashion shows and famous French couturiers. (What she hoped I might be able to do, what other lady's maids did, she said, was copy their designs. However, though I was handy with a needle and had made my own clothes, I wasn't sure my talent stretched that far.) And in London, we'd go shopping on Bond Street, and to Selfridges and Marshall and Snelgrove—which were both within minutes from the house in Chesterfield Gardens, she said.

Ottoline's definition of *shopping* was for me something of an abstract notion, and which had to date only ever involved staring through polished glass to admire items I knew I should never be able to afford, or own. And so the mere idea of it—going shopping— was as tantalizing as the thought of an ice cream on a hot day.

Unpacking Ottoline's toilette, I glanced at the labels—*Youth-Giving . . . Restores Beauty . . . Brings Vitality and Radiance to the Complexion.* And I shook my head as I lined up the jars and bottles on the small table in the small room Ottoline imaginatively called her bathroom, one that would have undoubtedly been classified as a cupboard at Birling, and where an old tin hip bath stood in a corner. For there was nothing remotely close to luxury here, and no running hot water. And I knew it would mean one of the maids— or me—having to carry cans of hot water up from the kitchen; those half-forgotten rituals and rigmaroles I'd so happily and quickly become unaccustomed to. I had become lazy, already spoiled by the modern conveniences at Birling—and by Ottoline. I had come a long way from carrying coals and slops up and down a candlelit back staircase, a long way from a bath every other week in a mouse-infested shared attic bedroom. I was a superior sort of girl now.

It was Billy who woke me. And I was embarrassed as I sat up. I'd fallen asleep on Ottoline's bed with her half-unpacked jewelry case tipped over next to me. I'd been waiting for the twilight, which had come and gone, and I had been dreaming of Kitty: I'd been sitting once more in the tiny kitchen of my grandfather's house, watching her as she busied herself with pots and pans; I'd been watching the bright orange embers beyond an iron door as it opened and then closed as my Kitty said, "There. There, now."

The room was dark but for the candle Billy held in his hand. And as he moved about, using it to light more candles, I tried to sort the jewels and untangle the ropes of pearls. He came next to me, scooping up the jewels and dumping them willy-nilly inside the case. "I think my mother's trinkets can wait until tomorrow."

"I don't know how I fell asleep like that," I said, rising to my feet, still a little disorientated.

"It's always a killer—that overnight journey. And the air here simply knocks one for six." He closed the case and carried it over to the dressing table. "Mother tells me you've traveled about a bit . . . in the South of England?"

It made me feel newly shy to think of Ottoline's speaking about me with her family. And whether Billy was simply being polite or was genuinely interested, I didn't know, but I said yes, I had worked in a number of counties.

"Good for you, I say. You know, I intend to travel," he said. "Not the way my parents do. I couldn't care less for fancy hotels, and I certainly won't be sending any trunks ahead—or taking lamp shades with me."

I smiled. By candlelight his features were childlike, his face innocent of any real experience, and yet his eyes shone with a fierce intensity I'd seen in another, not so long ago, at King's Cross station. And I was momentarily catapulted back and reminded.

"No, I'll take a knapsack and tent, that's all," Billy went on, staring beyond me into the dimness. "And then I'll wander . . . just wander wherever my fancy takes me."

At that moment Lolly appeared in the doorway. Billy picked her up and turned to me. "Do you like dogs, Pearl?"

"Yes," I said, because apart from Mister Darcy, I always had. He asked me if I liked *wild* animals. I wasn't sure how wild he meant, but I nodded. Then he asked if I'd ever seen deer, and I told him I had, in Hampshire, and before I knew it, I was telling him about the pet fox in Kent, and the mother and baby hedgehogs in Dorset.

"I think you're going to like it here."

He placed the dog down on Ottoline's bed and continued to tell me about the wildlife to be seen on the estate: capercaillies, red squirrels, hares and birds of prey. "There used to be ospreys, but I believe they're extinct now," he added.

I knew already that the estate encompassed some ten thousand acres of rivers, woodland, hills and fields. And I knew it had a history, too, for Ottoline had told me. People had lived there, she said, since the fourteenth century. The previous evening, over dinner on board the train, she had relished telling the story of a man who had been captured there one dark and stormy night by Cromwell's soldiers and then marched to Edinburgh to be executed. I wasn't pleased by the story, for I knew if there were to be ghosts at Delnasay, he'd be one of them.

"You know, I've even seen wildcats. And last summer I saw a golden eagle down by the castle rock," said Billy now, as though I knew the place. "It was incredible, Pearl . . . So majestic, so graceful . . ." He extended his arms outward, mimicking the bird's soaring movement. "I was with Raffy. You'll like him, I think. He prefers to stay in a cottage on the estate—uses it as his studio—but he knows the hills better than anyone, every path, exactly where to go . . . He knows how to light fires and skin rabbits, how to survive in the wild . . . He's a painter," he added, newly matter-of-fact.

One of the reasons I had a soft spot for Billy was because he seemed completely oblivious to my rank. He spoke to me as though I were his mother's friend, not maid; another guest, not a servant. And his innocence was humbling.

As we stepped onto the broad landing, Billy handed me the candle. "Good night, Pearl. I have a feeling you're going to sleep well."

He disappeared down the staircase, leaping beneath the multitudinous weapons and stuffed heads—now sinisterly illuminated by the oil lamps in the hallway below. A wave of noise swept out and up from the drawing room, then abated. I turned from the grinning stags and quickly made my way to my room.

The bedroom I'd been assigned was a long way from the other servants. Ottoline told me she'd put me there as a "little treat," and because of the views. And though it was late and I had missed the twilight, and though there was no discernible view, the moon was almost full and hung over the valley like a huge pearl, opalescent against the amethyst sky. And I blew out my candle and stood gazing up at it—trying to imagine myself viewed from the moon, framed in that window, lost in the wilderness, and thinking once again how very, very small was my existence. Until, at last, my eyelids grew too heavy to hold open and I climbed into bed.

I woke early the following morning, and it took me a few seconds to remember where I was and forget where I had been. Then I rose from my bed, pulled back the curtains and opened the window.

The air was mellow and soft. A purple mist blurred the line of the far hills, and a slanting light lay over the valley. Beyond the pathways and clipped hedges, a ribbon of bronze curled and threaded its way through grassy terraces and green pastures, here and there glistening gold. And amidst the sweet chorus of birdsong was the sound of water cascading over rocks and boulders in its hurry to join the fast-flowing, peaty river.

I dressed quickly, went downstairs and unbolted the door by the kitchen. The gritted path was rough beneath my bare feet, but the mossy flagstones by the lawn were already warm, and the grass soft and moist with dew. And as I breathed in that thin Highland air, my arms outstretched, exultant, Scotland smelled as sweet as anything my tongue had ever tasted. And I twirled about the lawn, relishing the privacy of the early hour and the vast surrounding wilderness.

I have no idea how long the man had been there, watching me, but when I saw the figure—the distant shape of a head and shoulders above the hedge at the bottom of the lawn—I stopped. He raised a hand to his hat, and then moved on, disappearing into the trees.

"Billy told me about last night," said Ottoline.

My heart trembled as I placed her breakfast tray down on the ottoman. "I'm very sorry, my lady. I was tired and . . . well, I don't know what happened."

She sat forward in her bed. "Oh, Pearl, you have no need to be sorry. We all get tired."

The distracting thing about Ottoline was her beauty. She woke up beautiful. I knew. I saw. Each morning, I saw what her husband did not. Ottoline slept on her left-hand side, one arm tucked beneath the pillow, the other stretched out; one leg bent, the other straight and pointed like a ballerina's; and her face, in repose, so childlike and serene that it seemed a shame to wake her. But I did, because I was paid to.

Those first few seconds and minutes of her day were the only time she had no notion of who she was expected to be, no idea of her role—or mine. Always, after I drew back the curtains, I watched her as she came to, stretched and blinked. Sleepy and in-nocent, she slowly sat up, and with her unmade-up hair and un-made-up face, her nightgown twisted about her, her first words were nearly always the same: "I was having a dream . . ." And then she'd regale me with that dream, and with names.

This day, our first in Scotland, as she buttered her toast, as I laid out her clothes for that morning, she said to me, "I feel quite awful, Pearl. Really, I do. I can't imagine how tired you are after yester-day . . . the last few days . . . and the news, all this talk of war . . . so very depleting, too. I should have known better, should have told you to leave things until today. I simply didn't think . . . but that's no excuse. I hope you'll accept my apology."

I said nothing. I felt my cheeks redden. It didn't feel right for Ottoline to be apologizing to me. And it was in fact the second time. I continued smoothing one of her favorite silk blouses and laid it out on the upholstered ottoman at the end of her bed.

"Did you sleep well?" she asked.

"Very well, my lady."

"That's the air—the altitude. It simply knocks one out," she said, shaking her head. "You'll be fine in a few days, once you ad-just, but until then you'll feel utterly, utterly exhausted. I suggest you try to grab a little siesta after luncheon. I always do during my first few days here . . . Couldn't get through otherwise . . . Oh no, not that skirt, Pearl. It makes my hips look so very large, and it itches . . . Let's try the dark green one . . . and that new belt from Liberty's—the one with the big butterfly buckle . . . I don't suppose you've had a chance to go outside yet?"

"Actually, I have. I went out very early this morning, my lady."

"Ah, and what did you think?" she said, crunching on her toast.

"I think it's . . . It's a stirring place, my lady."

Her blue eyes twinkled back at me as she lifted her teacup. "Did you by chance see my lovely Raffy?" she asked. "He's usually out and about early with his paints."

"No, I didn't see anyone, my lady."

It was later that same day, after Mr. Watts had informed us that Germany had declared war on Russia, and as I sat darning stockings and conducting an imaginary conversation with Stanley, persuading him not to sign up—because I knew his mood, how fed up he was with his job, and knew he would—there came a knock at my door. Billy appeared. He said, "Mother has asked me to come and fetch you."

I put down the stocking, the needle and thread, and followed him out of the room, along the corridor and then down the main staircase, beneath the stuffed heads and shields and swords. A number of guests had arrived at lunchtime, and I could hear the voices—and bursts of sudden clattering laughter—coming from the drawing room as we descended the stairs. But I really didn't want to go in there; drawing rooms were not and never had been my place. So I stopped in the hallway, by the door, and said to Billy, "I'll wait here, shall I?"

"No, come in," he said, opening the door and beckoning to me with his hand.

I saw Ottoline immediately: standing on the far side of the

room by the French doors out onto the garden. "No, no, dear . . . The whole place will end up filled with those beastly midges," she was saying to one of the boys' friends as he grappled about at her feet, wrestling with bolts.

She hadn't changed and wore the cream chiffon blouse and pale green checked skirt I'd laid out for her earlier. Her hair was piled up as I'd done it that morning, and in the loose style she favored; her face was devoid of any powder or rouge. But as I waited for her to look over and see me, I could tell she was a little on edge by the way she fiddled with the large cameo brooch fastened at her neck.

I wondered if Virginia—*Gigi*—Parker had arrived, and though I didn't want to be seen staring about or scrutinizing the assembled guests, I allowed myself a quick glance at a few of the ladies seated immediately in front of me, and decided on a long-jawed woman with a thin mouth and dead-fish eyes. The woman spoke to a silver-haired gentleman clad in green tweed, and I thought I heard her say the name Arabella, but at that same moment my attention was drawn back to Ottoline as she crossed the room, still fiddling with the brooch at her neck and wearing the very same smile she'd worn when I'd first set eyes on her at the Empress Club in London.

It was only when she sat down that I noticed the suntanned face, the unmistakable golden hair.

Chapter Six

"Ah, there you are, Pearl," said Ottoline, seeing me at last. "Raffy here seems to think you and he crossed paths at King's Cross station . . ."

And I tried to smile as I tried to breathe: *and in . . . and out . . . and in . . . and out . . .*

I wasn't sure what I was meant to do, whether I was expected to walk over to them and engage in conversation, or simply stand there and wait to be dismissed. But right at that moment, crossing over the great sea of tartan carpet and outstretched legs seemed like an epic and perilous journey, and one I wasn't prepared to make. So I remained where I was—just inside the doorway—and like the idiot I surely was, I smiled as I waited for Ottoline to say something more.

But she didn't. Instead, Mr. Stedman rose to his feet and walked toward me, and I was a little shocked by his attire, the sight of his muscular legs and bare knees. I'd seen picture postcards of Scottish men in short skirts, but I'd always supposed them to be a myth.

"We meet again," he said in a familiar deep voice, extending his hand, again.

And it all came together: Ralph Stedman, Raffy, the painter, the man who had watched me that very morning—dancing about the lawn in my bare feet. They were all one and the same person. And I was more than embarrassed: I was ashamed of myself. And not only for my stupid lies. The news was bleak, the world in chaos, and I had been seen—seen by him—dancing. *Dancing.* And, just to make matters worse, on a Sunday, too.

His skin was rough and calloused in my hand, and I longed to be dismissed. I glanced over to Ottoline, but she had moved alongside another man on the sofa and appeared to have forgotten all about me.

"I'm pleased you're here and not at Biarritz, Miss Gibson."

I kept my eyes on Ottoline.

"I understand this is your first visit to the Highlands."

I heard myself say, "Yes, though I have traveled extensively in England."

I'm not sure why I said such a thing. But I suppose in spite of my lies—about my name, my claim to relations in Northumberland and traveling to Biarritz—I wanted him to know that I *had* seen places.

"So I hear," he said.

Finally I looked back at him. And as his eyes crinkled up in a smile, I had the queerest sensation: a momentary but profound recognition, the feeling that all of this had happened before; that he and I had already stood in that room, on that carpet, looking back at each other, with Ottoline and war in the background.

"Do you always dance at dawn?"

"Only sometimes," I said, bolder and more uncertain than ever.

"Only sometimes," he repeated.

His gaze was fixed on me in a way I was unused to, and his teasing smile made me feel more awkward still. I was adrift, unsure what to say or how to navigate the conversation back to the place I belonged. Ottoline had summoned me, but she had not yet dismissed me, and I was used to being told what to do and where to go next. I was not used to standing in a drawing room making conversation with gentlemen—certainly not gentlemen in skirts.

Then came a drip of courage, and staying with the subject of dance, I said, "I was actually hoping to go to a tea dance in London, but I gather they're rather expensive."

His smile broadened. "Tea dances aren't for people like you."

At first I thought he was being patronizing, implying tea dances were only for moneyed people. But he went on. "Imagine it: You'd have to wear shoes and waltz about with some clumsy oaf in a suit."

And immediately I thought of Stanley.

"However, I'm at your disposal to teach you some Highland dancing . . . and as you can see," he said, stepping back from me, "I'm dressed for it."

I smiled.

He stepped nearer. "I hope I'll have the opportunity to dance with you one day, Miss Gibson," he whispered.

At that moment, the door behind me opened and His Lordship entered. The room fell silent as everyone turned to him for another update. And as he began to speak, I saw that I was right, for the dead-fish eyes positively lit up; the thin lips pouted and pursed. And I quietly left the room.

My third day in Scotland coincided with the third day of the month, and events were unfolding rapidly, and not just in Europe.

Initially, I thought the bare leg hanging over the edge of the bed belonged to Ottoline. But as I walked farther into the room, I saw that it was a distinctly male-looking limb, muscular, and covered with dark, wiry hairs, and that it belonged to the naked torso and head lying facedown and half hidden beneath a pillow; a head I knew was most definitely not attached to His Lordship's body.

Unsure what to do, I froze.

Was it Ralph Stedman, *my lovely Raffy?* Something told me it was, but I didn't want to look back at the bed. The bodies upon it were naked and parts were exposed. I glanced to the floor, saw Ottoline's discarded nightgown. I stared at the tray in my hands. I saw one cup, one egg, one teaspoon, and toast for one. I looked up at the curtains, wondered whether to pull them back and place the tray on the ottoman at the end of the bed, or whether to go back down to the kitchen and organize breakfast for two.

Averting my eyes, I turned, but as I left the room, I made sure to shut the door loudly and firmly. Then, clutching the tray, I loitered about the landing. Returning to the kitchen with Ottoline's breakfast tray would undoubtedly cause questions—and, perhaps, gossip. So I took a walk along the main landing and down another passageway where most of the guest bedrooms were situated—with a brass cardholder on each door and the name of the incumbent clearly printed in capital letters.

My heart was still beating fast and a little shakily, and I placed the tray down on a deep windowsill and stared out at the gardens. I jumped when I heard the voice behind me: "I say, can you remind me what time breakfast's served?"

I turned. "Mondays are as Sundays here, sir . . . Nine o'clock."

"Thank you, Pearl," said the young man, disappearing back into the room marked MR. F. COWPER.

I was astounded he knew my name until I remembered that Ottoline had announced it when she'd been sitting on the sofa with Ralph Stedman and another man—Mr. F. Cowper, I realized now.

I placed my hand on the silver teapot. Lukewarm, at best. I picked up the tray and headed back toward Ottoline's room. If Ralph Stedman was still there, I'd simply leave the tray on the ottoman at the foot of the bed, I decided. But as I marched down the corridor and turned a corner, near the door marked MRS. L. PARKER, His Lordship appeared.

"Good morning, Pearl."

His tone was distinctly somber, almost like a doctor's, and I wondered if Mrs. Parker had perhaps taken ill. I stood aside to let him pass by and then followed him toward the main landing, but when he paused outside Ottoline's bedroom door, I didn't think. I couldn't think. I simply shouted, *"Nooo!"*

Of course I shouldn't have called out like that and never would have normally. But what could I do? I thought His Lordship was about to open the door and enter the room.

"I'm very sorry, Your Lordship," I said, moving quickly to the bedroom door and standing in front of it. I held the tray between us like a shield. "Her Ladyship does not wish to be disturbed this morning," I added in a whisper.

"Then perhaps it would be more sensible for you not to be patrolling about these corridors shouting, hmm?"

"Yes, Your Lordship. I do apologize, Your Lordship."

He shook his head and walked off.

A potential catastrophe had been averted, but my heart continued to pound as I turned the handle, opened the door and entered the room for a second time.

Ralph Stedman had gone; Ottoline was sitting up in bed *and* in her nightgown. She said, "What on earth was that commotion? I heard someone shouting."

I placed the tray on the ottoman at the end of her bed. I said, "I'm afraid it was me, my lady. I'm afraid I raised my voice to His Lordship. I didn't think you wished to be disturbed."

It was the first time I'd seen her laugh. She said, "Oh my, I shouldn't worry about him . . . He has absolutely no interest in what happens within this room."

I drew back the curtains, opened the window. I rearranged the pillows and passed Ottoline her breakfast tray. "I hope you're not angry," she said as I walked away from her and into the dressing room.

I didn't say anything.

"You see, I know you came in earlier . . ."

I was looking through blouses and thought perhaps she'd think I'd not heard.

"I should have told you . . . warned you."

I picked out a salmon pink silk blouse and a dark brown tweed skirt. Underwear. Stockings. I carried them into the room.

"Have you ever been in love, Pearl?"

I felt my cheeks flush. "I'm not sure . . . I don't really know, my lady."

She moved the tray to one side, threw back the bedcovers and crossed her legs. "Then you've not been in love . . . You'd know, you see. You know when you're in love."

I nodded. Though I had longed for it, imagined it or how it must feel, I knew I had never been in love. Not with Stanley or anyone else. And yet, like a pool of wisdom just beyond my immediate understanding, it seemed closer to me now. If I could only allow myself to fall into *it*, I might fall in love with Stanley, I thought.

"Have you ever been touched by a man?"

I had. By Stanley, at the pictures. "Sort of."

"Sort of?" she repeated, and smiled. "There's no *sort of* to touch, real touch . . . real lovemaking."

And all I could think was that her tea would be cold by now, and her egg, and her toast.

"I'm going to share something with you, Pearl. Because I like you, I like you very much, and you're still young enough not to have to make mistakes. Sit down . . . Please, sit down," she repeated, gesturing to the end of her bed.

I sat down on the ottoman, taking care not to sit on the clothes I had just laid out. There was a small snag on the sleeve of her blouse, and as I reached out to it, made a mental note and wondered which color thread I could use, she said, "Please . . . Please look at me, Pearl."

I raised my eyes to her.

"Isn't it strange that we know so little about each other?"

There was nothing to say to that. So I nodded.

"You see, I respect *your* privacy, but I think it's important for you to know and understand at least a little about *me*."

I wasn't sure where we were heading. I felt as though we'd just boarded a boat together and were sailing into choppy, uncharted waters. I did not want any exchange of secrets, nor did I wish to hear about my lady's intimate, personal affairs. And yes, I was a little angry. I felt compromised, and more than a little disappointed.

"I married my husband when I was eighteen years old, shortly after I came out. It was what was expected," Ottoline began. "I was a child. I had no idea about men, or love or marriage. But Hector Campbell was dashing, and attentive . . . And most important to my mother, he rode beautifully, and most important to my father, he had money—lots of money." She paused for a moment. "After our marriage, I did fall in love, genuinely fall in love . . . But I've been married for over twenty years, and for most of that time, my husband's enjoyed a succession of mistresses." She paused and glanced over to the open window. "I have, I think, been a dutiful wife. I've given him his sons . . . an heir and a spare. I run his homes—our homes; I play my part. But my husband has always preferred to share himself with others, and I accepted that a long, long time ago. I had to . . . For these past two years or so it's been Virginia . . . And it'll be another, one day."

A shaft of sunlight fell on her, picking out the fine strands of silver in her dark hair, and as she lowered her head and looked downward, she appeared every one of her years, and nothing like the woman who had interviewed me in London.

She sighed. "I'm not sure what my husband and I have in common anymore. The only thing I'm certain of is our love for our boys. We're a family," she added, raising her eyes to me. "Family," she repeated.

I was relieved at hearing this word, her emphasis upon it, and I hoped we were about to paddle back to safer waters; that she'd tell me she really did love her husband and that she knew he loved her, and that what I'd witnessed that morning was a momentary slip, nothing more.

"It's taken me some time to forget about duty and allow myself the same freedom as men like my husband. It's taken me some time to allow myself to be loved . . . And the man you saw in my bed this morning? Well, he loves me—and loves me in a way I understand and need." She shrugged, and then she finally smiled. "He loves me," she said again, clearly relishing the sound of those three words.

But for some inexplicable reason my own heart sank.

And yet Ottoline deserved to be loved. Everyone did. And how could I damn her for her infidelity to a man who had abused her trust for so many years?

And she must have seen something in my expression, because she said, "Please don't be sad. Our lives are what we make them, and more and more as I get older, I realize this. We must all grab every chance for happiness with both hands, Pearl. Carpe diem," she said, reminding me of Stanley's *carpey-dee-um*. "Seize the day . . . Seize every day and every precious moment. We must. Particularly now."

Particularly now . . .

All day, Ottoline's words about grabbing happiness and seizing moments went round and round in my head. There I was in Scotland, another country, when we were about to go to war, when the man I planned to spend my life with was hundreds of miles away in London. All day, I pondered the complexities of marriage and the extraordinary muddles people got themselves into when there really was no need: Ottoline should have been with her husband at a time like this, not with Ralph Stedman; Lord Hector should have been with Ottoline—and not with Virginia Parker. And I should have been back in the South with my Stanley and not dancing about lawns and telling lies to a painter in a skirt.

All day, my thoughts clashed and simmered. All day, images sprang up in my mind. I saw Ottoline intentionally drop a towel to the floor, her dark hair stretching all the way down to her buttocks as she wandered about, as Ralph Stedman lay back on a bed, transfixed, his eyes fiercer than ever. And all day, bells rang out, announcing yet another telegram.

Though I still wasn't sure of His Lordship's role at the Foreign Office, I knew he must be important. For as isolated as we were, and whatever his role, *it* and *he* kept us up-to-date on unfolding events and news from London. And news traveled fast: The British fleet had been mobilized.

That evening, Mr. Watts led us in special prayers at supper.

And when he said, "God guard us and keep our great country safe and free," we repeated it in loud unison. Later, I returned to the servants' hall—with paper and pen, and the intention of writing another letter to Stanley. I couldn't very well do this in my room, not by the light from a single candle, but the hall was well lit by oil lamps and, though we were rather awash with lady's maids and valets, I thought it would be quiet by then. But it wasn't. Mr. Watts was patrolling the passageways, and Charles, Lord Hector's valet and Mrs. Parker's maid remained seated in the servants' hall.

As was the usual custom, we knew our guest lady's maids and valets only by the names of those they served. And I had learned earlier, at supper, that Parker was more loquacious than the others. That evening, late as it was, Parker was still in full flow, waving about an amber cigarette holder with a great length of ash arcing at its end, and talking about Mr. Asquith and what he might or might not do, as though she knew him intimately. But as I pulled up a chair, placed my writing pad and pen down on the table, she stopped. "Writing home, are we?" she said, stubbing out her cigarette.

"To my fiancé."

"Ah, and where's he?"

"London."

"In service?"

"He works at the Café Royal."

"I know it well. What does he do there? I might have met him." I didn't want to tell her. I said, "He's in management."

Parker widened her eyes, folded her arms: "I say, a fiancé in management. You'll be all right, then."

I smiled.

"So, what do you make of it?" she asked, quieter now and leaning toward me.

"I hope Germany will see sense."

She laughed. "I don't mean *that*. I mean the carrying on upstairs," she whispered.

"Parker," said Charles, smiling and a little too flirtatious to be serious, I thought.

"Forgive me if I'm speaking out of turn. I just wondered if it was the same at your last place."

"Oh no, I was with an elderly widow before I came here."

"Ha, old age doesn't always stop them," said Parker.

I tried to smile. I said, "Have you been with Mrs. Parker long?"

"Two years—and ready for a change as well. I suppose if you're going to be in service, it's a nice enough job, not too onerous, but I fancy something different."

"Like what?"

"Shop work, perhaps. Oh, I don't mean any old shop. I'm not planning to stand at the cash till in an ironmongers," she added, and laughed. "No, one of the London department stores, and ladies' fashions, I thought. They snap up people like us, lady's maids—who know how to sew and are familiar with the French fashions." She propped her head in her hands and stared back at me over the table. "What about you? Are you enjoying looking after Lady Ottoline?"

I nodded. "But it's still early days and I've a lot to learn."

"Hmm, I bet you've already learned who your lady prefers in her bed, though."

I said nothing. Charles winked an eye at me, then pushed back his chair and rose to his feet. "Time I went to bed . . . Good night, ladies."

Parker waited until Charles had left the room, then said, "I'm sorry. I didn't mean to be disrespectful about Her Ladyship . . . It's just, well, I happen to know things."

I smiled. "Yes, and so do I."

"Really?"

I nodded. "They're in love."

Parker rolled her eyes.

"He *loves* her," I said.

She stared at me. "I'm not so sure about that." She leaned over the table, and so I moved in, too. "He has someone else . . . In London . . . Considerably younger than Lady Ottoline . . . *Everyone* knows."

I stared back at her. "Idle gossip."

She shook her head. "No, not idle gossip. I've seen for myself."

I closed my eyes.

"I'm sorry. But best I tell you—especially as you'll be the one who has to pick up the pieces."

"Cad."

"Utter."

"He told her he loved her."

"Complete liar."

"Despicable."

"I'll say."

"And you know, I met him in London?"

"*No!*"

I nodded: "He carried my suitcase onto the train for me."

"Ha, narrow escape, I'd say."

At that moment came the sound of keys jangling in the passageway, a shuffling on the other side of the door. We locked eyes.

"Still up?" said Mr. Watts, peering into the room. "You know it's after midnight?"

"I was just saying good night," said Parker.

"And probably a very good idea . . . I've a feeling you might have an early start."

She smiled at me. "I'm pleased we had our little chat."

Dear Stanley,

I hope you are well. I am a little concerned to have heard nothing from you, but perhaps you did not receive my first letter—giving you the address in Northumberland? I know you must have my address here in Scotland, as I wrote to you twice before we came away.

We arrived here on Saturday & though I had no sleep at all on the journey & was very tired for the first day or so, I am well. I am also going to have quite a few tales to tell when I see you & am saving them all up—so be warned!

We are, it has to be said, quite isolated here, but there have been many telegrams to His Lordship—who is, I believe, quite important at The Foreign Office—and Mr. Watts (the butler) gives us bulletins each day. According to Mr. W., His Lordship thinks war is inevitable, and so everyone is understandably anxious & though I'm not sure what will happen, whether we will stay here for the full duration, all the boys—including Lady O.'s sons—say they'll sign up (Mr. W. reckons this is just young and foolish patriotism). I do hope you are not thinking the same? In fact, I would be grateful for a letter by return to reassure me of that.

Anyway, the main thing I want to tell you is that I have decided to give notice, and for reasons I do not wish to go into in this letter. As I say, I will explain all when I see you. I intend to wait until we are back in Northumberland to give formal notice. I've come to know Her Ladyship quite well & won't leave her until she has found my replacement. I need a good character—particularly after such a short time. But it'll mean I'll be in London, near you, & so I hope this pleases you.

Do write soon.

Fondest wishes,
Pearl

Chapter Seven

My maternal grandfather, Henry Gibson, was a blacksmith—like his father before him. He had a workshop and yard not far from the river, near St. Mary's Church in Battersea, which is where he married his sweetheart, Kate, and where each of their children was baptized, and later buried. Henry and Kate lost three sons in infancy and a daughter at five. By the time their youngest—my mother—walked into the Thames, Kate had already joined her children in the churchyard. My grandfather, Henry, passed away when I was seven, and his sister, Kitty, ten years later. She never saw me become a lady's maid.

The strange thing about my ambition to become a lady's maid was that, at the same time it happened—I don't really count my position with Mrs. B.—other things began to occur. Things almost in direct contradiction with everything I had previously thought. You see, I'd begun reading the newspaper, had started to think bigger than the counties of England.

I had been in service from the age of fifteen; an inquiring mind was not something that had been encouraged. But starting in Northumberland and continuing in Scotland, my desire for education, an ever-increasing thirst for knowledge, seemed to know no bounds. I wanted to know the history of the Balkans, know and understand what was happening there and how it affected the country in which I'd been born. I wanted to know about empires; not just the British Empire, but the Ottoman Empire, the French Empire, the Russian Empire—every empire there was or ever had been. And I wanted to know why the Prussian War had left so much undone; where Alsace-Lorraine was situated and what had actually taken place at Versailles.

But as Kitty used to say, *learning is a dangerous thing*, and everything I learned created only more questions—questions I wouldn't and couldn't have imagined months before. And it all made me realize how little I knew, how much I would never know, and it frightened me.

War seemed as unavoidable as the desperate forward motion of my mind. My heart was heavy with dread at the prospect of change—imminent change. So much so that I wanted to run back to Stanley, the sole representative of what I *had* been and knew. Confronted with uncertainty, I longed for familiarity, and in the absence of all others, it came in his shape.

❧

Each morning at around nine o'clock, the outbound post was collected from the polished mahogany and brass box in the main hallway, and the inbound post delivered and distributed. That morning, on the mantelshelf in the servants' hall, was a picture postcard cheerily proclaiming "Greetings from Scarborough." I glanced over at Mrs. Lister before picking it up. *Dear Rodney, I thought this might bring back some happy memories. Saw Derek yesterday and we had tea at the Grand. He says he intends to sign up. Can you please write to him? Fingers crossed for the sixteenth.* It was signed, *Love, Ethel,* and addressed to *Mr. R. Watts.*

It was only when I put down the postcard that I saw the small brown envelope addressed to me. I recognized the hand immediately and didn't think to take it to my room.

"That's funny," I said to Mrs. Lister as I sat down. "Here's a letter from my fiancé, and I've only just posted one to him."

"Well I never. I had no idea you were engaged to be married."

"Oh, well, it's not official. Not yet. It's . . . It's sort of secret, you see."

Mrs. Lister tapped her nose with her finger. "I won't say a thing. But it's lovely news and lovely that you're both thinking of each other—and understandably so at a time like this."

The envelope contained only one sheet of paper, one paragraph.

Dear Pearl,

This is not an easy letter for me to write. I have given much thought to our present circumstances & future, and if you had stayed in the South, I might have thought differently. But your decision to go North made me think, and now that it looks like there will be a War, I intend to sign up at the first opportunity

& do my Duty. Bearing in mind we didn't get to see much of each other anyway, and now with you up there & me down here—or even soon in France—there seems little point in us continuing. Suffice to say I feel I must end our liaison. I am very sorry and hope you won't be too sad. Plenty more fish in the sea, as they say.

Take care of yourself.

Best wishes,
Stanley

"Not bad news, I hope?" said Mrs. Lister, scrutinizing me.

I folded the page, put it back inside the envelope. "No, just a note for now."

Mrs. Lister winked at me. "The course of love never did run smooth," she said, laughing. "But don't worry, I won't ask what he said."

Plenty more fish in the sea . . . The cheek of it, I thought. But inside my head I heard the sea—the same gushing sound you hear when you put a shell to your ear. I rose to my feet and, clutching the letter in my hand and trying not to run, I went to the main hallway. But the postbox was empty, the letters all gone—including mine to Stanley. So I returned to the kitchen and waited until Mrs. Lister had gone to the larder before I opened the door of the range and threw in Stanley's letter. Then I closed the iron door and walked out of the house.

It was my own fault, I thought, as I fought back tears and headed down the driveway toward the old stone bridge and the river, that I had lost my suitor—my only suitor. I had been stubborn and selfish, trying to be the superior sort of girl Kitty wanted me to be—the lady's maid.

If I had stayed in the South, seen him more, gone to the pictures with him . . . If I had just been prepared to . . . to offer a little more of myself . . .

"Everything's about sex," I muttered, angry again as I clambered down the bank by the wall of the bridge. I hobbled across the washed-up stones and rocks and sat down on a large boulder near the water's edge. The sun was already high in the sky, the stone's surface smooth and warm beneath me. And though I knew—knew even then—that Stanley Morton wasn't worth my tears, at that moment a desperate longing, a longing I'd known all of my life, the desire to belong to someone or something, to have a home, a family, swamped me.

I didn't hear anyone approach. I felt a hand on my shoulder—a touch; that was all. Then I heard my name and I knew.

"Why so sad?" he asked, lowering himself and staring at me.

I shook my head, unable to summon any words. The only thing I knew for certain at that moment was that the world was bigger and far more dangerous than I'd ever realized, and I'd been abandoned, again.

"Is it all this talk of war?"

I didn't say anything, couldn't.

"Is it Delnasay?" he asked. "You know, you don't have to stay here if you're miserable and unhappy . . . I know Ottoline wouldn't want that. And I can speak to her, explain to her that you wish to go home."

Home . . .

He passed me his handkerchief, folded, freshly laundered. And as I took it from his hand, I heard someone call out in the distance; I turned in the direction of the house and then looked back to him.

"The boys," he said, staring back at me, frowning and smiling at the same time. "I'm supposed to be leading them on a hike, but I can't leave you here like this."

I rose to my feet. "You've been very kind, but I mustn't delay you . . . I'm fine now, Mr. Stedman. Really, I am."

As I stared ahead to the bank on the opposite side of the river, I felt a finger run down the thin cotton sleeve of my blouse. A touch so light, so lingering, so powerful, it took me back to something in my childhood: *There . . . there, now.*

When I at last turned my head, I saw him leap up the grassy bank and then pause to look back at me.

I waited a while before I returned to the house. Ottoline was nowhere to be found, and neither was anyone else. The place was deserted, abandoned, as though those who had been there—and only minutes before—had been summoned to the hills, perhaps to look upon that landscape once more, in *peace.*

I returned outside with my mending and my book. I fiddled with buttons and needles and threads, but my thoughts were awry; flitting back and forth from Stanley's cold missive to Ralph Stedman's warm touch, and then to Ottoline and again to her lover, Ralph Stedman; to the prospect of war and the possibility of a lifetime ahead of me in service. It would be my birthday in a few days' time. I would be twenty-four years old.

When Mr. Watts appeared from the side of the house, I quickly

got on with my sewing. He strolled over, remarking as he approached on the fine morning, and then sat down next to me on
the bench. I would have liked to ask him about his Ethel and
Derek, the significance of the sixteenth, but instead I inquired on
the whereabouts of the family and our guests. He informed me that
while the young men had taken to the hills on foot, His Lordship,
Mrs. Parker and others had gone out on horseback. He made no
mention of Ottoline, and I chose not to inquire on her whereabouts, but I did wonder if she had gone with Ralph Stedman and
the boys.

Mr. Watts went on. "His Lordship is always very generous with
his time, an excellent host, but I can tell he's finding it difficult . . . having to entertain and amuse so many guests under the
present circumstances." He paused and shook his head, "Yes, very
difficult."

Clearly, Mr. Watts knew nothing of His Lordship's true character, or of his tawdry extramarital affairs and current mistress. But
it wasn't my place to enlighten him. *Let him live in ignorance,* I
thought. In my opinion, Mrs. Parker was nothing in comparison to
Ottoline. And I had by that time seen enough to know that the
woman was adept in the art of simpering. I'd watched her in the
hallway the previous day, before she and His Lordship set off on a
walk. I'd pretended to be looking for Ottoline's favorite tam-o'-
shanter. And oh how that woman pandered to him! Hector this,
Hector that. Giggling like a young girl whenever he so much as
attempted to be funny. Pathetic, I thought. Why couldn't he see
through it? After all, he was reputed to be an intelligent man.

I said, "I think we're all finding it a little difficult, Mr. Watts."

Mr. Watts leaned forward and peered at the book lying next to me. "Taking the opportunity to catch up on some reading, I see." He stretched his legs out in front of him, placed his hands under his belly and squinted up at the sun. "I'm a Dickens man myself."

I said nothing. I wasn't in the mood to talk about books.

"Mrs. Lister tells me congratulations are in order . . . You're engaged to be married?"

So much for Mrs. Lister saying nothing. I said, "I was, sort of, but not now."

"Oh dear. I am sorry to hear that."

"There's no reason to be. It's for the best."

"Indeed. Marriage, family, personal commitments are always difficult when one is dedicated to a career in service." He turned to me. "I can tell you that Her Ladyship is very pleased with you thus far. Yes, very pleased. I think you have a fine career ahead of you, Gibson."

I nodded. "Actually, I prefer to be called Pearl, Mr. Watts—if you don't mind. It's what Her Ladyship and the rest of the family and everyone else here call me, so you may as well, too."

He bent down, picked a few blades of grass from the toes of his polished black shoes. "It's a little irregular, you know . . . in your position."

I couldn't help myself. I said, "But isn't everything a little irregular, Mr. Watts? Isn't today, here and now, a little *irregular*?"

He rose to his feet. "Well, there's work to be done—for some of us. I'll leave you in peace with your Mrs. Gaskell."

❧

Everyone returned by lunchtime, but the only sounds emanating from the dining room were the somber murmurings of wary voices.

His Lordship took luncheon on a tray in his study, and later, doors clanked shut and the house fell into silence once again.

Monday was always washday in every big house, though for me as lady's maid it went on all week. The washhouse, or laundry— where the copper bath was situated, along with the soda crystals, yellow soap, chalk for grease and oil stains and a small brown bottle of alcohol for grass—was where I spent a lot of my time. Ottoline said she couldn't possibly trust anyone else with her silks and chiffons, and of course her stockings and undergarments were very much my concern.

That afternoon, when I went to the kitchen to boil the kettle for Ottoline's laundry, Mr. Watts was sitting at the long pine table, bent over the newspaper, his head in his hands. He didn't look up at me, didn't speak. And minutes later, when I went outside to fill a pail from the pump in the yard, where a few of the girls stood about smoking, none of them spoke to me. But inside, as I filled the copper bath in the small washroom, I heard their conversation resume through the open window.

I recognized Mollie's voice immediately when she said, "I don't give a monkey what anyone says, particularly not old Watty. I'm getting the train in the morning and that's that."

"That'll be the end of your *career in service*, young lady," said another voice—one I couldn't place, but doing a rather fine impersonation of Mr. Watts.

I laid out items of clothing on the long wooden bench, applied the stick of chalk to a grease stain on a blouse.

"Listen, if all the men bugger off over there, there'll be plenty of jobs to be had—and *not* just in service. Sod this being in service lark."

I placed Ottoline's underwear and stockings into the warm soapy water, dribbled alcohol from the small brown bottle onto the hem of a cream skirt stained green from the grass. And then I stood staring at it.

I hadn't thought of the potential impact war might have on us servants, on our jobs; I hadn't thought about all the men in service who might sign up—hundreds, thousands, perhaps, up and down the country. Who would replace them? And who would replace *us* if we female servants were to give up our positions, too? How would these places manage? I glanced about the little room, the starched shirts hanging from the airer, the piles of folded white linen and napkins waiting to be pressed. I tried to imagine Ottoline, her silk sleeves rolled up as she worked the mangle. It would have been almost laughable if it hadn't been so frightening.

Then a voice beyond the window said, "There's no place like home . . . and home's where we should all be at a time like this."

But I had no home to go to, no mother or family, or any man to run to. And as I stood in that small warm room in an ancient building in Scotland, it came to me with new and absolute clarity: I was entirely alone in the world.

"What about *her* . . . madam?"

"Her Ladyship?"

"No! *Her* . . . Miss La-Di-Dah."

They all laughed. And I knew they were laughing at me.

"Tried to pretend she was engaged. Told Lister this morning and then told Watts something else."

"Typical!"

"Stuck-up bitch."

"Don't say that."

"Why not?"

"We don't know her . . . She might be all right for all we know. She's got quite a kind sort of face, really. And Mrs. Lister says she has no family."

"Everyone has family. Someone at least."

"Mollie's just jealous. Because she's pretty."

"Pretty stuck-up. Pretty if you like big puppy dog eyes."

"Give over. You're jealous."

"Listen, I've told you, I'm gone from here the morrow, and I don't give a hoot about any of them, including that one."

Those were Mollie's last words.

The next voice belonged to Mr. Watts: "Righty-oh, girls. Come along now. *No rest for the wicked* and all that. Just because the house is quiet doesn't mean there's no work to be done. *The devil makes work for idle hands.*"

I knew both of those. They were two of Kitty's favorites.

Shortly before six, before I attended to Ottoline, I took down her new cape that had arrived from Selfridges with that afternoon's post. The boys for some reason were all on the stairs, sitting about smoking, their rhetoric newly defiant, their spirits bold. And though our ultimatum did not expire until much later that evening, Germany—it seemed—was already *the enemy.*

"There's no question in it, old boy. We have to," Hugo was saying. "Every man must do his bit in this ghastly business. And the only way is to be fast and swift . . . Get it over with quickly," he added, punching a fist into his palm.

"What do you say, Pearl?" said Billy, looking up at me as I weaved my way between them. "Should we go? Should we all go and fight . . . ? Should we kill them?"

And I'm not sure why I did it, but I placed the cape under my arm and raised my fists up in the air.

They all laughed, apart from Billy, who turned away from me. And as I hung Ottoline's cape on a hook in the lobby, I caught him staring back at me, and with such fear and confusion in his eyes that I wanted to run to him, wrap my arms around him. I wanted to say, *No. No, you don't need to go, Billy. Not you. Never you.*

But I didn't. Instead, I walked down the passageway and went out to the yard. But outside, too, the air was full of bluster. A cooler wind swept down the hillside, bullying the heather and shivering trees. Newly arrogant and whistling. I circled the yard a few times—staring upward, challenging something; then, with my back against the wall, I closed my eyes and began a prayer.

"Feeling any better?"

Ralph Stedman. He had a gun in his hand, a couple of dead rabbits slung over his shoulder.

"Did *you* kill them?"

"I did. But I'm a good shot. They knew nothing," he said, raising his hand to the bloodied fur.

I reached into my pocket: "I have your handkerchief."

He smiled. "Please, keep it. I don't wish for your tears, but I rather like the notion of them on my handkerchief."

Was he flirting with me? Yes, most definitely. And so I offered no smile in return, and holding on to the linen inside my pocket, I said, "Oh, I must have left it down by the river."

"Shame."

"I'll replace it."

"There's really no need."

"Oh, but there is."

"You were sad this morning, and now you seem . . . a little angry. But perhaps that's progress. I hope so."

I shook my head. "I'm not angry."

But I *was* angry. I was angry with Stanley, angry with old men in London making decisions about boys, and angry with him, Ralph Stedman, for focusing on me in that way, for toying with me and making me feel in that instant as though my well-being mattered to him.

I'm not a fool. I know all about men like you.

He stepped nearer. I pushed back against the wall, spread my palms over the mossy stone. He said, "I'm not like the rest of them, you know. I'm on your side."

"I don't need you to be on my side, Mr. Stedman."

"The name's Ralph."

How is it that some people shine? How is it their mere presence brings warmth and comfort? Even with the bloodied animals draped over his shoulder—animals he admitted to killing—the aura around him, an aura slowly enveloping me, was soft and kind, as benign and gentle as Kitty. And I had to remind myself that this man was not to be trusted; I had to remind myself that this man was just another player. But, oh, I could understand why Ottoline needed him. I could understand why ladies from London to Paris and Biarritz fell for his charm. And it would have been as easy as falling off a log for me to fall as well.

But I wouldn't and couldn't. And I didn't. I got a grip. I said, "Mr. Stedman, while I appreciate your concern, I really don't think it would be fitting for me to be calling you by your Christian name. Furthermore," I said, grasping a word I thought suitably dignified and businesslike, but with no idea what I might add to it, and then, stepping away from the wall, finishing, "the horrendous situation is the only reason I was sad this morning. The news, Mr. Stedman . . . That was and is my only concern."

He nodded. "Of course. It's all of our concern."

"Indeed."

"But I don't believe you."

I affected a shrug. And knowing I had to extract myself, knowing I couldn't possibly allow myself another single minute of *him*, I turned and walked away.

But I heard him call after me: "And I know I'm right."

That evening, after supper, I did what everyone else had disappeared off to do: I wrote letters. I wrote one to Stanley, telling him—among other lies—that I'd already found another *fish*, and freshwater, not saltwater, this time. I wrote one to Mrs. B. And I even began one to Kitty. Then I tore them all up. Who was I kidding? I had no one to write to.

We knew early the next morning: Our ultimatum had expired and war had been declared. The fighting had already begun, Mr. Watts said at breakfast. He explained to us that Lord Hector would be returning to London, and that most of our guests would likely leave, too. And it all seemed to be unfolding fast, too fast, and for some reason I thought of Stanley, and of people in London and across the border in England, because Scotland was still a foreign country to me, and our distance from the capital served to distance me from *it*. Then we all bowed our heads and said more special prayers, and *Amen* became *Our Men*.

Later, when I went to Ottoline with her breakfast, there was no sign of her. I found her, eventually, in the small study—dressed and sitting at a desk, writing.

"Is there anything you need, my lady? Can I get you some tea?" I asked.

"No, thank you, Pearl."

"I'm very sorry . . . about the news, I mean."

She turned to me. Her eyes were shrunken and she twisted a handkerchief in her hands. She said, "The world is gone mad and I don't know what to do with myself, Pearl. I've been awake most of the night. I keep thinking about the boys . . . those beautiful boys sleeping on my linen, in my beds . . . dreaming." She looked up at me. "I don't want them to wake up to this war."

"The fighting's a long way from here, my lady, and it might all be resolved quicker than we think. I'm sure the boys won't be needed."

She stared at something beyond my shoulder, and with her eyes half closed and in little more than a whisper, she said, "No, they'll go. They'll all go because they believe it's their duty. Because old men will tell them it's an honor to serve one's country, to fight for it, die for it . . . A noble sacrifice." She fixed her eyes on me: "I'm quite sure you've heard them. They're all gung ho, all fired up."

I nodded. I knew. I thought of Billy, the fear in his eyes. His brother's determination.

"I won't be able to stop Hugo. It's what he was born for, like his father . . . But I think I can stop Billy." She straightened herself. "I've already written to Mr. Asquith. Yes. I've told him he can have one of my sons, but not both. Not both. In fact, I've suggested he enforce a rule . . . a rule of one son per family."

"That's a very good idea, my lady."

"It must start here," she said. "I'll allow Hugo to go—because I have no choice. And, if I *have* to send him, I shall send him with my love and my prayers, and even my blessing. But I can't let Billy go. I simply can't allow it. And so we must put those foolish notions out of his head." She paused, and there was a flicker of a smile. "You know what he's like . . . so idealistic, romantic . . . and so very easily influenced. We shall have to be vigilant, Pearl. We shall have to keep an eye on him."

"I'll do whatever I can, my lady," I said, remembering my raised fists and Billy's look of terror.

All day people departed: Lord Hector—accompanied by Charles and Hugo—for London, along with Virginia Parker, her husband and maid; and other houseguests for various counties in England. Later that afternoon, after beds had been stripped, fireplaces cleaned, names removed from brass plates on doors, Mr. Watts inspected and locked the bedrooms. Mollie and two other maids, given what they were due, left for the station, along with a groom and an under-gardener.

I stayed close to Billy. I watched him, checked his whereabouts by the hour, and that evening, when he came into his mother's dressing room and said he was going to a special service at a church in the nearby village, I immediately glanced to Ottoline and said, "Oh, perhaps I should go, too?"

"Yes! Yes, of course," she said. "You must go . . . Sadly, I can't."
She turned to her son. "I've invited a few of our neighbors to
dinner—and though our numbers are somewhat depleted, I didn't
think to cancel."

So I accompanied Billy to the service. We went on foot.

He said, "Isn't it strange to think we're at war?"

It was. That deliciously soft evening, our footsteps and the distant bleating of sheep spoke only of peace. I said, "It might all be
over quickly, Billy."

"Hmm, Hugo says only if we take swift action, only if we show
our strength and commitment. He says that's why everyone needs
to sign up."

"But not you, Billy. The army doesn't need schoolboys."

He laughed. "I'm not a schoolboy, Pearl, not any longer, and I
imagine there'll be boys far younger than me heading over there
right now."

"I don't understand why you would want to go, why anyone
would want to go and fight."

"It's not a question of *want*," he said, and though he sounded
about to say more, he left it at that.

We were almost at the top of the hill, the lofty strip of houses
known as Tomintoul, and I stopped, turned and stared back toward
Delnasay, its gray slate rooftops poking up from the evergreen trees.
I followed the meandering line of the river through the sleepy glen
to the whitewashed cottage where smoke rose up from a chimney.

"We won't be seeing Raffy at church," said Billy, moving alongside me and following my gaze. "He's an atheist. No, not an atheist," he added quickly, correcting himself. "An agnostic."

"Agnostic?"

"Can't make up his mind . . . needs proof."

"Well, you can't have proof about *everything*. Some things you just know. That's why it's called faith. And anyway, I don't suppose God has the time to go round proving himself to all and sundry . . . particularly now."

Billy laughed. "You need to tell Raffy that."

"Oh, but it's not my place to tell him."

"Why not?"

"Because I'm . . ." I was about to say *a servant*, but it didn't sound right, and for some reason I didn't want to remind Billy.

"You were about to say *a woman*, weren't you?"

I nodded.

"Well, for what it's worth, I happen to think most women are cleverer than men . . . No, really, I do. Look at the mess we're in now. Mother says if women were running things, it would never have come to this, and I rather think she's right."

I hadn't got to know Hugo, who was—perhaps understandably—a little dismissive of me, but I felt as though I knew Billy and that he would not patronize, judge or condemn me. There was not an iota of unkindness in his bones. And for the life of me, I really couldn't imagine him engaged in any fighting.

Billy turned his gaze toward a stretch of pine trees, through which a straggling line of low buildings was visible. "You know, it's said to be the highest village in the Scottish Highlands. Do you suppose the fact that we're nearer to heaven means God might better hear our prayers?" he asked.

I shrugged. "Perhaps . . . Let's hope so."

"Queen Victoria hated this village. She called it the most tumbledown, poor-looking place she'd ever seen, and the people who lived here—miserable and dirty. What a damned cheek, eh?" he added, turning to me.

"Did the queen stay at Delnasay?"

He laughed. "*No*, Delnasay's never had royalty. It's nowhere near grand enough. No, Her Maj was marauding about with her entourage. She came over from Balmoral—it's not far, but I pity the poor pony that had to carry her across the hills and glens. And she might have thought, might at least have wondered *why* the people were miserable and dirty, don't you think? Silly woman."

I smiled. "And you said women were intelligent."

"Ha, I said most. *Most*. And a pampered queen doesn't qualify . . . Anyway, we'd better get our skates on." And he took hold of my arm and placed it through his.

Arm in arm, we walked into the village and onto the main street, the only street. And though I felt a little awkward at first, with my arm through his—because I'd only ever walked out like that with Stanley—I thought it a lovely and kindly gesture. Typical Billy, I thought. And typical Billy that he'd know so many of those standing outside the church; typical of him to want to speak to them; typical of him to introduce me—and not as his mother's maid or any servant, but simply as "Miss Gibson." And when an old man with a cloud of snow-colored hair smiled broadly at Billy and then winked at me, I knew what he was thinking: I was Billy Campbell's sweetheart.

Later, as we all knelt down to pray, as I lowered my head to the varnished wood, I thought at first only of the boy kneeling next to me, and then of all the others: good men, young men, *fine laddies* . . . And what about the ones who needed proof? Would God give it to them? I wondered. And I reached into my coat pocket, felt for the handkerchief and ran my fingers over those embroidered initials: *RSS*.

Chapter Eight

Henry Gibson, my grandfather, fought in the Crimean War. Kitty told me it took him three months to walk back across a continent to the place he called home. But there were no flags flying, no bunting and no hero's welcome when he walked into Battersea Square late one afternoon in May, his clothes in tatters, his boots filled with holes. People mistook him for an outsider, a beggar, Kitty said. Old Man Tate, Peddler Palmer and even Mad Meg—who had never been right but had always known *things*—had all averted their eyes. Only Benny the Jew, said Kitty, knew and recognized Henry and had run up to him and kissed his beard and filthy hands.

Almost thirty-six hours after war had been declared, Billy disappeared.

He'd come down to breakfast, Mr. Watts reported; and there

was nothing at all unusual about Billy's appetite that morning, he said. But Ottoline, already fretful, wished to know exactly what Billy had had to eat; and when Mr. Watts reeled off the long list of items Billy had helped himself to from the sideboard, she shook her head and closed her eyes, as though it told her everything. Then Mr. Watts said he had seen Billy heading off down the valley with his knapsack, and suggested that he had as likely as not gone on a hike.

But Billy failed to appear at luncheon, and as teatime approached and the weather changed and it began to rain, Ottoline became more and more tense and agitated, drifting from room to room, window to window.

"You were meant to be keeping an eye on him, Pearl."

I wanted to say to her that I couldn't very well watch Billy every minute of every day *and* do my chores *and* attend her. But I didn't. I apologized.

She said, "I need Raffy . . . I need him to find Billy."

"But, my lady, Mr. Watts is probably right. Billy's no doubt simply gone on a hike and will be back soon."

"How do you know? How can Watts know?" she snapped. "While we're sitting about here, my son might already be on his way to . . . to war."

So I went to the kitchen, told Mr. Watts we needed to do something, or at least appear as though we were doing something, to locate Billy's whereabouts. Mr. Watts shook his head and rolled his eyes. He said, "That poor boy's not going to be able to leave his mother's side now."

"She wants Mr. Stedman to try to find him."

Mr. Watts nodded: "I'll go," he said with a sigh. "I'll go and seek Mr. Stedman, tell him what's what."

Then Ottoline appeared, along with Mr. Cowper, whom I hadn't seen all day. She was wearing her hat and gloves and new cape. She said, "We're taking the dogcart. We'll go to the village, find McNiven, ask him if he can go to the station—just in case."

As they all headed out of the door, I called after them, "I'll walk out down the valley, see if there's any sign of him."

Ottoline turned. "Yes, do that."

So I set off down the glen, following the path by the river. The rain had stopped and the air was fresh and sweet with the mingled scents of heather and pine. Clouds were dispersing and sunlight illuminated the tops of the hills and forested slopes to the east. The path was muddy, and the galoshes I'd put on over my shoes squeaked and squelched as I walked.

Was it to be like this every time Billy disappeared from her sight? I wondered. For like Mr. Watts, I was quite certain Billy Campbell had *not* gone, and Ottoline's reaction seemed unnecessarily dramatic. I had been walking for perhaps an hour, lost in the sound and rhythm of my stride, when the shape of Billy came leaping down the hillside.

"Here," he said, standing in front of me on the path, breathless, smiling, flushed. He handed me a small bunch of white heather. "It's for good luck."

The heather was wet in my hand. I said, "You've caused quite a panic at home, Billy."

"Really? Why's that?"

"No one knew where you were—and you've been gone all day."

"It's never bothered anyone before."

"Well, it does now. Everyone's been very worried."

He shook his head. "Then they're all rather stupid."

"Billy!"

"I'm sorry, but they are. All they know and understand is their own pathetic agenda . . . luncheon, tea, dinner," he added in a simpering voice, "and what to wear for each occasion. As though it even matters."

"I don't think—"

"The only one I trust," he interrupted, "the only one whose opinion matters to me, is Raffy. You see, he's different, Pearl. He's more like you and me."

I took a moment. Clearly, Billy had no idea of Ralph Stedman's duplicitous nature. No idea that the man he spoke of in such glowing terms was in fact his mother's lover. And the fact that Ralph Stedman had hoodwinked Billy, the fact that he had somehow inspired Billy to put him on a pedestal, made me want to loathe him more.

But I held my tongue. I said only, "I'm not sure about Mr. Stedman."

Billy turned to me. "That's because you don't know him yet, because he keeps to himself. But once you get to know him, once you understand who he is, what he stands for . . . well, I think you'll respect him as much as I do."

No, it most definitely wasn't the time, and though I already suspected—and felt in my heart—that there might never be another chance, I changed the subject and asked Billy where he'd been all day.

"Everywhere . . . over the hills and back again. Taking it all in." He turned away from me and stared down the valley, his hand to his brow. His hair was damp, slicked back from his forehead, and, transfixed for a moment by the beauty of him, I understood why Ottoline could not let go.

"Do you see it?" he said. "Over there, in the distance?"

He moved behind me, placed his chin on my shoulder and raised my arm. "There," he said, lifting my hand to a piece of the sky. "It's an eagle, a golden eagle. See it?"

And I could see something. A dark shape circling—just a bird, to me.

"Yes," I said. "I can see it now. But how do you know it's an eagle?"

"By the movement, the wingspan . . . and where it is. It's right above the aerie at the castle rock."

"Oh yes, that place."

"I'll take you. It's only a thirty-minute walk. Are you all right with heights?" he asked, moving round in front of me.

"I think so."

"Come on, then."

"Oh, but not now," I said. "We can't go now. We have to go back, Billy. Your mother . . . She's beside herself. She's gone out looking for you. Everyone's looking for you."

"Seriously? How embarrassing." He sighed. "Oh well, another time," he added, glancing back at me.

Another time.

❧

That evening, almost exactly forty-eight hours after war had been declared, and as I was sitting outside on the wall by the trees—still trying to fathom it all—I saw him, Ralph Stedman. Marching up the driveway, his head down, he seemed to have a new purpose to his stride. But when he looked up and saw me, he stopped. Then he took a few steps and stopped again. Finally he turned and crossed over the lawn toward me.

"Under the circumstances, it seems rather stupid to ask you again if you're any happier, and yet, bizarrely, I'm compelled to."

I wasn't inclined to climb down from the wall for him, so I stayed where I was, and I said, "And under the circumstances, I'd have to be an imbecile to be happy, Mr. Stedman."

I saw him staring at my ankles. "I'm waiting for the twilight," I said, as though I had an appointment with it.

He raised his eyes to me. "I hear there was quite a panic today. About Billy?"

I nodded. "But all's well that ends well."

He said nothing, and I watched him walk away toward the house. I wondered if he was planning to sign up, too, if he'd put down his paintbrushes and give up Ottoline's bed and lovers in London for his country, or if he'd be one of those Mr. Watts had already termed "shirkers." *Yes,* I thought, *he'll be one of those: Someone so duplicitous is bound to be. Probably say he's going off to war and then . . . then hide himself away in some woman's bedroom. Despicable.*

I got down from the wall, leaned against the stone and looked in the other direction. In the washed-out sunset hanging over the land, all was soft and still. *And yet we are at war,* I thought again; and then I said the word out loud: "War." It seemed completely inadequate, its one syllable a mere sound, like a bleat, and newly pathetic.

Ever optimistic, Mrs. Lister kept using the word *skirmish*, but something inside me scoffed at that word. Though the notion of war, the idea that men were already fighting and perhaps dying over in France, was still impossible for me to comprehend and imagine, I knew what lay ahead was not going to be any skirmish. It was simply too big a mess, with too many countries involved and tangled up in it for anything to be resolved quickly. It could last months, even a year—a whole year, I thought, staring up at the heavens; I might be twenty-five by the time it was over . . . twenty-six by the time I got to see France . . . Paris and Biarritz.

I had planned to be married by the time I was twenty-five. It had seemed a good age for it: not too old and not too young. And it allowed for me to have the first of my children at twenty-six; the second at twenty-eight; and a third at thirty. Nicely spaced. Not too many. Boy, girl, boy. Up until very recently, it had seemed possible, even likely. I would spend a year or two more in service, travel, see a bit of the world, or England at least, and then devote myself to . . . to Stanley? Had I really thought that?

"Yes, I had," I said out loud, half laughing, newly astonished.

"Had what?"

I turned. He stood on the grass, clutching a glass in each hand.

"Had . . . thought the Germans would see sense."

"Really?"

"Yes."

"Well, they didn't."

"No."

"No." He glanced at the glasses in each of his hands as though not quite sure how or why they were there. "Ah yes," he said, re-

membering, "my cousin and I thought your twilight might be en-
hanced by a glass of sherry."

"Your cousin?"

"Ottoline. Our mothers were sisters," he said, offering me a
glass.

I shook my head. "I don't drink."

"Never?"

"Only on special occasions . . . Christmas and such."

"Hmm. And the outbreak of war can hardly be described as a
special occasion."

He looked awkward for a moment, clutching the two glasses
and staring down at the grass. I said, "I had no idea you and my
lady were related . . . You must be very close?" I couldn't help myself.

"Not especially, not now—though we were when we were children." He raised his eyes to me. "Our lives and lifestyles are very
different. I see her when she's here, when I'm here, but I prefer not
to get too involved in affairs. That's why I stay at the cottage."

I was flabbergasted by his audacity. I said, "And what about
London, Mr. Stedman? Are affairs easier for you there?"

"Much. But it's entirely different. I'm quite often passing
through and tend not to tell Ottoline. I don't lie," he quickly
added—perhaps seeing my expression. "I simply don't tell her. It's
the only way. Otherwise, can you imagine? I'd be embroiled
there, too."

"She'll find out."

"Hopefully not . . . Not unless you tell her, of course," he added,
smiling. It all seemed to be something of a joke to him.

I stood up straighter. I said, "My lady has spoken to me about everything, Mr. Stedman, and, as I think you already know, I happen to have seen things for myself."

"No, I didn't know. But if you caught them together, I'm pleased. It eliminates doubt, and there's nothing worse."

Things were muddling, shifting about in my mind. I waited as he placed a glass on the wall, pulled out his packet of cigarettes and lit one. Then I said, "What do you mean, *them?*"

"Ottoline and Felix Cowper. Isn't that who we were speaking about?"

My heart performed a strange acrobatic feat in my diaphragm. I said, "Oh yes . . . Yes, indeed. Ottoline and Felix Cowper."

It was not Ralph Stedman. The liar, the cad, the man in Ottoline's bed was not he. It was Mr. Cowper, Felix Cowper. It was Mr. Cowper returning to his room when he asked me about breakfast; Mr. Cowper, who had disappeared off with Ottoline the following morning; Mr. Cowper, sitting with her now.

"You know, I think I will have that drink after all, Mr. Stedman."

He handed me a glass and raised his own. "To a short war . . . and to peace."

"To *peace,*" I repeated.

An exquisite silence fell over us, and as I sipped the warm liquid, I turned away from him, smiling at the shadows on the lawn, and at my own wonderful stupidity.

"Do you have cousins?" he asked after a while.

I shook my head.

"Siblings?"

I shook my head again.

"What about parents?"

"I never knew them, was brought up by my aunt, but she's gone, too."

He waited a moment, then asked, "So . . . where's home, exactly?"

I turned to him, still smiling. "I don't have one, Mr. Stedman."

"I see," he said, but I knew he didn't. I knew that to someone such as him, the idea of not having a home or family must be very strange. And I knew it even more by the lengthy silence that followed. For what can anyone say to that? There can be no further polite inquiries as to who or where. And though I'd experienced that same silence dozens of times before, and had sat in servants' halls listening to others speak about *home*, about mothers and fathers, sisters and brothers, grandparents, sweethearts and aunts, it felt different this time, perhaps because it was my birthday, or perhaps because we were at war, or perhaps because it was him.

Eventually he spoke. "A little dicky bird told me you were engaged to be married."

I took another sip from my glass, wondering who, exactly, his little dicky bird was. "No. That's wrong. I'm not . . . nor ever was," I added, and from the corner of my eye I saw him nod his head.

The sky had changed from a washed-out blue to a luminous pink. Behind the black silhouette of the hills the full moon had begun to rise.

I said, "Today was my birthday." He was the first person I'd told.

"*No!* . . . So it *is* a special occasion, and quite right, too, that you're having a drink. And though I know better than to ask a lady her age, I'm wondering . . . ," he said teasingly, tapping a finger on his chin.

A *lady*, I thought. "Twenty-four," I said.

"Does anyone know? Does Ottoline know? Has Mrs. Lister baked you a cake?"

"I haven't told anyone. It seemed . . . inappropriate, irrelevant."

"*Irrelevant?* Wait here," he said, and handed me his glass.

I watched his dark shape disappear inside the doorway, finished my drink and took a sip from his. But the air was turning damp and chilled, and so I followed his path across the grass toward the lamp-lit windows. We collided in the lobby. He took the empty glasses from my hands. "As you haven't given me much notice, I'm having to improvise. Do you have a dress, a birthday gown? Something you'd wear to a small soiree with a few reprobates?"

Soiree and *reprobates* were not words in my vocabulary, but I knew what he meant and so I said yes, I did. Because I had one good dress, never worn, and intended for some occasion in the future. It had been Mrs. B.'s Christmas present to me, and made by her dressmaker in Bournemouth.

"Well then, you have time to go upstairs and change. Celebrations commence in twenty minutes."

"Oh but, Mr. Stedman . . ."

"No *oh buts*. Off you go." He opened the door, and as I walked into the hallway, toward the staircase, he called after me: "And no more *Mr. Stedman*, please. My name is Ralph."

❧

I was standing in my underwear and wondering what to do, when Ottoline tapped on the door and walked into my room—carrying what appeared to be dozens of her gowns.

"You are naughty," she said. "I had no idea it was your birthday."

She off-loaded the pile of dresses from her arms onto the bed. "I wasn't sure if you had anything to wear, so I've brought you a few things to try on." She looked me up and down. "Yes, I think we're about the same size."

I had already taken my dress from the wardrobe, but when Ottoline saw it, hanging on the back of the bedroom door, she said, "You weren't planning to wear this, were you?"

"Oh no, not that old thing . . . That's just—"

"It looks like something my mother would have worn," she interrupted.

"It was a present, actually. From Mrs. Bart."

Ottoline rolled her eyes. "I might've guessed. You're twenty-four, Pearl, not sixty-four." Then she smiled and clapped her hands. "So, I've had the most marvelous idea. As it's your birthday, I want you to allow me to dress you . . . to be *your* maid. What do you think?"

But she didn't wait for a reply. She began rummaging through the pile of gowns she'd brought into the room with her, some of which I recognized. "Blue . . . No, too cold . . . Black?" She glanced over her shoulder at me. "No, definitely not."

"I'm really not sure about any of this, my lady. It's very kind of you and Mr. Stedman, but I'm not used to . . . and my birthday's almost over, anyway."

She rose up and turned to me. "But you must have a celebration of sorts . . . *please*," she added, clasping her hands together beseechingly, her eyes twinkling. "Your birthday is our tiny shred of normality. A frivolity, perhaps, but one we need . . . particularly now."

Particularly now . . . There it was again.

My life had become queer and mad. The whole world had become queer and mad.

"Try this one," said Ottoline, seemingly oblivious to the madness and lifting a gown up from the bed.

I had never worn a strap of pearls, never worn a diamond-encrusted headband—or any headband. I had never worn rouge, and I had certainly never worn—nor perhaps ever would wear again—a gown like the gold silk gown I wore that evening. But by the time Ottoline had finished with me, as I stood in front of the looking glass in my room, I appeared every inch a lady. And, for the first time in my life, I saw a thing of beauty staring back at me. Pearl Gibson, the once kitchen maid now lady's maid, had gone. Vanished. Instead, there was someone new, and though unrecognizable to myself at first, as soon as Ottoline moved behind me and appeared in the glass, I remembered.

Ottoline reached up, adjusted the headband and stared at me. "Beautiful," she said. She moved over to the door, but when I followed her, she stopped, and without turning to me, she said, "No, you must come down on your own, Pearl. You must make your own entrance tonight."

None of it was right. And as I descended the staircase, I felt as though I were on a stage, acting a part I was little suited to play and had not practiced. I stood for a moment, listening to the voices on the other side of the door. I heard Ottoline: "Of course she told me she had no family, told me when I interviewed her. But I hadn't realized she meant no one *at all*, and no home."

Then Ralph: "She thought her birthday was irrelevant. Inappropriate to mention."

"I really don't think one can be expected to remember every single servant's situation in life, or indeed birthday. And quite frankly, if you make a thing of one—you have to make a thing of them all, no?"

Then, quickly and sounding a little agitated, came Billy: "I'm sorry, but I have to disagree with you, Felix. If you employ people in your home, I think you have a moral obligation to find out their circumstances and look after them."

Someone clapped hands—Ralph I guessed. And I took a deep breath, turned the handle and opened the door.

There were only the four of them, and they had all dressed up: Ralph in a long, bright orange silk kimono; Billy in bow tie and a shorter but similar Chinese-looking jacket; Mr. Cowper in traditional white tie, and Ottoline in a dark purple gown with matching colored plumes in her hair. "And here she is!" said Ottoline, seeing me. Ralph leapt to his feet. He lifted a bottle from the silver ice bucket. Then came a loud pop, followed by a rendition of "Happy Birthday."

The only time anyone had made a toast to me before was when I turned sixteen. I had been working at a house in Kent at that time, and been desperately homesick, or rather, missing Kitty. I hadn't seen her in almost six months, and it was my first birthday without her. She sent me a picture postcard with roses on the front, and on the reverse it simply said, *Dear Pearl, Happy Birthday From Your Loving Aunt Kitty.* There was a smudged cross beneath her name, and that cross was infinitely more beautiful to me than the tinted roses on the other side.

And so I was thinking of her—Kitty—as I took my first sip of champagne, in a castle of sorts, in another country, with people I didn't know, and the likes of whom Kitty had never met, nor could ever have imagined. And I was wondering if she'd be proud of me, and if she'd still recognize me. And I thought I might be dreaming, but if I was, I didn't care. Because if it was a dream, I was determined to enjoy every single second of being treated as something more than I was: someone relevant.

As soon as Billy put a record on the gramophone, Mr. Cowper asked Ottoline to dance, and I wondered if Ralph might ask me. Then Mr. Watts entered the room. He filled up our glasses, and as he filled mine, he slid me a look that seemed to begin with, *In your position* . . . And as happens when one stirs from a dream, everything felt new and strange again, and I was embarrassed for him to see me sitting there, all dolled up, wearing Ottoline's jewels and gown, and drinking.

The door closed. Ottoline sat down next to me and patted my hand. "Don't worry about Watts. He's seen it all before—and far worse. And after all, it *is* your birthday." Then she got up to dance again, and I saw Mr. Cowper put his hand on her bottom and her lift it away. I looked over at Billy, wondered what he made of it all. His mother's lover was at least a decade younger than she was, and definitely nearer to Billy's age than her own. And it didn't seem right for Mr. Cowper to be behaving like that in front of Billy. But what was right? What was normal? We were at war and we were dancing, celebrating my birthday, an event rarely celebrated, and a bittersweet date to me—coinciding as it did with my mother's passing.

As I sipped my champagne, as I watched Ottoline and Mr. Cowper, I was for some reason reminded of Stanley and Eileen Poynter. "See you later," she'd said. Stan, she'd called him. I wondered if he'd taken *her* to a tea dance, if she had given him what *any normal fellow* expected. I had been a fool, I thought, closing my eyes for a moment. For I knew then that Stanley Morton had been two-timing me with the sticky-fingered Eileen; that he was no different to the fellow at the A.B.C., the one who'd blown smoke rings and winked at me. He, Stanley, Mr. Cowper, Lord Hector and even my absent father were all players.

"Who's a player?"

Ralph was leaning forward in his chair, staring at me.

"Stanley Morton," I said, feeling rather drunk.

"Stanley Morton," he repeated. "Did you care for him?"

I glanced down at my dark brown leather shoes, wishing again that my feet were smaller, that I'd been able to wear a pair of Ottoline's satin evening shoes. "Not really, not anymore."

At that moment, Billy sat down next to me on the arm of the sofa. He said, "It's a damned shame we're at war on your birthday, Pearl."

"Bloody good reason for a cease-fire," said Ralph, altering tempo and picking up the large silver lighter from the low table between us. He kept his eyes fixed on me as he held it up to his cigarette, sat back in his chair, crossed his legs and then exhaled a plume of smoke.

Billy picked up the lighter and began fiddling with it. *Flick-flick . . . flick-flick . . .* "Are you about tomorrow, old thing?" he asked Ralph. "It's just that I'd like to speak to you about something . . . a private matter."

"Of course," said Ralph, still watching me. "You know where to find me."

Billy put down the lighter. "And now, before I go to my bed and leave you lot to burn the midnight oil, I wonder if I can have the pleasure of a dance with the birthday girl."

I smiled. I'd been waiting for someone—Ralph—to ask me.

Billy took my hand, led me in a slow waltz, and when the music stopped, he lifted it to his lips: "Thank you. I shall have sweet dreams now."

After Billy retired, Mr. Cowper took over the gramophone, and as he and Ottoline continued with their intimate party for two, I thought Ralph Stedman—a man who had said he hoped to dance with me one day—was never going to ask me. But he must have heard this thought, because within seconds he put down his glass, rose to his feet and took hold of my hands. He never asked; he simply pulled me onto my feet. And perhaps he knew that my head was spinning, because he held me close.

He smelled of turpentine and warm wool, and suddenly everything shone brighter: china, glass, brocade and tasseled satin. Color and sound merged and blurred into one. And his warmth and his strength were newly familiar, and I thought, *I know nothing about you, and yet I know everything you are.* Then the music changed, became louder, and Ottoline shrieked and Ralph said, "Don't worry. You'll be fine . . . It'll all be fine." And as I placed my head on his chest, I thought, *Don't go; don't leave me.* And he said, "I won't. I promise."

Later, we all laughed, because everything was funny, strange and funny, but then Ottoline burst into tears and everything seemed to stop for a moment. And I almost cried, too. And Ralph took my hand and led me over to a table where rolls of smoked salmon and cheese lay on a silver platter. And he told me to eat, and so I ate.

"You must never again think your birthday is irrelevant," he said. And when he raised his hand to my brow and adjusted my headband, I saw that Ottoline and Mr. Cowper had gone.

I was staring at the clock, which was looking rather proud of itself on the table with fat ankles, when Ralph asked, "What are you doing?"

"Is that three o'clock or a quarter after midnight?"

"Does it matter?"

"No . . . But it is very quiet."

He got up from his chair, went over to the gramophone, rifled through the scattered records and put on some music. "Debussy," he said, bending down and unbuttoning my shoes. Then he sat back down, and he smiled as he watched me, as I twirled about the floor.

Chapter Nine

First there was the pain: a dull and incessant throb beneath my eyelids, in my temples and at the base of my head. Every muscle in my body ached. Then came the vision: one of me—dancing about my employer's drawing room, pausing from time to time to wag my finger at a china figurine, or at a clock. And I was mortified, lost in an anguish I had never before known. But then, slowly, came more: the vague recollection of climbing stairs while singing "Happy Birthday." To myself.

What had happened to me? How could I have fallen so far?

Because I knew better: I had been warned from a young age about Drinking. Kitty had told me. She was an ardent supporter of the Temperance Movement and a member of the Band of Hope; I had gone with her to meetings and on marches, trudging along streets beneath lofty banners and singing, "B. I. B. L. E.—that's the book for me!"

I knew. Yes, I knew. Drink was, quite literally, mother's ruin: a poison that obliterated good sense and sound judgment. A Good Time, Kitty said, was the start of any undoing. After that, it was a rapid downward spiral into immorality, depravity. Saving the souls of Good Time Girls had been one of her missions. I knew all of this. Or had, twenty-four hours earlier.

Self-pity was no use: I was my mother's daughter.

I raised my head and saw my gown—Ottoline's gown—draped over a chair; my discarded ugly brown shoes; my stockings and a headband lying on the floor. There was no question: My ruination was complete. I would have to resign.

Dear Ottoline . . .

No, that wasn't right.

My Dear Lady? My Lady? . . . It is with regret . . .

Profound regret, surely?

Then the door opened.

"No, please don't get up. Are you feeling quite horrid?" Ottoline asked.

I nodded. The inside of my mouth had a bitter metallic taste, and my tongue seemed to be coated with glue. And I tried not to breathe when I tried to say, "I'm sorry, my lady."

"I do feel for you," she said, staring down at me and frowning. "Champagne can make one feel quite beastly, particularly if one has a glass too many. I'll have Watts bring up my raw egg *cure.*"

A wave of nausea passed through me as I sat up. I said, "I'd rather not see Mr. Watts, if you don't mind . . . In fact, I'd rather not see anyone at all before I go."

"Go? But where are you going?"

"I'm not sure, my lady . . . Perhaps back to London."

She sat down on the bed, grabbed hold of my hand. "Oh, my dear, are you not happy here—with me?"

I was confused. I stared back at her. "Yes, but . . . well, after last night, and then now, this morning . . . I thought you'd want me to go, to leave."

It was Ottoline's turn to look confused. She shook her head. "Why ever would I want you to . . . Ah." She closed her eyes for a second or two. "I understand, I think. You thought I'd be angry with you because you've overslept?"

I nodded. "That . . . and last night. Drinking. Too much."

She smiled and gripped my hand tighter. "It was your birthday, and we had a jolly little party to ourselves—in spite of everything. If I'd for one moment thought it was going to make you feel wretched, well—I would never have entertained Ralph's idea. And as for drinking too much"—she shrugged—"one simply has to learn."

"So you don't want me to resign?"

She laughed. "Of course I don't want you to resign. However, I do want you to stay in bed and rest. Sleep it off. You'll feel better in a few hours. Billy and Felix have gone fishing, and I intend to put in a full day's writing . . . So there's really nothing spoiling," she added, rising to her feet. "And take a walk later. Fresh air always helps."

It was early afternoon by the time I rose from my bed. Stirred from my dreams by ravenous hunger, I dressed quickly, then took Ottoline's gown and headband and jewelry back to her dressing room

and put them away. I went down to the kitchen and stood in the
doorway, newly awkward and reluctant to enter. Mrs. Lister was
rolling out pastry, Mr. Watts polishing silver. A dwindling light fell
on the long pine table where he worked, quietly humming to himself. I moved on down the passageway, to the larder, where leftovers
from luncheon lay out on the slate bench, and where I closed the
door and stood for a while, tearing at a carcass, dipping chunks of
cold meat into an unctuous white sauce. I'd never tasted anything
so delicious.

Almost restored, almost revived, I took a handful of strawberries and went outside. Beyond the shadow of the house, sunlight
illuminated tiny particles of silver within the grit. And I thought:
We have all come from this, but only some of us catch the light.

And then I closed my eyes and concentrated.

*The hallway was dark but for one candle. Its flickering light danced
upon the walls. He handed me my shoes and said, "I must leave now."
But he didn't. He stared back at me, ran his finger across my brow,
down my cheek and onto my lips. And I wanted him to kiss me. And I
closed my eyes as I lifted my face to his. "Come and see me tomorrow,"
he said. And then a door closed . . .*

I walked under the archway and out of the yard, down the
driveway to the gap in the wall, the steps and overgrown path,
weaving my way through the long grass, tangled weeds and tall
thistles, until at last the cottage appeared, its whitewashed walls
peach tinted in the afternoon light.

Standing next to an easel, smoking a cigarette, he turned as I
approached. "Hello, you. I'm pleased you've come."

We sat side by side in a couple of old deck chairs. And as I gazed out across the glen, the river, beyond the alders and groves of silver birch to the mountains, the peace was overwhelming, newly extraordinary, deeper and more powerful than anything I'd known. And with it came a sense of belonging, a sort of contentment and connectedness. And I thought, even if nothing else happened in my life, this was enough: this sky, these hills, those high-up purples and blues, that dark bird's wing, those feathery clouds and *him*. I knew I'd remember it all for the rest of my life.

I turned, took in his profile: the line of his jaw and aquiline nose; his mouth, moving almost imperceptibly in thought; his long sandy lashes and sunburned cheeks. And his hands: the blond hairs that curled at his wrist, his fingers smeared blue and white with paint, and the paleness of his palms against his tan. And as I blinked and saved it to memory, I had an urge to reach out, take his hand and kiss it. Because I wanted him to know, this Ralph Stedman—a stranger who'd helped me board a train, who had watched me dance, sang "Happy Birthday" to me and later unfastened my shoes without unfastening me; for the first time in my life, I wanted someone to know everything about me.

In that illuminated moment came an understanding my whole being craved, and a quiet rapture flooded my soul, and I thought, *I am where I am meant to be.*

"Ralph, I just want you to know—"

"No, I don't need to know."

"But I want to thank you."

"For what?"

"For looking after me last night . . . for being kind."

He ran his hands through his hair and sighed. "Have I been kind to you? I'm not so sure about that."

The sun disappeared behind a cloud; a shadow passed over the hills. I watched its progress in silence, perplexed by his words and waiting for more. But none came.

Eventually I said, "Should I go?"

"Yes, you probably should . . . But I don't want you to."

He pointed to a buzzard circling high in the sky, to an oyster-catcher swooping over the shingle. He told me the names of the surrounding hills, the names of the pools in the river—the Avon, pronounced *A'an*, he said.

Slowly, we found our place again.

He teased me about the previous evening, telling me, yes, I had danced for quite a while.

"How long?" I asked, no longer embarrassed or shy.

"Oh, only for an hour or so," he said, turning to me, his eyes crinkling in a smile. "You accused a very ugly clock of being rather proud of itself, and then admonished it further for not being able to tell the correct time." And then, at last, he reached out and offered me his hand. He said, "You and I are kindred spirits."

"Wanderers."

"Weary wanderers."

"But I don't always want to wander. I'd like to have a home one day."

"And how do you see it, this home of yours?" he asked.

"It'll face due south," I began, assuredly. "The morning sun will come into the kitchen, on the eastern side; the evening sun, into the sitting room on the western side. It'll have three bedrooms and a modern bathroom. And I'll paint the walls of the sitting room a deep, dark pink, like a sunset . . . and the walls of my bedroom a golden color."

"And is the bedroom to be south facing?"

"I'm not sure."

"Gold might be a little too dazzling to the eye if it is."

"West facing?"

"Or south facing and . . . green?"

I shook my head. "No. I wouldn't want a green bedroom."

"Will there be a husband? . . . Children?"

I looked down, brushed an invisible fly off my dress. "I really haven't thought that far."

"You're being disingenuous, because I know you have. And so you should. You've pictured your home, how you wish it to look, and you need to populate it," he said.

I raised my eyes to him. "Well, of course, I'd like to think there'd be a family. I don't relish the thought of spinsterhood."

"I don't suppose you'll be a spinster, Pearl."

"I might . . . if there's to be a long war."

"Let's not talk about that," he said. "Have you eaten?"

We ate a rabbit stew he had made on the small stove inside and served on tin plates. He drank red wine from a jam jar; I drank water from a chipped china cup. And when he said, "You see, I know how to live in style," I laughed.

He asked me about Stanley, and I told him: "He was good-looking, sometimes funny. All the girls fell for him . . . and I suppose I was flattered. But we didn't really have much in common."

"Did you love him?"

"I thought I might. But I know now that I didn't."

"Did he hurt you?"

"No, my naïveté hurt me."

It was getting late, past the time I should be back, but I didn't want to go, didn't want to leave. And Ottoline had said she didn't need me. So I stayed on, watching him, listening to him, learning him.

Like me, Ralph had no siblings; like me, he had no home. The *S* stood for Sebastian, and Ralph Sebastian had been born in India, and then dispatched to a boarding school in England at five years old. School holidays had been spent with his housemaster or with Ottoline's family, and often there—at Delnasay. When Ralph reached the age of ten, his housemaster introduced him to a man he was told was his father, and from whom he learned that the woman he'd been writing to as *Mother* had in fact passed away some years before. More latterly, he'd spent time on the Continent, traveling, and studying the Great Masters, imitating them and producing portraits and pretty vistas for English and American tourists—most of whom were rich philistines, he said, and had no real understanding of art.

He was, he said, a disappointment to his father, who was a military man *through and through*, and had passed away some years ago. "I suspect I'm more like my mother. Certainly, having a painter for a son was an unspeakable embarrassment to my father. He'd have adored a son accomplished in sports or the sciences, not the arts . . . The last time I saw him, he asked me if I was batting for the other side," he added, staring back at me and raising an eyebrow.

I knew this term, and I suddenly wondered: Had I misread the signs? And so I took a moment and then said, "And do you . . . bat for the other side, I mean?"

He smiled.

"It wouldn't matter to me if you did—were," I said, picking up the chipped china cup and examining it as I pleaded with God.

"You really are adorable, you know?"

I looked up: "Am I?"

"Utterly." He took the china cup from my hand, ran his fingers over my open palm. "I could fall in love with this small hand," he said. "I could draw it from memory, imagine its touch, its innocence and industry . . ."

No one had ever said such things to me before, and I wasn't sure what to do or say. Only when he released my hand and sat back in his chair did the words come, the inevitable words: "Are you going to go?"

He sighed. "I'm not sure . . . I prefer to paint men rather than kill them."

"Does that mean you won't?"

"I can't promise you that. In fact, I can't promise you anything." He lifted his paint-smeared hand and stared at it: "But I'm not sure I'll be able to look Billy in the eye if I don't go."

"Oh, but Billy's not going. Ottoline's absolutely determined on that. And anyway, we have a pact."

"I'm not sure your pact will work. I rather think Billy's decided."

"But he can't have . . . When? It'll kill Ottoline if he goes."

"And it might kill Billy, but he's going—or more likely gone."

I thought of Ottoline and my words to her, my reassurance. "Do you know this? Do you know this for certain?"

Ralph nodded. "He came to see me earlier today. I'm sorry, Pearl, but I imagine he's already left."

I gasped. I rose to my feet. "I have to go . . ."

"Will you be coming back?"

"Yes . . . but I might be a while."

The air was filled with midges, and I stumbled more than once

as I ran back along the overgrown path toward Delnasay. I felt my
bun come undone, my stockings slide down, and my blouse, damp
beneath my arms and sticking to my back. The door by the kitchen
stood wide-open, and I paused for a moment, caught my breath and
adjusted my hair. Then, collected, I walked down the long passageway into the lamp-lit hallway, up the main staircase and toward
Ottoline's room.

She lay on her bed in the semidarkness, fully clothed and staring up at the ceiling.

"Billy," I said, "he's planning to go, my lady."

"Too late." She moved her hand across the bedcovers toward
the piece of paper: "Read it."

Dearest Mama,

*I know this will not please you, but haven't you always told
me I should follow my heart? And my heart tells me this: If my
brother, cousins & all of my friends are headed for France, I
must go, too. Because I can't stay here, hiding away when my
fellow countrymen, friends & family are all headed to fight for
Us & our Liberty. I can't live with it. And the only pain &
doubt I have right at this moment is about you. But rest assured,
I will do my utmost to stay safe.*

Please forgive me, and keep us all in your prayers.

Billy

I put down the letter, asked Ottoline if she knew when Billy
had left. "We might still have time," I said, thinking someone—

perhaps Mr. McNiven—could get to the station at Boat of Garten quickly enough to stop him.

Ottoline closed her eyes and shook her head. "He left hours ago, Pearl. I imagine he's already boarded the overnight train from Edinburgh to London."

I thought for a moment; then I said, "But His Lordship's in London! Perhaps he can intervene—do something?"

"Yes, perhaps," murmured Ottoline. "Felix is going to try to put a call in to him first thing tomorrow." She opened her eyes and turned to me. "You didn't know, did you? Billy didn't say anything?"

"No, I had no idea, my lady."

"And Ralph?" she asked. "Do you think he knew? It's just that . . . well, he and Billy are very close, and I'm not sure I could ever forgive him if he knew and hadn't told me, warned me."

"I'm quite sure he didn't know."

"He's only just turned nineteen, Pearl."

I waited a moment; then I asked if she wished me to help her undress. She shook her head. I asked her if she needed anything. She shook her head again. Then came a knock at the door. Mr. Cowper appeared. He walked over to Ottoline's bed, sat down on the edge of it and took hold of her hand. "Darling," he said. And as Ottoline began to cry, I left the room.

That night, a dark shape circled the twilit skies above Delnasay. I watched it from my open window. "He's not here; he's gone," I whispered to it.

Chapter Ten

Hector Campbell went to King's Cross, and to Waterloo and Charing Cross stations in search of Billy. He spoke to Billy's friends, but none of them had any information, or at least nothing they were prepared to impart to Lord Hector at that time. He spoke to his own friends, including Mr. Asquith and Lord Kitchener—who put out an alert.

And then hopes turned to Hugo, who was already in France with the British Expeditionary Force and might be able to somehow trace and find his brother, and persuade him to return home— because Billy was under twenty-one and had gone without his parents' permission, as Ottoline repeatedly said. But then Lord Kitchener appealed for another one hundred thousand men and every country in Europe seemed to be declaring war, and Mrs. Lister said trying to find Billy would be like trying to find a needle in a haystack.

So the waiting continued like a long prayer, and I began to see how the war was already reshaping lives and altering destinies. I began to understand that there was no escape from it, even in the Highlands of Scotland. For those of us left were all a little at odds with one another, and the paradise surrounding us, and even the peace—that exquisite peace enveloping the glen—began to feel *un*natural.

For a while Ottoline seemed to have no use for me. She rose early and spent her mornings studying the newspapers: underlining names, places in France, cutting up pages and columns, inserting them into envelopes later to be addressed and added to with notes and letters. Her correspondence became all-consuming, and in response to a daily deluge of shock and horror, she feverishly filled sheet after sheet of paper—murmuring to herself as she scrawled words to friends and relations, and to other mothers of sons.

She scoured the map of France His Lordship had sent her, running her finger along some invisible line, nodding to herself when she saw a name she recognized from the newspaper and then, sometimes, marking it in ink with an X. There was never any mention of her novel, and the clothbound notebooks she'd brought with her from Northumberland remained stacked up where I'd placed them on the day of our arrival.

Her afternoons and evenings were invariably spent with Felix Cowper—who usually rose at lunchtime. I suppose she was afraid to let him out of her sight—lest he, too, disappear. But I knew his departure was as inevitable as Ralph's; I knew it was only a matter of time. Even in our isolation, I could almost hear the drums, sweeping through towns and villages and calling up men. They would go, I thought. How could they not?

And Ralph? Ralph remained conspicuous by his absence. And aware as I was of his betrayal of Ottoline, and my own lie to her, aware as I was by then of my feelings, I was reluctant to go to him.

And so the hours were slow and heavy, each one imbued with the still and melancholy air of an early Sunday evening. And we all remained indoors. As though to go outside, to disconnect for just one moment from *it*—the War—was in some way disrespectful and unpatriotic. No one wished to be caught staring appreciatively at any views—*not at a time like this*. Instead, we waited. We waited for a telegram from Lord Hector about Billy, or a letter from Hugo; we waited for updates—about Britain, about France, about Belgium. We waited for news.

News . . .

But the Belgians were holding out well against the Germans, and Liege remained well guarded. Then, on what should have been a Glorious Twelfth, Britain declared war on Austria. The following day, Mr. Cowper left, and Ottoline entered a new phase, one in which she took refuge in playing gramophone records very loudly, and indulged in her newly acquired habit of smoking. And as my last shreds of optimism sank, I took a rusting bicycle from the coach house and headed up the potholed road for the church in the nearby village. At the top of the hill, I stopped and turned. Across the valley, smoke rose from the chimney of a whitewashed cottage. He had not gone. Not yet.

I sat in the church alone. And I tried to pray for peace, and for Billy's safety and for Hugo's. But my thoughts were littered with fighting words: *combat . . . conflict . . . campaign . . . casualties . . .* And muddled in with them—and above and beyond them, and selfishly, I know—was one name. And as the sun streamed in through the stained glass, I asked Kitty once again for guidance: *Tell me what to do.*

Though she never married, Kitty had once had a sweetheart called Joe. She had been engaged to him for almost nine years by the time she learned about the barmaid at the Raven, a nearby public house, and realized she had kept herself for a wedding night that would never be.

Magnanimous, ever generous, Kitty always spoke to the woman who stole her Joe, even when she bumped into her with yet another infant in the perambulator. I think she knew she had wasted her years, but her extraordinary capacity for forgiveness allowed her to smile through the pain.

'Tis better to have loved and lost than never to have loved at all.

It was almost seven by the time I arrived back at Delnasay. I dropped the bicycle onto the grit in the courtyard, entered the house and almost collided with Mr. Watts emerging from the butler's pantry. I heard him say, "Ah, Gibson," but I ignored him and raced down the passageway toward the music coming from the drawing room.

Ottoline sat with a glass in one hand and a cigarette in the other. Seemingly oblivious and in a world of her own, she moved her shoulders back and forth to the music. When at last she saw me, she said, "This is one of Billy's favorites."

And so I waited, watching her as she quietly sang along to the chorus: "Come on and hear, come on and hear, Alexander's rag-time band . . . They can play a bugle call like you never heard before, so natural that you want to go to war . . ." I waited until the music ended and the crackling began. Then I asked if she could spare me for an hour or so.

"An hour . . . a day . . . a week," she said, quietly, nonsensically, and without so much as looking at me. "What does it matter?"

"I shan't be long, I just—"

"You just *have* to go to him, I know . . . I know what it feels like." She turned to me then. "Are you in love with him?"

I didn't know what to say.

She stubbed out her half-smoked cigarette, put down her glass and went over to the gramophone. She lifted the needle and the crackling stopped. And as she stood with her back to me, she said, "I don't want him to break your heart."

I shook my head. "He won't."

"How can you be so sure?"

"Because he's a good person."

Then, turning to me, she said, "Oh, Pearl . . . I *know* he's a good person." And I saw a new sympathy in her eyes, and I had a strange fluttering in my stomach: a feeling you get when you know something's coming. "He hasn't told you, has he?"

"I'm not sure," I said, hoping yet knowing and waiting for it to come.

The room tensed itself. My throat felt as tight as a coil about to spring.

"He's married, Pearl."

Married. The word bounced about the room, reverberating off

the blue-painted walls and china figurines. And with its reverberation came that gushing sound, flooding my ears and head like a
great wave. And though Ottoline went on speaking, though I
could see her mouth moving, her voice drifted away; and down and
down I sank, until all I could hear was the distant drum of my own
heartbeat.

Then loud and clear came Kitty: *Stand up straight and look at
Her Ladyship when she's speaking to you.* And thus, I surfaced.

". . . So it's a learning curve," Ottoline was saying. She moved
over the room to the sofa, sighed as she sat down. "Men do tend
to miss out the small detail of a wife when they want something . . . someone," she said, raising her eyes and glancing over at
me. "Of course, it's not a conventional marriage—never was. She's
older than he is, French . . . Her name is Marie Therese."

She beckoned me over to where she sat. And so I went, and I
sat down, next to her. She took hold of my hand, gripped it tightly
in hers. Her rings pressed into my fingers. "They married some
eight years ago, when Raffy was on his first trip to the Continent.
French, Roman Catholic—she wouldn't allow him to touch her
without a ring on her finger. Silly boy . . . But perhaps he wanted a
mother figure. Anyhow, initially, it seemed they were happy-*ish*.
They moved about . . . France, Spain, Italy. Came to England once
or twice . . . and then, well, his letters and postcards were signed
off just from him. *From Ralph.*"

Finally, I thought of a word to say: "Divorced?"

Ottoline gasped. "*Divorced?* My dear, Marie Therese Stedman
is French, a Catholic . . . She'll never countenance divorce. No, she
and Ralph have to live with their mistake. They will never divorce.

Ralph will never be able to remarry—no matter how much he loves someone," she added, looking me in the eye.

"Children?" I said, after a moment or two.

"Thankfully not."

I lowered my gaze to our hands, Ottoline's fingers intertwined with my own. "I've embarrassed you and made a fool of myself. If you'd like me to leave—"

"Stop! You haven't embarrassed me. Not at all . . . And I don't believe you've made a fool of yourself, at least I hope not," she said, scrutinizing me.

I said nothing. I knew I had made a fool of myself.

"I know only too well that we can't choose whom we fall in love with," Ottoline began again, "or when and how it will happen. We can only make decisions based on *what* we know, the facts of the matter, and the facts of the matter are Ralph's situation. He's married, taken." She squeezed my hand. "And as for leaving, well, where would you go, hmm? Your home is here, now—here and in Northumberland. Your home is with me, Pearl."

We sat in silence for some time, staring out at the still and sunlit gardens beyond the French doors. And she kept hold of my hand, and it didn't feel remotely strange; it felt steadying, comforting and maternal. And I thought, *This is what a mother would do. This is how a mother would be.*

We were still sitting side by side and holding hands when Mr. Watts came in to ask Ottoline about dinner. She hadn't eaten in the dining room since the day Felix Cowper left, and this evening once again she asked for a tray in her room, "In a little while, Watts, if you don't mind . . . Around eight o'clock will be fine."

I knew Mr. Watts didn't like *arounds*, and *abouts*, and *little whiles*. He was a man of punctuality and precision. Vagueness was not his style, and I could see his discomfiture give way to mild alarm when he glanced to our hands and said, "Very well, Your Ladyship." And, of course, trays to Ottoline were my job, not his.

As the door closed, I said, "Thank you for your kindness, my lady." And I was about to go on, was about to explain to her that I would go to the kitchen and arrange her supper tray, attend her in the usual way, when she said, "Kindness? My motto in life has always been *Do unto others as you would have them do unto you*. I'm not sure that necessarily qualifies as kindness."

"Oh, but it does, I think, and it's what my aunt used to say . . . and *You reap what you sow*," I added, and then wondered why.

Ottoline smiled, and as she finally let go of my hand, she said, "And what's that other one? *Let not the sun go down on your wrath*? I don't need you tonight, and I rather think you should go to him— to Ralph. You need to have your say. And I want you to. It's important for you to express what's in your heart, to release it. Otherwise it will fester there, and that's not good. Not good at all." She rose to her feet and I quickly rose, too; then I waited as she walked over to the window.

"Life's so short, Pearl, so very precious and short," she said, newly quiet. "I look out on these lawns, and it seems only a moment ago I ran across them and into my grandfather's arms; only a moment ago that I watched Hugo and Billy playing on them." She turned to me. "That's all we have, you see, in the end: a handful of moments . . . and that's why we must seize and hold on to each one of them," she added, clenching a fist out in front of her. "Otherwise . . . well, they simply slip away."

As I opened the door for her, she smiled and placed her hand on my arm. She said, "Do whatever you have to do. Say what you have to say. But please come back to me. I need you."

I watched her cross over the hallway, watched her climb the stairs, and I thought, *I'll come back to you. I'll come back to you and I'll never leave you. Never.*

And then I walked out into the golden light of an August evening.

Chapter Eleven

It was a golden evening in August when Henry Gibson sat down in the mud on the banks of the Thames. He wept beneath a bruised heaven. For the sky over London was like one of Mr. Turner's paintings, Kitty said, all purple and mauve and yellow. And it had taken my mother's body six days to float upstream to Mortlake. Six days since Henry had found the baby wrapped up in a blanket at the back of his workshop. Six days since he'd carried the small bundle in to his sister.

They had both remarked on the luminescence of the baby's skin: "Like a pearl," said Kitty, "a precious little pearl."

And thus, I became.

The door stood open. He lay on the daybed beneath the window on the other side of the room.

"Good evening, Mr. Stedman."

He looked up and smiled, put down his pencil and paper. "Ah, so we're back to formalities, are we, *Miss Gibson*? You know, when you said you might be a while, I didn't realize you meant almost a week."

"And when you told me about your family, I didn't realize you had a *wife*."

He sat up, swung his legs off the bed. "Ah yes, my wife," he said, staring down at the paint-splattered floorboards. "My wife," he said again, running brown fingers through yellow hair. "Dear Marie Therese, whom I haven't set eyes on in over a year, whom I married in haste." He paused, glanced up at me. "Young and foolish haste."

I shook my head. "It doesn't matter how young you were or how foolish. You're married, Ralph . . . and you didn't tell me. You danced with me, you—you took off my shoes and held my hand. You held my hand here, and you told me nothing . . . *nothing.*"

That gushing sound was back inside my head. And I wanted him to get up, to walk over to me and take me in his arms, to hold me and tell me . . . tell me something that would make it stop. Tell me something that would make sense of everything. But he didn't. He stared up at me through that long yellow hair of his, and in that fine deep voice he said, "I'm sorry. I was going to tell you, Pearl. I intended to tell you."

"Oh really? And would that have been before or after you'd seduced the lady's maid?"

He shook his head. "It's not like that and you know it. And if you hadn't run off that night in search of Billy . . ."

I heard him call after me as I ran back along the path. Heard him as I leaped over the little stream. And then I stopped, and I waited. Why, I'm not sure.

No, that's not true. I stopped because I knew time was slipping. I stopped because I had never known anyone like him—and knew I never would again.

And the air was thick and syrupy, and my head was still gushing, gushing with the sound of water, and I thought of my mother—drowning with her desperate love, drowning as she bled. And of Kitty's smudged cross and unrequited love, and of Billy's pure heart, and Ottoline's unhappy marriage and sense of duty. *Duty.* Duty, honor, service and sacrifice, peace and goodwill . . . Peace and goodwill to all men and all women, and those boys, those boys sinking into the mud of another country.

And the scream that came out of me echoed all around the valley. And in the silence that came after, my body trembled and shook.

Then all was still, perfectly still and perfectly quiet. And an indeterminable time passed as we stood staring at each other. He held my gaze as he stepped over the stream. One of us said, *Don't go.* One of us said, *Stay.* One of us reached out. And I was rescued. Anchored in his arms, steady once more.

When he lifted my face from his chest, he said, "I *was* going to tell you," and I nodded; I knew. And as he continued to hold me, I continued to listen. "Despite your cynicism, I'm not in the habit of seduction—of ladies, maids, or lady's maids. In fact, I've led a celibate life for the last few years, preferring to concentrate on my painting. Not that it appears to have done me much good. I've lived a nomadic existence. I have nothing to offer anyone—any woman, and, as you now know, certainly not marriage." He paused, and I felt the warmth of his breath, his mouth on my hair. "The last thing you need is someone like me, a penniless painter, a less-than-mediocre imitator of masters. The last thing you need is a Ralph Stedman." His arms tightened. "It was never my intention to hurt you, Pearl. I would rather die than hurt you."

The road to hell is paved with good intentions . . .

It was not my intention to fall in love with a married man. I knew only too well the heartbreaking ramifications of such a liaison. I had not intended to be like my mother. Not for me the tawdry title of *mistress*. I intended to have a life bound in respectability, *for better or worse, for richer or poorer*. I wanted *in sickness and in health*; I wanted *till death us do part*. I wanted the white gown and confetti. And, accordingly, I had planned and thought through to the last detail how my own life would be—the hardworking devoted husband, the three well-mannered children, the clean and tidy house. A happy home.

But history has a habit of repeating itself—no matter how much we wish otherwise—and that evening, that quiet, sun-drenched evening in Scotland, I abandoned every plan and aspiration, and I intentionally and wholeheartedly entered into an illicit love affair. I made the decision consciously, knowingly, acutely aware of that moment, and the future.

Hand in hand we walked back to the cottage, crossed its threshold, closed the door. The lowering sun played in slants through the small window, casting stripes onto the splattered floorboards and paneled walls. And amidst the dust and painterly debris of brush-filled jars, unfinished canvases and strewn rags, I allowed Ralph to undress me.

Slowly and in silence he unbuttoned my blouse, draped it and then my skirt over the back of a chair. Slowly and in silence he unfastened my shoes, lifted my feet out from them and unrolled my stockings. He stared into my eyes as he loosened my bun, and so close, so close—studying my features as though they were of incalculable value, barely touching, breathing me in, he moved his mouth over my hair, my shoulders, my neck, until I could bear it no longer. And with our lips sealed, our bodies locked in a dance as old as time, we moved across the room—certain, knowing and sure of our fall. Then came a tangle—of breath and hands, of limbs and warm flesh; and wave after wave of new sensation, and a sudden burning pain.

Afterward, as we lay in each other's arms, and perhaps seeing my tears, he asked, "Did I hurt you?"

But I couldn't speak. *This is the beginning,* I thought. And I closed my eyes and smiled as a single finger crossed over my brow, down my nose to my lips.

"Do you know how long I've been waiting for you?" he said. "Not days . . . and not weeks. *Years.*"

I lifted his hand and pressed my lips to his palm. "I'm here now."

He sighed. "I wish you'd been here earlier. Ten years earlier."

"I was fourteen, Ralph. Still with Kitty, and I don't suppose she'd have been too happy for me to run off with a painter . . . a *reprobate,*" I added, smiling as I used his word. But I didn't want to think about that time, and I didn't want to think about Kitty. I wanted to think only about us, and because we could not speak of any future, I went back to the beginning and I said, "Ralph, you know the day we first met, that day at the station in London?"

"Mm . . ."

I glanced to him, his head on the pillow next to me, his eyes half closed. "Did you see me in the refreshment room? Was that when you noticed me?"

He pulled his arm from under my head, reached over me to his packet of cigarettes, struck a match and lit one.

"Well?" I said as he lay back down beside me. "Did you?"

"I'm not sure I should tell you."

"Oh, please . . . Please tell."

He sucked on his cigarette, exhaled. "I sort of followed you there," he said, staring up at the cobwebbed ceiling. "Of course, I was also heading to King's Cross—so that was fortuitous—but it was on the Underground that I first saw you."

"The Underground," I mused. "But I never saw you . . ."

"An interesting face, I thought . . . A little too symmetrical, perhaps, but interesting all the same. A face with a story. Eyes like a wary young fox, and mouth quite set, determined."

"You barely looked at me in the refreshment room."

He slid me a glance. "I know how to do these things," he said. "And anyway, I didn't want you to see that I was drawing you. You might have slapped me."

"Drawing *me*?"

"Mm, it's somewhere here."

"Can I see it?"

"You can when it's finished. It's still quite rough, but I think I caught the essence of you." He went on. "Of course, it *was* more than a little strange when you introduced yourself to me as my cousin." He smiled. "But that's when I guessed who you were."

"You knew?"

"There was a letter waiting for me when I arrived at the Hotel du Palais at Biarritz. It's a place my family has visited—and one of Ottoline's favorites. I'd told her I'd be spending a few nights there en route home. Her letter to me was mainly about arrangements for Scotland, but she also mentioned that she'd finally found a new maid. Rather quirky and a bit of a gamble, she said."

I was a little rankled by that. And perhaps he sensed this, because he quickly added, "She also said she knew I'd like you."

I smiled.

"It wasn't exactly hard to figure out. You used Ottoline's name and you *were* heading to Northumberland. And let's face it, my darling, that suitcase of yours was far too large and heavy to be visiting any aunt for a few days."

"That was Kitty," I said, as though that particular lie had been her fault.

"I rather admired your ingenuity and wit. Clever creature, I thought. Why not *be* someone else on a journey? And you inspired me . . . I later introduced myself to someone as Hector Campbell, and enjoyed a very pleasant trip imagining a rendezvous with my own Ottoline."

He reached over me, stubbed out his cigarette, and, still working it all through my mind, I said, "You knew . . . You knew and you played with me. All those lines about having met before. You knew you'd be seeing me again. You knew and I didn't."

"That's how life works sometimes. But think of it this way—you made an impoverished painter very happy on that long journey north. I had something to look forward to. And I didn't even know about the dancing. That was a wonderful surprise."

And he stared at my mouth as I pulled him to me.

Chapter Twelve

The Germans seized Brussels; Namur fell; and then came news of the Battle of Mons. British casualties were estimated to be two thousand, and I thought, *Two thousand? In one day?* It seemed impossible, and I said so. I told Mr. Watts that I thought the newspapers had got it wrong; maybe it was two hundred, I suggested, and even that sounded two hundred too many. But no, Mr. Watts said, the newspaper's figure would be correct, and the final toll significantly more.

August ended and September began. We read British losses were estimated to be in the region of fifteen thousand, that more nurses were needed, and more horses, and more men—always *more men*. We read that the French government had moved to Bordeaux, that Indian troops had arrived, and then, that the Allies were forcing Germany back; the enemy was in retreat. Mr. Watts poured us a glass of sherry and we toasted, "To victory!" He reckoned it would all be over by Christmas.

And still Ottoline said nothing about returning south. Mr. Watts asked me if I knew anything, and I said no. Then Mrs. Lister asked me, and I said no. Their questions rankled me, reminding me as they did that, sooner or later, there would and had to be change. But I had no desire to head south, no desire to be anywhere other than close to Ralph. Despite all our prayers and hopes, despite my determination to be optimistic, I knew that beyond the hills, beyond the quiet wilderness surrounding us, the tentacles of war were spreading and moments had to be seized. *He who hesitates is lost.* I would not be lost.

Meanwhile, that still and sleepy peace continued to envelop the glen, and routines went on. Clocks were wound, fires laid, and as Mrs. Lister stood watch over steaming pans as though her life depended on it, and filled enough jars with jam to feed an army, Ottoline studied troop movements and battles, and continued with her letters to friends in government. I'm not sure what she wrote, though I'd sometimes hear her quietly reading her words out loud before she folded the pages and placed them inside an envelope.

For my own part, I tried to hold on to Mr. Watts's view that the fighting would cease, be over by the end of the year. I tried to convince myself that Ralph would not be needed after all; that Billy would return, along with Hugo; that the country would somehow untangle itself from the horrible mess, and that Kitty would be proved right: The newspapers had got it all wrong. And I took comfort from the landscape, for its brightening colors seemed to reflect that hope.

Each evening, my lover waited for me by the trees next to the bridge, and hand in hand we walked back to the dusty cottage. I no longer cared who saw us, or what anyone thought . . . and who was there to see? Ottoline, Mrs. Lister and Mr. Watts hardly ever left the house, preferring to keep a vigil there among the fading headlines and within earshot of the doorbell or any telegram. A couple of local girls had been employed to replace the five who had returned south in the preceding weeks, and they were quite different; friendlier, less gossipy and judgmental, I thought. Altogether nicer.

However, from time to time I got the impression that Mr. Watts thought I was perhaps being a little neglectful of my duties. He made a number of comments about Ottoline's previous maid, how *devoted* she had been to Her Ladyship before she left to get married, what a fine upstanding woman she had been—that sort of thing. Then one day, a Sunday—my day off—he said, "Off again, are we?" as I passed by the kitchen door.

I made no reply, but as I paused by the back door to pick up the wicker basket I'd earlier packed with rolls, cheese, cold chicken and ham, he stepped out from the kitchen and came toward me.

"Off for a picnic, I see."

"Yes, going down the valley."

"With Mr. Stedman—*again?*"

"Yes, with Mr. Stedman again."

Mr. Watts didn't say anything. He turned and disappeared back into the kitchen.

Ralph laughed when I told him. "The old bugger knows."

"You think so?"

"Definitely." Then, after a moment or two: "I wonder . . . I wonder . . ."

"Mm, wonder what?"

"If old Watts isn't just a little in love with you himself," he said, sounding almost excited by the notion.

"*No!* Don't say that. He's old enough to be my father!"

It was an unseasonably warm day, and we walked for miles down the valley, following the course of the river until we at last found the spot, another "Eden" Ralph wished me to see. I sat among harebells and watched him dive naked from a rock, disappearing into the river's dark pool, before emerging noisily, euphorically, beneath its clear waterfall.

"You should come in. It's perfect," he called over.

"I've told you already, I can't swim."

"But, sweetheart, I won't let you drown."

Ralph knew about Kitty, about my childhood, the places I'd worked and people I'd known. He knew about Stanley. But I had yet to tell him the truth about my mother's end; that she had not died in childbirth—as he and most others presumed. I had yet to explain why stepping into a river—any river—was anathema to me. And I would tell him, but not that day, I decided.

Later, after we had eaten our picnic, we lay side by side on the grassy bank. Soothed by the sound of the water, staring up at the cloudless sky, I said, "Here, now, on a day like this, it's impossible to comprehend or even to imagine any war, isn't it?"

"Yes. But let's not speak about it."

He sat up, took hold of my hand and slid the gold band he wore on his pinkie onto my wedding finger. "With my body I thee worship."

I raised my hand to the sky, stared up at the ring.

"It was my mother's," he said. "I want you to have it."

"So are we married now?" I asked, turning to him and smiling.

"We can pretend, can't we? And when this war's over, we'll have a honeymoon. I'll take you away . . . Where would you like to go?"

"Biarritz."

"Biarritz?" he repeated, sounding vaguely amused as he lay back down next to me on the grass.

"Yes, to that hotel."

He turned onto his side, propped his head in his hand. "And which hotel is that, my darling?"

"The one you were at when Ottoline wrote to you about me."

"Ah, the Hotel du Palais."

I nodded. "Yes, that one. Don't they have a glamorous cocktail bar there?"

"Indeed they do, and with dancing," he said, lifting my hand and pressing my fingers to his lips. "But what is it about you and Biarritz?"

"I'm not sure. I'd never heard of the place before Ottoline mentioned it. And then, when I met you and you said you'd been there . . . I could sort of picture it. See us there."

He laughed. "There are places far more beautiful than Biarritz, though I suppose we could call in there, en route."

"En route? En route where?"

"Anywhere, everywhere."

After a minute or two, I said, "You're not going to go, are you?"

"Go where?"

"You know where . . ."

"I thought we agreed not to speak about it?"

"You brought it up."

"I was talking about *after* . . . when it's over."

"Well, it's going to be over very soon, so there's no point in you going. You won't be needed."

"And this is according to whom?"

"Everyone."

"Everyone?"

"Mr. Watts."

"Ah, Mr. Watts, a man incubated in domestic service. Well, of course he would know. Yes, he would certainly know what's happening in France and how and when it'll end. I imagine Kitchener consults him regularly for his opinion."

I didn't like his tone, his sarcasm or his cynicism. I'd never heard him speak like that before, and though I was no great admirer of Mr. Watts, I didn't like Ralph sneering at his being "in domestic service." I said, "Don't be like that. He's optimistic . . . and I need that. We all need that, Ralph."

He didn't say any more, and we dressed and packed away the remnants of our picnic in silence.

He walked ahead of me all the way back to Delnasay, occasionally stopping to look up at the sky or the hillside, but offering little in the way of conversation and replying monosyllabically to me. And as I watched him—his long legs striding the narrow path through the heather, his golden hair catching the sun, hanging in soft curls over his shirt collar—I had a hideous feeling in the pit of my stomach. For he seemed to be already marching away from me.

But as we neared the road, the driveway back to the house, he put down the basket, turned and reached out for me. "Come here." He held my face in his hands, stared into my eyes. "I'm sorry."

I lowered my head to his chest, wrapped my arms around him, relieved. "Will I see you later?"

"No, I think not. Not tonight. I'm going to paint . . . and I need to if I'm ever going to get those bloody canvases finished."

I knew this was important. Ralph had come to Scotland to paint, and with the intention of completing no fewer than six decent pictures to sell at a gallery in London. It was how he made money, survived. He'd recently received a check from the gallery for some of his paintings of Spain. If he could sell another half dozen pictures during the coming winter, he'd have enough money to rent a small studio in London, money with which to buy more canvases, paint more pictures. That's how it worked.

I watched him as he walked away—taking small steps backward. Watched him as he blew me a kiss, turned and disappeared into the trees. Then I picked up the basket and headed up the sun-dappled driveway, my heart filled with love, and his ring on my finger.

It was the afternoon of the following day, and I was hanging Ottoline's stockings on the line in the small yard when Mr. Watts walked up to me. "Mr. Stedman asked me to give you this," he said, handing me an envelope.

My stomach lurched; the earth tilted. And I knew. "When?"

"He was very explicit on his instructions and asked me not to pass it on to you until after luncheon."

"When?"

"Early this morning."

It was almost three o'clock.

I put the letter inside my pocket and tried to continue with my task, but my hands were shaking and that gushing noise was back inside my head. Mr. Watts stood crunching the grit with his polished shoes, staring up and around, not speaking. Then, finally, he turned and walked back to the house. I dropped the pegs and stockings, and pulled the envelope from my pocket.

My Darling,

I'm a coward already by electing to write these words rather than look you in the eye and say them. But you see, I know that if I looked into your eyes, I'd never leave. And though I loathe & detest war, every war, I particularly detest this war for taking me away from you. These past few weeks have undoubtedly been my happiest & best. One blissful month in Scotland with you was worth waiting for—worth all the lonely months & years, and I will feed on it. I will nourish myself with those sweet memories and grow fat on my remembrances of Us.

And oh, my darling, please don't be sad, because it kills me, kills me even now to think of you shedding tears, and I am truly not worth them. It struck me yesterday at the end of our picnic how selfish I have been. Selfish because I cannot offer you anything, and all the more selfish because I know how much you deserve to be loved and cherished.

So please don't wait for me. Don't waste your days & months waiting for a man who can't give you what you want & should have. If I have meant anything to you, do this for me:

Marry, have children, be happy! *This is what I want for you, Pearl. Have that house, paint your bedroom gold and never ever change.*

Take care of yourself, and take care of Ottoline. Remember, she's not like you and me. And walk forward, my darling girl, walk forward and walk tall.

Always,
RSS

Another page; a few lines.

Wee, modest, crimson-tipped flow'r,
Thou's met me in an evil hour;
For I maun crush amang the stoure
Thy slender stem:
To spare thee now is past my pow'r,
Thou bonie gem.

Calmly, I folded the pages, pushed them back into the envelope and put the envelope inside my pocket. Calmly, I turned and walked through the gardens in the direction of the river. Calmly, I followed the path.

There was birdsong, the sun was high and it was Monday—the start of a new week. But Ralph had gone; my love was done and over. And his words and that *Always*—like the full stop at the end of a long and beautiful sentence—had to be enough. And so, calmly, I sat down on the spiky ground beneath the trees, lay back and wept.

Eventually, when no more tears would come, I opened my eyes and looked up at the blue that pricked here and there through a canopy of fading green. I could feel the wetness on my temples, in my hair; the comforting warmth of the earth beneath me. But already I was changed; already it seemed as though a hundred years might have passed between the previous day and that moment.

Chapter Thirteen

A veil had fallen. Colors faded and sounds were muted. Never again would life be as vivid. Never again would I love in the same way or give myself so completely. My best had been, was already in the past. Ahead of me were years of something less than I had known. Ahead of me were compromise, acceptance and a small and infinitely private place I would be able to return to in quiet moments alone. But I knew its flame, like a beacon once burning and bright, would slowly diminish and cool, that my memories of Ralph—like those of Kitty—would eventually fade.

And so I tried to take comfort in the fact that I had known love, and been worthy, and that this abandonment was different. Because, I reasoned, if he could have, if circumstances had been otherwise . . .

And then would come darkness once again, and without any death, I'd slip into grief.

And yet, that inextinguishable flicker of an optimist's heart inevitably reignited, rose up and whispered, *Maybe*. Maybe. And that possibility was enough. Enough for me to hope, enough for me to challenge the Universe, to plead and bargain with it, offering up heart, mind and soul, anything and everything, to keep one man safe and alive, and somehow bring him back to me.

And thus the days of September fell away, each one removing me further from what I'd believed to be a beginning but had in fact been an end. The senseless sun blazed as brightly as ever, hours melted and time moved on, offering space. And almost unhearing, almost unseeing, almost but not quite numb, I drifted with it. I continued perfunctorily with my duties, as abstracted as Ottoline, each of us quiet and lost in her thoughts. She made no mention of any return south, and it seemed to me as though we might very well stay there forever; that perhaps each of us couldn't bear to leave that place, to part with it or them. And sometimes, in the echo of twilight, I heard Ralph say my name: *Pearl . . .*

Reality came in black and white, and I studied it—the News— with a newfound, albeit quiet, appetite for detail. I read that more women were needed—to work in factories, train as nurses, drive ambulances. I knew I could be more useful; knew I *should* be more useful. But how could I leave Ottoline after her kindness to me? I couldn't. Not then. I was aware, vaguely at first, but then clearly, of that fragility I'd first sensed the day I arrived to work for her. My lady needed me.

Then, one afternoon, as I was lying on my bed, wearing Ralph's ring and thinking of him, again—because I wanted to remember every single second of our time together, because I didn't want time to erase his features from my memory, or for the war to blot *Us* out—Mrs. Lister came to my room. She said, "I'm sorry to disturb you, but being as Mr. Watts has had to go to Grantown . . ."

"What is it, Mrs. Lister?" I said, removing the ring, resenting the intrusion, reluctantly sitting up.

"Well, I'm not sure, but it's a bit funny if you ask me . . . Perhaps you need to come and see for yourself?"

I had no idea what she was talking about. I wondered if one of her cakes had sunk. She said, "*She's* in the drawing room."

I could hear the music before I reached the top of the stairs.

I swept down the staircase, across the hallway, opened the door and saw for myself.

With rouge smeared across her cheeks and wearing enough jewelry to sink a ship, Ottoline danced about the floor with an invisible partner, half laughing and mouthing words. It took a moment or two for her to notice me, and when she did, she adopted the demeanor of a child caught in some naughty act.

I said, "The music's a little loud, my lady. Shall I turn it down?"

She waved her hand dismissively. "Take it off . . . Take it off, Pearl."

I walked over to the gramophone and turned down the volume so that it became soft and quiet, a background noise.

Ottoline stared down at the carpet. She said, "I was just thinking . . . thinking and imagining . . . Billy loves dancing."

Her words were slurred, I saw the glass on the table and I knew then that I *had* been neglectful, and that in my absence something had happened—a shift, a tilt. A small and unnoticed downward spiral born of too much time alone. I walked over and took hold of Ottoline's hand. "Would you like to continue dancing?" I asked.

She looked back at me and nodded. And so we danced. We waltzed about the room with me as the man and she the lady, and though I knew it was—as Mr. Watts would say—irregular, it didn't matter. How could it? How could anything now?

Later, I carried two large cans of hot water up the back staircase and filled the old tin bath. I poured in some scented oil, helped Ottoline undress and then helped her into the bath. I knelt down next to it and cleaned the rouge from her face with a flannel. And as she sat in the scented water, her hands wrapped around her knees, she raised her eyes to me and said, "Am I going mad, Pearl?"

I shook my head. "No, my lady. We're *all* going mad."

She began to cry. "I don't want to go back to Northumberland. And I can't go back there now. You know why, you understand, don't you?"

And I was about to shake my head, I was about to say, *No, I don't understand,* when she went on. "I've not been regular for a few years, but it's been almost three months, I think . . . which would be right."

I had been with Ottoline only for a short time, was still unsure of her exact age, and had not given any thought to her menstrual cycle. Or, if I had, had supposed her to be going through what I'd heard referred to as *the change,* that time when a woman's ability to conceive a baby diminishes and the bleeding stops.

"Hector will know. He'll know it's not his. He'll know it's Felix Cowper's," she said, lowering her head to her knees. "Oh God, what a mess. What am I going to do?"

I reached out, took hold of her wet hands. "Don't worry. We'll think of something. We will. We have to."

She stared back at me: "You won't leave me, will you?"

"Of course I won't leave you."

"Do you promise?"

"I promise."

The veil lifted. By September's end the landscape had altered to a rampant frenzy of pale bronze, dark copper and bright yellow, burnished gold and brilliant red. Impossible to ignore, impossible to turn away from. And I wished Ralph had been there to see it, paint it. I wished everyone, including Lord Hector, had still been there, because maybe then he'd have noticed his wife; maybe then he'd have seen the colors reflected in her eyes and seen, too, how dull Mrs. Parker's were by comparison.

But what of Ottoline's condition? In the days immediately after her confession, we had not spoken of it again, and though I had racked my brain to come up with a plan, the only answer seemed to be for the two of us to go away for a while—for her baby to be born in a place where no one knew the Campbells. I hadn't thought any further than that, but I knew there was no way Ottoline could keep her baby. We would need to find a family.

Meanwhile, and as ever adding to the complications, there was Mr. Watts to contend with. He told me that *we* were late. The time to head south was overdue. "It's the usual course of events. Has been for years," he said. "We always return south at the end of September."

And it came to me. We would and should return to Birling, and in the New Year, Ottoline and I could come back to Delnasay— alone. She could spend her confinement there, with me, and when the time came, we'd employ a midwife, and pay her handsomely. We could surely find a family there just as easily as anywhere else, I reasoned.

I wasn't sure how much Mr. Watts knew—had seen or perceived—about Ottoline's state, how fragile she was. But I knew Mrs. Lister understood something of what was going on. The day after she'd come to my room, after I'd gone down and found Ottoline made up and dancing, she had told me that such occurrences were not new. They had happened before, she said.

"She's always been a bit . . . well, flighty, if you know what I mean. A bit too much up and down," Mrs. Lister said, shaking her head. "High-strung, I suppose, like a lot of them are. And of course he's always away," she added, tutting to herself. "I sometimes wonder why he married her. I mean, why marry someone and then spend your life away from them, eh?"

I agreed. *Why?*

"And as you know, she's ever such a kind soul. And clever as well, but perhaps too clever . . . I think too many brains makes you go a bit queer, don't you?"

Ottoline received a letter from her husband once a week, usually in the second post on Monday afternoon. I often wondered what he said to her in those letters; if he ever told her he cared, or that he loved her. For how could he not? And I'd seen him watching her, seen him that day in her bathroom at Birling, when his mouth had twitched. Strange, I thought, that he had allowed himself to lose her, and to the rather puny Mr. Cowper.

I had often imagined having my own telephone and calling people up—Lord Hector and a few others as well, not all of them alive . . . a call to London, heaven or hell, depending. It was a wonderful fantasy, the notion of speaking my mind without having to look back at them, my betters *and* my worse: surprising them all with a *"Hello, Pearl here!"* Liberating. I'd imagined one such call to Stanley after I'd received his last letter, and just to tell him what a feckless individual he was, and how much better-suited he was to a sticky-fingered chambermaid. He didn't have a lot to say, but it was cathartic.

In reality, I'd only ever used a telephone once, when Mrs. B. had sent me to the post office to call up her eldest son and tell him she was dying. It wasn't long before I left her, and she was delirious, seeing people who weren't there and having conversations with the furniture. The doctor said it was hallucinations caused by dehydration, possibly too many boiled eggs and not enough water, he said, after quizzing me on her diet.

But my imagined telephone calls to Lord Hector were different . . .

"Hello . . . Hello?"

"It's Pearl Gibson, Your Lordship."

"Pearl who?"

"Pearl Gibson. Your wife's maid?"

"Wife? Ah yes, my wife . . . What do you want, Gibson?"

"I want to tell you what an ass you are."

"An ass? What are you on about?"

"It's a hoofed mammal, Your Lordship, and looks a bit like one of those horses you like to ride about on, but a little smaller and with longer ears. Like a donkey."

"For God's sake, Gibson, get to the point."

"Of course, Your Lordship. The point is, you're an idiot."

"How dare you!"

"Yes, I do!"

Clunk.

And my many imagined telephone calls to Ralph were altogether different again . . .

"It's me."

"I thought it would be you. Hello, darling."

"Where are you?"

"I can't tell you that."

"I miss you so much . . ."

"And I miss you, too."

"Have you been thinking of me?"

"All the time."

"Are you coming back soon?"

"As soon as I can. I promise."

"I love you."

"And I love you, my darling girl."

"Stay safe for me."

"I will."

Though I had imagined telephone conversations, I was not—
unlike so many other servants I'd known—a seasoned eavesdrop-
per. Nor was I in the habit of reading other people's correspondence,
except a postcard, which seemed to me altogether different and
more public. But when I saw the opened envelope—lying next to

the glinting paper knife on the desk in the small study and in Ralph's hand and postmarked London—I had to read it.

His paltry lines gave little away: He was training with the Artists Rifles and anticipated serving with a unit of the Seventh Division. He would try to keep in touch, and would do his utmost to find Billy, he assured Ottoline.

There was no mention of me, but it wasn't Ralph's style to discuss personal matters; certainly not in a brief letter like that. Nor did it trouble me that he'd elected to write to Ottoline rather than me. After all, he'd told me not to wait for him, told me to move on with my life. *Get married, have children, be happy,* he'd said. But as I refolded the small sheet of paper and placed it back inside the envelope, I pictured him as he'd been that first time I'd seen him at the station, and I smiled in the knowledge that he'd followed me there, and that our paths had been destined. Whatever the future held, I knew I'd survive, and now, I hoped with all my heart that Ralph had given me reason to.

But there was no time for idle romanticism and dreaming, not now. I had to look after Ottoline. There was more than one war to win.

"Hector says I have to return south," Ottoline announced one morning as I collected the newspapers that littered the floor and surrounded her desk. I folded the crumpled, cut-out sheets and put them in a pile, for I wasn't allowed to remove them, or to hand them over to Mr. Watts for the fires, which had caused another sort of friction between him and me.

I said, "Well, the weather *is* changing, my lady . . . and I think perhaps we should."

Ottoline shook her head. "No, I don't want to. I don't want to. And anyway, what does it matter to him? He'll not be there. He'll be with Virginia. In London."

"But that's a good thing, surely?"

She shrugged her shoulders. "Mm, perhaps . . ."

She was drifting, unanchored, and I wondered if she'd forgotten her state: that she was carrying Felix Cowper's child, and, from what she'd told me and by my own calculation, she was already almost four months gone. I said, "I think it's perhaps better if His Lordship stays in London, don't you? After all, isn't he more likely to hear about Billy there?"

"Oh, I'm quite sure he knows more than he's told me. In fact, I'm certain of it . . . I think he probably sanctioned it all."

She still hadn't caught on to my motives, so I said, "You know, you're not really showing yet, my lady, not at all. And it'll be Christmas soon. People always eat a lot at Christmas."

She blinked, took a moment and then she smiled. "Ah, you mean I have to get fat?"

I nodded.

"And then what? Give birth to a Christmas pudding?"

I laughed, and she did, too. I couldn't recall the last time I'd seen her laugh. I said, "Then we go away for a while . . . and return here. We could come back in . . . February?"

Her expression changed. "No, that's the very worst time. We'd never get through the snow, and we'd certainly not survive *here*."

My heart sank momentarily. I thought of Biarritz, then said, "What about the South of France?"

Ottoline shook her head: "We're at war, Pearl. It'll be very difficult if not impossible to gain permission to travel overseas."

"Dorset?"

"Hector's cousin lives there, and makes it her business to know *everyone*—and everything."

"The Lake District?"

Her eyes widened, her smile returned. "The Lake District," she repeated. "Yes, yes . . . I suppose I could have a friend, or even some distant, forgotten member of my family. It's a little irregular, but . . ."

"So is life."

We didn't plan any further than that. But it was enough to assuage Ottoline's immediate fears about returning south.

❧

Our final days at Delnasay were eerily quiet. The gramophone was broken, and the man who repaired such things had gone to war. The only sound came from the bitter northeasterly wind whistling beneath doors and down chimneys, tapping at glass panes, beyond which final remnants of summer fluttered to the ground. At night, the cold air whispered, flickering candles and creaking branches in the blackness outside. Dusk fell earlier; rooms shivered. But the news kept coming: Antwerp had been evacuated; the Germans occupied Lille; the Belgian government had moved to Le Havre; the Allies occupied Ypres; and Canadian troops had arrived in England.

Then, finally, the news stopped and the house was silenced.

Mrs. Lister and I spread sheets over furniture; we stripped beds, swept out grates, closed shutters and locked doors. And the longings and prayers and voices of that summer were packed away and became a thing of the past. And as I stepped out into the drizzle, I breathed in the scents of peat and pine and heather, and placed my palm on the wet stone. This place had offered me a lifeline—and a lifetime. Those granite walls had been my home, and I knew something of me would remain there forever.

I climbed onto the waiting pony and trap, and we moved off down the driveway, beneath the arching limbs and dripping branches, over the bridge and fast-flowing river. I glanced back only once: for my eyes to find and know that whitewashed building, sitting forlornly in the mist. It *had* happened; it was *not* a dream. Ralph Stedman existed. And he was alive, I knew. I knew that. And I also knew with reasonable certainty by then that I was carrying his child.

In love, my lady and I were no different. We were each of us flawed by our sex, each of us *fallen.*

PART TWO

Chapter Fourteen

"*Harry?* . . . But that can't be right. He's only just turned fourteen."

Harry had disappeared days before our arrival back at Birling, leaving some penciled words about Duty and England for his mother. She had told Mrs. Lister that the family was proud of him, and comforted by the fact that he had gone with his two cousins—also still *bairns*, according to Mrs. Lister.

I pictured Harry in his old man's oversize suit. He had longed for a uniform, as though it would offer him some magical status and place in the world. Now he would have one, and might very well die in it.

Minutes later, after I'd run out of the kitchen, Mrs. Lister came to the servants' cloakroom where I was ill, having vomited. She said, "Ah, I knew you'd be upset about young Harry. But you mustn't let it get you down."

I wasn't sure if it was Harry or my condition that had made me ill, but I appreciated her kindness.

Throughout November the air was stagnant, filled with the scent of rotting leaves and wood smoke. Nothing moved. It was as though our small part of Northumberland slept on as war raged, as perfect limbs and adored smiles were blown like dust into the ether. But the newspapers continued with their lists and numbers. And Lord Kitchener asked for more. And I thought, *There'll be none left.*

Then came the first flurry of snow, and everyone spoke of a "White Christmas" as though a frozen white world could make things better, as though it would somehow distract us from the slaughter across that thin stretch of water, the English Channel. But it did distract some, and so did the nearby army training camp, and the village hall dances where the soldiers were more than will- ing partners to the local girls, including a few of the young maids at Birling. And amidst the excitement of snow and soldiers, there was still speculation it might all end in time for Christmas.

But no pretty snowfall could convince me, nor could it dis- tract me from Ottoline's condition and my own. And as I sat in the murky yellow glow of my lamp-lit room, extending waist- bands, sewing in new elastic and moving buttons, I wondered when and where and how to tell Ottoline my own news, and how she'd react.

Yes, I was anxious. Yes, I was worried. I was quietly terrified of what Ottoline might say and do. That my child would be her blood relation meant nothing in those moments of fear and doubt. I'd heard plenty of tales in my time about the fate of female servants who'd succumbed to the advances of the gentlemen of the house. Plenty of stories about maids who'd left carrying more than their bundle of aprons. All of us servants knew what happened to girls like that, for their sad stories were passed on to us as a warning.

But would I be one? Would Ottoline dismiss me? Without any father, husband or brother—I had nowhere to go. I would quite literally be out on the street. And so all of this kept me awake at night. All of this kept me pacing that soft green and gold carpet. For what would I do? Where would I go? Who would employ me? In those small hours, I often thought of my Kitty and felt only shame. I had let her down. I was not after all a Superior Sort of Girl. I was no different to my mother.

It was early December and late in the afternoon when Ottoline began to bleed.

I knew what was happening, had seen it before—years before, when my roommate, a parlormaid with a penchant for footmen, had lowered herself over a chamber pot, moaning and reeking of gin. I'd been the one who'd taken the pot down the back stairs and out of the house. "Chuck it . . . Chuck it somewhere in the garden," she'd said, sobbing. I buried it a long way from the house, next to a stream and a weeping willow.

It couldn't be like that for Ottoline, and I suggested we send for the doctor. But no, she didn't want any doctor, least of all their family doctor. Like everyone else, he knew nothing of Ottoline's state. The only comments made had been on my lady's fuller figure: She had gained weight and it suited her, they said. Her long sojourn in Scotland had been beneficial; she looked well.

By midnight it was over. But I stayed by her side. I sat in a chair by her bed, mopped her brow with cold flannels, held her hand and watched her drift, moan and murmur names.

At one point in her delirium she saw not me but her mother and cried out, "Don't go, Mama. Don't leave me." And I gripped her hand tighter. Later, I was stirred from my own fretful dreams by the sound of her voice calling out, "Hector." And her situation came to me with new and powerful understanding. For she had been alone for years in a quiet place of fitted carpets and ticking clocks; she had been alone for years with her polished antiques and pristine uniformed staff. Lost in luxury without any comfort.

Shortly before six, I carried the covered pail downstairs. I went to the servants' cloakroom, put on my hat, coat and gloves, took the flashlight from the shelf by the kitchen door and left the house. The moon was almost full; the ground glistened with frost. Beyond the shadow of the house, its rooftop and chimney, the monkey puzzle tree cast its design over the frozen lawn and a solitary owl called out from the deodar.

I left the pail by the gate to the woods, went to the potting shed and returned with a shovel. It took some time for me to unsettle the earth where Ottoline had asked, where a succession of snowdrops, primroses, daffodils and bluebells came up each spring. But eventually the earth gave way and became softer, as though opening up for my sad offering.

I knelt down, placed the blood-soaked nightgown containing the tiny scrap of life into the hollowed ground. I said, "Our Father, who art in heaven, hallowed be thy name. Thy Kingdom come, thy will be done . . ." Then I stopped. The words didn't sound right, and what good had any of our recent prayers done? No one had heard them.

As I rose to my feet, I picked up the shovel and glanced back at the house, the dim light of Ottoline's room. I thought of my mother and that fateful day, the day of my birth. For I, too, had been discarded—the discarded remnant of an illicit love affair—and my life had been defined by that day. And for a moment I was overwhelmed with sadness for the unacknowledged and unnamed, the secret burials and unmentioned births, souls who'd never known sunlight or love.

And then I thought of the birth announcement I'd found circled in Kitty's hand. *Arabella Godley* . . . How wanted she must have been for her name to be placed in the newspaper. Celebrated. Cherished. Rocked and cradled. Each gurgle and flickering smile adored.

I was still thinking of her, Arabella Godley—wondering who she was, where she was, and trying to picture her—when Mr. Watts walked into the washroom. "You're up early."

"Couldn't sleep, Mr. Watts."

"And is Her Ladyship . . . a little better, do you know?"

"Oh yes. Time of the month, Mr. Watts, that's all."

He stood staring into the sink where the water still flowed pink. "What you women have to endure," he said, shaking his head, and then he walked away.

In the days and weeks that followed, Ottoline slowly recovered. She never once spoke about the events of that night and instead resumed her campaign of letters—to Mr. Asquith and Lord Kitchener, and anyone else she knew or could think of in government, strangely humming rather than speaking the words as she reread them. She was obsessed with finding Billy, and thought everyone—Asquith and Kitchener included—should do their bit to locate him and return him home safely. She spent her afternoons in the drawing room, reading and rereading accounts of troop movements and battles in the *Times*, poring over murky images and casualty lists with the magnifying glass, quietly reciting names out loud.

Then, shortly before Christmas, I was dispatched to Newcastle to purchase Christmas presents for the staff, along with two scrapbooks—later to be marked *Hugo* and *Billy*. It snowed heavily all day, and my return train was canceled. After a telephone call to Birling, I checked in to a hotel by the station, and then caught a train back the next day, shivering all the way and staring out at endless fields blanketed in white. No one could meet me; the roads were impassable. I had to walk all the way back to Birling through the snow—my feet numb, my back aching—laden with parcels. But I was thankful Ottoline had changed her mind about books in favor of Jacquard scarves for the female servants, and ties for the men.

On my return, Ottoline was more interested in the scrapbooks than in any gifts—or my well-being. And later, I helped her with them, pasting handwritten notes and her sons' first letters to her from school, including one from Billy, which read: *Dear Mama, I hope you are well. The other boys here are all show-offs. I am doing Archery and Henry Paterson has a verooka. His mother sent him a quarter of sherbets and lickorish. Matron's dog is called Susan. Yours faithfully, Billy Campbell.*

And beneath each photograph, Ottoline carefully penned names and a date:

Hugo & Ottoline—Delnasay, Summer 1895.
Hugo, Billy & Nurse Phillips—Birling, Christmas 1898.
The Family—Delnasay, Summer 1905.
Hugo & Billy—Delnasay, Summer 1909.
Ottoline, Hugo & Billy—Delnasay, Summer 1912.

These scrapbooks became Ottoline's passion. As she stared through the magnifying glass at the small photographs and I busied myself with scissors and glue, we listened to records on the gramophone. Her latest favorite was entitled "Are We Downhearted? No!" And it was a catchy song, the sort that stays in your head and you find yourself humming, singing or whistling; the sort that actually makes you feel a bit better. And it became quite the thing below stairs during the run-up to that Christmas for one of us to sing, "Are we downhearted?" and another—or and more usually a few—to shout back, "No!"

But then that all changed, and the War finally arrived at Birling Hall.

"Mrs. Watts?" I repeated, staring back at Ottoline, dumbfounded.

I'm not sure why I'd assumed Mr. Watts to be devoid of any lover, wife or family. But in hindsight, I realize I'd simply been caught up in the unfolding events of my own life and the war, and that I hadn't been interested enough to find out. I had too quickly judged the man; sensed only an intensely private person who believed in the *old ways* and gave everything to his profession. All I'd seen was the conscientious butler—a man in tailcoat and striped trousers.

Ottoline went on. "She's been residing at Scarborough since . . . oh, shortly before war was declared. It's where she grew up, and . . . well, he thought she'd be safer there than in Newcastle." She paused and shook her head. "I did tell him. I said to him in Scotland—and as soon as war was declared—that she must come to Birling. But no, he said she wanted to go *there* to stay with her brother. He thought that was best."

But it hadn't been best, and Mrs. Watts hadn't been safe. Far from the battlefields of the western front, ten days before Christmas, and under the cover of the early-morning mist, German battleships had broken through minefields in the North Sea and launched an attack on the seaside town. Ethel Watts and her brother had both died in the house in which they were born, killed at home.

Later that same evening, I went down to the kitchen in search of Mr. Watts. I sat with him and listened. He and his wife had met, he said, when he was still a footman and she a parlormaid. "And far too good for me." After they'd wed, they had planned for both of them to leave service, planned to set up a nursery garden. But the business they had planned did not come about. "And then came Derek . . . and it made sense for me to stay on in service. But we planned . . . oh yes, we always planned," he said. "We only ever thought of the future."

Derek Watts was now fighting in France, alongside Hugo and Billy Campbell and their friends, and Mrs. Lister's three sons. And yet Mr. Watts had kept this knowledge to himself, beneath his starched shirt and buttoned-up waistcoat. But it was the loss of his sweetheart and wife that tormented him and made him weep, because he had told her to go there, assured her she'd be *safe*.

"But I still have Derek," he said, glancing up at me. "And he's the image of her, you know? Oh yes, so like her . . . so like his mother," he added, looking away, smiling, remembering. "And I'm very much aware you have no family," he added, reaching over the table and patting my hand.

"No, I have no one to lose," I said, albeit disingenuously and without looking at him.

"Oh, Pearl, I know that's not quite true."

It was the first time he'd called me by my given name. And after that, he could only ever be Rodney to me.

More snow fell, and the news came thick and fast. Mrs. Lister received a telegram and then a letter about her middle son, Peter: *Valiant to the end . . . A credit to his country.* She read these words out loud more times than I can remember, and looked up at us, smiling and weeping at the same time. We learned, too, that a gillie from Delnasay—a man I'd met and liked, a man whose family had worked for Ottoline's for many years—had also been killed, leaving a wife and four young children. And then Ottoline told me about Virginia Parker's eldest son—a *heartbreaker*—"notoriously handsome," she said. And she wrote to Virginia, and I posted the letter.

Throughout all of this, each and every day I thought of Ralph.

And I waited until last to search the List of Wounded and Roll of Honor. Because everyone knew I had no one. Everyone, it seemed, apart from Rodney Watts, who often smiled and winked at me as he rose up from the paper, as if to say, *No Ralph Stedman*.

I continued in my conundrum about when and how to tell Ottoline about my condition. And then I decided to leave it until the New Year.

Christmas came, with holly and carols and church as usual, and I'd never been in a house as beautiful or as atmospheric. Ottoline *loved* Christmas and was determined that it should be the same as always. Thus, a tree went up, festooned in baubles. Candles flickered in a hallway scented with pine, eucalyptus and cinnamon, and each evening I went to look at the tree, to take in the rarefied atmosphere—made more magical by the white world outside and the shimmering colors and heavenly aroma inside. It was impossible to imagine war, or any evil. Good *would* prevail. How could it not? It had to.

Then, finally, and rightly, on Christmas Eve, Ottoline received the letter she had been waiting for, along with a photograph. Billy was alive and well. And for a moment the war stopped and nothing mattered other than Billy Campbell and his well-being. Like a beacon, that photograph—of a smiling, uninjured, completely recognizable Billy in uniform—lifted our hearts and shone a light ahead. And later, when we heard of a truce, that the soldiers at the front had exchanged gifts, sung carols and played football together, it lifted us further.

But then it began again.

On January the first, we read that the *Formidable* had been sunk and, two weeks later, that German aircraft dropped bombs on Great Yarmouth. And Rodney Watts, still unable to come to terms with his wife's death, went again to the Yorkshire coast—the seaside town of Scarborough—as though he'd been mistaken, as though the funeral had been a figment and he'd find her there. We all wondered if he'd come back. But he did.

And on the day he came back to Birling, as I reached over Ottoline to pick up her hairbrush, my waistband button, already moved once, popped and fell onto the carpet. She looked up at me, my face, and then lowered her eyes to my stomach and said, "Oh, Pearl . . ."

And I told her. And I cried.

She stood up, took me in her arms and held me. "Just as you looked after me, so I promise to look after you."

"But I don't want to give away my baby."

"Nor will you . . . Nor will you. This is your home, Pearl, and it will be your child's home, too. Don't forget, I'm a blood relation to your baby."

I stared back at her. "But Lord Hector . . . the others . . ."

"Do you trust me?" she asked.

I nodded. I did.

"Amidst war and death and destruction, you carry life. And with life there is hope. You carry hope, Pearl."

It was all Ottoline's idea.

She had thought it all through, she said, and the only impediment to my keeping my child was my unmarried status. If I could find myself a husband, become married, all would be well.

At first, I thought she was having one of her turns.

"How can I find a husband, my lady? I can hardly summon one out of thin air. Added to which, there's a war on and few men around."

And I was waiting for her to come to, waiting for her to say, *Ah yes, good point.* But instead, she said, "Exactly. And this plays into our hands. Don't you see?"

I didn't. But I would.

Chapter Fifteen

Ottoline drove me to the station herself. A nerve-racking experience at the best of times, made worse by the snowy conditions. However, we made it, and as Ottoline exclaimed as she pulled on the hand brake, "Still in one piece!"

There was no sign of the greasy chap I'd encountered months before. We stood alone on the platform. Ottoline said, "Remember, Pearl, all you have to do is come back married . . . Mrs. Whatever. The name doesn't really matter, so long as everyone *thinks* you're married."

The plan—Ottoline's plan—was actually very simple: I'd go to London for a rendezvous with my "secret sweetheart" and then return to Birling a few days later, a respectably married woman. *Voilà!*—as she'd said.

Ottoline left me in order to get home in time for a meeting of her Working Party. She had established it early in the New Year. The group was an unlikely mix of local gentry, estate workers and

servants, who, within the sumptuous confines of the green drawing room—the winter drawing room—knitted and sewed, and
packed parcels to *our boys* and our prisoners of war. The parcels
contained books, magazines and food; balaclavas and scarves, and
socks and mittens. Along with her war-chronicling scrapbooks,
which had become more like journals and now numbered some
half dozen, Ottoline's Working Party had given her a focus. It
offered her a distraction from her own recent and very private loss,
and perhaps a distraction, too, from my situation.

For despite her kindness and support, despite her acknowledg-
ment of my condition, and her knowledge of the facts, Ottoline
never mentioned Ralph's name. And neither did I. It was as though
he had never existed, or had died years before and been forgotten.
And yet, I believed—had to believe—that she would have told me
if she had heard anything.

London was noisy. The city now belonged to Lord Kitchener and
men in uniform. King's Cross station heaved with them, and the
Underground was a sea of khaki, male odor and voices. I was shocked
by their number, shocked by their sound and shocked by the reality
of war. For unlike Scotland and Northumberland, the great mobili-
zation was here, in the capital, and London was very much *at* war.
Ambulance bells rang out in the streets, where a steady stream of
Red Cross vehicles moved up and down, carrying wounded newly
delivered from the front. This was the scene even in the once quiet
confines of Mayfair, and even on Dover Street, where Ottoline had
kindly arranged for me to stay at the Empress Club.

The seemingly never-ending procession of ambulances would stop, in a while, the gentleman on the front desk told me. The problem was, he said, three hospital trains had come within minutes of one another that afternoon, which was unusual, he added, unless there had been a great battle. It would quieten down in a while, until later, around midnight, he thought, when the next trains were due. "They usually come in at that time, when there's less people about and it's quiet . . . Grim business," he added, shaking his head.

Then, smiling, overly cheery, he asked me what time I would like to dine. But the thought of food made me feel sick, and the thought of stepping into the palatial dining room there sicker still. So I told him I'd be taking my meals elsewhere.

"I see. I should perhaps warn you that quite a number of restaurants have closed for the duration. But if you'd like me to make a reservation for you, Miss Gibson, I know of a few that remain open and would be suitable for a young lady dining alone."

I smiled. "There's no need. I shall be dining with my aunt. She lives not far from here."

A porter took my bag and showed me to my room on the third floor, overlooking Dover Street, and the moving canvas rooftops. The man on the desk was right: The ambulance procession did eventually cease, and by the time I stepped out onto the street once more, things were calmer and quieter. A fine drizzle had begun to fall, turning the smog a murky yellow beneath the glow of gas streetlamps. I bought a newspaper and headed for the A.B.C., and there, with Ralph's ring on my finger, and pretending to read, I watched sweethearts: khaki-clad Tommies and their girls, all locked eyes and clutching hands, impervious to their surroundings, and me. The only thing I recall reading was that a man had been arrested for dancing in the street. But by then there were so many rules, mainly to do with the Defense of the Realm Act, DORA, and many of them designed to keep women out of public houses, restaurants and hotels—away from soldiers—at night.

Later, walking back through the rumbling metropolis, past public houses filled with song, and darkened shop doorways with couples pressed up tight, I realized DORA's rules couldn't stop a *Good Time*; it was all that mattered now. Kitty's world had been swept away.

It was on the morning of my second day, finding myself on Regent Street—and right outside the place—that I stepped into the Café Royal Hotel. I went to the desk, asked for Miss Eileen Poynter. I was told that no one of that name worked there and was in the revolving door, about to step out onto the street, when I had another thought, and came back round.

"Silly me," I said to the man on the desk. "I forgot about the wedding. I think dear Eileen's perhaps better known now as Mrs. Morton."

I was led from the main lobby down some stairs and then via a door disguised in the paneling to a passageway that stank of eggs and boiled cabbage, and where I was told to wait. I wasn't altogether sure what I intended to say to Eileen. I suppose I was just curious about her, the two of them, but even then, as I waited, I realized my suspicions had been accurate.

After a short while, a fair-haired woman—the wrong shape and older-looking than I remembered Eileen—emerged from double swing doors at the end of the passage. She looked me up and down, then came next to me. We stood side by side against the wall as uniformed staff wheeled trolleys of laundry past us. Eventually she said, "You're not waiting for me, are you?"

"I'm not sure. I don't think so . . . not unless you're Mrs. Morton?"

"And what if I am?" she asked, folding her arms.

It *was* Eileen, and quite clearly she didn't recognize me, had no idea who I was. So I improvised: "Stanley's sister," I said, extending my hand.

"Oh my. I do apologize. But you have to be so careful these days, don't you? It's Cynthia, isn't it?"

I nodded. "Have you heard anything?" I asked.

"Not a single word . . . Not in over four weeks." She opened her eyes wider: "That's not why you're here, is it? He's not dead, is he?"

I began to laugh and then I said, "*No!* Well, not that I'm aware of, anyway."

"Good. I'd be bloody furious if he was." She slid along the wall nearer to me. "Listen, Cynthia, I think you should know—I had a baby last year. Little boy. Stan Junior. He'll be a year old in a couple of months, and already a handful, I can tell you. Anyway, that's why I use the name," she whispered. "I'd have been thrown out of here otherwise."

"I understand," I said. And of course I did, and far more than she knew. But as I computed the numbers, I realized that she had already given birth to Stanley's child when I'd last seen him—eight months ago. It felt like eight years.

"Look here, I'll be finished in an hour. If you fancy, we can go and have a little drink somewhere. What do you say?"

"I'm afraid I can't. I promised to call in on my aunt."

"Nellie?"

"No, Kitty."

"Oh, Stanley never mentioned her."

"No, well, she and Stanley have never quite seen eye to eye."

"Shame. I could've written to old bugger-lugs and told him we'd been out together painting the town red." She smiled and unfolded her arms.

"Why not tell him that anyway? Tell him me and you went out on the town and had a jolly good time to ourselves."

"Oh, Cynth—you are a one!"

Warming to my theme, I went on. "You could even tell him that we met up with that lady's maid friend of his . . . What was her name? . . . Gibson?"

Eileen gripped my arm. "*Yes*, I think it was. Miss Gibson. You know, he worked with her someplace down in Hampshire. Reckoned she was a bit obsessed with him." She paused, wrinkled her nose. "Said she kept turning up here and demanding to see him. And you know, I think I met her once . . ." She stared back at me with new curiosity, and for a moment I thought my cover had been blown. But then she shook her head. "I can't rightly remember her."

I feigned a little laugh, and as I put on my gloves I said, "The last I heard, she'd married a rich artist and was living in a castle in Scotland."

"*No!*"

"Yes. In fact, now I come to think of it, the wedding was in the newspaper . . . photographs and everything."

"Blimey, that'll give him something to think about," said Eileen, looking away again and ever so slightly dazzled. "A castle in Scotland," she repeated. "Well, I never . . ."

I couldn't help myself; I had to add more. "I think there's a baby due as well . . . Yes, I'm sure I read an announcement in the newspaper."

"Really? I thought they only put that in once they were born."

I shrugged: "Scottish custom, I suppose."

"My word, Scotch newspapers must be chocka!"

I laughed. She laughed. I said, "Well, I'd better get on now. But it's been nice to see you, Eileen . . . and do give Stanley my best, and be sure to tell him about Pearl."

"Pearl?"

"Miss Gibson. I just remembered her first name. It was in the newspaper."

She nodded, gulped, and for a moment I thought she might cry. Her eyes glistened with tears and she grabbed hold of my hand: "It's ever so kind of you to come and see me, Cynth."

And I thought, *It's not her fault; it has nothing to do with her.* And I reached into my purse, took out the pound note Ottoline had given me and pushed it into her hand. "For my nephew," I said. "For Stanley Junior."

I waved back at the chap on the desk as I walked across the lobby and into the revolving door. And then I headed to the A.B.C., where I found a suitable corner to watch people from and ordered the Three-Course Special.

After four days—spent mainly in bookshops or wandering about, or sitting in cafés watching people—I returned north. Ottoline was waiting on the platform, huddled in fox fur, smoking a cigarette and breathing fumes into the frosty night air. As I stepped down from the train, she said, "I feel as though you've been gone for absolute months."

We walked to the motorcar. I wound the starter handle. Then, juddering, we turned out of the empty station and headed down the narrow lanes toward Birling. It was a particularly dark night and the headlights didn't seem bright enough, but Ottoline was in ebullient spirits. "So," she said, "tell me all." Just as though I'd had a rendezvous with a real lover.

"Well, I went to the A.B.C. . . . ," I began.

"No, no, *no!*" she said, cigarette still in hand and ash falling. "I want to know who you are now. Mrs. . . . ?"

So I told her.

"Mrs. Gaskell?" she said. "Isn't that . . . a little literary?"

Of course it was a literary name. But I couldn't very well be Mrs. Stedman. Almost everyone at Birling knew that name, and there was one already, somewhere in France. It wasn't until I had been on board the train and heading back to Northumberland that I'd given my newly married name any thought. And the inspiration was right there on my lap, in the form of *Sylvia's Lovers*.

"No, I'm afraid you can't be Mrs. Gaskell," said Ottoline, more to herself than to me.

We turned off the road and into the driveway. Snow was beginning to fall, and as we drew to a halt and Ottoline pulled on the hand brake, she said, "We need to think fast."

So we remained seated inside the car, and when Rodney emerged from the house, peering at us from a distance from beneath a large black umbrella, Ottoline simply smiled and waved at him, and he returned inside. She said, "Is there no one you've been romantically involved with—apart from Ralph?"

It was strange for me to hear her say the name; strange for me to hear anyone say the name. I said, "Yes, there was someone. But I really don't wish to use *his* name."

She turned to me. "What is it?" she asked. "What's his name?"

"Morton. Stanley Morton. But there's already someone posing as his wife."

She clapped her hands. "Perfect! That makes it all the more justifiable . . . He's still alive, I presume?"

I nodded.

"A cad?"

I nodded.

"In France?"

"So I believe."

"Don't worry, we'll have you widowed in no time."

I wasn't sure about that last comment. As much as I resented Stanley, I didn't wish him any harm. After all, he had a son. I said, "You do mean *pretend*, don't you?"

"Good gracious, I'm capable of many things, Pearl—but not murder." She lifted my hand: "Ah, I see you managed to find yourself a ring. Good. Now try this." She handed me another ring, a ruby set with small diamonds. "Ah, *quel dommage* . . . I thought it might fit. Oh well. You can wear it on your middle finger and tell everyone it was old Mrs. Morton's and that you haven't had time to have it sized."

"I can't take this."

"Yes, you can. My husband gave it to me years ago, and rubies were never me."

"But what if His Lordship notices it on my finger?"

"Pearl, a man who's had as many mistresses as my husband will have purchased enough diamonds to render one small ruby entirely forgettable . . . And now, Mrs. Morton, let's go inside and tell everyone your news."

Without wasting any time, Ottoline gathered together her depleted staff and announced my new status. Rodney smiled a little too knowingly for my liking, and I could tell Mrs. Lister was suspicious, for as soon as Ottoline disappeared, she said, "Well I never, that was a quick courtship."

But Rodney stepped in. "Not all that quick, Mrs. Lister. You've known your husband some time, haven't you, Pearl? You were engaged to be married when you came here, weren't you?"

"Yes, I was. That's right. It was a little bit on and off for a while, and I kept it all quiet because . . . because of the war . . . and everything," I said, petering out.

"Must have cost your fella a bob or two," said Mrs. Lister, examining the ruby ring.

"Actually it was his mother's. We didn't have time to get it sized."

"No, I bet you didn't," she said, nudging me with her elbow and winking.

The next evening, they threw a little party for me in the servants' hall. An iced cake and sherry, and three white balloons hanging from the gilt-framed picture of the King. Rodney made a toast, "To Pearl and Stanley." And though I felt like a fraud—and was one—I went with it, because I had no choice. Married was respectable; married was the only way for a woman in my condition.

Because of my ever-thickening waist and changing shape, my other *Happy News* was announced only a month after my "wedding." And if Rodney Watts suspected anything, he didn't say. Though Mrs. Lister did. "I had a funny feeling about it all—what with it being that quick," she said as soon as she got me on my own. And then, eyeing my belly and computing something further, she whispered, "But when—when did you see him, your Stanley? When did you get the chance?" Luckily, she helped me out: "Aha, it was when you stayed at Newcastle before Christmas, wasn't it?"

I winked an eye at her.

But it didn't matter what anyone thought. I was—to all intents and purposes—respectably married, and by that time it had already been decided where my baby would be born. Once again, Ottoline had thought it all through and taken control.

She'd said to me, "By my calculation *and* yours, this baby is due in June. And babies don't wait to fit in with lies . . ."

I shook my head. "What do you mean?"

"What I *mean* is, we have a slight problem with a baby that is due in September—or even later—arriving in June."

"I'll say it's come early."

"Really? . . . *Two months* early?"

I shrugged. "Why not?"

Ottoline fluttered her eyes and sighed. Then she spoke to me very slowly. "Pearl, a baby born two months prematurely looks quite

different to a full-term baby. A baby born two months prematurely
will be tiny, weak and frail, and very likely require medical care.
Do you understand?"

I nodded.

"If your baby arrives when it's due, in June—and regardless of
anything you say or claim—people will see and know that it is *not*
a premature baby. Calculations will be made, conclusions drawn.
Your reputation will be more than a little tarnished—and I'll be
incriminated," she added quietly. "But they're going to suspect anyway if they see you get too much bigger. Added to that, there's the
complication of the doctor . . ." She paused and muttered something to herself. "No, he can't be involved. And you're still neat—
very neat," she added, reaching out and running her hand over my
small rounded belly. "But just you wait. It's always in the last couple
of months one goes . . ." And as she blew out her cheeks and extended her hands out over her own stomach, I couldn't help but
laugh.

Ottoline continued. "Easter's early this year. I've always adored
Scotland at that time. So we shall have a trip—you and I, at Easter.
Then, because it's so glorious, and because there's nothing to rush
back for, and because you're *blooming* with all that Highland air
and your baby is not due for another few months, we'll extend our
stay. By the time we return here, our little darling will have gained
weight and be positively thriving."

So that was that. My baby *would* be born early, but not there.
It would be born in the Highlands.

Chapter Sixteen

Ottoline informed the couple who lived in the gatehouse that we were on a *religious retreat*, and that we required complete solitude for our prayers. It wasn't implausible; everyone was praying.

It was early April and the blue-iced mountains had begun their thaw. The river was in spate, the greening woods filled with bird-song and the sound of a hundred streams gushing down into the valley where sheep and lambs and languid cows grazed. And I was grateful that my child would be born in a place of such vibrant life.

And yet, it was all so strange. Strange to witness the indestructible beauty of Mother Nature—going on regardless, delivering another season, one associated with hope and promise into a world so dark and troubled—and strange to be back there; strange to see that whitewashed cottage. For despite all my efforts, Ralph's features had faded and become indistinct, and my memories of that time—and of him—now had a dreamlike quality to them. More than anything else, it was strange to be carrying new life amidst the incessant news of death. For the war raged on, insatiable in its appetite, and another three million men were needed.

We had been at Delnasay for only a few weeks when we heard that the *Lusitania* had been sunk with a great loss of life. Shortly after this, we learned that German airships had raided the south coast of England, dropping bombs on Southend, Leigh-on-Sea and Westcliff; and that a German zeppelin had attacked Ramsgate. In the middle of May, we read about the effects of asphyxiating gases, and that Italy had declared war on Austria. There were zeppelin raids on London and the east coast. British casualties were estimated to be a quarter of a million.

Ottoline had predicted—told me on board the train north—that going back would *stir things up* for me. And it did. For so many months I had been strong. For so many months I had avoided self-pity. There were people suffering far, far worse than I was, I knew. But returning to Delnasay plunged me back into memory, and into my unquestionable love for one person. And so, despite the bright skies and unfolding leaves, my heart was heavy, and that landscape—no matter how sweet or fresh—served only to remind me of Ralph, and his absence.

Ottoline said, "You must not go to the cottage. You must put yourself in a happy place . . . Think happy thoughts for your baby."

And I tried. I sat in the blue-walled drawing room, sometimes with my feet up—as instructed—and instead of scanning lists and searching for surnames beginning with *S*, I flicked through old copies of *Punch, The Field, Bystander,* and *The Lady* and *Country Life* magazines from before the war. I listened to Ottoline as she read to me and recited poetry, often Robbie Burns, and usually with what even I knew to be quite appalling pronunciation.

We fended for ourselves. Or rather, Ottoline fended for us both. And I was more than surprised; I was astounded by her knowledge and ingenuity and resourcefulness. For where and when had she learned to lay and light fires or fill oil lamps? Who had taught her how to manage a range and to cook? And what must it be like, I wondered, to be able but not allowed?

And so, one afternoon, as she crouched down by the fire, snapping the twigs she had gathered outside, I asked her, "Who taught you all of this?"

She glanced over her shoulder at me and smiled. "My mother, of course."

"Ah yes," I said, as though it had been a stupid question.

But still it made no sense. I'd seen the portrait of Ottoline's mother at Birling, and she did not strike me as a woman whose hands had ever been blackened with coal. And though I wanted to ask more, I wasn't sure how, or indeed if I should. But then Ottoline put down the kindling, knelt back and went on.

"My mother was not of the same stock as my father . . . had not grown up with an army of servants. She was from a rather bohemian family—artistic and talented, but invariably penniless and with absolutely no idea about money, or how to manage it. Fortunes wavered, came and went with the seasons. She spent most of her childhood moving from house to house, witnessing celebratory spending one minute and feverish selling the next. It was by all accounts a precarious existence. But one that undoubtedly taught her, made her resourceful and fiercely independent . . . She used to tell me never to take anything for granted. Never to assume that just because things *are*, they will remain so . . ."

"She sounds very wise."

"She was," said Ottoline, her back to me, facing the half-made-up fire. "She was wise and wonderful, and a tad rebellious and not quite of her time. Unconventional, I suppose." She paused and turned to me. "She refused to employ a governess, insisted on teaching me herself. So in addition to some history, a little geography, English and French, as well as learning the piano and how to draw, I also learned how to light fires and how to cook. And while rolling out pastry or . . . or poaching fish, she spoke to me about life—about art and philosophy, or hats and shoes, or *men!*" She shook her head and smiled. "Yes, she was unconventional."

I felt for the gold band on my finger. I said, "And your mother's sister, was she the same?"

"Aunt Connie? I never knew her. But Mother always said that where Constance had inherited the talent, she had learned from its waste."

"Constance," I repeated, clinging to the notion of *her* and her ring. "She went to India . . ."

Ottoline nodded. "Yes, and my poor mother was heartbroken— to lose her only sister. She never saw Connie again . . . And she loathed *him*, her brother-in-law, Major Stedman. Said he was a ty- rant and a bully and that his neglect of Ra—" She stopped. She looked away from me. "This wood won't do," she said after a mo- ment. "It's still damp."

She rose to her feet, brushed down her skirt. "I shall have to go and fetch some more. And then I'll make us tea. Yes, that's what I'll do," she murmured, and left the room.

Almost every morning Ottoline bicycled to the village for newspapers, bread, milk and other provisions, and returned pink cheeked and full of gossip about people I did not know. And I could only imagine what they thought of her—Lady Ottoline Campbell, as she flew down the main street in her tam-o'-shanter and long tartan socks, ringing the bell of that familiar rusting bicycle. Each afternoon, we walked along the valley, following the path of the river, and each evening, she busied herself in the kitchen, rattling pans and sometimes swearing loudly. We both agreed that if Ottoline had been in service, she'd have been a far better lady's maid than cook.

One evening, as we sat quietly, each of us pretending to read, she said, "You know the reason I don't mention him is because it's better for *you* that way. You do understand, don't you?"

"Not really," I said, without raising my eyes to her.

I heard her sigh. "I blame myself."

I looked up. "Blame yourself? But for what?"

She closed her book. "You and *him* . . . this situation. I brought you here, and I had a duty of care. But I was too caught up in . . . in my own affairs, I suppose, and the war. This wretched, bloody war. I'm sorry, forgive me. It's just that I'm angry. And not just with Kitchener and Asquith and this useless coalition, but with myself—and with Ralph."

"But I don't want you to be angry. Not with Ralph, and particularly not with yourself. I knew what I was doing."

She shook her head. "No, you didn't. You were already in love with him by the time you learned he was married. And now you're to have a child, a child without a father, and I must share that responsibility. I wish to," she quickly added.

"You've been more than kind to me."

She smiled. "I'm afraid we're going to have to kill off poor Stanley after we return to Birling, otherwise it'll all get too tricky. You'll be a widow—but you'll be able to marry, hopefully, one day. In the meantime, you and your child will be provided for, so I don't want you to worry about that. But you must try to forget about Ralph. Put him behind you. Look forward."

I nodded.

She glanced about the room, then back at me. "Of course, if it really *is* meant to be—decreed by the universe and all that," she added, raising her arms in a dramatic gesture, "then it will be. He'll come back to you . . . He'll ride back into your life and you'll be together, but together *in sin*. And that won't be easy, Pearl. Not for you or for him, and certainly not for your child."

She paused and I smiled. She had no idea, I thought. Because living *in sin* with Ralph was not only preferable to a life outside of sin and without him; it was what I had come to hope for. Then she went on. "It's very easy to be romantic, you know, particularly now." And there it was again: that phrase, one I'd come to loathe. "Yes, very easy when the object of one's affection and longing is absent . . . But the reality will be different, quite different. You see, even if Ralph does return—well, he could be maimed, crippled, and then what? He has no money, Pearl. And you'll have a child, an illegitimate child—and a damaged man, one you barely know, to look after."

"I know him and he knows me. He knows me better than any other person in this world."

She stared at me, frowning: "No, he knew you for a moment,

Pearl. And though you may relive it a thousand times over in your mind, that's all it was—and all it will ever be."

In that instant I almost hated her. She had no idea about love, real love, I thought. She knew nothing. Nothing at all.

So, minutes later, I didn't hesitate when she said, "And please, do promise me you won't go to the cottage."

"Yes, I promise," I said, flicking the pages of an already ancient magazine.

The path had narrowed, become more overgrown, but as I pictured him—his long stride and feet on that track, his paint-smeared hands reaching out and brushing over the long grass—I sensed his presence. And so strongly, so acutely, that by the time the white building emerged, I thought, maybe . . . just maybe.

The door was unlocked, the interior empty and stripped of furnishings. Cobwebs hung down from the beamed ceiling, drifting aimlessly in the musty, damp air. An empty jam jar lay on a fly-covered windowsill, its base stained dark red—the only trace, only clue. I stepped back outside, overwhelmed by the emptiness, overwhelmed by a new sense of desolation. It had been September when I'd last seen him. Now it was May. Eight months, I thought; only two seasons. And yet a thousand years might have passed. And I sat down on the grass and wept.

"You promised me . . . Yes, you did. You promised you'd not come here."

Ottoline marched toward me, her tam-o'-shanter askew, her skirt still hitched up into her belt from her bicycle ride. She helped me to my feet. She said, "I told you, didn't I? Didn't I try to warn you?" She threw back her head in disgust. "You *silly* girl . . . What am I to do with you? Haven't I said—and over and over—that you have to be strong? You have to accept that he's gone and that he might never come back."

"But where are his things—his paints and canvases?"

"They're safe, in storage. I promised I'd keep it all for him."

Still holding on to my hand, she led me at a march back down the path, toward the house, muttering all the way about the price she'd had to pay for some butter and the nonappearance of the butcher from Elgin, and the state of the road and a puncture. And I thought, *Puncture?* However did she know how to mend a puncture? Was that her mother, too?

Later, she carried the old tin bath downstairs to the kitchen, then boiled kettles of water to fill it. She helped me to undress, helped me into it. And as I sat in the bath, she stood smoking a cigarette, talking to herself as she surveyed the lined-up jars of spices she had found in a cupboard; from time to time stirring the pan of something she said she had "invented" earlier that day on her unfortunate bike ride.

"You know, I rather like the name Paprika," she said, sprinkling, then turning and smiling back at me.

And I thought, *Hector Campbell—you silly, silly man. You have absolutely no idea.*

My contractions started shortly after luncheon, which we had taken together in the kitchen, and where Ottoline remained for some time, cleaning up. When she finally came into the drawing room and saw me—standing with my head down and gripping the marble mantelpiece—she rubbed my back and told me it was just the beginning. I was irritated by this comment, by her touch and even her wisdom.

Then the pains stopped. Stopped completely. And we sat looking at each other, waiting. "You have to brace yourself, dear. It could go on like this for days," Ottoline said, smiling at me as she picked up the newspaper.

I was dozing, flitting in and out of dreams, half listening to a wood pigeon in the trees outside and the ticking of the clock within the room, when a great wave convulsed my body and threw me out of my slumber. And this time I buckled and cried out in pain.

"Breathe . . . You must breathe through it, dear," said Ottoline, sitting down next to me and grabbing hold of my hand.

And I tried, and I tried, and as it subsided, I said, "I think . . . you need . . . to fetch . . ."

"The midwife—Mrs. Grant? Yes, I think you're right. Do you want me to help you upstairs—to my room? It might be more comfortable for you there."

I shook my head. "I want to stay here."

She plumped up the cushions behind me, suggested that I lie down. But I couldn't. Instead, as she left the room, I rose to my feet and paced about the carpet, waiting for the next wave to come. I saw her through the window, pedaling like fury up the driveway, disappearing into the peach-colored evening. And then, as pain seized me and shot up my spine, I banged my fist on the glass pane and cried out: "Ottoline! . . . Ottoline!"

I'm not sure how long she was gone, but by the time she

reappeared, I was half undressed and crawling about the tartan carpet on my hands and knees. I knew the design, each shade and almost every one of those checks. She dropped some towels to the floor and knelt down beside me, and I placed my head on her shoulder and cried—with relief, and fear, and exhaustion, knowing the worst was still to come.

She placed a cool flannel to my brow. "Mrs. Grant will be here soon, very soon."

"Have you ever delivered a baby?" I asked.

"No. But I have given birth to three."

"*Three?*"

Then it came again, more intense than the last time. And like an injured animal, I panted and moaned and whimpered. And as Ottoline spread out towels and pulled cushions down from the sofa beside us, I felt a strange tingling sensation, something warm and wet running down my legs. She said, "Ah yes. I think your waters have broken."

"Three?" I said again. "You had three?"

"Yes, there was another—after Billy. A girl. She lived for only a few days. A hole in her heart, they said."

"A girl . . . You had a daughter?"

Another wave of pain. I gripped hold of Ottoline's hand. And when she reminded me yet again to breathe, I told her she sounded like Mrs. *Bloody Bart*, and she said, "Yes, that's it . . . Release it all. Say whatever you feel." And I heard myself scream Ralph's name.

Then wave after wave it came, flooding my senses, drowning out who I was, where I was and everything that had come before or could come after, until there was only *it*, and an overwhelming desire to expel it from my body.

But Ottoline said, "No, not yet . . . not yet . . ."

And I thought I would die. And I shouted and screamed that at her.

Then, finally: "*Now!* Now, Pearl."

My daughter entered this world shortly after nine o'clock on Midsummer Day, screaming just as passionately as her mother, and a week late—according to Ottoline's calculation. Minutes later, the elderly midwife arrived. I was checked. My baby was checked. "A bonnie bairn, Mrs. Morton," she declared. "Seven pounds, six ounces."

And later that evening, after the midwife had left us and as dusk began to fall, I sat with my feet up on the sofa—feeling proud and swamped with a sort of contentment I'd never before imagined or known. Drinking a cup of deliciously sweet tea, I watched Ottoline as she cradled my baby in her arms.

"So, is she to be Kitty?"

"No. Nor is she going to be Paprika."

Ottoline raised her eyes to me and smiled.

Quietly, privately, in the days leading up to my daughter's birth, I had for some reason kept thinking on the name Arabella. It was a pretty name, a fine name, I thought, for a daughter—Ralph's daughter. But *Arabella Godley* was quite different to *Bella Morton*, and I had known too many Bellas in service, and my daughter would never be in service, I decided. Arabella Godley was a notion, a mere idea, and a missing piece of a jigsaw, and Bella Morton would only ever be my reaction to it.

After my daughter's birth, there could only be one name. Or at least one name she would be known by.

"She's to be named after the person who brought her into this world . . . She's Lila."

Lila. She was to me the most perfect creation. Ever. Adorable from the start, and comical, too; with a rather large head covered with a down of fine golden hair, bright inquisitive blue eyes, neat button nose and enormously fat cheeks. She had a tiny rosebud mouth that twisted and turned and offered up every nuance of feeling without any words, and long slender fingers like her father—artistic fingers, which she liked to stretch out or sometimes clench and wave in anger. And skin so soft and mouthwateringly delicious that Ottoline and I often fought over whose turn it was to press our lips to it.

When Ottoline produced an ancient-looking perambulator from one of the outbuildings, I laughed. "I'm not putting her in *that*."

"Oh, but it'll scrub up fine," she said, wheeling the thing into the kitchen.

And it did.

Each day my Lila grew fatter and more beautiful. Each day I loved her a little more. Very quickly, I couldn't imagine my life without her. For almost eight weeks Ottoline and I watched her, sighed, cooed and fussed over her—as though she were a present to us both from the gods, a miracle. We set clocks by her, watched clocks for her, listened for her stirrings and whimpers. And using the newly scrubbed perambulator—or "baby carriage" as Ottoline called it—we wheeled her along the banks of the A'an, sat next to it beneath the pines on the lawn, looked back at each other and

smiled, for together we had brought Lila into this world, this un-
imaginably beautiful and troubled world.

It was during this time that Ottoline said, "Can we share her?
Will you allow me to love her, just a little? Because we're much
more than lady and lady's maid now. We're friends—dear friends.
You and Lila are like family to me. And I am after all her blood
relation."

It was only right that Ottoline be Lila's godmother, and I decided on Billy and Rodney Watts to be her godfathers. I wrote to
Billy to ask him and received some sweet words in return: *I can't
begin to tell you how deeply honored I feel. And though I can't promise
to be at the christening in person, I shall be there in spirit—and simply
can't wait to meet her.*

We headed south earlier than planned. It was not long after the
first anniversary of the beginning of the war and shortly after Ottoline received word from Lord Hector that Hugo was to come
home on leave. There was great interest in us—now three—when
we arrived back at Birling. *Yes, Lila had come early . . . Yes, she was
indeed a robust little thing . . .* Something of a celebratory atmosphere drifted around the house. Hugo was coming home, and a
baby, it seemed, was what everyone needed—and, as Rodney said,
a most welcome and happy addition. But it was Mrs. Lister I was
most concerned with and needed to seek out alone.

So, on the evening of our arrival, after I had settled Lila, I returned to the kitchen in search of Mrs. Lister. Tentatively, I inquired if she would be willing to look after my baby for a few hours

each day, so that I could attend to Ottoline—continue my duties as her maid. Mrs. Lister's face went pink; for a moment she appeared to have stopped breathing, and I thought she might very well explode.

I said, "You'll be paid, of course. And Her Ladyship is happy if you are . . . But I can find someone else if it's not—"

"No!" she yelled in a great gasp, then took a gulp of air. "You don't need to find anyone else." Another gulp. "I love bairns . . ." A brief pause and another gulp, and then it came: "You ask my Frank. Love them I do. Wished I had more. And him as well. Oh yes, him as well. But it weren't to be, you see. And you don't need to worry. No. Don't need to worry about a thing. Treat her like one of my own, so I will. Just like one of my own. Well innocent, aren't they? Yes, innocent and from God. Precious little mites. No, you don't need to worry about a thing. Your little Lila will be fine with me. And you know I've had a few. Oh yes. Not that it was easy with my last, mind you. Lost ten gallons of blood, I did. Frank thought I was a gona. Sent for my mother, he did. They had my grave dug. Beside himself, he was. Beside himself."

Eventually she stopped. I went to tell Ottoline, who smiled and said, "Did she go on and on?"

"Yes."

"I told you."

She had.

But what I hoped for, what mattered to me more than anything, was for my daughter not just to be accepted, but to be cared for and loved. And that night, with Lila sleeping soundly in her cot—Billy's old cot—next to me, I felt relieved and happy that Mrs.

Lister would be looking after her when I was not. And happy, too, that despite my circumstances, I was to continue as Ottoline's maid.

Hugo's leave was delayed. But the fine weather held out for the final day of the Feast Week celebrations at Warkworth. All of us at Birling went, on foot, and en masse. For Feast Weeks were part of summer in every village and town, in every county, like flower shows and cricket, or strawberries and cream. And there were strawberries, and ice cream, and a fancy dress pageant at the castle, with music and dancing, and where Mrs. Lister—dressed in medieval costume—sang "The Ballad of Chevy Chase." There was a carnival on the river, with streamers and flags and colorful floats, and a rowing race, during which we almost burst our lungs, and then burst them again when our young under-gardener with a clubfoot took first prize. And there was what Mrs. Lister referred to as "the Hoppings": a funfair and amusements in the market square, with shuggy boats and a roundabout, a coconut shy and endless stalls.

"What a grand day," said Mrs. Lister, out of costume and in charge of the perambulator once again as we trailed behind the others down the dusty road home. "Just like old times."

But there was a war on; husbands were absent, children fatherless and servants in short supply. As a consequence, a doubling up of roles had come about. Instead of housemaids and parlormaids, we now had house-parlormaids, and instead of a head gardener, under-gardeners and grooms, we now had gardener-grooms; and no footmen, none at all. And so I suppose it was inevitable that my own role should also expand. Though I have to admit, when Ottoline first suggested it to me, I felt a little insulted. It was a man's job, I thought, and I had no idea how to drive a motorcar, added to which, it had taken me a long time to earn my position as lady's maid. But Ottoline assured me that it would be only for the duration of the war, because after that, everything would get back to normal. And an ability to drive, she said, would be another string to my bow. She would teach me.

"It's really terribly easy. The main thing one has to remember— concentrate on—is the steering," she said, moving her hands as though controlling a horse's reins.

Easy it was not—not for me. I spent five consecutive afternoons driving one of Lord Hector's motorcars up and down the driveways and lanes around Birling with Ottoline in the passenger seat, smoking incessantly as she pointed out obstacles and trees, issuing instructions like a sergeant major. More than once we bounced along a grass verge, but only once did we end up in a ditch. A local farmer pulled us out. Eventually, I got the hang of it, and we drove all the way to the nearby market town of Alnwick and back— without glitches, hitches or ditches. And thus, I became a lady's maid–chauffeur, or something of that sort.

My very first trip out alone in the motorcar was to collect Lord Hector and Hugo from the station. "Not too far. An easy one," Ottoline said. I set off extra early, drove slowly, and then had to wait a full half hour at the station, wrapped in a rug from the back of the car. But when the train eventually rattled in and drew to a halt, only Lord Hector appeared on the platform. Perhaps not surprisingly, he seemed a little disconcerted to see me there—waiting for him. So I explained how Ottoline had taught me to drive, and then I helped him into the car and offered him the rug. I didn't ask about Hugo, didn't want to.

As we turned out of the station, it seemed unusually dark and gloomy until His Lordship mentioned that it was in fact dusk and suggested I turn on the headlights. But I wasn't sure how to, where the switch was. So we had to stop, briefly, for him to show me. After that, he sat up front with me, and I drove back even slower than I'd driven there. But when we drew to a halt outside the house, as I switched off the engine, His Lordship said, "Excellent, Pearl. Very well done." And I felt proud.

I learned about Hugo's absence at supper. Rodney told us that Lord Hector had received a telegram only that morning—and only hours before he was due to meet his son. Hugo had been injured in an ambush and taken to a casualty clearing station somewhere near Loos. Details of his injuries were vague: leg and head wounds, Rodney said, but nothing life threatening.

Two days later, after the harvest festival, Lila's christening took place as scheduled, with Ottoline and Rodney as the attendant godparents.

"Ottoline Constance Katherine Charlotte Wilhelmina," said the vicar, in a slow, somber monotone, and eyeing me. But nothing could rankle me that day. I was proud of my daughter and of her names; all five of them. Each one of them meant something, honored someone, and whereas I had only the one name, snatched at random and meaning nothing, my daughter had five—*and* a christening.

Afterward, we returned to Birling—chattering noisily and ready for a celebration. But as sherry and cake were served and passed round the drawing room, a telegram arrived for Lord Hector.

He moved over to the window, and there was a lull in the proceedings as he lowered his eyes, read the words and then carefully folded the paper and pushed it into the pocket of his waistcoat. He stood perfectly still for a while, staring out at the gardens. And it would have been easy to think it was nothing more than an update from the Foreign Office. But as I watched him, I sensed something new in his features and stillness. He waited until conversation and clatter resumed before he walked over to Ottoline, who was holding Lila. I saw him look down at my baby, place his hand on Ottoline's arm. "I need to speak with you in private, darling."

Calmly, Ottoline handed Lila to Mrs. Lister—resplendent in pink—and left the room with her husband.

A short while after this, as I sat with Mrs. Lister, who was still clutching a sleeping Lila to her bosom, Rodney, too, left the room. And though Mrs. Lister and I looked at each other, we said nothing. To speak a name would be tempting fate. But as the minutes passed, Mrs. Lister's nerves got the better of her; she had to fill up the waiting.

"Might not be anything . . . as likely as not . . . Ah, and look at her now, little mite . . . worn-out, worn-out she is, and who can blame her . . . Yes, as likely as not some business of His Lordship's . . . But you haven't had any cake . . . Go on, have a piece . . . It'll all disappear later . . . You know what them girls are like."

I lifted the china plate from the table in front of me, picked some icing from the slice of cake. Then the door opened. Rodney entered and sat down. It was Hugo, he said, staring at Lila. He had died of his wounds. I spat the icing into my hand.

Hugo's remains took a week to arrive in Northumberland. The undertaker collected the coffin from the station. After the funeral, we all followed the flag-draped hearse on foot, through a biting wind and falling elm leaves, to a cemetery near the beach.

Ottoline was surprisingly stoical. Once more her grief was quiet, intensely private and dignified, her tears silent. She told me she found comfort in the knowledge that Hugo had joined a number of his friends—including one that had been with us at Delnasay. Once more she distracted herself with correspondence, writing to Billy, penning replies to each of the black-edged "in sympathy" letters she and His Lordship had received, and there were quite literally hundreds. And she threw herself into her own *war effort* with new commitment, writing to our prisoners of war and shopping for them.

Almost every day I drove past the road to the beach and cemetery where Hugo lay, over the ancient bridge and through the towered archway into Warkworth. I parked Ottoline's car in the market square. And sometimes, as I walked up the hill, beneath the looming castle and toward the post office, I thought I could sense the Gray Lady watching me. I didn't like to look up at the castle, or its dark tower. And I didn't hang about. After I'd handed in the letters and parcels, I hurried back down the hill with the list for Thompson's, the grocers. And such was my imagination that I would often heave a sigh of relief as I drove back over the bridge and headed home to Birling, as though I had escaped the clutches of some supernatural force.

Later, safe, all ghosts forgotten, we received the provisions from

Thompson's. And as Ottoline checked them, reading items and prices out loud, I recorded in one of her scrapbooks what we had sent, and spent:

Golden Syrup—7d
Potted Meat—6d
Cake—1s 2d
Biscuits—1s 6d
Chocolate—1s
Cigarettes—1s 2d
Sardines—5d
Marmalade—7d
Soap—1d
Tea—1s 10d
Tobacco—5d

It was in the late autumn, not long after Hugo's death, that Ottoline went to London. I'm not sure how Lord Hector did it, but he had managed to secure a three-day pass for Billy. It wasn't Billy's first leave: Lord Hector had seen him earlier that spring, when Ottoline and I were in Scotland and Billy had turned up out of the blue at the Foreign Office. His Lordship didn't tell Ottoline until after we'd returned to Birling, and she was understandably sad. At that time, the news of Billy's leave had made me feel guilty: If it hadn't been for me, Ottoline could have perhaps traveled to London and met her son, I thought. So I was very happy for her when she told me.

"I'm going to see him, Pearl . . . I'm going to see my boy," she kept on saying as I packed her bag.

Naturally, she was excited, and yet I sensed some trepidation, too, when she said, "It'll be the first time we have been together as three. Just three now."

Because of Lila, and because the trip south was only a matter of a few nights, I was to stay at Birling. But I knew by then that Ottoline was perfectly capable of looking after herself. The house in London had been requisitioned and was now a military hospital, and Ottoline was to stay at her club.

I took her to the station and saw her onto the train, and four days later I collected her.

"So handsome in his uniform, Pearl. And still so darling, so sweet . . . A little tired, perhaps . . . yes, tired. And thinner . . . Well, they don't get much, you know . . . And such ghastly conditions . . . like your worst nightmare, he said . . . We took him to the theater, twice, dinner at the Savoy and the little Italian place round the corner. You'd think he hadn't eaten in months. Well, he probably hadn't, you know, not properly . . . and so tired . . . And sad, of course . . . Yes, immensely sad about Hugo. And sad about so many of his friends. But so darling, so sweet . . ."

Seeing Billy had been both good and bad. A mother had been reunited with her boy, able to touch him, hold him and spend time with him. But it was an infinitely more fragile Ottoline I collected from the station that day. It was one thing to read about battles, gaze upon numbers and names, but quite another, it seemed, to see the effects of war firsthand—particularly on one you loved. Seeing Billy again had shaken Ottoline, and for a while after her return, though she rallied in front of the other servants when they inquired after Billy—"so handsome in his uniform"—she was unusually subdued. Her scrapbooks were abandoned, and there were no parcels for me to post.

I later discovered that Billy's account of life in the trenches was not necessarily what was printed in the newspapers. He had told his parents of the appalling and squalid conditions, of a lack of equipment, resources and properly trained men; he had spoken of poor communication, and mistakes being made—resulting in killing our own; and he had talked of the corpses, the half-dead and dead and body parts left lying in the mud; and of the crippling fear that sometimes took hold, and of deserters being shot.

Yes, it had been too much for Ottoline; it was too much for anyone to comprehend. And I wondered if and how those inhabiting that hell—should they survive—would be able to resume normal life. Would they ever be able to put it behind them? And would we, those of us who had spent the duration at home, who had waved *our boys* off with flags and banners, ever be able to understand, or forgive ourselves? For they would all be damaged, I thought, even those still able to smile.

I tried not to think of Ralph in that place of suffering and carnage. In my mind, I placed him elsewhere: an office, London, a sun-drenched field away from the fighting, anywhere but that dark hole. And I was resolute in my belief that he remained alive, for I knew Ottoline would have told me if she had heard anything, and she had not. I had never seen his hand on any envelope again, and I had been vigilant.

I was lucky: I had a constant reminder of him in Lila, and she—

along with Mrs. Lister's intransigent patriotism—pulled me back from any hideous contemplation. Day by day my daughter grew bigger and stronger and more beautiful. She thrived on Mrs. Lister's hip as the cook moved about the kitchen—stirring, tasting and always adding more salt.

And so another Christmas passed and another year began, cold and bitter and black as coal. In February everything turned white and froze. Spears of ice hung from the guttering outside my window, pipes burst and for more than a week we were housebound. Snow turned to sleet and then rain, and Easter was shrouded in fog. But May brought longer days and daffodils. The hazel catkins came out overnight, the boughs of cherry trees burst pink, hawthorn hedges pricked green and we heard the first cuckoo. Each day the sky stretched farther over the ripening fields where larks soared and corncrakes rattled their song.

In June we celebrated Lila's first birthday. A few days later she took her first steps, staggering barefoot across the lawn into Ottoline's outstretched arms as I looked out from an upstairs window.

Then came July. The month Ottoline stopped reading the newspapers.

Chapter Seventeen

I was below stairs in the laundry when I heard the howling. And at
first I thought it was the dog, Lolly—or another animal, injured, in
great pain, and somehow inside the house. But as it went on, and I
put down the iron and moved out into the passageway, I realized
that the sound was human and that it contained a word, repeated
over and over, and that the word was a name and that the sound
belonged to Ottoline.

And so I knew. Knew before a silence fell over the house. Knew
before Rodney appeared at the end of the passageway. Knew before
he said it: "It's Billy."

And I didn't run. I stood stock-still for a moment, deafened by
the new soundlessness, frozen in the sudden inevitability. Then,
slowly, I walked up the stairs and into the hallway. I saw the telegram lying on the floor by her feet, but I didn't pick it up. I wrapped
my arms around her—so still, so quiet, it was as though she had
stopped breathing. I held her for some time, and then with my arm

around her, I led her up to her room. I removed her shoes, helped her onto the bed, pulled up a chair and sat holding her hand. She didn't speak, didn't utter a word, and neither did I. For what was there to say? They were gone, both of them. Lives not yet started, extinguished. Unspent decades snatched.

I'm not sure how long I sat with her, but her continued stillness and the blankness of her eyes concerned me. So I whispered to her that I was going downstairs, and that I'd be back in a short while. I'm not sure if she even heard me.

Rodney was standing at the bottom of the stairs. "How is she?"

"Quiet. *Too* quiet . . . I think we should send for the doctor."

I hovered over him as he made the telephone call, closed my eyes as I listened to his words: "Yes, Master William . . . Oh, only today—minutes ago . . . Lying down, in her bedroom . . . Shock, yes . . . Of course . . . See you then, sir."

Rodney put down the receiver. "The doctor will be here in the next hour . . . Meanwhile, I think I should make an announcement, don't you? Gather us all in the servants' hall?"

"Yes. You need to inform everyone."

I went back to the laundry. I scrubbed down the wooden bench, over and over until my hands were almost raw, until I heard the handbell in the servants' hall. It was a formality, but one that had to be observed. And we were a raggle-taggle lineup of old and new, of differing shapes and ages and sizes, of differing worlds. Brought together for yet more bad news, another death. And I was pleased Mrs. Lister had taken Lila out on a walk and was not there. She had by that time lost two of her three sons, and I knew it would hit her hard and be better for Rodney to tell her in private.

Rodney held a piece of paper in his hand. I suppose he wanted to get the facts right. He stared down at it as he officially informed us what we already knew: Billy Campbell had been killed. In a steady voice, a voice measured by experience, he said Billy had died on the first day of July, and during the first hours of a new offensive in the region of the Somme.

One of the newly hired gardener-grooms shook his head: "Bad luck."

Rodney raised his eyes: "No, not bad luck. Bad luck is when you don't have a winning number in a raffle. Billy Campbell—along with his brother and countless others—has sacrificed his life for you and me, for all of us."

Then our young kitchen maid, Sissy, asked Rodney if he was sure, quite sure, because she'd heard that soldiers reported killed often turned up again. A ripple of murmurings swept through the lineup; oh yes, that's right; others had heard such things, too.

Rodney waited. Then he said, "I'm afraid we're quite certain, Sissy."

"Will he come back for his funeral—like Mr. Hugo did?" she asked.

Rodney shook his head. "Sadly, there is no body for us to bid adieu to."

I closed my eyes as Rodney went on. He explained that many of those who had perished in France could not be recovered. He said the day Billy died, a truce had been negotiated in order for both sides to recover their dead and wounded from No-Man's-Land. But, unfortunately, Billy Campbell's body had not been found. Then he thanked everyone in advance for their understanding and left the room. And I returned upstairs to sit with Ottoline.

❧

Lord Hector arrived home in a taxicab later that evening, by which time the doctor had been to the house and attended Ottoline.

"I'm so sorry, so very sorry," I said.

We stood together at the foot of Ottoline's bed, watching her.

"I caught the first train," he whispered. "How is she?"

Ottoline remained very still. She lay with her hands by her sides, staring past us at nothing. She had not spoken, not said anything at all. Not even when the doctor quietly whispered his condolences. The only movement I'd seen her make was when, from time to time, she closed her eyes, turned her head and clutched at the bedcovers, desperate, uncomprehending of a world in which it was possible for her children to die.

"The doctor has given her something."

Lord Hector nodded and moved away from me. He sat down by his wife's bedside and took hold of her hand. "My darling . . ."

For days Ottoline stayed in her bed, in her room. And there was little for me to do. I was shut out; her bedroom door remained closed with Lord Hector on the other side of it. I knocked, I asked and inquired, and then passed over trays to His Lordship and later collected them. In grief, at least, Ottoline's husband was strangely protective and possessive of her, and no one, not even I—her maid—was allowed entry.

Sometimes, waiting outside the door, I heard his voice—quiet, murmuring, tender. Once, I heard her scream, "No! No! You did not! You weren't there!" I heard her weeping; heard him weeping. And

though it was impossible for me to understand the nature of a marriage such as theirs, I knew they had been reconciled in grief, and
that it was something raw, profoundly intimate and deeply private.

They say things come in threes, but *they* didn't account for this
war. And that summer, the summer of 1916, the summer of my
daughter's first unsteady steps, would forever in my mind be associated with a place called the Somme.

And death did not always wait for ominous clouds or bad
weather. Nor did it arrive with bells and telegrams. It came unan-
nounced on fragrant mornings when dust motes danced and birdsong drifted in through open windows. It came amidst whistling
and humming, the scents and sounds and industry of an ordered
house, working at normality.

So, when I heard the familiar shuffle and tread behind me in
the kitchen, I didn't turn. I was, I think, probably daydreaming,
because we all—even I—continued to cling to that very fine
thread of a still-beautiful and extraordinary thing called life. And
I can't remember now what Mrs. Lister said, exactly, about Harry's
death, but it was the Somme again; I heard that much. And I
couldn't recall—was Harry fourteen, fifteen or sixteen years old?
The only thing I could see at that moment was a gaping collar and
the aching vulnerability of a young pale neck. And like that tender
stalk, something snapped in me, and for the first time in my life I
felt the burning passion of hatred. Real hatred. But I said nothing.
It wasn't done to give way to emotion. To do so would signify some
sort of surrender, or worse still, *defeat*.

A short while later we were once again summoned to the servants' hall, and once again Rodney carried out his grim duty. Afterward, I informed His Lordship, who said he would pass on the news to Ottoline—*when the time is right.*

I presumed His Lordship must have decided that the time was indeed right later that day, because that same evening Ottoline appeared downstairs for the first time since Billy's death. She came to the kitchen, where Rodney, Mrs. Lister and I sat with our cocoa. She was dressed in a purple gown—one I'd not seen before, and which was definitely not suitable mourning attire. Her face was pale, her eyes unusually bright, and when she began to extend her sympathy to Rodney in a quiet, monotone voice, Mrs. Lister couldn't help herself. She interrupted, "No, it's not Derek, Your Ladyship. It's Harry . . ."

Ottoline appeared confused.

"Little Harry—our hallboy . . . Mollie Rankin's brother?" Mrs. Lister went on.

"But that can't be right," said Ottoline. "He's still a child . . . He can't possibly have been over there." She pulled out a chair and sat down at the table. "Please, do sit down," she said. For some minutes we sat in silence. Then, "How's Lila?" she asked, glancing over to the perambulator where my baby lay sleeping.

"She's very well, my lady. Completely spoiled by Mrs. Lister here."

Ottoline placed her hand on Mrs. Lister's. "Whatever would we do without you, Mrs. Lister? And whatever would *I* do without the three of you?"

"It's always been a pleasure to serve Your Ladyship," said Rodney.

Ottoline frowned. "That's what they did, isn't it—*serve?*"

"Aye, they all served their country proud," said Mrs. Lister, newly tearful.

"Serve," said Ottoline again. "Yes, I suppose they did their duty. They laid down their lives for . . . for something. I'm not sure what."

"Well, for king and country and empire, Your Ladyship," said Mrs. Lister. "They laid down their lives for all of us. And that's why we have to be strong. Yes, we have to. We owe it to them."

Ottoline smiled vaguely; Rodney slid me a look. And Mrs. Lister, still sounding a little put out, said again, "They laid down their lives for their country, they did."

"Perhaps," said Ottoline, quieter and abstracted now. "But you see, I just need to know . . . I just need to know . . ."

She didn't finish her sentence. Lord Hector appeared in the doorway: "Ah, there you are."

Quickly, we rose to our feet. Ottoline remained seated, moving her index finger over the pine table as though writing something on it.

"Sweetheart . . ." He moved over to her, frowning as he watched her finger and waiting until she had finished. Then he helped her to her feet. As he led her out, she turned back to us. "Thank you," she said, smiling—just as though she'd been at a tea party.

"Still not right," said Mrs. Lister, gathering up our cups and shaking her head.

The next morning, I was summoned to His Lordship's study. He asked me what Ottoline had said in the kitchen the previous evening, and so I told him what little there was to tell. He said it was very *early days*, that Ottoline's grief was not just for Billy but for Hugo, too—a delayed grief. She needed time, he said, to adjust to the fact that both of their sons had gone.

"I'm afraid she's still in denial, but eventually she'll come to understand and accept the reality of the situation."

"Are you sure?" I asked him.

He thought for a moment and then said, "No, I'm not sure. How can I be? But I have to hope."

However, in the weeks that followed, Ottoline did indeed seem to recover a little, begin to grasp the awful tragedy of her sons' deaths, and slowly return to something of her former self. I reestablished our old routine: taking her breakfast to her on a tray each morning, laying out her clothes, helping her to bathe and dress. She never so much as glanced at a newspaper, but she did resume her scrapbooks, and, now united in grief, she often held court with Mrs. Lister in the almost aptly named morning room. Meanwhile, Lord Hector remained in residence at Birling, and I wondered if he'd ever return to London. But in the middle of October, prior to Trafalgar Day, Lord Hector did return to the city, to stay at his club for a few days and attend a memorial service. And it was then that Ottoline told me of her plan to commune with Billy and Hugo.

Mrs. Reed was delivered to Birling by taxicab on the Sunday evening after His Lordship's departure. I was extended an invitation to the *meeting* in the dining room. Ottoline said, "I'd like you to be there." She was nervous and excited. Desperate, I suppose, and who could blame her? Mrs. Lister was also invited, and seemed keen on the whole experiment until she heard the woman was from Amble, another nearby town whose inhabitants filled her with suspicion.

Ancient, pencil thin, with badly died hair and a broad accent, Mrs. Reed sat smoking as Rodney, Mrs. Lister and I filed into the room. I sat between Ottoline and Mrs. Lister. Rodney dimmed the lights, and we all joined hands over the polished mahogany table. Mrs. Reed asked for silence—this, even though the room was already deathly quiet. Then she closed her eyes, began to breathe deeply. And I was surprised by Mrs. Lister, who seemed to have put aside her antipathy and quickly followed suit. After no more than a minute or so, Mrs. Reed spoke: "Aytch, I am getting the letter aytch."

"That'll be Hugo," Mrs. Lister whispered loudly.

"Yes, Hugo, my eldest," said Ottoline, eager.

"Is that you, Hugo?" said Mrs. Reed, newly deep, newly solemn. Then, "Yes, it is *he*," she said, and I heard Ottoline gasp. "Do you have a message for your mother, Hugo?" asked Mrs. Reed.

The message was simple, really: Hugo was at peace *on the other side*; he felt no pain and sent his mother his love and blessing. Ottoline held my hand tightly as she asked Mrs. Reed, "Is Billy with him?"

Mrs. Reed repeated the question: "Is Billy with you, Hugo?" Then she lowered and slowly nodded her head as she listened to a voice we could not hear. Eventually, she said, "Yes, Billy is with his elder brother. He is surrounded by light, and wishes his mother to know that he is safe and at peace. He feels no pain, only love."

Ottoline whimpered.

(Mrs. Reed later told Ottoline that, though she had heard Billy's voice, it had been very weak and faint, but that this was normal. Billy hadn't yet fully transcended; his voice would become stronger in time.)

After this, letters of the alphabet were thrown about at random. And there was a K, but I didn't say anything. If it was Kitty—and I very much doubted it—I didn't want her spilling out anything to those present, or chastising me on any illicit love affair. When Mrs. Reed said, "P . . . Paul, Peter?" Mrs. Lister almost rose to her feet: "Yes, that's mine! That's my Peter."

Needless to say, Peter Lister, too, was at peace and happy on the other side. He told his mother he missed her roast beef and Yorkshire puddings. Ottoline gasped once more; Mrs. Lister began to cry. They both seemed to have forgotten Ottoline's earlier introduction: "And this is Mrs. Lister—our cook here at Birling."

We were amateurs, I thought, and Mrs. Reed a charlatan, preying on the emotions of recently grieved, desperate parents.

Then she said, "The K is still with us . . . and quite determined. A female presence, I think . . . yes, a woman. And passed over some time ago."

Ottoline turned to me. She said, "Your aunt? Her name was Kitty."

"It is *she*," said Mrs. Reed. Then, after a moment, "Your aunt wishes you to know that she is very proud of you." I smiled, albeit a little reluctantly. Mrs. Reed breathed in deeply once more. "But there is another," she said, rolling her head and now gasping. She spoke of water, a drowning, someone who had taken *her* own life and wished for forgiveness. I said nothing and joined with the others as we all shook our heads.

"There's to be a meeting . . . a meeting with the man who is in some way linked to this . . . this sad ending. He is related to one here," Mrs. Reed went on insistently.

A shiver went down my spine. But my mother's suicide was at that moment—and every moment that had come before—too shaming for me to own up to. From that point on, things unraveled, and little else came that made any sense: a woman, possibly in Ireland—sitting sidesaddle upon a gray mare; a man in a flying uniform; and another—a girl—who had once worked at the house. And we all shook our heads again.

Later, as flurries of hail tapped at the windows, Mrs. Reed asked for candles to be lit and prayers said. For there were many, she claimed, lost in a limbo between this world and the next, unable to see the light and move on. Then she had a cup of tea and a cigarette and talked about a new hairdresser, the one who had done her hair. When the taxicab arrived to take her home, I saw Ottoline hand over ten shillings.

After that and all through the winter, Mrs. Reed came once a week, usually on a Wednesday at eight o'clock. And though I never attended another of these meetings, the others did—and brought along more: Mrs. Lister's two widowed sisters; a few friends of Ottoline's who had also lost sons; and our kitchen maid Sissy's mother. Invariably, the Other World broke through. Invariably, Ottoline was connected to her lost boys. On almost each occasion, the Campbell boys brought Mrs. Lister's two sons with them. The departed, it seemed, came together for ten shillings.

It was in the early spring and after one such meeting—one that had lasted longer than usual, and after I had waited up for her in her bedroom, and then, perhaps foolishly, alluded to Mrs. Reed's thriving business, that Ottoline turned on me.

"And what would *you* know about loss?" she asked, smiling queerly and staring back at me in her mirror. "You've not lost anyone—apart from an elderly aunt. And though that was sad for you—and I understand that—it's quite different. And you have a daughter, a beautiful daughter sleeping soundly in this house. You've not lost sons—or any husband as far as I'm aware, or have you?"

"No, my lady, I have not."

"Exactly. So please do not speak to me about Mrs. Reed's credentials. And please do not speak to me about loss or grief." She paused for a moment. "You need to remember your station, Pearl. You're my maid . . . and many would have thrown you out."

I said nothing. I continued brushing my lady's hair. As I did so, I once again contemplated Mrs. Reed's unearthly connections—which granted her such earthly power and price. And I think I knew then that I was at the beginning of another end and that Ottoline would forevermore choose the dead over the living. My mistake, misinterpreted perhaps, had been to cross over a line and question the validity of Mrs. Reed's power. In doing so, I had—certainly as far as Ottoline was concerned—not only questioned Mrs. Reed's credentials, but Ottoline's love for her sons, and even the validity of their existence.

Minutes later, when Ottoline rose up from the dressing table, she said, "Oh, by the way, *my cousin's wife* is arriving tomorrow."

"Cousin?" I repeated.

"Her name is Marie Therese. She isn't bringing a maid, so I'm afraid you will have to look after her."

"Yes, my lady."

I can't be sure, but I think I bowed my head before leaving the room.

Chapter Eighteen

Blood is thicker than water, to some. Loyalty fluctuates, ebbs and flows, and all passion gets spent, eventually. This is what I was thinking as I waited for the train carrying my lover's wife.

Marie Therese Stedman would be staying at Birling for a week, Ottoline had told me that morning. Her manner had been different to the previous evening. She was softer, conciliatory, more like her old self. She told me that she had had no choice in the matter; the woman had come to England to escape her own war-ravaged country and was *floating about the way foreigners do*.

Only one person stepped down from the train. Tall, dark haired, dressed in what I assumed to be late French fashions, she saw me immediately. There was no one else.

"Moor-ton?"

I nodded.

She handed me her bag. "Such a long journey," she said. "And ze train—not so nice."

We walked to the car. I put her bag in the boot. We drove out of the station. She said, "Iz strange, no? Lady drivers. But in Paris ze same. Yes. All over. All ze same. Women must do ze men's work. All ze same."

I looked back at her—briefly—in the mirror, smiled and nodded. And as we came onto the long road that led up to the driveway of the house, she sighed loudly and said, "So long, so long since my husband and I came here."

Luckily, Rodney was hovering about in the hallway, and he took over—and took her bag. But as I walked away, Madame Stedman called after me: "Moor-ton!"

I turned. She beckoned. I went back. Into my hand she slipped a few coins (*centimes*, Rodney later said, peering at them through the magnifying glass).

I waited a while before I went upstairs to the appointed guest room to unpack and hang away Marie Therese Stedman's clothes. The silver-framed photograph was at the very bottom of the bag, wrapped in a long white nightgown. My hands shook when I saw him, as I held the photograph, as I took it over to the window to look at it more closely in the light. They stood outside a church, she smiling, Ralph with his head tilted to one side and staring at the camera with questioning eyes. I placed the photograph on the bedside table next to her Bible, and then stepped back from it, my heart aching. Was he still alive? I'd be able to find out, I thought. Sometime during the course of that week, I'd find out.

But that evening, when I knocked on the door and offered to attend to her before dinner, Marie Therese Stedman informed me she did not need my help. She had not had a maid, she said, since before the war, and was long used to dressing herself and doing her own hair. And the following morning when I took in her tea, she once again told me she would not be requiring my help. Then she smiled as she said, "I am not a baby, and I understand you have one already to look after . . ."

"Yes, I do."

"Well then, spend time with ze baby . . . I can look after myself."

For a number of days I saw very little of Marie Therese, or indeed of Ottoline. The two women went out in the motorcar—sightseeing, visiting nearby castles, villages and towns, leaving in the morning and not arriving back until late afternoon or early evening. Then, one afternoon as I played on the lawn with Lila, I heard the distant but unmistakable sound of Ottoline's driving—the acceleration, honking horn and crunch of wheels on gravel. Minutes later, Marie Therese appeared by my side.

I flinched as she reached down and stroked Lila's cheek. She spoke some words to her in French and then told me how very pretty my daughter was. "Gold, her hair is gold," she said. "Not like yours . . . She is like her father, no?"

She was. Just like her father.

She said, "Your husband—he is in France?"

I nodded. Amidst so many real deaths, the fictitious one Ottoline and I had planned for Stanley—making me a widow—had been forgotten.

"Ah, so difficult for you with ze baby . . . And my husband also. Away. Fighting." We walked on, side by side. She said, "But I am hoping I will see him soon—in London."

I stopped, turned to her. "He is alive?"

"Yes, alive and well, thank God. Oh but please . . ." She placed her hand on my arm: "You must forgive me for my . . . how do you say, thoughtlessness? Ottoline, she tells me you have not heard any-thing from Monsieur Moor-ton in a very long time."

"No, not in a long time."

She shook her head. "Is so bad, ze not knowing . . . Which regiment is Monsieur Moor-ton?"

I turned away from her. "I'm not sure . . . I can't quite remem-ber now."

"No matter. I will ask my husband. I will ask him if he has heard anything of Monsieur Moor-ton and I will tell him about ze baby." She bent down, stroked Lila's cheek once again and spoke more words in French to her. Lila held out her hand and offered the woman a crumpled daisy.

"For me?" said Marie Therese, clutching a hand to her breast and feigning amazement.

Lila chuckled and staggered off.

"You have a beautiful little girl, Madame Moor-ton. Her father will be very proud—I am sure of that."

"Yes, I'm sure," I said, watching my daughter, her husband's child.

Days later, I drove Marie Therese back to the station. And as we waited on the platform, she said, "I will not forget, Madame Moor-ton. No, I will not forget. I will ask my husband about your own." She opened her purse, took out a crown and pushed it into my hand. "For ze baby," she said. "For little Lila."

The train rattled in. I handed Marie Therese her bag.

"Good-bye, Madame Moor-ton."

I watched it trundle off, heading south. She would see him; I would not. I had been the mistress and she would always be the wife. And yet, and in spite of my shame, I was grateful. For I had a part of Ralph his wife would never have.

Autumn crept in early, scattering the shriveled remnants of another summer and tossing leaves through the smoke-filled air. October blew wet into November, turning the lanes to brown, pebble-strewn rivers. And as redwings edged and battled against the squall, the weather vane spun round and round. Then came stillness. The sky lowered itself further and daylight dwindled, until dusk came at three and winter descended, tapping at pipes and whistling its cold tune beneath doors. Trees stood out stark against the low sky, and as squirrels danced on their naked limbs, birds froze in the snow. Only the robin's red breast was visible, bobbing about in the flattened alabaster borders.

Each night, I lay in my bed listening to the distant roar of the sea, throwing itself upon rocks and sand, upon anything. Desperate. Crashing. Crushing. And just like the sea, the war went on, a relentless background noise we had become accustomed to. And though we continued to pray, we no longer said *special* prayers; and though the newspapers continued to arrive, no one raced to read them. Disenchanted with *King and Country*, disillusioned with God, we had grown accustomed to long numbers, missing faces and bad news; accustomed to deprivation, food shortages and rationing. Our time was wartime. And though I sometimes felt guilty about my coldness and detachment, it was the only way.

And yet, I knew—we all knew, had to believe—that *it* would end one day and that some sort of vaguely remembered normality would be restored. But it could never be the same. For it was not only Kitty's world that had been swept away, but some of mine, too. Being in service, it seemed, was no longer something to be proud of, and the whirligig of our ever-changing maids, young women determined *not* to have a life in service, proved this. Their ambitions echoed a few of the ladies' magazines, newly defiant and pugnacious with words about feminism, equality and independence. A modern world was dawning, I read, and in it, women would have the same rights as men; be entitled to the same jobs and earn the same money; they would have a voice, and a vote.

Ottoline was right: *Our day* was coming.

And what of her, of Ottoline? She had delivered my daughter into this world, been inordinately kind to me, and—certainly, after Hugo's death—she had been dignified and stoical, had talked of honor and sacrifice, of duty and service. But after the loss of Billy, that changed. For a while her world shriveled into a dark hole and she was cemented in her grief, and cemented in that place with Lord Hector. But later, after she reemerged and began to pick at the pieces of her life, she was not the same Ottoline.

The things that had counted to her had gone, and the great sorrow that had claimed her heart remained there, heavy as a stone, and sometimes sending tears dripping down her cheeks as she stared ahead in wordless fury. Often, the only one able to assuage her grief was Lila, now a little person and able to speak.

The doctor had prescribed pills, a tranquilizer of some sort, but she took others, too, not prescribed: pills to help her sleep, pills to help her wake up, pills to ease her many—and imaginary, I sometimes thought—headaches. And she drank more than ever. A small sherry, often before luncheon, a glass of wine with luncheon, and then later in the day, her favorite malt whisky. Everyone knew, but no one said anything. Ottoline's drinking was the elephant in any room.

Physically, Ottoline was not unrecognizable from the woman she had been. She had simply aged. Grief had turned her hair gray, her eyes dull, and though she had, eventually, a year after Billy's death, stopped wearing black, her preference for somber colors made her once youthful complexion more sallow. She had no interest in fashion, and I wondered if the bright, colorful gowns in her closets would ever again be worn. Would Felix Cowper still recognize her? I wasn't sure. She never mentioned his name. And when her beloved dog, Lolly, finally passed away—ancient, deaf and blind, but for so long cherished—Ottoline barely noticed. It was as though she had slipped beneath the surface of life to a place where nothing could reach her.

The shift for me—the final shift, if you like—came in October 1918.

I had been to Newcastle, shopping at Fenwick department store for fabric with which to make arm covers for some of the worn-out chairs in Ottoline's sitting room. There, I had taken tea among impatient mothers and their patient offspring, watching innocent eyes follow waitresses carrying trays with tall glasses and long spoons, pastel ices flowing in cochineal syrup. Afterward, I'd walked down Northumberland Street staring into shopwindows at shiny new gramophones and gadgets for the home. Things I could never afford, for a home I would never have. And yet, despite the depravations of wartime, the city's streets seemed to contain a collective optimism and a contagious ebullient energy, an energy completely lacking at Birling. And later, as I was motoring northward on the Great North Road, it came to me with sudden clarity how isolated I was and had been, and how much I needed to get myself and Lila away from that place—so drenched in grief.

But as soon as I saw Rodney emerge from the house, eager to greet me, I had second thoughts. For this place was my home, *our* home—and those within its walls the only family we had. How could we leave them?

"Successful trip?"

"Yes, and most enjoyable."

"I'm afraid we're all caught up in a rather queer occurrence," said Rodney, sounding unusually awkward.

"Oh yes, and what's that?" I asked, lifting the packages from the back of the motorcar and handing them to him.

"Well, it seems Her Ladyship has taken Lila on a little excursion . . ."

I turned to him. "What do you mean, *a little excursion?*"

"A day out."

"Was Ottoline driving?"

"I believe so. They left not long after—"

"But Ottoline's not well enough, Rodney—and her driving is quite appalling at the best of times."

"I don't imagine they'll be too much longer. In fact, when I heard the motor, I thought they were—"

I didn't wait for any more. I ran to the house and marched into

Hector Campbell's study, and not like any lady's maid—and certainly not like the young woman who had appeared in that same room with blisters so many years before—but like a mother whose daughter had been abducted, kidnapped.

I said, "Your wife has taken my daughter. She has taken her out in the car."

He placed his head in his hands. "Yes, I know."

"What are you going to do about it? Because I want her back . . . I want my daughter back now."

He raised his eyes to me. "Look here, you and I both know that Lila's quite safe. You and I both know how much Ottoline adores her."

"No. It's not right. *I* am her mother. And Ottoline took her without my permission. I don't want to have to call the police."

He sighed, removed his spectacles and looked down at them. He said, "Pearl . . . Pearl . . . You, more than anyone, perhaps even more than me, know Ottoline. She wouldn't hurt a fly. Couldn't. And yes, fragile she may be, but she is *not* irresponsible." He looked up at me. "Those she loves, she holds dear, keeps safe. Would defend with her life. It's her nature. You know that. Love is all that matters to her."

"And isn't it a shame that you didn't realize this years ago?"

His eyes widened.

"She's not well enough to be driving herself, let alone a child—*my* child."

"I'm quite sure," he began again, his voice like a doctor's, perfectly pitched, perfectly measured.

"Do you have any idea what is happening in this house? Do you not see? Ottoline is slowly killing herself . . . drinking herself to death, popping pills to make her forget, to make her sleep, to take away her pain."

He closed his eyes. "I really do think you're overreacting, my dear."

That *my dear* triggered something. Something I had pushed down and gulped back for years, and now it rose up—and rose up in a great torrent.

"Men like you, Lord Hector, are everything that's wrong with this world. You spend your life pretending—pretending everything is fine in order not to have to deal with the truth. You turn your wives into jewelry-clad imbeciles and keep your mistresses in the shadows. Then, one day, one of those women you've . . . you've bedded has a child—*your* child. And without any hope of a life, without any financial support or status, they unravel, and walk into a river. That's what your sort do to women."

"I think you've said enough."

But I hadn't; there was more.

"You abandoned your wife—and no doubt countless others—but what you need to realize is that you also let down your sons. What sort of example were *you* to Billy, to Hugo? How does it feel to have sent your boys off to their deaths and still be here, sitting in the comfort of your study, smoking cigars, shuffling papers—and telling me about *love*?"

He stared at me. "How dare you?"

I was spent. My heart slowed, the room took shape once more and the man in front of me changed from every villain in every nightmare to something else, something pathetic: a relic, a throwback; another old man with a stiff collar and a sad past. And then, with regret too ancient for this lifetime etched in his features, he whispered, "I loved my sons . . . I love my wife." And I turned and walked out.

Even now, I'm shocked by how I spoke to Lord Hector that day. I had never in my life spoken to anyone like that. And though I was vaguely aware that the hypocrisy belonged to us all, that I, too, was culpable in the great deceit of love—for hadn't I knowingly slept with another woman's husband?—my fury that day was not just with Lord Hector, but with almost every man I had ever known—and one I had not: my absent father.

After I left His Lordship's study, I stood in the hallway, staring about and wondering what to do. Hector Campbell was as deluded as his wife, I reasoned. My words—no matter how impassioned—would mean little to him. After all, I was a woman *and* a servant. In the eyes of men like him, there could surely be no cheaper combination. For the next hour or so, I wandered about the garden, up and down the driveway—listening for the sound of a car as I attempted to repair my relationship with God, promising him everything if he kept my daughter safe and brought her back to me. Then I went to the kitchen where a contrite Mrs. Lister told me she had had no idea that Her Ladyship was taking Lila out in the motorcar; she had thought they were going for a little walk. That was all.

She said, "Now you sit down, and I'll make us a nice cup of tea."

"I don't want a cup of tea."

"I'm sure they'll be back soon . . . won't have gone far."

"They've been gone *all* day," I said, wringing my hands and walking in circles.

"Her Ladyship will—"

"Her Ladyship is not fit to be at the wheel—and you know that."

"Yes."

At that moment my ear pricked up at the distant honking of a horn, and I ran out of the kitchen and up the stairs, along the passageway toward the hallway, colliding with Rodney. "They're back," he said, breathless, all smiles.

As I walked into the marble hallway, Lila appeared. "Mama! Look! See what I have for you!"

My daughter handed me a package. I didn't look at it, nor did I wait for Ottoline to emerge through the doorway. Instead, gripping Lila's hand tightly and amidst much protesting and the onset of tears, I marched her away and up to our room. There, I closed the door, fell to my knees and held her. When I finally released my hold on her, she stared at me, her tearstained face set in a pronounced frown, her bottom lip stuck out in displeasure. Then, full of new sympathy: "Don't cry, Mama." She reached down, lifted the package from the floor. "Look, see what Auntie got you . . . Look, Mama." She took my hands, carefully placed the gift into them.

I said, "She is not your auntie, Lila."

"She is."

"She is *not.*"

"She *is!*"

Slowly, I unwrapped the package: a first edition of *Wuthering Heights.*

"It's a book, Mama."

I had a passionate impulse to pack our bags, to leave there and then and burn every one of my bridges. But then what? Heaven only knew, because I had nowhere to go.

Later, as I lay on the bed next to my daughter, stroking her precious golden curls, I heard all about her day out with *Auntie*: They had been to the beach, to see the sea, had lunch at someone's house (this, I later learned, was in fact a restaurant), and then gone shopping in the big town, where they had had ice cream.

Eventually I said, "I don't want you to go out in the motorcar again without me." And to the inevitable *why?* I replied, "Because I say so."

There was no explanation, no apology from Ottoline when I attended her later that same evening. She simply said, "We had the most wonderful time, you know," and then recounted some of their day in more intelligible terms than Lila's earlier account. "I do adore her," she said, smiling at herself in the mirror. "Little Lila . . . She's like one of my own. Yes, truly, just like one of my own." She laughed. "In fact, a number of people today thought that she was. Yes, they thought she was mine. They said, 'So like you . . . so like her mama.'"

My anger had subsided and I had my daughter back—she was safely upstairs, in our bed, asleep—and I had decided not to confront Ottoline on the matter, because there was little point, I thought. But I was newly unsettled by this. I said, "And did you tell them? Did you tell them that she is not yours?"

Ottoline thought for a moment, then shook her head. "No, I don't believe I did. Why would I?"

"Because it's the truth?" I suggested.

She swiveled round to face me. "But I thought she belonged to us both. I thought we agreed to that?"

"Well, I named her after you . . . and I made you her godmother—"

"No, no," Ottoline interrupted. "In Scotland, after she was born, we agreed—yes, we did, we agreed that she would be brought up here at Birling and that we would share her. You can't go back on that promise now, you know, just because it suits you. Jealousy is a very destructive emotion, Pearl. Very destructive." She snatched the hairbrush from my hand, turned back to the mirror and began brushing her hair. "You're jealous because Lila loves me. You're jealous because I gave her such a wonderful day out."

I didn't say anything. There was no point in fighting delusions. I turned back the bedcovers and bid her good night. Then I returned to my own room—weary, wrung out by the events of that day. I held on to Lila's small body as though it were the crown jewels and I were the guard. The *woo-woo* from owls beyond my window failed to soothe me, and the familiar rattling of corncrakes in the moonlit meadows sounded newly jarring. I fell into a fitful sleep, waking from nightmares and reaching for Lila, until at last another day dawned.

It wasn't yet nine, but I was as usual in the laundry when I heard the distinctive footsteps upon the long, stone-flagged passageway and some scurrying in the kitchen.

"I think we need to have a chat," said His Lordship, standing in the doorway.

I dried my hands. I knew what was coming, and I was ready for it, or so I thought. Thus, I followed him back along the passageway, up the stairs, across the marble hallway, down the corridor and into his study. He closed the door after me.

"Please, do take a seat," he said, gesturing to the chair in front of his desk.

I sat down. He sat down.

"I'm troubled, Pearl. We need to clear the air . . ."

He took off his spectacles, reached inside a drawer, pulled out a cloth and began polishing them. "It's not easy," he said. Then he put his spectacles back on, swiveled his chair and looked out of the window. And I waited. And I waited.

The shelves in his study were lined with leather-bound books— books I'd never once had the opportunity to survey or been invited to borrow. Amidst these were framed photographs of young men with differing hats and beards: some standing, some seated; dressed for cricket, rugby, rowing, hunting or shooting. On his desk, I saw a single photograph: Ottoline.

"I knew when I married her," he began eventually. "Her father was honest, perfectly honest. He told me, explained everything. She had her first breakdown at sixteen. Spent time in a nursing home." He paused here, and I saw him lower his head for a moment. "No, let's not pretend—they're called asylums. She had tried to kill herself. Can you imagine? At sixteen . . ."

I said nothing. I was forewarned, and *forewarned is forearmed*, and *a leopard does not change his spots*, I thought, falling back once again on Kitty's proverbs.

He went on. "But she was different, so different to other girls . . . unpredictable, a touch wild perhaps, but exciting all the same. And I fell in love with her. I adored her. I knew the moment we met that I wanted her to be mine—and not to own, but to love and make happy. That was all I wanted, you see, to make Ottoline happy. Her happiness and well-being meant more to me than anything. Still do." There was another pause; he lowered his head again. "The first affair came shortly after Hugo—a young army officer, and very handsome, as I recall. Of course it ended, the way these things inevitably do. She came back to me, as I'd hoped, and for a time we were happy. Then came Billy. It was not long after . . . I knew the chap, saw it unfolding, thought I had no choice but to let it run its course. But this time it was different; there was a child. A girl."

He turned to me, removed his spectacles. "Has she ever told you?"

I nodded. "Yes, sort of."

He stared down at the papers on his desk. "It was a difficult time for her. She'd always longed for a daughter . . . and afterward, well, she was told there could be no more babies. The affair had ended—oh, long before the baby—and she sort of . . . sort of unraveled and fell apart. I took her away, to Switzerland. On our return, she told me that she hated me, hated me for marrying her. Said she had never loved me, never could or would." He glanced up at me. "But time passes; we move on. I still love her, and I have to believe she loves me. Otherwise, my life has been meaningless."

"She told me it was you. She told me you'd had affairs from the start."

He closed his eyes.

"What about Mrs. Parker?" I asked.

"The Parkers have been devoted friends to us *both* . . . In fact, it was Virginia Parker who cared for Ottoline after she lost her daughter, who came to stay here and nursed her. Throughout all of it, Virginia was stalwart in her support—indeed, in her defense of Ottoline." He raised his eyes to me. "I'm not sure why she turned on Virginia. But Ottoline does that—with people, places, causes. She falls in love very quickly, and falls out of love just as fast."

That strange word-filled, sun-filled morning helped me at last begin to understand Ottoline, her nature and the nature of her marriage. But it was too late. Something inside me had snapped and was broken. Lord Hector knew it and I knew it. We both knew my time was done. And yet, his humility, his honesty and, perhaps more than anything else, his undoubted love for Ottoline, touched me. And so when he rose to his feet, when he came toward me, his hand outstretched, I not only took hold of it—I took hold of him. He smelled of cedarwood cologne.

"Do I really seem like a Lothario to you?" he asked, stepping away and peering at me over his spectacles.

No. He didn't. And never had.

In the end, I left quietly, and not until the day after the armistice, which was in itself a queer day at Birling, because no one seemed to be aware of it, or to care. There was no celebration, no party. It was just another day, another day at the end of a very long four years. Lord Hector remained in his study; Ottoline pored over her scrapbooks; Mrs. Lister rolled out pastry and Rodney wound clocks. So it was, really, just another day in the great sweep of days that would see them all on and take them to an end.

It was not yet light when I picked up my pen. And it was hard to know what to say, where to begin, and I was pleased to have Lila there in the room to distract me from what I knew could so easily become a lengthy letter of love, and regret, and recrimination. Thus, fast, and without too much thought, I wrote:

My Lady, Ottoline,

I hope you can find it in your heart to forgive me for what will seem to you a hasty departure. But I have given much thought to this and over a long period of time. I hope you will be able to understand my need to establish a life for Lila and myself, away from Birling, and understand that Lila needs more than you & me, and Mrs. Lister & Mr. Watts as playmates. In the not-too-distant future she will be starting school, and it is important to me that she have friends & learn about life, real life.

There is so much I wish to say and tell you, and it is my dearest wish that we will one day be able to meet and speak as friends. In the meantime, I am grateful for everything you have done for us, and I remain—

Yours,
Pearl

I folded the sheet of paper and put it inside the envelope along with the ring—the ruby and diamond ring she had given me, loaned me. I took a last look around my room, my yellow room, picked up my suitcase—empty of novels, Bible and encyclopedia—and glanced over at the bookcase where a dog-eared pamphlet titled *The Private Shadow* remained. And then I followed Lila along the darkened corridor and down the staircase.

"Wait here," I said as I put down the suitcase.

I pushed the envelope beneath Ottoline's door, and then I stood for a moment with my forehead rested on it. I felt like a mother abandoning a child—abandoning a helpless child without a good-bye. And for a moment I vacillated: *What will she do? Who will look after her? How will she cope?* Then I heard Lila, my own child, the real child, and I turned and walked back to her.

The house was quiet, but a few lamps were already lit downstairs. Rodney and Mrs. Lister were up and about. In the kitchen, Mrs. Lister cried, said she'd had no idea and that it was all such a shock, and what about Lila? And what about Her Ladyship—did she know? And where was I to go? On and on it went, as I knew it would. Then she mentioned Stanley, saying she could sort of understand it, imagine that I'd wish to be reunited with him now that the war was over.

I said, "Unfortunately, that can't happen. He died."

She looked horrified. "But when?"

"Oh, a while ago now . . . I didn't say anything because of . . . Billy and Hugo, and your boys."

She flung her arms around me and began to cry again. And yes, I felt guilty, but I couldn't pretend about him anymore. And as I held her, as Rodney smiled at me, I knew he knew.

Eventually I stepped away, out of the kitchen, and called down the passageway for Lila.

Rodney accompanied us outside, where the taxicab sat waiting with its headlights shining into the rain and mist and falling leaves. He placed my suitcase in the boot, gripped me by the shoulders and said, "Are you sure? Are you quite certain?"

I nodded.

"You don't want to wait a little longer—see them and say good-bye?"

"No, it's better like this. His Lordship won't be surprised. And I've left my lady a note . . . As I told you, I decided a while ago that

I'd leave when the war ended—and now it has ended. And I don't wish to spend another winter in the country. In fact, I don't want to stay another week."

"Are we really that bad?"

"You know what I mean. It's time for me to move on."

"Look, this may seem a little impudent, but—" Rodney reached into the inside pocket of his jacket and pulled out his wallet.

"No, I don't need any money, Rodney," I said, and I pushed away his hand. "I've managed to save up quite a bit over the last four years. But thank you anyway. It's very kind of you . . ."

"What will you do? For work, I mean. Your savings won't last forever, you know. It's prudent to keep something set aside."

"I'm not sure. Shop work, perhaps. I've seen advertisements, and it seems to pay quite well."

"You will let me know if you need anything—any help?"

"Yes, I will."

"I'll miss you—and her," he added, nodding at Lila, already sitting in the back of the taxi and singing happily to her doll.

I tried to smile. "We must keep in touch, you and I."

He lowered his hands, stared down at his shoes. "Yes, indeed."

And then, because I knew so much and felt for him—and because a million moments had passed since he had first opened that door to me—I flung my arms around him and held on to him for longer than was usual.

"A little irregular, Mr. Watts," I said, stepping back, wiping away tears.

"A little irregular, Pearl . . . But isn't today, here and now and everything? And won't it always be so?"

"Take care of yourself."

"And you. Write to me. Let me know . . . Let me know how you're both getting on and all that."

"I will, I promise. And I'll keep my fingers crossed about Derek, but I'm sure you'll hear something soon. They'll be releasing prisoners of war. He'll turn up."

"Oh yes," he said, ever brave and standing taller.

I climbed into the waiting motorcar, and as I held on to my daughter, as our taxicab swept down the treelined driveway, I turned and looked back at Rodney Watts—singular, unchanged, standing on the driveway in his tailcoat and striped trousers—and beyond him, the house: a house I had arrived at as a silly girl with blistered feet, a case of books and head filled with romantic notions. A place I had arrived at with swollen ideals and inflated ambition, and was now, four years later, leaving as a mother, a woman of limited means and meager expectations, but a woman who had known love.

I watched Rodney raise his hand, watched him disappear behind the rhododendrons. Then I turned, fixed my eyes ahead and pulled my daughter's small body closer. And for a moment I could see it all: the sky, the hills, those high-up purples and blues, that dark bird's wing, those feathery clouds and *him*, sitting under the apricot light of another country and time.

PART THREE

Chapter Nineteen

Yes, Memory is a cruel thing. For it knows our struggle to remember, and to forget, and it ignores Time. It whispers or withholds, suggesting more, or less, secure in the knowledge that it will have the final say. Secure in the knowledge that it can—at any time it so wishes—erase, adapt or rewrite our story. Redeeming, damning, it thrusts upon us, altering statements to questions and shrinking our vistas.

And so we cling onto the slow days of our youth, rich and golden and soft beneath our feet, heavy with promise and the blue skies of an eternal summer. Then we remember our autumn, when the skies lowered and the song stopped and dusk began to fall. And we knew that summer had an end, and that we would, also.

My life had not turned out as I'd once imagined, but I could have no regrets; I had Lila. And I took strength and comfort from her—her smile, her touch, and each time she wrapped her arms around my waist and told me she loved me. Each time she lifted my hands and pressed her mouth to my palms, each time I lowered my face to her hair, her sweet-smelling golden hair, I was grateful. And when she was good, I'd say, "Your father would be very proud of you, Lila." And when she was naughty, I'd say, "Your father would be *so* disappointed."

But there was no father. I had no husband—dead or alive—and no war widow's pension. Lila and I belonged nowhere and to no one. And I still yearned for that, to belong, for us both to belong. I wanted to believe that my life—begun the day my mother chose to abandon me on a dirty workshop floor, the day she decided to walk into the Thames—would amount to something more than this today, tomorrow and the day after. With all my heart I wanted to believe that I was *not* the continuum of my mother's end, and that the future would prove it; that there would be an alteration, a change in the circumstances of my life.

On our arrival in London, I reverted to my own name, or rather, my maternal grandfather's name. I had never wanted the name Morton and could not allow my daughter to grow up with it. Thus I became *Mrs.* Gibson, another war widow. The city was full of them, and I was just another, I thought.

Lila and I spent one night at our first boarding house. It was the only place I could find advertising vacancies. And it was cheap and close to the station. But I should have known. I should have known by the sign offering rooms by the hour and by the seedy characters hanging about the lobby. And I should have known by the London-bound revelers singing on board the train and those dancing—

drunkenly, wearily and still draped in flags—about the station concourse that there was a party going on in London: a victory party.

The walls of our room were paper thin and amidst the alcohol-infused revelry and arguments, amidst clanking beds and constant thunder on the staircase, I didn't get any sleep. None at all. Traffic flowed past all night, rattling windows as horns honked and bells rang out and lights flashed across the torn wallpaper. The sudden and deafening clatter of life: so different to Northumberland.

The following day I secured lodgings in Bayswater, led by another sign in another window: NO GENTLEMEN, WOMEN ONLY—WIDOWS WELCOME. However, I learned very quickly that a woman on her own with a child was something to be viewed with suspicion—particularly by those inherently suspicious, even in the aftermath of war. We had been there for less than a week when I was asked to leave because another widow had told the landlady she suspected that I was not a widow at all, that I was an unmarried mother. I had been caught out on technicalities, the details of my husband's regiment and my war widow's pension. My landlady said she had no choice; she *had* to take such complaints seriously—otherwise what would people say? They would say she was lowering the tone of the neighborhood, and then what?

So Lila and I moved on again—to another room in Bayswater, with meals, a shared bathroom and, crucially, a sympathetic landlady. It was a clean, quiet and calm household, but beyond it, the city remained engulfed in a hysterical atmosphere of patriotic fervor. There were demands for vengeance against Germany, demands to *Hang the Kaiser*. And there was about to be a general election,

in which recent legislation decreed women over the age of thirty
be allowed the right to vote.

I was twenty-eight.

A few days after the election, I secured a part-time job a short
bus ride away at Selfridges department store, where I spent three
days a week spraying scent on diamond-clad wrists. My landlady's
daughter, Myrtle, looked after Lila while I worked, and we spent
our Christmas there, with Mrs. Dalby and Myrtle, in the gaslit
front parlor decorated with paper chains made from old newspapers. I received a card from Rodney and one from Mrs. Lister, but
I heard nothing from Ottoline.

The year 1919: It sounded bizarrely futuristic. But I'd heard
people say that there was good luck to be had in that double number. And there was.

Early that year, I was offered full-time work at the store, and
moved upstairs—to lingerie. Trying to sell corsets and brassieres to
women with bound chests made no sense, but by then little made
sense anyway. I spent my days staring at painted smiles and expensive faces, watching women clutching onto the arms of men with
glass eyes and stiff legs, and surveying French lace and frills as
though such things mattered. However, working full-time brought
in a little more money, and a few months later, in the summer, Lila
and I moved out of our lodgings and into a two-bedroom flat in
Fulham. It was sparsely furnished, and without a bathroom—just
the usual shared lavatory outside, and a tin bath in the kitchen—
but it offered us privacy and more space.

Myrtle continued to look after my daughter, and each evening
after she left, after I'd put Lila to bed, I'd do my chores and then sit

beneath the gaslight, sewing—patching, mending and adapting Lila's clothes. She was growing quickly, and though I didn't have the money to buy new clothes for her—or for myself—I did have an eagle eye at jumble sales. Lila always looked smart; everyone said so . . . *Smart as a carrot.*

I didn't need luxuries because I had my memories of Ralph, and they were enough, I thought. Night after night, I closed my eyes to that dim, colorless room and returned to the hills—still purple and blue—and to him: long sandy lashes and sunburned cheeks, fingers smeared with paint. But I could no longer see the color of his eyes. Like my romantic heart, my memories had shriveled.

I no longer prayed and had stopped going to church. Toward the end of the war, I had struggled with my faith, and then, after the Spanish flu epidemic took hold, I knew I couldn't subscribe to a god capable of inflicting more suffering. I wasn't the only one to give up on him. Most of the people I worked with thought the same: *What good had all those prayers done?* The god Kitty had taught me to believe in, that magnanimous deity who absolved and forgave, granted miracles and made the world better, had gone, presupposing he had ever been there.

Though the war officially ended that summer, with the signing of the Treaty of Versailles, reminders of it were everywhere. *Heroes,* the newspapers called them: HEROES, EACH AND EVERY ONE. More than three and a half million men had been demobilized. War torn, twitchy, hungry and filthy, our heroes flooded the capital, lingering outside Tube stations, in squares and on street corners, dazed by normality, and in the absence of orders, unsure what to do or where to go next. They stood in line not for a medal, but a cup of tea or lump of stale bread; they slept on park benches, on flagstones and in gutters. Some wore tin masks lest their missing mouths and noses offend our sensibilities, while others, those without limbs, sat about in wheelchairs, waiting for a penny to be dropped into a hat. As those they had fought for wrinkled their own perfect noses and murmured, *Something really ought to be done.*

I was on my midmorning break, hurrying back from the bank, when I heard the first stroke of eleven and everything stopped—as if by magic. Horse-drawn delivery wagons, tramcars, taxicabs, motors and cyclists all came to a halt. Delivery boys skidded to a standstill, road sweepers paused in their work, men removed hats and stared downward, and veterans saluted. Like an eerie photograph, Oxford Street froze into the November mist and within the silence, which second by second deepened and spread out over the city, was a deafening agony. But for two minutes the universe stopped as we paused and remembered. For two minutes we dreamed of another time.

How could we forget?

But by then, even by then, I struggled to remember Ralph's voice. Only very occasionally and in silence would it come to me, like a scrap of music played in the distance and always too far away to hear properly. All of him belonged to another time, and London was noisy, too noisy to hear a single voice from years before. For the most part, I was content to be amidst that cacophony, content for ringing bells and honking horns to silence my ghosts. But at the end of each day, as I weaved my way home, past couples linking arms and heading to bright lights and warm fires, I dreaded the oncoming quietude, those lonely hours after Lila had gone to bed.

The act of living had become a great effort, and I wondered if there was something wrong with me physically. I had reached the end of my spiritual resources, the end of my pathetic optimism, and I had held my breath for so long that emotionally I had ceased to exist. The notion of the future—once bright and exciting, and filled with possibility—caused only anxiety, and that sense of separateness I had always known had become amplified.

Reflecting on my life, I realized I was a failure. There was nothing special or superior about me; nor would there ever be. Self-pity tapped late at night, brought on, I suppose, by nothing more than loneliness. Then, afterward, I would fall into self-loathing: *I am a selfish, self-centered creature*, I'd think. After all, I had Lila, and I was alive.

It was sometime after that two-minute silence, perhaps a few days or a week, that I decided I needed to break out of my malaise— my grief that wasn't actually grief. My life, but for a few all-too-short months, had been a long, monotonous routine and—outwardly, at least—it had taken its toll. I was the reflection of disappointment and thwarted hopes, the unextraordinary result of extraordinary circumstances. Shackled by shame and burdened with what Kitty had once called a brave heart.

I considered my assets: I was still attractive—pretty by most standards, and I had that quality often remarked on called poise— and I wasn't stupid. I had a reasonable general knowledge, could talk about a variety of subjects including literature, people and places. I reviewed my weaknesses: an untrusting nature, perhaps; a predisposition toward loneliness; an inherent romanticism . . . an agonizing, lifelong feeling of unworthiness; a lack of worldliness; a confused understanding of who I was, and where I fitted in; a tendency to bolt and run from difficult situations . . .

At the end of my brief, amateur self-analysis, I knew it was time to adopt a different demeanor, a more positive approach. It would start externally, with a new look, I decided, knowing that would be the easy part. Two days later, I had my hair cut. Almost twelve inches fell to the floor of the salon. That same evening, after Lila had stopped squealing and running her hands over my shorn hair—*Can I just touch it again, Mummy?*—after I'd finally got her to bed, I applied my new makeup. I practiced in front of the mirror . . . starting with a smile and leading on through unmistakable shades of gayness to silent laughter. I could be happy. I would be happy. I would take myself out into the battlefield of life and fight for my share—no matter how small. I would not sink without a fight; I would not be like my mother, or like Ottoline.

I'm not sure if it was my hair or my lipstick, but the new me certainly evoked more attention than the old me, and not just from the road sweepers and workmen—so fond of a wolf whistle and tawdry one-liners—but from men on the sixth floor, including one called Leo Holland.

Leo, or Mr. Holland as he was to me then, had recently arrived from Manchester to take up a managerial position in the accounts department at the store. He was a few years older than I was, a bachelor. My colleague, Mary—also from the North—introduced us, telling him that I, too, had spent time "up there." He asked me where, exactly. And so I told him, and he knew that part of Northumberland. It was where his grandmother had been born. And thus my friendship with him began.

And at first, it was just that, a friendship—and very much a work friendship, involving nothing more than the occasional lunch together in the staff dining room. But then it moved on and away from the confines of the store. He asked me out to the pictures, and I went. Then he asked me again, and I went again. And at the end of that second time, as he waited with me at the bus stop, he said, "What are you doing on Sunday?"

"Nothing much," I said, truthfully. Because Sundays were always quiet days—depressing and indeterminably long.

"I wondered if you and your daughter might like to come to the Natural History Museum . . . It's a great place for children."

By that time, I had answered his questions, told him of my late husband, Henry, fallen at Gallipoli, and of my daughter, who had never known her father. My lies were to me necessary and consistent with what I had told others. We agreed early on not to talk about the war; agreed it was important to look forward, not back. Leo had been in an administrative position in the army and had not seen any active service, and I knew, could tell, that he was perhaps a little bitter about this. As for marriage, he'd simply never met *the right girl*, he said.

After our visit to the Natural History Museum, we went to Gunter's for tea. The afternoon was a success. Lila liked Leo, and so did I. Our Sunday afternoon outing—a trip to a museum or gallery followed by tea—became an almost regular thing, and would no doubt have been more regular but for his elderly and frail mother, to whom he returned to Manchester to visit every other weekend.

Eventually, after one of our Sunday outings, I invited Leo back to the flat, which was strange—as I'd never had anyone back there before. The space, up until then uniquely feminine, seemed not only to shrink with a male presence but to appear browner and gloomier than ever. I saw it all through his eyes: the small sitting room with its gaslight hanging from the grimy ceiling, the tatty furnishings, impoverished curtains, and worn-out-linoleum-covered steps leading down to the windowless kitchen. All of it was drab, and though none of it was *me*, it was my life.

Leo was, I suppose, quite old-fashioned in his attitude toward our courtship, perhaps because there was the extra complication of a child, or because he simply wasn't sure. Either way, it took some time for him to make the first move—which was in itself an old-fashioned gesture: to take my hand and kiss it. And yet I appreciated his genteel manner and slow pace, his consideration and the fact that, even after he had seen inside my colorless life, he still wished to kiss my hand. He was a gentleman, and he dressed like one, too: always immaculate in his suit, starched white collar and silk tie, homburg hat and camel hair overcoat. A dandy, the girls at work said, a regular dandy.

Of course he wasn't like Ralph, not in any way at all. But I did not need or want a penniless bohemian, or another married man. If I was going to have someone in my life—potentially, a father for Lila—I wanted someone like Leo Holland: respectable, hardworking and yes, conventional. That he was older, middle-aged, did not bother me in the least. In fact, I thought his silvering hair and mustache very distinguished-looking, and after all, I was quite middle-aged myself. Yes, I was proud to walk out with him.

One Sunday, when he stayed later than usual, and after I'd put Lila to bed, he said, "One of the things I most admire about you, Pearl, is your dignity."

I smiled. "That makes me sound old—and very unfashionable." Because it sometimes seemed to me as though dignity went out with the war, as dated and revealing as a garment from another era. And yet I also knew—knew only too well—that it was a luxury to call anything old-fashioned.

"Not at all," said Leo. "You've coped with adversity, tragedy— and you continue to hold your head high."

"My late husband told me always to walk forward and walk tall," I said.

And then I wondered if Leo would still think me dignified if he knew the truth. That the only Henry Gibson I had ever known had died long before the war, that I had never had any husband and that my daughter—like me—was the result of an illicit affair. No, I wasn't dignified. Unlike my poor mother, I'd simply learned how to swim.

Initially, after I'd first left Birling, I had corresponded with Rodney Watts quite regularly. His son, Derek, was one of those *missing in action.* He'd never been found, but somehow—and for the life of me I don't know how—Rodney clung to the hope that his son would one day turn up. I learned from Rodney that Ottoline had taken on a new maid called April, that the house in London had been sold and that Lord Hector had retired. And while Mrs. Lister remained *in situ,* other maids came and went *like guests passing through the revolving door of a hotel.*

Then, and in the way these things inevitably do, our correspondence became less frequent. And perhaps I made it so. That link with Birling was also a link with the past, and with Ralph, and in order to move forward, I knew I had to sever what came before—no matter how painful. And so Birling, its inhabitants, ancient routines and quiet customs, were like a dream—and sometimes like a nightmare, too, because my war had been spent there, and I associated that place only with death and grief.

That Christmas, the second after the end of the war, I received another card from Rodney, along with a letter, in which he told me that many of the rooms at Birling had been shut up and staff numbers reduced further. Ottoline was once again *very fragile*, but she and His Lordship were going away to France in the New Year, to pay homage to their sons. A holiday on the Continent would do Her Ladyship *the power of good*, he said.

Chapter Twenty

It was a few months after Rodney's Christmas letter, and sometime in the early spring of 1920, when I saw her. She was sitting alone at a table in the staff dining room, her head bent over a magazine. At first I wasn't sure. Her hair—once mousy—was now champagne colored and cut short, like mine; her face fuller, puffier. Then I saw the amber cigarette holder, a length of ash threatening to fall onto her open magazine.

I had only ever known her as "Parker," but it wasn't enough. So I said, "Scotland . . . Delnasay? . . . Summer 'fourteen?"

"Oh my word . . . Ottoline Campbell's maid . . . You've changed a bit. It's Pearl, isn't it? Well I never. What on earth are you doing here?"

An inch of cigarette ash fell onto a black-and-white image of a voluptuous woman in a corset.

"Lingerie," I said. "And you?"

"Ladies' fashions—French Salon, of course—but only recently. I just moved over from Gamage's . . . And it's Amy, by the way. Amy Patrick. Please, sit down, join me."

I sat down, she closed her magazine and we spent the next few minutes recalling the names of those who had been at Delnasay that summer—a grim roll call of who had died and who had survived.

"What about Mr. Cowper? Do you know what happened to him?" I asked.

Amy stubbed out her cigarette. "Awarded the Military Cross . . . but lost both of his legs, poor sod," she added, wincing. "Living in a home in Putney the last I heard—with nurses round the clock, of course. Has to." She reached over the table, placed her hand on mine: "And such a shock about the Campbells . . . Makes me feel sick to think about *them*," she said, staring down at a gravy-smeared plate and shaking her head.

"Hugo and Billy?" I said, thinking we'd gone back to them.

"No, Ottoline and Hector."

"What do you mean?"

"You don't know?"

I shook my head.

"Oh, my dear . . . Well, it was a while ago now. The first I knew was when I read about it in the newspaper." At that moment someone bumped past her. "Excuse *me*!" she called after them. "*Really*, I sometimes wonder what happened to good manners." She rifled through her bag, and I waited as she put another cigarette into the holder and lit it. "It was an accident, a horrible accident . . . And somewhere in France as well, but no other cars involved, thank goodness. They had been on one of those tours. You know, one of those motoring tours of battle sites? Though why anyone would want to go on one of those is beyond me. Anyhow, I think it said they had visited the Somme."

I nodded.

"It didn't say so in the newspaper, but I happen to know it was Her Ladyship at the wheel."

"How do you know this?"

"From Mrs. Parker. I see her quite often. She's one of my best customers. Always liked the French fashions, you see . . . Impeccable taste."

"What did she tell you, Amy?"

She took a long drag on her cigarette. "It's all a bit of a mystery how it happened," she said, her voice filled with smoke. "The weather was fine that day, and they had not long left their hotel, were heading to another, heading south, I think Mrs. Parker said . . . perhaps to the Riviera. Anyway, the car went off the road—must've skidded or something—and then plunged down a ravine into trees. *Boom.* Ottoline would have been killed instantly, Mrs. Parker said, because . . . well, her body was quite broken up. But Lord Hector . . . He was found some yards away from the car."

"Going to get help . . ."

"Or thrown."

I put my head in my hands.

"I'm so sorry. I thought you'd know."

We went to the powder room. I stood with my back against a door, listening to Amy as she peed, smoked and spoke, then flushed, unlocked and turned on taps. "Yes, all very sad. Tragic, really . . . the whole lot of them gone."

I opened the door. I said, "I don't suppose you know what happened to Ottoline's cousin . . . He was a painter—and also at Delnasay that summer. His name was Stedman . . . Ralph Stedman?"

She lowered her lipstick, stared at me in the mirror. "Was he the one from India—the captain mentioned in dispatches?"

I nodded. "Yes, India," I said, moving nearer.

She ran a slick of red over her lips, pressed them together and pouted. And as she put the makeup away in her bag, she said, "He was on that list. You know the one I mean, the one from Geneva . . . the Red Cross list of dead. Mrs. P. saw it. She said it wasn't as sad as some, because he was a bit older and had no children."

I turned on a tap and stood staring at it.

"I'd better get going," said Amy. "But let's do lunch tomorrow. I always take mine at one thirty. What about you?"

"Yes. One thirty."

As she made for the door, I called after her. "Amy, that list, the one from Geneva, is it an official thing . . . an official proof of death?"

"I should say. Unless you're Jesus Christ and rise up again." She laughed. "See you tomorrow."

I spent the afternoon in a daze, staring at French lace but seeing only French roads and French mud, and, more abstractly still, wondering if this reality—my life—was all an illusion, and if I'd eventually wake up in another time. I don't recall measuring or fitting anyone, and I don't recall speaking to anyone, though I'm sure I did. Over and over I shook my head, as though that action alone could shake out Amy's words, or dislodge a name on a list someone in Geneva had decided to call *Dead*. But I knew, and I think I had known for some time. Ralph was gone, and gone forever.

Later that day, I stood outside the staff entrance. Waiting in the drizzle without an umbrella, I felt strangely reconciled to Ralph's death, but I still couldn't grasp Ottoline's violent end, and my mind was awash: I saw a car slam into a tree; saw Lord Hector come to and then turn to his love, his life, that fragile *but all the same exciting* girl he had married in another century. I saw him reach out to her shattered body and speak to her. *Darling* . . . Saw him struggle to open a crushed car door; tell her that he was going to get help.

"Sorry I'm late." Leo held his newspaper above my damp hair. "One of these days I'm going to buy you a big umbrella," he said, smiling. Then, "Oh dear, has something happened?"

And so I told him about Ottoline, or tried to.

He said, "Let's go and have a drink."

"It's just a shock," I said, sitting in the gloomy pub with a gin and orange in my hand.

"Of course."

"You see, I haven't heard from Rodney—Rodney Watts. He's the butler. You remember, I told you about him?"

Leo looked back me, vague, but then nodded.

"I haven't heard anything," I said again. "And it happened some time ago."

"Not everyone likes to deliver bad news, and I imagine he's been very busy. There'll have been the repatriation of the bodies to organize, a complicated process. And then the funeral arrangements . . . trustees and executors to deal with . . ."

"I missed the funeral," I said, suddenly realizing.

"You didn't know."

"It would have been in the newspapers."

"You don't read them."

Later, we caught the number 19. We sat at the front of the upper deck, and Leo held my hand. He said, "I'm seeing you home and that's that."

As soon as we arrived back at the flat, Myrtle said, "That man's been again, Mrs. Gibson."

"Oh, and which man is that?" I asked.

Lila pulled at my arm. "Mummy . . . Mummy . . ."

"You, missy, should be in bed."

"The smart one," said Myrtle, folding her arms beneath her bosom. "The one in the suit."

"Yes, but *which* one?"

"I'll put on the kettle," said Leo.

"*Mummy!*"

"Lila, please don't interrupt. You must wait until Mummy has finished speaking to Myrtle."

"That one in the suit, the one I told you about . . . Says he has to speak to you in person, says he's going to come back next week, on Thursday."

"Well, that's all right, then. Thursday's your day off," said Leo, coming into the room, picking up Lila and twirling her about in a way I knew would make it hard for me to settle her.

I wondered briefly who the man was. But quite often on my return from work Myrtle said the same thing: "A man has been, Mrs. Gibson." And then offered the very same limited description: *a man in a suit.* It had happened before, would happen again, and whether milkman, grocer or gasman—what did it matter? The bills would be paid, eventually.

Myrtle left. I put Lila back to bed and read to her for a while, a very short while, for her eyes closed before I had finished a page. Then I sat for a few minutes, staring at her and thinking of Ralph. I'd tell her about him one day. I'd take her to Scotland, to Delnasay; show her the cottage, the river.

I returned to the sitting room, sat down next to Leo, and as we drank our tea, he said, "You mustn't let it get you down. About Ottoline, I mean. I know you worked for her for a few years, but it's not as though she was family—a blood relation."

I closed my eyes for a moment. I said, "She was Lila's godmother."

"Yes, I know, and I understand that you and she were quite close for a time, but let's be honest—what's she ever done for you?"

I turned to him, was about to speak, but the words wouldn't come. I couldn't tell him.

He took hold of my hand. He said, "She was your employer— your *employer*, Pearl; that's all. And you honored her by making her Lila's godmother . . . But I think she let you down, and Lila, too. I mean, *look*—look around you. Can you imagine *her* here—in this room?"

I shook my head.

"No, exactly. She got far more out of you than you got from her. And now she's gone and . . . well, sad as it is, that's that."

We made love there on the sofa. It was the first time since Ralph. And though it was quick and clumsy, it satiated something. Afterward, we sat side by side, disheveled, awkward, each of us staring at the burned-out fire. He said, "I'm sorry. That wasn't quite how I'd planned."

No, and it wasn't how I remembered.

The next day, I met Amy for lunch. I selected our table, a quiet spot tucked away in a corner, and I led her into the conversation. I needed her advice, and I knew she'd be open. I said, "Do you happen to know anything about how to stop babies?"

She looked back at me, wide-eyed.

I feigned a little laugh. I said, "Oh, not for me. I have a friend who's in a predicament . . ."

"Pregnant?"

"No, I don't think so. Well, she hopes not, but she might be."

"What's her situation?" asked Amy, dunking bread into a bowl of glutinous soup.

"It's a bit complicated . . ."

"It always is," she said, without looking up at me. "Is she married? I'm guessing not."

"No, she's not married, but she's seeing someone. Well, she's been seeing him for a while, I think, but nothing had happened, you see . . . and then, just last night, or maybe the night before, they sort of . . ."

Amy looked up. "They had sex—and now she's worried that she's pregnant."

"Exactly."

"How old is she—this friend of yours?"

"Oh well, she's about—"

"I mean, she should know if she's likely to be pregnant—'cause there's that safe time, isn't there?"

"Yes," I said, "when's that?"

"Straight after your period, isn't it? Lasts about a week or so."

I tried not to smile.

"I don't know what to advise if she's pregnant . . . Will this chap marry her, do you think?"

I shrugged. Then I said, "I really don't think she's pregnant."

"Well, she still needs to get herself sorted, get herself one of those Dutch caps."

"Do you know where she'd be able to get one?"

Amy nodded. "I'll give you the address."

Chapter Twenty-one

It was around ten when the doorbell rang.

"Mrs. Morton?"

"Gibson. I am Mrs. Gibson."

The man pulled a piece of paper from his pocket. "Ah yes, I have that name here also." He handed me his card: *Theodore Godley and Company . . . Solicitors . . . EC4.*

A shiver ran down my spine at the sight of that name, Godley, the name I'd seen on a birth announcement so many years before.

"It's with regard to the estate of the late Lady Ottoline Campbell. I've called a number of times . . . May I come in?"

He followed me upstairs and into my small sitting room. "Please," I said, my heart pounding as I stared at him, and gesturing to the sofa, "do sit down, Mr. Godley."

"Ah, I'm afraid I am not Mr. Godley. He's my boss. My name is Jacobson—Roger Jacobson." He sat down. "This shouldn't take too

long, Mrs. Gibson. My first task was to locate you, which I was able
to do with the help of His late Lordship's former butler."

Former. That word sounded so strange. His life must have fallen
apart. I said, "I haven't heard from Mr. Watts in some time."

"Mr. Watts has been most helpful. As I say, it was he who informed us of your address. In cases such as this we prefer to establish contact in person—face-to-face, so to speak—rather than by
letter. Letters can so easily go astray and fall into the wrong hands,"
he added, and smiled. "I'm afraid my next task is . . . a little sensitive. Legal protocol demands I see some proof of identity—but a
birth or marriage certificate will suffice."

I had neither. And I told him. "They're lost, I'm afraid. But I
have plenty of other documents—mainly bills."

At first, he wasn't sure about this, but then he relented. So I
reached for the unpaid bills on the mantelpiece and handed them
to him.

"Oh dear, final reminders . . ."

"I also have this," I said, handing him my post office savings
book.

He looked at the name, the balance, then raised his eyes to me
and smiled. "You know, it's at times like this that I love my job," he
said.

I was still on my feet and standing in front of him, and it was
his turn to say, "Please sit down, Mrs. Gibson."

So I sat down and he told me. Told me I had come into some
money, a considerable amount of money. At first, I thought I heard
him say *five thousand pounds.* And I stared at him as he said it again:
"The sum of five thousand pounds—to you, Mrs. Gibson." Then he

said, "And for your daughter . . ." Here, he paused and checked his paperwork, and I pinched the flesh on the back of my hand—once, twice, thrice. I kept thinking *five thousand pounds, five thousand pounds* . . . "Yes, for your daughter—the late Lady Ottoline's goddaughter—the sum of thirty thousand pounds."

Yes, it was a dream, had to be. That name Godley and thirty thousand pounds . . .

"Mrs. Gibson . . . Are you quite all right?"

"Can you just tell me all of that again, please?"

And so he did. And afterward, when I opened my mouth, tried to speak, the words wouldn't come. But then, at last, eventually, I heard myself say, "Thirty thousand . . ." And my voice sounded far away, and not like my voice at all.

"Thirty thousand," repeated Mr. Jacobson.

"Thirty *thousand?*"

Mr. Jacobson smiled. "Thirty thousand pounds, Mrs. Gibson."

At some point he must have gone through to the kitchen, because the next thing I knew he was handing me a glass of water, and as he did so, he said, "This is one of the reasons why we prefer to deliver news like this face-to-face."

Mr. Jacobson sat back down. "Do tell me when you're ready for me to continue, Mrs. Gibson."

"You mean there's more?"

I took a few sips of water, then looked up at him and nodded.

"The other part of Her late Ladyship's bequest to your daughter concerns a property in Scotland. A place named Delnasay . . ."

Mr. Jacobson unfolded a large sheet of paper, a map. He went on to explain that Ottoline's bequest to Lila was not the entire estate but included the house, formal gardens, and land amounting to some fifteen acres. He then took time to explain more about the money Ottoline had left to Lila. It would be held in a trust until she reached the age of twenty-one, he said. However, the terms of Ottoline's will stipulated that Lila and I should receive an income from the capital sum until that time. According to Mr. Jacobson, the money would guarantee us a generous income—easily enough, he said, to cover the costs of maintaining Delnasay.

"When your daughter reaches the age of twenty-one, the capital sum along with any interest not taken as income will legally become hers. She'll be able to reinvest it, spend it—do whatever she wishes; it'll be up to her, her decision. But I'd very much hope that you'd guide her in moderation and prudence, and that by then you'll have excellent advisers in place. You see, she'll be a very rich young woman, Mrs. Gibson, and these waters are—as I'm sure you already know—filled with sharks all too hungry for rich young women."

I had concentrated hard on his words. I said, "My daughter isn't yet five. It is a long time away, twenty-one."

"Rest assured, sixteen years will go in the blink of an eye, Mrs. Gibson."

"But what if I'm not here—what if something happens to me? My daughter might have money now, but she has no other relations, no family. We're on our own . . . Who will advise her then?"

He laughed at this. "You're still young. I'm quite sure nothing is going to happen to you, Mrs. Gibson." Then he became more serious. "But, in the unlikely event that something were to happen to you, the trustees—of which Mr. Godley is one—would continue to ensure your daughter's money was safely and wisely invested. In fact, I can assure you here and now that Mr. Godley would personally see to it, and would continue to advise her—and yes, even after she reached the age of twenty-one." He smiled.

"And will I meet him . . . this Mr. Godley?"

"Oh yes. I am simply the messenger, Mrs. Gibson. In due course, once probate is granted, we'll need you to come to our offices, meet with Mr. Godley, sign the relevant paperwork—and, of course, be issued with your money."

I glanced at the map on his knee. "Is the cottage—the one near the house—included in the bequest to my daughter?"

He wasn't sure which cottage I meant. So I moved over to him to view the map of the estate. I saw the house and gardens—now Lila's—clearly marked in red. And saw, too, that the cottage was beyond the boundary of Ottoline's bequest.

Even so, I placed my finger on the shape.

"Ah, the old gamekeeper's cottage . . . No, that property is not included."

"But what is to happen to the rest of the land? Is it to be sold—broken up?"

"Possibly, but I'm afraid I'm not at liberty to disclose any further details, Mrs. Gibson. At this stage, our task is simply to locate the beneficiaries—which, with the exception of your good self, has not been at all easy," he added.

"But there *are* others?"

"There were. However, it seems the war claimed them." He looked at me. "It's the ongoing tragedy of the times we live in, Mrs. Gibson . . . So many wills were not amended during and after the war. And why would they be? I imagine the last thing on any grief-stricken mind is administration, the updating of a last will and testament. Increasingly, we find ourselves having to stretch the net wider and wider in order to locate a beneficiary still alive. Death was always a sad business, but it seems to me all the sadder now, in the absence of so many sons and heirs."

I would never again need to worry about money. *Reminders* were a thing of the past. Ottoline had seen to that. And though I was grateful, immeasurably grateful, seeing the map of the estate, that tiny, almost insignificant oblong shape, had made me realize: I would have handed back all of it—every single penny and piece of granite—if Lila and I could have had Ralph with us. We might have been poor, Lila might have grown up in rags, but she would have had her father. We would have been together. A family.

Bittersweet was my good fortune.

It was later that fateful Thursday and early in the evening when Leo arrived. He brought a bottle of wine, and made a thing of it, its vintage and cost. Then he asked me if I'd had a nice day. But I was in a strange place, an unreal place: caught in the limbo of disbelief, soaring and crashing with each exhalation. Everything around me appeared tawdry and cheap; everything, including him, Leo Holland.

And so I didn't look at him. I said, "Oh, just the usual, you know . . . nothing special."

And when he reached out and touched me, I pulled away.

Then, "What's this?" he asked.

"Steak."

He laughed. "You must be flush," he said, and he rubbed his hands together. "But I'm not complaining," he added, winking at Lila, who was sitting on the linoleum step in her dressing gown and a moth-eaten fur hat, once Ottoline's, and drawing a picture of me.

I had already decided not to tell anyone—at least for the time being—about Ottoline's bequests. And in truth there was no one *to* tell, apart from Amy and Leo. I certainly couldn't tell—or even begin to explain to—my almost-five-year-old daughter that she had just come into a fortune and been left a house in Scotland. Money to her was copper pennies; a silver sixpence was *rich*. Thirty thousand pounds was . . . unimaginable. And not just to her, but to me.

Earlier that day, after Mr. Jacobson had left, I'd poured myself a glass of sherry from the bottle at the back of the cupboard, the one left over from Christmas. At first it tasted disgusting, and I'd winced and shivered, but then—and like all alcohol, it seemed to me—it got better. So I'd had another and sat with my feet up on the sofa and cried, and laughed, and then cried again. For I was rich and I was poor. I had money, but I didn't have Ralph—and never would again.

I comforted myself. I had enough money to buy a home, to furnish and decorate *that* sitting room, *that* bedroom. I had enough money to buy a motorcar, and still enough to travel abroad—first-class. I'd take Lila to Biarritz. Yes, Biarritz, I thought. The Hotel du Palais . . . We'd take a suite, make friends, dine with them each evening at eight, and I'd invite them all to Delnasay—where *we tend to spend our summers* . . .

I saw ocean liners and pictured New York: the Statue of Liberty, skyscrapers and streets more bustling than in London. I saw an open road, the green patchwork of counties. And with windows wound down and the wind in our hair, Lila and me—crossing borders and heading north. Always heading north—back to him.

And muddled in with all of this, and interrupting each imagined trip, was that name, Godley.

Bittersweet was my good fortune.

Leo and I waited until Lila had gone to bed before we sat down at the table. He poured the wine and I served our supper. He spoke about the store, those people who did not pay their bills, and went on about one in particular, a duke, no less.

He said, "I hope you haven't forgotten—I'm going away next week."

"When?"

"On Saturday . . . I told you, remember?"

"No, I don't recall you telling me. Where are you going?"

"Home—Manchester—to visit my mother."

"But you only just visited her."

"She's not well . . . very frail."

"Yes, I know, you said that last time. And the time before that."

We finished our meal in silence, and then I picked up our plates and took them through to the kitchen. I'm not sure what irked me, why I was suspicious—if I was. Perhaps it was simply that Leo's trips north were something apart from me, a former life I still knew little about and felt excluded from. He'd never invited me to meet his mother, and it was telling, I thought. If I'd been important to him, if he'd had even the vaguest notion of making me his wife, surely he'd want me to meet this frail lady—before it was too late?

My emotions were undoubtedly out of kilter that evening, and yet, in some other way, I felt stronger and clearer headed. I had never had a father, brother or husband to look after me, and now I no longer needed one—or any man. I was, as they say, of independent means, and with the dawning of that knowledge came a strange new courage. And so, when I went back into the room, sat down, watched Leo pick up his lighter, hold it to a cigarette, when I said, "I hope you don't have a fancy woman up there," I was not angry or insecure. I was, though Leo could hardly have known it, curiously dispassionate. My passion had been ring-fenced years before; my passion belonged to one name.

Leo smiled and rolled his eyes. "As if."

"You do go up there quite a lot," I said, reaching for a cigarette from his packet and then pouring myself another glass of wine.

"You're in a funny mood tonight."

"Not really."

"I've never seen you smoke before."

I shrugged.

"Has something happened today?"

I shook my head.

"I have to see my mother, Pearl. And I have some holiday to take—and she's not well. It seemed like a good opportunity for me to spend some time with her . . . I'm sure you'll cope without me for a week."

I stared at him: "I'm sure. Actually, I'm planning on having a holiday myself . . . I'm going to buy a motorcar, take Lila on a trip."

He raised his hand to his mustache and stroked it, as though weighing up the likelihood of this happening. "Really? And just *how* are you going to buy a motorcar?"

I looked away from him, tapping my cigarette on the edge of the ashtray: "With money, of course. I have some savings . . . some money I'd forgotten about." I raised my eyes to him and smiled. "I thought I might visit Rodney Watts in Northumberland . . . and then head on, to Scotland."

At this, he laughed. He stubbed out his cigarette, rose up, moved round the table and stood behind me. He rubbed his hands over my neck, my shoulders, and then down over my blouse to my breasts. "I'll take you away, Pearl . . . I'll take you to Scotland if that's where you'd like to go . . ."

And I closed my eyes to shut it all out. That room. Him. Me. All of it. But later, in my bed, as I felt hands and then tongue, as I closed my eyes again, I saw a fierce gaze not years away but inches away; I saw golden hair falling over a suntanned brow: a fantasy no longer indistinct, still there for me to hold.

Chapter Twenty-two

Dear Pearl,

I hope you are well. Thank you for your kind letter and condolences. You must forgive me for not having written to you sooner, but as I'm sure you can imagine, it has been a very sad and busy time for those of us still here at Birling. Everything happened so very quickly—the accident itself, such a sudden and violent ending, and then the funeral, an impossibly sad day.

Yes, the house is to be sold—in fact, I think it is to feature in the Country Life magazine. Meanwhile, I have been assisting the local auctioneers in preparation for the sale of furniture & artifacts, and various personal effects. Listing it all, checking and then checking again for the catalog. (I enclose a copy for your perusal. I am sure many of the items listed will bring back memories and be familiar to you.) But it is a grim & heart-breaking task, to take a final glance upon everything—still in one place, belonging to one family—and know it is to be scattered without any true provenance or story. And yes, as you so rightly say, the end of an era.

Other than a few of the outdoor staff, everyone has been paid what they were due, and all have gone. Mrs. Lister's final day was today. We took our time to walk about the house together, and we remembered the family & the happy times we shared with them. So many Christmases, Master Hugo's and Master Billy's birthday parties, and in particular, the New Year's Eve party at the dawn of a new century—1900. We both agreed that was the very best evening the house had seen, at least in our day.

As I think you know, Mrs. Lister's husband recently passed away, and she has, albeit somewhat reluctantly, decided to live with her sister. But she was most grateful for your picture postcard of Old Vistas of London—and, I'm sure, will write to you in due course. As regards my own future, I have given my word to the executors that I shall stay on here until after the auction; then I shall return to the county of my birth, Yorkshire. I'm not sure if I ever told you, but I recently acquired a bungalow at Scarborough—a modest but spacious place, with a good-size garden & an uninterrupted view of the sea. I very much hope you & Lila will come and visit me. Rest assured, you will always be most welcome.

Yes, it is irregular, dear Pearl—all of it. And I still wonder—what are we to make of this, our journey in life? What are we

*meant to learn? And each and every time I come back to one
thing, and one thing only. And it is this: Love is the only thing
that matters, and without it, we learn nothing.*

*I enclose my new address at Scarborough and look forward
to hearing from you.*

Very best wishes,
Rodney Watts

I saw from the catalog Rodney had enclosed with his letter that the
sale was to take place in three days' time, and I decided then and
there I had to go. I had missed the funeral, but I wanted to pay my
respects, to see Rodney and take a look about the house once more.
I told my supervisor at work that my elderly aunt in Northumberland had taken seriously ill. I was all she had. I asked Myrtle if she
could stay at the flat for a few nights—earn a few extra shillings.
She could. I found out train times, sent a postcard to Rodney, and
the next morning I headed to King's Cross.

Memories came flooding back to me on that journey north. It
had been summer, early July, and the countryside had been a patchwork of green and gold, church steeples bathed in sunshine, sleepy
villages unaware of what was to come. And I, as green as the fields,
as innocent as those white-smocked people working in them, and
entirely oblivious that I had just met my destiny.

This time, thanks to Rodney, there was a taxicab waiting for
me at the station. It followed the usual route, the one I had walked
seven years before—carrying a ton of romance and dressed for the
wrong season. And I smiled and shook my head as I remembered.

Then the stone facade came into view—solid and unchanged. But it could not be the same, I knew, and as we turned into the driveway, trepidation took hold.

"Sad business," said my driver, shaking his head as I paid him. "Just have to hope someone buys the old place and it doesn't go to wrack and ruin like the rest of them."

As the vehicle drove away, I took a look around me. The gardens bore testament to the cuts in staff Rodney had mentioned. Even at the end of the war, when I had last seen them, the grounds had been better tended . . . Or had they? I wondered. Had I been so preoccupied with what was happening *inside* that I had simply not noticed what was happening outside?

There was no sign of Rodney, but I pulled on the doorbell before I stepped into the lobby and opened the inner door.

The hallway was all of a muddle—with gardening tools laid out on the small velvet sofa from Ottoline's dressing room, and random items from the kitchen spread over the mahogany table next to His Lordship's hats and canes. There were trays of silver cutlery, boxes of miscellaneous china and crockery, some of it wrapped in newspaper and a few pieces displayed on the top, presumably to show what each box contained. I moved on, peering through doorways at more chaos and muddlement. Things from bedrooms were placed willy-nilly in sitting rooms, and hatboxes, trunks and other items of luggage lay about the passageways as though another inmate had just arrived into the madness. Like an old lady who had forgotten her age, the season, occasion or country, I found each part of the house incongruous and all wrong. Only Lord Hector's study felt calm, felt sane. Like him, I thought, placing my hand upon one of the empty shelves. All that remained were his desk and chair, and the lingering faint scent of cigars.

I walked back to the hallway, and my voice echoed as I called out as I climbed the stairs. I waited a moment before turning the glass handle and opening the door.

Gardenia.

Sunlight flooded in through the tall windows—now stripped of their voluminous curtains. The bed, too, had been stripped, and the bedside tables, with their paraphernalia I was used to seeing—the books, the pills, the glass decanter and tumbler, the photographs of Billy and Hugo—were gone. The dressing table had been moved away from the window and for some reason placed at the other side of the room, deserted of the Minton china bowls that had each evening contained rings, earrings and straps of pearls, and of the silver-topped perfume bottles—and brushes and combs I had once used on my lady's hair. The closets in the dressing room were empty, the marble bathroom cleared. Ottoline had been packed away into cardboard boxes and crates, cataloged, numbered and tagged. To be sold to the highest bidder. Nothing less.

I opened a window, leaned out of it, my arms resting on the peeling paint, my mouth already hungry for that familiar salty air. And as my gaze hovered and then found the woods in the distance—carpeted in bluebells—I recalled the night I had gone there with a shovel, in the depths of winter, in the depths of war, a lifetime ago. Then I raised my eyes from that budding green to the great big blue, and two skylarks, singing in flight.

I wiped away tears as Rodney approached. He held me in his arms. He said, "Yes, it's all very sad, isn't it?"

"It's coming back . . . seeing it again, like this . . . without her, without them. And the state of the house," I said, gathering myself and stepping back from him. "Everything all over the place."

"I know, I know, but that's how it's done. That's the way the auctioneers wish it to be, and it's all in their hands now, you see." He glanced down and placed his palms flat on the windowsill, then raised his eyes and stared out across the gardens. "Such a tranquil spot, isn't it?" he said. "Hard to fathom . . . Hard to believe they've all gone."

I moved alongside Rodney and looked out again. He had been there for almost three decades. This was his home. That was his view on the world. He had nothing and no one, and I knew how that felt.

"I'm very grateful to you for coming back."

I moved my hand, placed it over his. "I would have been here earlier had I known."

"Taxi was there—and everything?"

"Yes."

"Good journey?"

"Yes, fine."

He glanced at me. "You have a new look . . . Very glamorous, if I may say."

I smiled. I'd never in my life thought of myself as *glamorous*.

I waited a moment, then said, "I've had an idea, something I want to discuss with you, but not now."

"Sounds intriguing."

"It's a sort of proposition."

"Not marriage, I hope."

"No, Rodney, not marriage—at least, not yet."

He laughed, and then he turned to me. "It's good to see you again, Pearl. You have no idea how much I appreciate—"

"No," I interrupted. "You don't need to say. I'm here because I want to be here, because I wanted to be here with you."

That evening, Rodney and I took our humble supper—a slice of pork pie, and new potatoes and salad from the garden—to the dining room, along with a bottle of wine from the cellar. "Well, why not?" said Rodney, striking a match and lighting a silver candelabra. Amidst boxes and crates, picnic hampers and fishing rods, and with the unnerving presence of a tailor's dummy dressed in one of Ottoline's gowns, we tried to steer our conversation, tried to recall the funnier incidents from our time together in service. But each one delivered us back to that room and a tragedy.

Eventually I said, "Why didn't you write to me, Rodney?"

"I did. You were the first person I thought of, and I wrote to you. But then, when I remembered your sad departure from here, and how difficult Her Ladyship had been with you, it seemed wrong— unfair of me to even so much as inadvertently put pressure on you to come north . . . the expense of traveling all this way, and Lila, and your job . . . Well, I decided it would be selfish of me to burden you."

"Were there many there—at the funeral?"

He shook his head.

"I imagined the church would be packed. They knew so many, were so well connected . . ."

"Used to be," he said, "before the war. But it's been a long time since we entertained. In fact, I can't recall the last time we had any houseguests—or even so much as a dinner party." He sighed. "And unfortunately, it didn't go into the newspaper, not until after the event. You see, it was all so unexpected . . . and in the absence of any family, well, it simply slipped my mind. I suppose I was in shock."

"But who organized it—the funeral? Who made all the arrangements?"

"Oh, I saw to most of that, and the Foreign Office dealt with the repatriation of the remains."

The remains, I thought, and I closed my eyes for a second or two, and then I said, "And there were no family members—none at all?"

"There was a cousin of His Lordship's—and a woman, Dorothy something or other. Distant relation of Her Ladyship's, she told me. Though it sounded very distant to me. There was the family lawyer who traveled up from London with two gentlemen from the Foreign Office to attend, and representatives from various local charities His Lordship and Her Ladyship had been involved with and supported . . . But of course many of their friends reside in London and would have had no knowledge—until later, as I say. And, sadly, there weren't many staff . . . Well, so many of you have moved on, moved away." He paused for a moment. "I was very sorry to hear about Mr. Stedman—Captain Stedman. I know you and he were . . . were close."

I tried to smile. I half wondered whether to cut through our polite pretense there and then. But it felt wrong and disrespectful to speak to Rodney Watts—still wearing his tailcoat and striped trousers—about my illicit affair.

Rodney continued. "Of course, there are many still missing and unaccounted for, you know—not necessarily dead. Only last week—and not far from here—a young fellow turned up. Turned up out of the blue at his parents' farm . . . Yes, just like that, and having been missing for over two years. Imagine."

I knew from his letters that Rodney hung on to this everthinning thread of hope. I said, "Well, that's wonderful, and I've heard such tales myself"—I lied. Then I asked, "The lawyer, the man you mentioned who came up from London for the funeral, do you know his name?"

"Godley. Theodore Godley. But he wasn't just Lord Hector's lawyer; he was a dear friend. They had known each other since their school days."

"And what is he like—this Mr. Godley?" I asked with studied new nonchalance.

"Oh, uncommonly kind," said Rodney. "Like His Lordship."

"Is he married, do you know? Does he have a family?"

"He's a widower . . . but I believe he has one child. A daughter."

My heart fluttered; I looked away from him.

He reached over and patted my hand. "I shouldn't say anything, but I have a feeling you'll be meeting Mr. Godley for yourself one day soon."

And I smiled, because of course I already knew this.

Later, in my old yellow room—where Rodney had kindly made up the bed for me—I read through the sale catalog again and circled the lots I intended to bid for. Rodney's advice about keeping something aside meant I still had a little of my savings left. But as I turned off the lamp, I remembered: I no longer needed to worry about money.

～

All that glitters is not gold, I thought as I sat in the drawing room on a chair from a guest bedroom. And I watched as I waited. The auctioneer rattled at a fast pace through the contents of the house, like a race through the lives of Ottoline and Hector Campbell: "And from His Lordship's time at university . . . purchased on their honeymoon in Paris . . . on the occasion of the birth of their first son . . . from the turn of the century, I believe . . . bought at Christie's of London shortly before the war . . ." On and on it went, punctuated by hands flying up and the slam of a hammer.

"Our next lot—number two-six-seven . . . A collection of scrap-books and various memorabilia belonging to the late Lady Ottoline . . . Can I start the bidding at . . . sixpence?"

I held up my card.

"Sixpence to the lady at the front."

Someone else held up a card.

"One shilling to the gentleman in the tweed jacket," the auctioneer said, pointing his finger to the back of the room.

I held up my card again.

"One and six to the lady at the front."

I turned to the man in the tweed jacket, saw him raise his card and immediately raised my own.

And so it went on: two shillings . . . two and six . . . three shillings . . . three and six . . . Then: "Going-going-gone." *Slam.* "To the lady at the front."

I waited awhile for my next lot number. The item was the gold gown I had worn for my twenty-fourth birthday, which, as I had seen in the catalog, was from Worth of Paris. Bidding was fast. A woman from London was buying up all of Ottoline's gowns, and though her determination almost matched mine, I got it. *Two pounds*, I wrote, next to the circled lot number in the catalog.

Next, the photograph from Lord Hector's desk, the one of Ottoline at eighteen, and taken around the time of her coming out. And again, my hand went up and down and up and down, until at last the auctioneer slammed down his hammer, and we smiled and nodded at each other once again.

The man in the tweed jacket—the one who had been after the scrapbooks—bought a portrait of Ottoline by a painter named Sargent, and I couldn't help but wonder who the man was. But Rodney would no doubt know, and I'd ask him later, I decided. By teatime, we were racing through jewelry. I lost the ruby and diamond ring Ottoline had given me on the occasion of my "marriage" to Stanley to *the woman in the brown coat*. I wasn't too upset. I'd decided to bid on it only because Ottoline had given it to me. But, and perhaps like Ottoline, I'd also decided bloodred rubies were not really me. I caught my stride in miscellanea and won a number of cardboard boxes filled with what the auctioneer termed *general artifacts* and *bric-a-brac* from the house.

That night, Rodney and I compared notes. We sat at the kitchen table and went through the entire catalog. He had bought a number of Lord Hector's natural history books, one of his canes, a pair of binoculars, two prints, a silver coffeepot, two armchairs, a card table and a decanter and a half dozen wineglasses. And we talked about the other bidders, and the items we had lost out on.

"What about that fellow in the tweed?" I asked. "The one who bought the portrait of Ottoline. Who was he?"

Rodney thought for a moment. "Ah, I think you mean Cecil Armstrong . . ."

I shrugged.

And Rodney, who had never been one for gossip, stared at me. Then he said, "It was a difficult time, that . . ."

I closed my catalog. "Was he the father of Ottoline's daughter?"

Rodney nodded. And it was, I knew, as much as I'd ever get from him. His loyalty to Lord Hector and Ottoline was lifelong and unbreakable—even in death—and I respected Rodney all the more for it, and I hoped that Hector and Ottoline had known, and shown their appreciation.

Thus, tentatively, I began, "I know we shouldn't speak about it, that it's confidential, and not necessarily something you wish to discuss with me, but I just wondered . . . Well, I hope that they remembered you in their wills, that's all."

Rodney smiled. "His Lordship has been very generous . . . and indeed was before any bequest. You see, he knew I wished to retire to Scarborough. Have a place with a garden and a view of the sea. It was his gift to me."

I had forgotten all about Rodney's bungalow, and though I was delighted to learn that he had been provided for, my plan—the proposition I had mentioned to him—suddenly seemed pointless. Even so, I decided to run it past him: "Rodney, you know I mentioned that I'd had an idea . . ."

I didn't cry when I left Birling—and Rodney. I knew I'd see him again. I didn't cry until I was on the train, and not until after York. And I'm not sure what triggered my tears. But perhaps it was nothing more than the sky—that vast northern sky hanging over the

Yorkshire Dales: a place Billy had spoken to me about and intended to visit; a place Ralph had been.

Staring out of the smeared window, I was once again overwhelmed by the notion of their absence in the world. And by the cruel shafts of light falling through curtains of rain onto already flooded fields.

Chapter Twenty-three

"But would you really—even if you thought he might be married?"

"Ha, I'm not proud. I'll take the crumbs from the table," said Amy.

She was being disingenuous, I thought, falling back on her usual humor. We were sitting on a bench in the park, watching Lila play with the new hoop Amy had bought her. It was Sunday, Leo was once again in Manchester and I'd been trying to broach the subject of sex outside of marriage. But Amy's attitude was hard to fathom. Like other single women I knew, and not unlike me, she was possessed with a contradictory mix of old-fashioned values and new morality; one that upheld and craved the respectability of marriage and at the same time embraced notions of equality and new freedoms. It was a muddled modern world.

I said, "My friend—that one I told you about?—she had an affair with a married man, once, during the war."

"Everyone did during the war, dear . . . By the way, what happened to her?" asked Amy. "Did she get herself sorted?"

"I believe so."

"Are they going to get married?"

"I'm not sure."

"She's a fool to let it go on too long without a ring on her
finger."

"He goes away a lot," I said absently, watching Lila.

"Aye aye, sounds like she's fallen for another married one."

I turned to her. "Really?"

"Well, what do you think? He's getting his oats without any
commitment and then buggering off. Does she know much about
him—has she ever been to his place?"

I shook my head.

"There you go. Probably got a wife and family. Six kids, I'll bet.
And another girl shacked up somewhere."

"She *is* a little suspicious, I think," I said after a moment or two.

"I don't blame her."

"But he's very nice—or so she tells me."

"I bet he is," said Amy. "They always are. And I know the type.
They have one rule for themselves, another for the mistress and yet
another for the wife. It's all about control, you see. Oh yes, I can
spot them a mile off . . . They're always the quiet ones, well dressed,
impeccable manners, seem like gentlemen and call themselves
bachelors. They pretend to be old-fashioned, and if you talk to
them about feminism, they call it newfangled jargon, and if you
make any demands—to hell with you. They're tricksters of the first
order . . . She should have it out with him—or chuck the blighter.
I would."

"Maybe she doesn't want to be on her own."

"Or maybe she can't imagine life without him," said Amy, in an overly dramatic and affected voice and raising her hand to her brow.

"Oh no, it's not like that. She's not in love with him. At least, I don't think she is."

Amy swiveled round to face me. "For the sake of argument, and on a scale of one to ten, just how keen is she on this fellow?"

I looked around me and then back at her. "Five . . . maybe six."

"It hardly sounds like grand passion—though I'm not sure that exists."

"Oh, but it does," I said quickly. "It does exist, Amy."

Her eyes widened. "Henry?"

Henry. "Yes."

"Well, you're lucky to have had that . . . and you're lucky to have her," she added, smiling at Lila as she ran toward us.

I watched Amy as she took Lila's hand and led her over to the ice-cream seller. I had been lucky; I was lucky—far luckier than Amy knew. And yet, it struck me that each time fate handed me something, it also took something away: It had granted me life but taken away my mother; given me Lila but taken Ralph; and now, now I was to have money but no one to share my good fortune with.

The three of us sat in silence as we ate our ice creams, and after I'd wiped Lila's face and she'd climbed down from the bench, Amy said, "As regards your friend—and by the way, does she have a name?"

I stared ahead, saw a sign: EELBROOK.

"Ellie," I said, "Ellie Brook."

"Well, your Ellie will just have to use her own judgment. No point in rattling the old blighter's cage if all she wants is a bit of hanky-panky and the illusion of love. But to be honest, she sounds pretty spineless to me . . . Not that I blame her, I suppose. Hundreds and thousands of women in this country would give their eyeteeth to have a man, even if it has to be an illicit affair."

That term made me shudder.

"She'll feel wretched when it ends, but at least she'll have had an *affair*, unlike the rest of us. And what has she got to lose?"

I thought for a moment. "Well, she does have children."

"You didn't say . . . *Whose* children?"

I shook my head. "I forgot to say. She was married—before the war. Yes, her husband died, you see."

"How many children?"

"Three."

"And the first affair—the other one you mentioned—was that when she was still married?"

"Oh no, that was afterward. After her husband died."

"Sounds like she's been busy."

I shook my head: "No, not really."

"Well, credit where credit's due, I suppose. At least she waited . . . But still, the fact that she has children, well, it paints a very different scenario," said Amy, her voice almost chastising.

"I don't know why I forgot to say . . ."

"Yes, a *very* different scenario . . ."

"I think the children are fine. I've not met them, but—"

"Has he?" Amy interrupted. "Has this new fella of hers met them?"

"You know, I think he has . . . Well, one of them, anyway."

Amy fired up a cigarette and shook her head. "Her first responsibility has to be to her children. Those poor babies who lost their father, and have already—and probably unknowingly—witnessed their mother's infidelity to his memory. But quite frankly, Pearl, it sounds a mess."

I cringed. I wanted to ask, *What if it is only one child? Does that make any difference?*

Amy leaned nearer and went on in a whisper. "Forgive me for saying so, but this Ellie of yours sounds a bit sex-mad, and to be honest, I shouldn't think your advice would do any good. From what you've told me, she sounds very selfish."

"Oh, but she's not—not at all. She adores her daughter—and her sons," I quickly added. "She really has done her best for them—all three of them."

"Hmm. Well, I've said it already and I'll say it again: She sounds like a sex addict to me. I've read about them, you know—women like her. And there's a lot of it about nowadays," she added, with an air of being above that sort of thing. "It all started with the war, khaki fever . . . But anyway, regardless, if she has anything about her, she'll confront this chap, tell him what's what and remind him that she has responsibilities, namely her three children."

We sat in silence for a moment, and then Amy asked, "So, what's she like, then—this Ellie Brook? I mean, is she very attractive? I imagine she must be."

"Oh, she's really quite average. Yes, I'd say she's an average woman."

"She doesn't sound very average to me."

"No? . . . Well, I suppose in some ways she's not."

I glanced away, wishing I'd never mentioned my fictitious friend. I had painted a picture of some sexually voracious, predatory

female; a widow with three children who had had at least two affairs with married men. I said, "You know, I think I've done poor
Ellie a great disservice, because she's not at all what she seems,
what I have told you . . . and what I've told you is only a tiny part,
the worst part."

"So tell me the best part," said Amy, eager now. And for a moment I thought she knew. Then she said, "You see, I'm amazed you
and she are even friends, because she sounds absolutely nothing
like you."

I smiled. "No, I suppose we're quite different," I said, and feigned
a little laugh.

"Describe her to me," said Amy.

"Well, she's quite tall, darkish haired, and she carries herself
very well."

"I bet she has a good figure."

I nodded. "Yes, she does."

"Even after three children?"

I nodded again.

"And breasts? I bet she has breasts. They all love them, you
know. Oh yes, while we're busy binding our chests, the men—what
few there are—are all after bosoms."

"She does have fine breasts," I said.

I wasn't entirely comfortable with the conversation, but picturing Ottoline removed any dilemma or hesitation in my description.

"And her eyes," Amy said. "What color are they?"

But I could see only one pair of eyes. And at first I floundered.
Then I said, "Indescribable."

"Hmm, I might've guessed."

Chapter Twenty-four

Whenever I thought of Arabella Godley, my mind summoned a pale-skinned, delicate creature with fair hair, a whispering voice and flesh as soft as a newborn baby's. My Arabella was serious, contemplative, principled and earnest. She had no time for fools, was intolerant of prejudice and injustice. My Arabella was a voracious reader and had spent time in Italy where she had learned all there was to know about art and architecture. She played the piano most afternoons and then walked out, writing poetry in her head beneath the dwindling twilight.

Had circumstances been different, we might have been sisters.

It was early October when I caught a tramcar to the city to meet with Mr. Theodore Godley. One of those early autumn days with a sky bleached of blue and a low sun. I sat on the top deck, right at the front, looking out at copper-hued trees, glistening buildings, and traffic and life. And I wasn't nervous; I was curious—and queerly excited.

I was pleased to see Mr. Jacobson, who greeted me in the lobby and then led me into the oak-paneled room to introduce me.

Theodore Godley's hand was soft and warm, his eyes kind and dark, the edge of each brown iris turning to gray, like his hair, which remained thick and was swept back from his forehead. His skin was tanned as though he had recently returned from a foreign country, and the measured and mellow tone of his voice reminded me of Lord Hector. And there was something about him so familiar that I half wondered if our paths had somehow crossed before.

Mr. Jacobson remained with us as Theodore Godley read out various clauses and subclauses, things he said he was legally bound to tell me. And I was mesmerized by him, this Godley—so handsome and fine, so uncommonly kind.

I signed my name at the foot of some pages, and then Theodore Godley signed his name as well. A secretary brought in coffee, and Theodore Godley smiled at her and said thank you, and as we drank our coffee, he asked me what I intended to do with the place in Scotland. I told him that I wasn't sure, but as Delnasay belonged to my daughter—and not to me—it would be up to her to decide, one day.

"Well, you'll be able to go up there and enjoy the place very soon . . . Though perhaps better to wait until next spring. It's certainly a beautiful spot," he added.

"You know it?"

He widened his eyes. "Indeed. I was lucky enough to spend

some very happy times at Delnasay . . . Though I haven't been for a long time. Not since the war."

Had he been there when I was? I wondered. Had he been one of the houseguests, a face I'd seen and perhaps smiled at—said good morning to?

"Not since 1914?" I asked.

"Yes. That was the last time I was there—when war was declared. Not the happiest of visits, of course, and unfortunately cut short."

"I was there, too."

"Were you really? How very rude of me not to remember you, Mrs. Gibson—and to think we may have sat next to each other at luncheon or dinner," he said, and laughed. "*No*, don't tell me we did?" he added, glancing over at his colleague in mock horror.

I shook my head. "No, I don't think we did."

Clearly, he had no idea, no idea that I was Ottoline's former maid.

"Feels like a lifetime ago, eh? And I imagine it'll be very strange for you to go back there."

"Yes, it will. But I'm in no hurry."

And then I took the plunge, for my mother and for me: "How is Arabella?"

His eyes widened. "You know my daughter?"

And as the room closed in, as I realized and knew at last, I heard my voice—steady, calm: "We were born the same month, only a few days apart . . . in August 1890."

A smile flickered. He said, "It's a wretched thing, having one's only child living on the other side of the world. Arabella's been in Malaya for almost ten years. She has three boys now, you know . . . Grand little chaps, all very . . . But tell me, how did you meet?"

I shook my head. "We never met. I simply know *of* her."

"Ah, I see. Mutual acquaintances?"

"No, not really . . . Not until now."

Confusion clouded his eyes. He glanced to Mr. Jacobson, then back at me. And then he smiled and said, "Well, all I can tell you is that my daughter is . . . happy. She has a husband who loves her, and she adores being a mother."

"Being a mother is indeed a privilege. Unfortunately, it was a privilege my own mother was unable to enjoy."

Mr. Jacobson spoke. "We have that loss in common, Mrs. Gibson. And it is surely the worst."

"Yes, the worst, and all the more grievous when one knows that it has been caused by a broken heart," I said.

And as Theodore Godley stared back at me, silence fell over the oak-paneled room, and a bolt of sunlight illuminated the dust-filled air between us. And for a moment, just a moment, I thought I sensed my mother's presence.

But our business was done, and I had said my piece. I put on my gloves and stood up. The gentlemen both rose to their feet. Theodore Godley came round the desk, and altering tempo, regaining control, he laughed and said, "So, does little Ottoline know anything of her inheritance?"

"She's known as Lila—and no, she doesn't."

"Lila? That's an unusual abbreviation of the name if you don't mind me saying."

"Yes, not like Charlotte and Lottie . . . Not like that," I said, staring once more into those kind brown eyes.

And I saw it happen, saw the circles close one within another, the pieces come together: the name Charlotte Gibson, the remembrance of the young maid at his house on Cheyne Walk in Chelsea, the unwanted pregnancy, the suicide, the half-forgotten potential scandal that had once threatened to topple his marriage, reputation and career. Buried for three decades, it all surfaced now, on a sun-filled and seemingly ordinary October morning.

Mr. Jacobson broke the spell. "Mr. Godley?"

Theodore Godley took my hand. He held it firmly in both of his. Then, in a quiet voice, one weighted by convention and respectability, he said, "I hope you'll keep in touch, Mrs. Gibson. And any questions you might have—any questions at all—please do not hesitate. I am here for you—at your service. Always."

I walked out with my head high. I had finally met my father. Met him, looked him in the eye and reminded him. And that was enough. After all, I was thirty years old and had, I thought—as I walked down the pavement—done quite all right without him. And yet, he had not been at all how I'd imagined. For my mother's doomed and illicit love—and the timing of her death—had not only made him a villainous caricature but also frozen him in time. I had envisaged someone younger, and arrogant; a *ladies' man*, a charmer, an identifiable philanderer. But he was none of these things, and if circumstances had been different, I might have called him a gentleman.

As I stood at the bus stop, the synchronicity of it all struck me again. For Theodore Godley had been at Delnasay; our paths had been destined and had already crossed; and though he would be looking after his granddaughter's interests, and mine, though I might at some stage in the future have to meet with him again, I would never need to say anything more. Any future dealings with the man would be of a business nature, I decided.

And then I thought of my mother, and I saw things differently. It was not a momentary lapse; it had been a planned and premeditated ending. She had waited to give birth to me before killing herself. Knowing she could never be with the man she loved, the father of her child, thinking the circumstances of her life were to be fixed in ignominy, Charlotte—my mother, *sweet Lottie* to some—had elected not to continue with this life. And on that August evening so golden, as she walked into the water, before she lowered herself into the high tide, she must have looked across the river, toward the lamp-lit windows of Cheyne Walk where another woman had recently given birth to a legitimate child, one whose name would be Godley.

But I, too, had Godley blood running through my veins, and perhaps I was more like *him* than her—for I could never abandon my child. And yet I had to forgive her, my mother; I had to let her go, release myself from the burden of her rejection. And so I decided there and then that my mother was from that day a complete and finished part of the past. And as I stood at the bus stop, as the traffic passed by, churning up dust, I closed my eyes to a woman I'd never known. I closed my eyes to a woman I had for a lifetime longed for and missed.

As for my half sister, Arabella, she had only ever been a vision, a fantasy: the whispered notion of a more perfect version of me.

The legitimate, educated, accomplished and loved version. I would in all likelihood never know whether my Arabella was the real Arabella. But I was pleased to know that she was happy and, stranger still, that she had known Theodore Godley as a father. And yet the scales of the Universe had decreed some rebalancing— of proximity, at least, for I was the one in his orbit, and I knew something of my future lay in his hands.

Initially, the only thing I'd told Leo was that Ottoline had left me some money; a small amount, I'd said. But he had gone on and on: "Fifty? . . . A hundred? . . . Come on, tell me, how much?"

Eventually, and just to shut him up, I said, "Thirty-five. Thirty-five pounds."

"*Thirty-five pounds* . . . She could easily have afforded to leave you a bit more than that."

So, later that day, after my meeting with Theodore Godley, when I met Leo at the usual place—the pub round the corner from work—and he asked, "How did it go?" I said, "Fine, all tickety-boo."

"Did you get your money?"

"Oh yes," I said, sipping my gin and orange. "It goes into an account tomorrow."

"Hark you. An account, eh? And all for thirty-five quid," he added, laughing.

I smiled. "How is your mother?"

"A little better . . . but it's up and down, as you know."

"Very up and down," I said. "The doctors must be alarmed by just how up and down she is . . ."

"Old people do linger."

"A bit like wives."

He stared back at me. "I wouldn't know about that," he said, smooth as velvet.

I smiled. "I think you do."

My colleague Mary had confirmed what Amy thought, and what deep down I had known for some time.

"I really don't want to be the one to have to tell you," Mary had begun, "but I think you ought to know—especially after what you went through with Henry. The thing is, well, it's Mr. Holland. He's married, you see . . . Has a wife up in Manchester . . . and well, what with him taking you out and not coming clean, a few of us . . . Well, we decided you should know."

Pride kicked in once again. And I pretended to Mary—dear sweet Mary, with her soft heart and good intentions. I said, "Oh, but we are not an *item*, you know. No, not at all . . . His poor wife is an invalid, and we simply drown our sorrows together, Mary, nothing more. Good gracious, we are not *courting* . . ."

Her relief went some way to assuage the guilt of my duplicity. And when she rolled her eyes, shook her head and said, "Well, what are we like, eh? We got that one wrong," I laughed.

"And what do you mean by that?" asked Leo now, pulling at his collar, his chest puffed up—all ready for a great debate, a fight to clear his name.

"Please, let's not lie anymore," I said—and once again I was taken aback by the steadiness of my voice. "We've both lied . . . both of us. You have a wife you didn't tell me about, but one who is alive and exists. And I have a husband I *have* told you about, but a husband who never was."

"You're making no sense . . . I don't know what you're talking about."

"Yes, you do. You're married, Leo. You have a wife. That's why you go back to Manchester . . . not because of any frail mother."

He looked around, took a moment; then he turned back to me and said, "And you—you were *never* married?"

I shook my head. "Never."

"No man who fell at Gallipoli?"

"None."

"But Henry—you described him so well."

"My grandfather."

"And I thought you were so dignified," he said, laughing now.

"And I knew I wasn't . . . *Quid pro quo*," I added, remembering one of Stanley Morton's Latin terms.

"So that's it—we're finished?"

"Of course we're finished." I looked down at Ralph's ring. "I may have lied, but I only lied to protect my daughter. It was never my intention to hurt anyone . . . And just because I invented a husband doesn't mean I'm happy to be a lie myself. I'm not prepared to be anyone's mistress."

"That's rich—considering you were someone's tart once, and long before me."

"You're right," I said, raising my eyes to him. "I was someone's mistress, briefly."

"And what if I tell you that you have been again?"

"I tell you I'm worth more than that."

"More than thirty-five quid?"

I stared at him, his thin smile and lying eyes. And I was tempted to throw my gin and orange in his face. But I didn't. Instead, I stood up, and as I put on my gloves and picked up my bag, I said, "Actually, you may as well know . . . It wasn't thirty-five *quid*; it's thirty-five thousand. That's what Ottoline left us—Lila and me— thirty-five thousand pounds." I was about to walk away, when I remembered Delnasay. "Oh, and also a castle in Scotland."

I wished I'd had a camera, because his face really was a picture.

Chapter Twenty-five

I wasn't sure what Leo would do after our meeting that day. I half wondered if he'd appear at my door, or come and find me in the store. But he didn't. And I realized I'd made it difficult for him by telling him about Ottoline's bequests. He might have been a charlatan, but he was also a proud man, and I knew the term *adulterer* was enough without the tawdry addition of *opportunist*.

Nor had I been sure about what to do regarding my job at the store. It seemed reckless—imprudent, Rodney would say—to give it up. Jobs were hard to come by, particularly jobs like mine—clean work, with regular hours and the added benefits of a free lunch and staff discount. But with so many unemployed and in need of work, it felt wrong to be paid money I didn't need—and for a job I didn't even enjoy. So I handed in my notice.

I knew all too well how a fool and his money were soon parted; and though I now had *it*, I wasn't sure what to do with it, how best to use it. And I could have done with Leo Holland's professional advice, but there was no way I was going to ask him, or Theodore Godley. And so I wondered if Amy might know of someone able to advise me.

"Every lady's maid's dream," she said when I told her of my conundrum. "But good for her, I say. She didn't forget you, Pearl— or Lila."

We were sitting in the staff dining room, a place I'd avoided for a number of days for fear of running into Leo. And I hadn't mentioned figures; I'd simply told Amy that Ottoline had left Lila and me a nice sum, and that I needed advice.

"It's not a problem I've ever had myself," said Amy, smiling. "Though I don't suppose I'd have too much trouble spending anything that came my way . . . But you're very sensible, you know, in adopting such a cautious approach."

"But do you know of anyone?" I asked again.

"Well, I can think of one chap." Her eyes twinkled. "He works here in accounts . . . and I've gotten to know him quite well," she added.

"Not Leo Holland?"

"Yes! Do you know him?"

I didn't answer her question. I took a moment, and then I said, "How well do you know him, Amy?"

She smiled. "Let's just say we have a friendship."

"A friendship? Has he taken you out?"

She nodded. Then she leaned over the table. "I didn't tell you because I haven't been seeing him long, only a few weeks," she whispered. "And please keep it quiet. He says it wouldn't do for it to get out. Not with him being in management and, you know, all

those rules about fraternizing. Anyway, he's as straight as a die—
well, you have to be in that job, but I can ask him if you'd like."

"No. I don't want you to ask him," I said quickly. "In fact, I'd
rather you didn't mention my name or anything at all about me
to him."

Her expression changed. She said, "Is there a particular reason?"

I looked away from her, across the packed room. And that was
when I caught sight of him—or rather, the back of his head—
seated next to a palm at the table reserved for management in the
large alcove. A wife in Manchester, me, Amy . . . I wondered how
many more he'd tricked. Then I stared at Amy.

"Come on, dear . . . You're getting me worried now." She opened
her cigarette case, and I watched her place the cigarette in the
holder and light it.

"If I knew something—something bad—about Leo Holland,
would you want to know?"

"Of course I would."

"Think, Amy, because not everyone does. Some prefer to live
in ignorance."

At first she didn't say anything; she kept her eyes fixed on me as
she raised a now shaky cigarette holder to her lips. Then, "I would
most certainly want to know. Yes, I would want you to tell me," she
said, and exhaled a thick plume of smoke.

"Are you in love with him?" I asked.

"I'm not sure."

"Then you're not. You see, you know when you're in love."

And it made it easier, I thought, bracing myself. But she beat
me to it.

"You're going to tell me he's married, aren't you?"

I nodded.

"Manchester?"

I nodded again.

She glanced away from me. "*Bastard,*" she hissed. "Lying bloody bastard." Then she turned to me. "But how do you know?" she asked. "*No,* don't tell me. Don't tell me. I can guess . . . Yes, I can guess."

"I think we may have overlapped, you and me. And who knows—maybe others as well."

She stared at me. "That friend of yours, the one having the affair, Ellie what's-her-name—it was you, wasn't it?"

"I'm sorry. I don't know why I lied, why I didn't tell you . . . I suppose I felt ashamed, embarrassed."

She lowered her eyes. "*Men* . . . What is it with them?"

I didn't say anything.

She sighed heavily as she stubbed out her cigarette, decapitating it in the ashtray; then she shook her head and laughed. "You know what? I can't bloody wait to see him."

"You don't have to—he's over there."

Where I had held back, Amy did not. She rose to her feet, stalked across to the palmed alcove, the management table, and in a voice loud enough to silence the entire room, she said, "I'm so pleased to find you and your colleagues here, Mr. Holland. You see, it saves me the bother of having to go up to the sixth floor to inform them that you're a *cheat,* an *adulterer* and a *liar.*"

The gasps were audible. A few people had already risen to their feet. And as others dropped cutlery, craning their necks to peer round into the alcove, Leo Holland tried to stand up, too. But Amy pushed him back down. Then she picked up a bowl of something with custard and tipped it into his lap. "Enjoy your pudding," she said, and walked out of the dining room.

For a moment or two the hush continued. Then, as people sat back down, and amidst murmuring and whispering, and as someone emerged from the kitchens with an armful of towels, I picked up my own bag and Amy's and made for the powder room.

There, Amy and I grabbed hold of each other. We winced, screamed and laughed. And then—newly serious—Amy said, "That'll be it for me. But I don't care if I'm sacked. He had to have his comeuppance."

"And your revenge was indeed *sweet*," I said, and we both giggled again at the thought of Leo Holland's custard-covered crotch.

It was only a short while later, I discovered, that Amy was summoned to the sixth floor. There, she was interviewed by two very senior managers, Mr. Selfridge's right and left hands, she said. She told them what they almost certainly already knew: that Leo Holland was married. And then she told them what they almost certainly did not know: that he had actively pursued, lied to and seduced a number of female employees. She refused to give any names on grounds of confidentiality, and played her final hand well, assuring the two men that she would not go to the newspapers with such a damaging story. That was the clincher, she said.

And it was. For in the absence of war, certain newspaper editors seemed to be desperate and trawling the gutters for stories. And there was a new sort of magazine, salacious gossip and scandal its only interest, and what they couldn't find, they invented. But certainly, within the store it was quite the talking point for a few days, and the rumors were rife and grew out of all proportion to the truth: Mr. Holland had defrauded the company, was a bigamist and had seduced dozens of female staff. I was almost tempted to feel sorry for the man, Leo Holland; a man I had allowed into my bed and introduced to my daughter. He had lost his job and returned to Manchester, I heard on the grapevine. But I hoped Amy was right, and that, having been served his comeuppance, he had learned something and would never again trick another woman.

The same day I finished at the store, Amy was promoted to manager of the French Salon. After work, we went out for a drink to celebrate. It was a Friday evening, and the pub round the corner was packed, too noisy to hear ourselves speak—even in the saloon bar. So we quickly moved on, to "somewhere more civilized," Amy said, a hotel off Bond Street she had once been to with Leo.

We sat on a plush velvet couch in the cocktail bar, and when the waiter came up, Amy put on a voice and asked for the wine list. She pored over it for some time, then ordered two glasses of something called *hyse wayte*. As the waiter walked off, as she rifled in her bag for her cigarette case, she whispered to me that gin and orange was a bit common—all right in pubs perhaps, but not in posh places.

I whispered back, "Well, now you're in management, Miss Patrick, it really wouldn't do for you to be seen doing anything common . . . And I'm sure public houses are a thing of the past. It'll be cocktail bars and posh places for you from now on."

She threw back her head and laughed. Then, after she lit her cigarette, she said, "Seriously, isn't it strange to think that not so very long ago we couldn't have done this?"

"You mean coming out for a drink—*unaccompanied?*"

"Yes! My father would turn in his grave to think of me entering a public house—or even sitting here in this bar with you."

I nodded. "My aunt, too. She'd think we needed rescuing."

The waiter placed our wine on the table; we clinked glasses. "To a new era," said Amy.

"You know, the first time I ever got drunk was at Delnasay. Just after I met you."

"*No.*"

"It was my birthday. I was twenty-four. They organized a party for me . . . champagne," I said, remembering as I glanced across the softly lit room.

"Champagne in the servants' hall?"

"No, I was with Ottoline, and Billy, and Felix Cowper . . . and Ralph."

"Ralph? Now remind me again—which one was he?"

"He was Ottoline's cousin . . . the painter."

"Ah, the one from India—the one mentioned in dispatches?"

I nodded. "He didn't stay at the house. Preferred to stay at a cottage on the estate."

"So where exactly *was* this little soiree?"

I looked at her and smiled. "That's funny. That's what he called it—a soiree. A soiree with a few reprobates."

"Who?"

"Ralph."

She leaned toward me. "You've gone a bit misty-eyed, if you don't mind me saying . . . Were you frightfully smitten?" she asked, sounding more like one of them than us.

Vaguely, I nodded.

"Don't tell me you were in love with him?"

I didn't say anything. Amy was my friend, and yet I still hadn't told her about Ralph. Like everyone else, she believed I'd been married to a man called Henry. A man who'd died in the war.

"If you don't wish to tell me, that's fine. We all have our little secrets," she said.

But it wasn't a little secret. It was a once-gaping wound that had, over time, scabbed and healed, and then left a scar—hidden from view. And it was, along with my mother's suicide and her abandonment of me, something pushed down so deep that it was terrifying to contemplate speaking of.

So I shrugged. "It was nothing," I said. "A little flirtation, that's all."

But Amy, wily Amy, must have seen something in my eyes, or heard it in my voice. Because the atmosphere in the bar changed, and when a man sat down at the piano and began to play something familiar—something sad and familiar—Amy offered me a cigarette. And as I took it, as she held out her lighter, as I raised my eyes to hers, she said, "It was him, wasn't it? Ralph was *the one*—not Henry."

I'm not sure what I said first, what order it all came out in, but over the next hour—and another glass of wine—Amy heard everything. She was the first person I'd told, and the relief was immense. To say his name, be able to talk about him at last—my love, my one and only experience of real love—was extraordinary, liberating and cathartic.

Eventually, I said, "So that's it. And now you know."

Amy sat in silence for a while. Then she reached over the table, took hold of my hand and squeezed it. "Dear Pearl, you've been through so much . . . so much more than I ever knew. But at least you've known real love."

And at that moment I felt guilty. I realized how much I'd had by comparison. Because Amy was right: I had known love, real love; and I had my daughter—the living embodiment of that love. And what did she have? Oh, she had a title at work—and, unlike me, that meant a lot to her—but she had little else. And she had already admitted, accepted the fact, that she would probably never marry or have children. "Not enough men to go round," she'd said, without any trace of self-pity.

And it was true. No matter how cruel it seemed, there probably weren't—simply couldn't be—enough men to go round. Those who had survived, and who were fit and able, had their pick of bright young things, younger women—gay with unspent energy, untarnished by deprivation and loss. We Victorian daughters were destined to be the wallflowers. Even then, I think we knew that.

Later that evening, as we linked arms and walked back onto Oxford Street, toward the bus stop, Amy said, "To be honest, I'm a bit fed up with love. I suppose it's been all the waiting . . . Waiting since I was sixteen, seventeen—whatever. Now it just makes me angry. It makes me so angry, Pearl, to know that I've waited for nothing, that the man I was destined for was probably killed in the war."

Amy's bus came first, and as it approached, she said, "Are you going to the funeral?"

"Funeral? Whose funeral?"

"The soldier they're bringing back from France. The *unknown* soldier."

Myrtle wasn't bothered. It would be too crowded anyway, she said; there'd be nothing to see. So it was agreed; she'd come a little earlier to look after Lila.

The procession was to begin at Victoria station, where the soldier's body had arrived the previous day and had been guarded overnight. From there, it was to head via Whitehall—where the King would be, and the new monument unveiled—to Westminster Abbey for burial.

It was shortly after seven when I walked out into the pale morning light. I followed the others on foot, silent and solemn, some carrying wreaths and flowers, all of us dressed in black. Heading east and then southward toward Belgravia, picking up more on the way. At intervals, the throng thinned and then swelled again, some heading for the Mall, Trafalgar Square and Whitehall. I went in the direction of Parliament Square and Westminster Abbey, where Amy had said she'd be and look out for me.

I heard the gun salute signaling the start of the procession, and nearer the abbey, where the crowd bulged and thickened, policemen and soldiers lined the roadside. A few people tried to get ahead, elbowing their way forward as others called out after them about *pushing in*. Using a megaphone, a policeman asked for respect, and seeing the look of alarm on the face of an elderly woman walking alongside me, I took her arm. The policeman must have seen her panic, too, and perhaps thought we were together, because he came forward and led us both through the crowd to a spot opposite a door to the abbey.

For almost two hours, I watched and waited. I listened to the intermittent chatter around me, the speculation as to the identity of the soldier—for whom we had all shaken out our mothballed mourning clothes and traveled miles to pay our respects. And I, too, wondered who he was—this soldier all of London and beyond had come together for. Was it little Harry Rankin? Or one of Mrs. Lister's boys? Or was he Billy Campbell? Or Ralph? It was a soldier who'd fallen in the early days of the war, someone said. But what were *the early days*—the first weeks, first months or first years? And did it matter—when and who and how? In death, he belonged to every one of us.

Toward eleven, the chatter abated, and there came the muffled sound of drums and the heartbreaking strains of a funeral march. Then, the clip-clop of hooves brought into view the gun carriage, borne by six black stallions and carrying the flag-draped coffin. Alongside it walked the pallbearers, those field marshals and generals who'd escaped death—in the fight *for King and Country*. And following the cortège, there came the man himself, the King, and behind him, a sea of uniformed ex-servicemen.

Someone nudged me. "See that one over there? That's Field Marshal Haig, that is."

I knew the name, of course, but I had no idea to which of the uniformed men he referred. They all looked the same—and all equally guilty.

I watched the coffin as it was lifted onto medaled shoulders, and as Big Ben began to strike eleven, I heard someone quietly sobbing. And I realized it was me.

Chapter Twenty-six

The year 1921 was certainly going to be different: I had no job, but I didn't need one; I had no man, but I didn't need one. Instead, I had money and plans. And I had my daughter, and Amy.

It was Amy who accompanied Lila and me when we went to look over a house in Putney early that year; Amy who witnessed my signature on the leasehold. But before that, and perhaps more important, it was my father, Theodore Godley, who looked over the lease.

I had received a Christmas card from him, an address on Cheyne Walk printed beneath the handwritten *With Very Best Wishes, Theodore G.* At first, the card and sight of his name had unsettled and irked me. Did he really think we could be friends— or that I would ever address him as Theodore? The man was more presumptuous than I'd thought. He would remain Mr. Godley, and there could be no Christmas card in return.

However, curiosity got the better of me, and not long after Christmas, I found myself standing outside that address. It was a murky afternoon and the traffic along the Embankment moved slowly. Blackened coal barges sounded their horns on the Thames, and beyond them, across the river, the vague outline of St. Mary's Church, where my mother and Kitty lay, rose up in the gloom. So close, I thought. And moving my eyes to the Albert Bridge, following the pavement back toward the fine redbrick house, and me, I imagined my mother's hurried tread.

But I did not go to the door that day. Instead, I walked home. Only later, when Amy sensibly suggested I should have a lawyer look over the leasehold, did my thoughts once again turn to Theodore Godley. For a few days I pondered, working through the potential ramifications, the turmoil and disturbance it might cause to my newfound equilibrium. But Amy was right: I needed advice— and I knew no one else.

I stepped from the cold winter's night into the warm hallway. A maid took my coat, hat and gloves. She showed me to the first-floor drawing room, told me, "Mr. Godley won't be long." And I could hear his mellow tones, strangely warm, drifting up from a room below.

And the place was exactly as I'd pictured it: filled with polished antiques and gilt-framed paintings. A woman upon a gray mare peered down at me from above the black marble fireplace. She sat sidesaddle, dressed in an old-fashioned riding habit, with a top hat, and a sprig of white heather pinned to the lapel of her jacket. I stared at her haughty expression—her smile that wasn't quite a smile, her dark eyes—which seemed so knowingly fixed upon me. But I was nervous, and my imagination was playing tricks on me, because there was something uncannily familiar about her mouth, her nose and even the shape of the eyes.

"Do you see . . . see the resemblance?"

I turned to Theodore Godley and made a point of shaking my head.

"*Really?* But you look so like her."

"Who is she?" I asked.

"Your grandmother. Georgiana Godley."

He moved over to a table, a silver tray with a decanter, and poured something into two glasses. Then he came and stood next to me. And as he handed me a glass, I asked, "Where is that place?"

"Ireland."

"You grew up there?"

"No, but my mother did. I grew up in Somerset."

"I've always wanted to visit Somerset."

He smiled. "I was hoping . . . Well, I'm very pleased you've come."

I wanted to tell him that my call was strictly business. I wanted to say that I had come to him only to ask if he'd look over the document inside my bag. But already we had broken a boundary and crossed over into new and uncharted territory. And any such statement from me would have been disingenuous. With or without any documents, I would have found a reason, an excuse to step inside my father's house.

"Please, do sit down."

I sat. He stood.

I said, "I'd always assumed I looked like my mother. My aunt said I wasn't like her, but . . . Well, I thought that was because of what happened."

"Lottie was fair," he said, frowning and looking down at his shoes. "With pale skin that freckled in summer, a soft voice and serious nature . . ." He paused, glanced up at me. "She was a sensitive soul, overly contemplative . . . and perhaps too principled. And she was bright, very bright, articulate and intelligent, and quite wasted in her role as . . ." He petered out, looking away from me again. "Yes, fair and bright," he whispered.

And thus, the shape of my mother finally emerged. And I realized that my vision, my fantasy, the more perfect version of me—the earnest girl with pale skin and a soft, whispering voice—was not Arabella Godley; it was and always had been my mother.

He sat down. "When did you first learn about me?" he asked.

"I'm not sure. I suppose the first clue was when I found the announcement of Arabella's birth among my aunt's possessions. But that was a long time ago . . . and for some reason I became fixated on her name and not yours."

"And I had no idea."

"No idea about me? Or about my mother and what happened to her?"

"I knew she'd passed away," he said, staring into his glass.

"She didn't *pass away*; she killed herself. Drowned herself—out there in the river," I added, gesturing to the window.

"Yes."

"And what about me? Did you know? Did you not know she'd given birth to a daughter only hours before she took her own life?"

He ignored my question. He rose to his feet and said, "It's important that you know I cared about her. I cared about her very much."

I bit my tongue. Already I was angry. I wanted to shout, to say again, *And what about me? Did you not know? Did you not care?*

But in the hour that followed, I said little. Instead, I listened as Theodore Godley told me more about my mother. He had employed her as a parlormaid, and she had been with him for almost a year when he married, by which time they had given in to what he called *a rare chemistry*. The affair had stopped around the time of his marriage, but not my mother's employment. And perhaps that was the mistake, he suggested. Because the affair began again not long after.

"I was an adulterer. I was weak. I betrayed my wife, my wedding vows. But Lottie . . . Well, she was special, beautiful inside and out." He paused, sighed loudly; put down his glass, and then picked it up again. "When she told me she was expecting a child, my child, I went into shock. I panicked." He shook his head. "But I assured her I'd help—financially."

"But it wasn't enough."

"No. And she was right. She deserved more."

"And so?"

"And so . . . she resigned from my employ. I came back one day and found out. Later that same evening, I confessed everything to Diana—my wife."

"And she forgave you."

"Forgiveness takes time. Has to be earned. But yes, over time I regained my wife's trust, and love."

He had paced about the room, intermittently sitting down and then rising back to his feet as he spoke. Now he sat down once more. He said, "It was then, during that time, I learned about my wife, who she really was . . . Yes, I think that's when I truly began to love her. You see, her reaction was not as I'd anticipated. Her perspective was different. Her main concern was Lottie, her well-being, and the well-being of her unborn child," he added, glancing at me. "She spoke about *our* predicament, *our* moral duty . . . as though my transgression were something she had a share in, had played a part in. The child's future had to involve us both, she said."

"What did she mean by that?"

He smiled. "She meant exactly what she said. That she wished to be involved—to know you."

I said nothing. He went on. "So, one evening, a few days later, I went to your grandfather's house. He wouldn't allow me inside, to see or speak to Lottie . . . He called me an arrogant toff; told me he'd like to string me up. And I didn't blame him."

"Henry," I said, imagining the scene.

"Yes, Henry Gibson . . . I explained to him that my wife knew everything, that we had talked it all through and that it was our wish for Lottie's child—my child—to grow up in our home, be part of our family."

It was time for me to pace. I rose from my chair. "What did he say?"

"Only that he'd have to talk to his sister."

I turned to him. "Did you meet her—Kitty?"

"No, not that night, but I later did. It was Kitty who told me what had happened—to Lottie. She came to my office . . . Came all the way to the city to tell me in person," he added, wincing at the memory.

"And your offer—your offer to take me in? What was said about that?"

He stared at me. "Kitty told me the child had died."

I shook my head. "But I don't understand. Why—why would she tell you that?"

"I've pondered on this a great deal since you came to my office. And you're right; it makes no sense. Not until one remembers your great-aunt's situation."

I sat down. "Her situation?"

"Her childlessness. You see, I can only conclude that she simply wasn't prepared to give you up, to part with you."

My father kissed my hands and asked me to forgive him, then saw me into a taxicab. But the only person I thought of on that short journey home was Kitty. And the only person I thought of as I lay in my bed later that night was Kitty: God-fearing, honest and abstemious Kitty. My beacon, my light; a woman whose example I could never live up to. She had kept me for herself and invented a lie, a lie that had lasted seventeen years and taken another thirteen to uncover. That night, her betrayal seemed so great that I hated her—and I cursed her out loud, because I could have had a different life, I thought; I could have been someone.

The next day, my thoughts and emotions shifted and settled. Forgiveness began to creep in. I realized that without Kitty, I wouldn't be *me*. There would be no Pearl, Kitty's *precious pearl*. I would never have gone into service; never have known Ottoline, or Ralph. Never have had Lila.

A few weeks later, shortly before Easter, I moved in to my new home in Putney. Amy helped me choose the furnishings. She helped me paint my new sitting room pink and my bedroom gold, and when I asked her if she'd like to move out of her Maida Vale lodgings and live with us, she did.

At around the same time, I began voluntary work at a home for ex-servicemen situated nearby. Each afternoon, I wheeled a trolley of books through the wards and convalescent rooms, helping the men to select something, and then later, after my rounds, reading to those who'd lost their sight or for whatever reason found it difficult to hold a book or focus. It was infinitely more rewarding than selling overpriced brassieres, and I enjoyed it immensely. I made a note of anything requested that we didn't have, and others— mainly classic novels—I thought should be there.

Almost every day I arrived laden with books—until the trolley was too small for the collection and Matron suggested I shouldn't bring in any more. But then, happily, someone called Ellie Brook donated a bigger trolley: a proper library trolley with shelves so that the men were better able to survey the titles. And she kindly sent a fine selection of English novels with it, including many of the works of Dickens, Hardy, Trollope, Eliot, Austen and the Brontës. We were all very grateful to Miss Brook, particularly those men who thirsted for escape.

I couldn't help it; I had my favorites and had ended up on a first-name basis with a few. But there was one, a youngish man whom face burns had disfigured and who had lost both legs. He refused any books—and never spoke; simply shook his head each time I wheeled the trolley toward him. He stared out from his bath chair, which was always situated by a window. And I had been there for some time when I heard the matron say his name and realized.

I never said anything, never acknowledged that we'd met or had known each other before, and, at first, neither did he. But one day, after I'd persuaded him to allow me to read him some poetry, and without looking at me, without so much as turning to me, he said, "We know each other, don't we?"

I nodded. "Yes."

"Scotland, wasn't it? . . . Delnasay?"

"Yes."

"Do you still see her, Ottoline?" he asked.

I hesitated. "No, not anymore."

"Well, if you do, if you do happen to meet with her, don't tell her. Please, don't tell her about me. I wouldn't want her to see me like this. You understand, don't you?"

"Of course, Mr. Cowper."

I didn't want to leave, not even for a few weeks, but I had—as I say—made plans. So I called on Myrtle Dalby and asked if she'd be prepared to cover for the duration of my *holiday*. Like me, she was a bookish sort, and in the absence of any other work, and with the added incentive of a few shillings *and* travel expenses, she agreed.

I had delayed my trip for long enough—and mainly because of Lila's school. But I waited a little while longer, until the first week of June. It was almost the end of term anyway, and my great-aunt who resided in Scotland had taken ill, I told the head teacher; Lila and I were all she had. The following day, Lila, our new spaniel puppy and I climbed into the Lagonda motorcar I'd purchased a few weeks before—and which came with various warranties and an RAC membership. And with windows wound down and the wind in our hair, we headed for the Great North Road.

Chapter Twenty-seven

I have to say, Rodney's bungalow was immaculate—by any standards, but particularly by comparison to the house I'd left Amy in charge of. But as soon as we arrived, as soon as Rodney showed me about the place—with its newly fitted pale-colored carpets—I was worried about our yet-to-be-trained puppy, Sammy, a dog possessed by the spirit of a kangaroo and with no idea of propriety.

"He can sleep in the car."

"Oh, he'll be fine."

"He can sleep in the car."

"Sammy can't sleep in the car, Mummy—he'll be all alone and scared."

"I'm sure he'll be fine," said Rodney again.

I set my alarm. Took Sammy outside minutes after the ringing of each hour.

Rodney's new carpets remained unstained, and after only one

night we journeyed on—playing I Spy and singing old songs like "Pack Up Your Troubles," "Keep the Home Fires Burning," and "After the Ball Is Over." Lila knew them all word for word and sang each one with gusto.

North of Newcastle, and without so much as thinking, I turned off the Great North Road. I picked up the familiar lanes of my memory. I knew each incline and bend, every cottage, copse and tree. And when Lila asked, "Where are we going, Mummy?" I said, "I'm going to show you the place we used to live."

But the gates were closed, chained and padlocked, with a sign: PRIVATE—TRESPASSERS WILL BE PROSECUTED. "I don't like it," said Lila, pulling a face and shaking her head as though she had been asked to taste something unappetizing.

"No, it doesn't look very inviting. But no need for you to get out, darling," I said, turning to her as I tied on my rain cap. "You stay here; I'll take Sammy. We'll only be a minute or two."

I stepped out of the car and into the Northumbrian drizzle. As Sammy ran about the overgrown verge, I walked up to the chained gates and placed my hands on the cold, peeling paint. A sea fret rolled in over the weedy driveway; its damp air diffused the light, coating the stone of the old building and rendering it darker. And as I held the wet iron in my hands, as I stared back at the place—chained, sealed, shuttered and seemingly dead—a queer reverberation took hold of me. I felt a raw stinging on the back of one of my heels, heard the clip-clap of a delivery wagon, and then the faint echo of whistling—someone whistling in the distance.

Sad, silent, forgotten, the place belonged to time now, and I turned away from it and to the small face staring at me through a wet windscreen. It wasn't what I had wanted her to see. But what had I wanted her to see? The place as I had once seen it—as it had been that day I'd arrived in the summer of 1914? Pristine and loved, with velvet striped lawns bathed in dappled light, and windows pulled open and draped in gold, and Rodney, and Ottoline . . . Sweet, fragile Ottoline? Yes, perhaps that's what I had imagined my daughter would somehow see. But like her, I saw only a sad, gloomy place, abandoned and belonging to another era.

"I'm very glad that we don't live here anymore," said Lila as I climbed back into the car and handed her wet dog over to her. "It's horrible, Mummy. It looks like a haunted house."

It did, and it was. But I couldn't give up.

And so from there we drove down the dripping lanes to Mrs. Lister's sister's house. Rodney had given me the address, and we found it easily enough. We left Sammy in the car, for it was a small place with small windows, and so dim and universally brown inside that even Mrs. Lister confided in whispers she liked to spend as little time as possible there. She was, however, delighted to see us, and completely mesmerized by Lila—the baby she had looked after so devotedly.

She served us tea in *the front parlor*, a room so cramped with furniture and china ornamentation that one had to move very carefully and slowly as one squeezed into it, to an antimacassar-covered armchair. Then, without pausing, she brought me up-to-date.

"Mollie Rankin's just had her fourth. Another boy, mind you. But I suppose we need them now. Called her first one Harry, she did. But he had rickets, had to be put on a special diet. And little

Sissy Fender—I think you'll remember her—she married the butcher's boy . . . the one with the spots and funny eyes? And Mrs. Carney—now I don't think you ever met her—she's working for a titled family in Yorkshire. Big house. Huge place, she says. John was killed, of course. She says they've had such trouble with servants, they're going to try having all men now. Well, I suppose you have to do something . . ."

As Mrs. Lister went on, Lila kept springing up, to look and see and touch, and my heart leaped into my cake-filled mouth, and I heard myself saying, just like one of those mothers in Fenwick department store, "*Please*, do sit down . . . Do sit still."

"Oh, let her have a look," said Mrs. Lister, smiling, enchanted. "Those are *my* dolls," she said. "I've been collecting them since before I got married."

I could tell Lila liked the china-faced dolls. And I could see that Mrs. Lister could tell, too.

"Which one's your favorite, pet?" Mrs. Lister asked Lila.

Lila thought for a moment, then pointed to one.

"Ah yes, she's lovely, isn't she?"

Lila nodded. "She looks like a princess."

"And you know, she probably was, pet—oh yes, she probably was."

Lila turned to me. "Can we stay here, Mummy?"

"No. We can't—we have to get on."

"You could, you know," said Mrs. Lister, glancing about her and wondering how it might be done.

"No, really, that's very kind of you. But we have the dog, and I have a reservation at a hotel at Berwick."

"Ooh, Berwick indeed!" said Mrs. Lister, as though the border town were the French Riviera. "Well, I can't compete with
that."

"I don't want to go to Berwick," said Lila. "I want to stay here."

I smiled at Mrs. Lister, already tearful. And then I rose to my
feet.

It was too many cakes and biscuits and all those china dolls, I
thought as I finally got Lila into the car. But Mrs. Lister hadn't
made it easy, and now, as she bent down and tapped at the passenger window, blowing kisses to Lila, and as I tried to say good-bye
to her, she suddenly said, "Hold your horses a minute," and scurried
back into the cottage.

She emerged a few moments later with something shrouded in
a linen tea towel, and I had an idea what it was. She opened the
car door, lifted the towel and placed the doll in Lila's eager hands.
"That's from me to you, my pet," she said, wrapping her arms about
Lila and shedding tears into her hair.

As we drove away, as Lila held her doll and looked back at Mrs.
Lister—standing in the middle of the road and waving the towel
in her hand—she sobbed. And I was surprised and unnerved by
the strength of her emotion. I handed her my handkerchief; I said,
"Sweetheart, why are you so upset?"

"Because she was lovely . . . That's all."

I nodded. She was; had always been. And as Lila's tears abated,
as she settled and then fell asleep, I decided I'd write a letter that
very night. After all, Mrs. Lister did not like her sister's house, and
a summer in the Highlands with Lila, Rodney and me might be just
the ticket.

∾

We set off from Perth early and before lunchtime drew up outside the village store. When I emerged with our groceries, the first person I saw—the first person I recognized and remembered—was Mr. McNiven. With a hand pressed up to the window, he peered into the car, at the dashboard. Another motoring enthusiast, I thought, for even when I spoke—addressed him by name—he seemed more interested in the machine than in me. When he eventually turned, I could tell he didn't know me, and why would he? But after I jogged his memory, he shook my hand so vigorously, I thought my arm might drop off. And as Lila skipped about the pavement with Sammy—the dog yapping excitedly and jumping up at the piece of shortbread in Lila's hand—Mr. McNiven offered me his belated condolences, and then asked about Delnasay.

It was ours, I told him—nodding my head in the direction of Lila. Well, that was good, he said, because there had been rumors, lots of rumors. In fact, he himself had heard that the place had been sold to Germans, and his brother had heard it was to be turned into a hotel. No, I assured him, that was not going to happen. And then I was honest and told him that though I wasn't sure how much time Lila and I would spend at the house, it would certainly not be sold. That was most reassuring also, he said, because the whole area was changing with new people—many of them *foreigners*—coming in, buying up places going cheap, and all of them with too much money and queer ideas. At least I think that's what he said.

As he spoke, the woman who had served me inside the shop

appeared in the doorway. She stood with her arms folded as I tried to reassure Mr. McNiven once more. "The old butler, Mr. Watts? And also the former cook—Mrs. Lister?" I said, trying to jog his memory. "They'll be joining me soon . . . I'm sure you'll remember them when you see them."

"Aye, well, good luck to you," said McNiven grimly, watching me as I opened the boot of the car and placed the groceries inside.

"I'm sure we'll be fine, Mr. McNiven," I said, slamming the boot shut.

Then the woman spoke. She said, "They came back, you know, the Campbells—after the war. But only the once . . . only the one time."

I nodded. Rodney had told me he had returned to Delnasay with Hector and Ottoline the summer after the war's end. But Ottoline hadn't been well enough to entertain any houseguests, and returning there had not been a good idea. The place had been *too* quiet, held too many memories, he said.

"Aye, it's a sad thing for such a bonnie place to have been deserted," muttered McNiven, watching Lila and scratching his beard. "And not a living soul within its walls for two years."

"Och, that's not strictly true, Fraser McNiven," said the woman. "Mr. and Mrs. Baxter have continued to look after the place regardless. Mind you, they'll be anxious to speak with you—to know what's happening," she added, eyeing me.

"Yes, of course."

I knew I needed to see the couple, the old retainers—the former gamekeeper and his wife—who lived at the gatehouse. I wanted to reassure them, wanted them to stay on.

"And there's him down at the cottage."

I stared at her: "*Him*—at the cottage?"

"Aye, keeps himself to himself. Bit of a recluse—a hermit, isn't he, Fraser?"

"Shell shock, I reckon," murmured McNiven.

"Which cottage?" I asked, looking from him to her.

"The old gamekeeper's place," said the woman. "He's been there for a wee while now. How long would you say?" she asked McNiven.

The man scratched his beard again and drifted into ponderance. Lila skipped toward us with Sammy.

"Bonnie wee thing," said the woman. I wasn't sure if she meant the dog or Lila. "We do deliveries now, you know. You can even telephone in your order."

"Six months? . . . Aye, maybe six," said McNiven.

"Mummy?"

I looked at the woman. She seemed more compos mentis than McNiven—who continued with his calculations and murmurings about months. I said, "The man at the cottage—do you know his name?"

"Och, I wouldn't know that, dearie. He's only come in here the odd time . . . you know, for this and that," she replied, wrinkling her nose.

I turned to McNiven, focusing on his tobacco-stained fingers as he worked them through his gray beard. And despite knowing it was impossible, despite knowing the name had been on a list, a *list of dead*, I still said it: "It's not Mr. Stedman, is it?"

"Now then," said McNiven, holding up a finger, determined not to be hurried, "was he Lady Ottoline's cousin?"

"Yes—Ottoline's cousin. Ralph Stedman." My voice sounded desperate.

McNiven squinted up at the overcast sky; I stepped forward; he shook his head. "No, it's not him. He was killed in the war. And both her sons as well."

"*Mummy!*"

I opened the car door. Lila climbed inside with Sammy.

I raised my hand to McNiven and the woman. Or maybe I raised my hand to no one. Because they had both gone—disappeared by the time I climbed inside the car. And as Lila giggled and covered Sammy with kisses, I stared down at the dashboard, the steering wheel. But my mind had gone blank. I couldn't remember what to do next, how to drive. I heard Lila say, "Come on, Mummy."

I turned to her. "I just need a moment."

She reached over, placed a small sticky hand on mine. Tenderly, she said, "We're nearly there . . . Not too much further now." Words I had said to her for the last two hours.

Then, finally, it came to me: ignition, hand brake, clutch, gearshift and accelerator.

All the way up the street and then on, along the hillside and narrow winding road, I replayed words, over and over. Yes, it was a man. *He*—not she. A hermit, she'd said. Shell shock, he'd said. And then I slowed, and then I stopped. Sure enough, smoke rose from the chimney. The place was inhabited. Someone was there. But *he was killed in the war* . . .

"What are you looking at?" asked Lila, sitting forward and peering through the windscreen.

"Just the view," I said. "Isn't it pretty?"

"I like the sheep," she said. "*Baa!*"

I tried to laugh as we drove on—down the steep hill, over the bridge, through the pillared gateway, toward the castellated gables and oak front door.

"Here we are," I said, coming to a halt.

And I was waiting for her to say, Mummy, *I don't like it*, but instead she said, "Ooh, I like it. Yes, I like this place."

I took the key from the envelope and unlocked the door. Walking back into that place was like walking back into a dream. Nothing had changed. The same boots were lined up on one side of the stone floor; the same tweed cloaks and raincoats hung on the stand; shooting sticks and canes huddled in the compartments beneath them. The walls in the main hallway were still painted yellow, still festooned with stuffed heads, antlers and weapons.

But the Baxters had done a good job, for although the place smelled musty and a little damp, it was surprisingly clean and tidy. I would get rid of the stag heads, and the weapons, I thought as I followed Lila up and down the stairs, as we unpacked the car and carried bags to our rooms, Sammy trailing in and out after us. And I would repaint it all—in time.

I took the bedroom I'd had before, and put Lila's bag in the one next to it. Then I went down to the kitchen and did some reconnaissance, checking out the larder and cupboards. I wiped down the dusty surfaces before I unpacked our groceries; then I made us a meat paste sandwich and sat down at the pine table with Lila.

"It's a bit bigger than home," I said.

"But it has a nice feeling."

"Really? Do you think so?"

"Mm." She nodded, her mouth stuffed full. I waited as she chewed, watching her tiny, sweet jaw. "It doesn't feel *too* big," she said, agreeing with herself and then shaking her head: "Not like that other place."

"Birling?"

"Yes, that place . . . That was a *sad* place."

After lunch, I went to find the Baxters, but there was no one home, and so Lila and I took Sammy for a walk down the valley, following the rough road that ran adjacent to the river and turned into a track, then a path. We walked for an hour or so through sunlit pastures and shaded groves of birch and elder, their branches dipping into the crystal water, until we finally came to the clearing, the spot where Ralph and I had spent our last afternoon together. There we paused, and I sat down and watched Lila as she stood on the grassy bank, staring down into the river.

"Can we come here for a picnic, Mummy?"

And I longed to tell her. I longed to tell her about her father, how it was one of his favorite places, how alive and beautiful he'd been when he'd dived into that water and swum there—the last time I had seen him.

We walked back following the same path, and I watched Lila as I had watched Ralph—striding ahead, from time to time stopping to bend down and examine an insect, a cobweb, or look up at the hills. And as I stared at her long golden hair, hanging loose and already down to her waist, my heart performed an acrobatic flip—once, twice, thrice. Could McNiven be wrong? Could Ralph be alive and living at the cottage? Had he gone back there?

There was only one way to find out. But I couldn't take Lila; I'd have to wait, find someone to mind her for an hour or so. Mrs. Baxter?

But the Baxters were still not at home, and so we returned to the house, removed dust sheets, brought in logs and laid fires. Around five we had tea, and sat outside with it so I could better see the gatehouse and the Baxters' return. Around six, we made a list of everything we needed to buy for the place—and do. And then another: of our five most favorite people in the world. "But only grown-ups, Mummy."

Lila's list ran thus: *Mummy, Sammy, Misses Lister, Amy, Mister Watts, Mertel.*

And mine: *Kitty, Ottoline, Amy, Rodney, Mrs. Lister.* I missed out only one name.

Around seven, I suggested to Lila that she have a little explore of the gardens before bedtime and take Sammy with her. I gave her the whistle I'd bought at the shop. I said, "Don't go far. Stay in the garden, please."

I returned to the kitchen and fiddled about for a time, trying to quell an ever-growing nervous anticipation. Then I went back outside. I'd wait a little while longer, then try the gatehouse again, I thought. And I began pulling at weeds, deadheading the geraniums in the tubs on the step outside the front door. I could hear Lila—out of sight, but somewhere nearby—chastising Sammy for not doing as he was told. I smiled as I turned. The plunging sun was still warm, flickering above the hills and flickering beneath my eyelids when I closed them.

When I saw Mr. McNiven—walking up the gritted driveway,

beneath the trees—I put my hand to my brow. And blinking into the sun, still smiling, I called out, "Hello again!" But nothing came in return. And then, slowly, as my eyes focused, as the figure emerged from the shadows and into the light, I saw that it was not McNiven. The man walking toward me was Ralph.

Chapter Twenty-eight

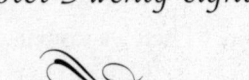

Golden-haired youth had gone, along with a broad-shouldered, muscular frame. It had been replaced with something leaner, more fragile and perhaps finer. A gray beard obscured his features, and yet that gaze, unforgettable and for so long cherished, was as intense as ever. I have no idea how long we stood there, staring at each other without any words. For both of us—and even time itself—seemed to seize up in that instant: Seasons unraveled in backward motion, too many to count. Years froze to seconds. And where and how could we begin? I was different to the girl he'd known in 1914, and he was a changed man.

"The geraniums . . . ," he said at last, looking away from me to them, and without finishing the sentence.

"Yes," I said, as though he had.

Then, after a second or two: "You've had your hair cut."

"Yes."

"It suits you."

"Yes."

"Very *du temps*, as they say in France."

"Do they?"

"*Moderne*."

"Yes, *moderne*. I suppose it is," I said, locked, already lost, and then, reaching for my hair—and something else, something to keep me afloat—I went on. "There's a woman. Well, not a woman. She's more of a girl, really . . . who does it. Does it for me. In London. Where I live. Was living . . . What I mean is, before I came here."

My stumbling was agony, but his eyes crinkled up into a smile, the lines around them etched deep. And because he didn't speak, I continued on in that inane and meaningless staccato. "She's really very good. Not at all expensive. Her mother takes in laundry, you know. And her father, he has—"

"Pearl," he said, interrupting me. And that was all he said. My name. But the sound of it on his lips brought me back to the here and now, and to him.

I said, "I had no idea that you were . . ."

"Alive? Oh yes, still alive—*just*."

"But you were on a list. One from Geneva."

"So I heard. But it was an R. M. Stedman. And I am R. S.," he said, as though I needed reminding.

From the flagstones down onto the grit, I moved. And he, too, took another step—smiling, frowning—as unsure as I was.

Then came Lila's voice: "Mummy . . . Sammy's being *very* naughty."

Ralph turned his head. I watched him take her in.

"He won't come, Mummy . . . and this stupid whistle doesn't work."

Sulky-faced, bored and swinging the whistle about on its long string, Lila walked toward me. She wore the new floral dress I had bought for her at Liberty, violet colored like her eyes; her once white socks hanging about her thin ankles and brown with dust from our walk.

"This is Lila," I said, and then, as she wrapped her arms around me: "Lila, this is Mr. Stedman. He is—*was*—Ottoline's cousin."

"Pleased to meet you," she said, wearily, perfunctorily.

Ralph stared down at her. "And it is a pleasure to meet you, Miss Morton."

"*Morton?*" she repeated, unwrapping herself, wrinkling up her nose and giggling. "I am not Morton . . . I am *Gibson!*"

Ralph glanced at me, already a question in his eyes. I said, "We are Gibson, of course . . . Perhaps you have forgotten."

"I heard otherwise," he replied quickly.

"Morton!" said Lila again, still giggling. "*Who* is Morton?"

"Sweetheart, you really should go and find Sammy, you know."

"Oh, he'll come back," she said, twirling the string and whistle about, staring at Ralph.

"Is Sammy your brother?" Ralph asked her.

Another peal of laughter. "*No*, you silly—"

"Lila!"

She glanced at me—and then she turned and looked at Ralph with new sympathy. "Sammy's only a dog, really."

Ralph slapped his forehead with his hand. "You're right, I am a silly Billy, a complete and utter silly Billy." Lila's expression changed.

She smiled at him in a different way. And I could tell already that she liked him, this disheveled, confused, self-confessed silly Billy called Mr. Stedman. She said, "Don't worry, we all make mistakes—don't we, Mummy?"

I nodded.

"And so tell me, how old are you, Miss Gibson?"

I could tell she liked this also—being addressed as *Miss Gibson*. "Nearly six," she replied, with great emphasis on the number.

"Six," repeated Ralph. "My, that's a lot. That really is quite old."

"But it's two weeks away," she said, turning to me. "It's still two weeks—isn't it, Mummy—till my six birthday?"

"Six*th*," I corrected. "Yes, two weeks."

"You know, I was even born on Midsummer Day," she said proudly.

"*Really?*"

"Yes, and even right here as well . . . Even right here in this place," she added with outstretched arms. "Because my daddy was at the war, you see, and—"

"Lila," I interrupted, "what about Sammy?"

But she wouldn't stop.

"Were you at the war?" she asked Ralph now.

"Yes, I was," he said.

"Did you see my daddy there? He was a painter, wasn't he, Mummy?"

I closed my eyes. Heard Ralph say, "I'm not sure . . . What was his name?"

"Henry Gibson," she said. Then, quieter: "But he died in the *gally-polly*."

I opened my eyes. I couldn't look at Ralph. I knew his gaze was fixed on me. And although it had been quick and unplanned, I was grateful to Lila, for she had in that exchange told him everything he needed to know, and everything I would have struggled to tell him. And Ralph knew only too well about Henry Gibson, my grandfather, who had fought in the Crimean War.

"I look just like him, don't I, Mummy?"

"Sweetheart, *please*—you really do need to go and find Sammy. We don't want to lose him now, do we?"

We both watched her walk away, and even after she had disappeared around the side of the house, we kept looking in that direction.

Then, eventually, he said, "Why didn't you tell me?"

"I couldn't. You'd gone. You'd told me to get on with my life."

"I thought you had. I heard you'd married that idiot Morton and that you'd had a child to him . . . and Marie Therese, she confirmed that."

"I needed a husband and I used his name for a while. That's all."

"That's all?"

"I didn't know where you were . . . and *you said*, you said, *Get on with your life*; you said, *Don't wait for me*. You said, *Get married, have children*. You said that, Ralph."

He shook his head. "You should've written; you should've told me."

"You never wrote to *me*," I replied, louder than I'd intended.

I heard him inhale, exhale. And then, before he turned away, as he looked up at the sky, he said, "I didn't expect this . . . wasn't prepared. And I'm sorry, but it's too much . . . too much."

I watched him walk back down the driveway. I didn't call after him or follow him. I knew he needed time, and so did I.

❧

"I like Mr. Stedman," said Lila, wiping crumbs from her mouth as she sat eating toast in the kitchen. "He's funny."

"Mm, he can be."

"Do you think he knew Daddy?"

I shrugged. "Possibly."

"I think he did." She took a gulp of milk. "Mr. Stedman was a soldier, too. He probably knew my daddy," she said, full of self-importance and with the addition of a creamy white mustache.

"There were lots of soldiers, Lila—they didn't *all* know one another."

"Did you know him before the war?"

"Who?" I asked, pretending.

"*Mr. Stedman!*"

"Yes . . . I did. For a short time."

"Was he different?"

"Everyone was different, darling."

"Were you?"

"Yes, even me."

"How were you different?"

"I just was."

"But *how?*"

"Well, I was younger, and more romantic, I suppose."

"What does that mean—romantic?" she asked, picking up the large knife in her small hand and smearing more jam on her toast.

"It means . . . believing in love, and the power of it. Believing in *good*."

"Do you not believe in good now, Mummy?"

"Yes, of course I do. But it was different then."

"You say that a lot . . . *It was different*," she said, mimicking my voice.

I laughed.

Then, "Was *he* romantic?"

"Who?" again pretending.

"Mr. Stedman!"

"What a very strange question to ask . . ."

"I saw him looking at you."

"And . . ."

With a mouthful of toast, she raised her head and fluttered her eyelids. And I laughed—again. I said, "Mr. Stedman was Ottoline's cousin. I met him here, Lila . . . I met him here the summer war was declared."

"Was my daddy here, too?"

I rose to my feet, began to clear the table. *So many questions,* I thought. But she had a right to know the answers to them, a right to know the truth. I said, "Perhaps tomorrow I'll tell you all about it."

"About what?"

"About Mr. Stedman—and your father."

"So they *did* know each other!"

I would tell Lila; of course I would. She deserved to know—with or without Ralph's agreement. I could not lie to her. Like me, she had met her father; unlike me, it had happened early in her life, and at a time when I was with her and able to explain. I would not and could not leave her with unfinished business, secrets and loose ends.

I had expected days, not hours, but later that same evening—as the sky changed and grew ever more ominous, and after I had put an exhausted Lila to bed—there came the sound of a fist banging determinedly on wood. I peered out of the tiny window in the lobby before I unbolted the door.

"I think we need to talk," he said as he stepped inside, shaking the rain from his hair and smelling of whisky.

Chapter Twenty-nine

We stood in the blue-walled room of my twenty-fourth birthday, staring about and not at each other. I'd lit a lamp in there earlier, and now I lit another. As I did so, I could feel his eyes on me. "There," I said, turning to him and attempting a smile.

He said nothing. He reached into his pocket and pulled out his cigarettes.

I said, "I thought you might need some time. I know this is all a shock."

"Time," he repeated, without looking at me. "I think I've lost enough of that as it is, don't you?"

He lifted his cigarette to his lips. His hand was shaking, and I longed to reach out and touch him; tell him that I had thought of him every single day and night of those missing years; tell him that nothing had changed, that nothing mattered to me other than Lila and him—his well-being.

"Is there any whisky in this place?" he asked, gruff, abrupt.

I'd already noted a full bottle in the larder and so went off to fetch it, and a glass.

I was nervous, I was excited and I was also afraid. The man I'd opened the door to, the man I'd seen and spoken with earlier, *was* Ralph. But a different Ralph, I reminded myself in the larder in whispers, and how could he be the same? For a moment, just a moment, panic took hold of me: I didn't know this man, had no idea how badly damaged he was. Shell shock? I knew little about it.

When I returned to the room, as I handed him the bottle and glass, he said, "I knew you'd come—eventually. You see, I knew Ottoline had left this place to you."

"To Lila," I corrected.

"Yes," he said, pouring the honey-colored liquid into the glass, "that was the bit I didn't understand. Why would my cousin leave Delnasay to Morton's child? It didn't make much sense—but then again, very little does these days," he added, offering me a tight smile. He raised his glass. "Good health," he said, then limped toward one of the windows and stood with his back to me, staring out at the stormy twilight.

"Ottoline was Lila's godmother," I began quietly. "I came back here with her—the summer after we met, after the war began. In fact, Lila was born in this room, Ralph, right where you're standing. That very spot is where Ottoline delivered our daughter into the world."

"*Ottoline?* Ottoline delivered her?"

"There were only the two of us. By the time the midwife arrived, well, Lila was here."

"She never told me."

"How could she? No one had heard from you. No one knew where you were."

"Ottoline knew."

"No, I don't think she—"

"She knew," he interrupted, loudly, turning to me. Then, quieter, "She knew and she lied to me. She wrote and told me that you'd married Morton. Told me you'd had a child, a daughter . . . But no, that was later," he said, shaking his head and trying to remember, "not until after Billy, after I wrote to her . . ." He glanced up at me. "Then I heard from Marie Therese, heard that she'd met you— met Mrs. Morton in Northumberland. And I have to say, she was quite enamored by your . . . *our* daughter," he added, closing his eyes for a moment. "But I didn't know, didn't know any dates— when you'd married, when the child had been born—and to be frank, I didn't particularly wish to hear anything more."

"But did you never wonder? Did it never occur to you? And how could you think I'd marry Stanley Morton? How could you think that?"

He stared back at me. "I didn't. I didn't think. Not for four years. I was too busy trying to stay alive."

"Why don't we sit down?" I said.

"I don't wish to sit down."

So I sat down and he remained on his feet by the window, sucking the last dregs from his cigarette. Then he walked over to the marble fireplace, flicked his butt into the grate and, staring down at it, said, "It must have been hard for her, Marie Therese, seeing the child like that, realizing."

"What on earth do you mean? Marie Therese can't have known." I saw him pick up the remnants of a bunch of white heather I'd carefully placed on the mantelshelf earlier, and I said, "Oh, please don't touch that. It's very precious to me."

He moved his hand away. "Somehow, I think she did. I think Marie Therese knew Lila was mine." He turned to face me: "And now that I've seen her, too—well, I'd have to be an imbecile not to recognize my own likeness."

"Ralph, I'm quite sure Marie Therese would have said something had she known—or even suspected."

"She did." He smiled. "She's a very clever woman, my wife."

"What did she say?"

"Yes, very clever," he said again—thinking aloud, remembering. "What did she say?" he repeated. "Only that you were clearly very much in love with your husband; and that your child was sweet and dark haired, and the image of the man in a photograph you'd shown her—a wedding photograph of you and your husband."

I laughed. "But that's a complete lie. There is no photograph."

"As I say, my wife's very clever."

"And Ottoline?" I said after a moment. "Why would she lie to you?"

"Revenge," he said. "She never forgave me for not telling her about Billy . . . You remember, that day he left, after he'd been to see me? She viewed it as a breach of loyalty, almost an act of war," he added, half laughing.

"But how did she know? I never told her."

"No, I told her. My conscience got the better of me after Billy's death. I felt as though I was partly to blame."

"But you weren't. Billy would have gone anyway."

"You're right. But in Ottoline's mind, had I told her, she might have been able to stop him . . . or delay the timing enough so that he wasn't in that place—on the day he was killed."

I shook my head.

"But it wasn't just about Billy," he said. "I think she wanted to protect you, keep me away. Shortly before I left here, she asked—no, no, not asked—*told*—told me that it was in your best interests, and my own, for me to go, and stay away." In reply to my expression, he went on. "She said I was being cruel and selfish, that I couldn't and shouldn't mislead you, no matter what I felt. And she was right, I thought; I was being selfish."

"Ottoline was a hypocrite."

"I don't think she was."

"How can you say that? What about *her* affairs? Her unfaithfulness to Hector?"

He stared at me: "Hector was her rock."

Outside, the storm gathered pace, rushing, fearful, spluttering combative drops against the glass panes, whistling half-forgotten tunes beneath doors and down chimneys.

"Without *him*," said Ralph, continuing, "she would never have survived. You see, Hector understood her . . . her propensity for romance. He understood that she was in love with love, in love with *being* in love. And he understood that it made her extraordinarily vulnerable."

"But why lie about him? To absolve her own guilt?"

"I think it was more complex than that," he said, quieter now, more pensive. And then finally he sat down—on the other sofa, directly opposite me. "Perhaps adding romance and drama to what had been an almost arranged marriage brought some sort of strange freedom to her life . . . And I can't be sure, but I imagine it began as some sort of game—to inspire Hector's jealousy, reignite some passion . . . But with a mind so fragile, a heart so needy, it became an addiction."

"She was like a child."

"Yes, she wanted everyone to live happily ever after, and Hector knew that was impossible. He knew every one of her love affairs— real or imaginary—could only end in separation and sadness. And I think he felt guilty. Guilty that he'd married her . . . And then spent most of their marriage indulging her, trying to make up for robbing her of some happy ending of her own."

"She fell apart after Billy."

"Not completely," he said. "She was sane enough—and cared enough—to make sure you and Lila were provided for. And I'm immensely grateful to her for that."

And when he smiled, my heart leaped, and I felt my solar plexus tighten, my throat close. But that gaze, and his proximity to me, was suddenly too much. I rose to my feet, and, glancing about the room as though searching for something, I said, "Well, it's all very queer, isn't it?"

I moved over to the fireplace, and as I stood clutching the white marble ledge, I remembered the last time I'd hung on there like that, and later—when I'd crawled about on all fours, whimpering like an animal; and how Ottoline—then, *my lady*—had mopped my brow, held my hands and told me to breathe: *Breathe, Pearl!* And I felt myself begin to shake. Not my hands, or my legs, but my whole body.

"I didn't even say good-bye to her."

"She understood."

You don't know that. And then, realizing something more, I turned to him. "You saw her?"

He nodded. "In France . . . I stayed on there after the war."

"With your wife?"

"No, Marie Therese returned to Paris at the end of the war. I was living in Provence—a tiny place north of Avignon. I had no reason, I thought, to come back to England."

"How were they? How was she?"

He stared at me as though weighing something up in his mind. Then he said, "She was dying, Pearl."

As I sat down, I heard him say the words *tumor* and *inoperable.*

"So she knew, she knew she was dying . . ."

"No, Hector told me. He told me she had no idea. No one knew, he said. He had spoken with the doctors alone and asked them not to tell her . . . I didn't see them for long. They made a detour to call in on me . . . She was frail, painfully thin. They had been to the Somme and she spoke about that, and the vast number of crosses—line upon line, she said. In a strange way, I think seeing so many graves helped her. She seemed . . ." He paused and glanced away. "Well, she seemed at peace with everything, reconciled."

"So perhaps she did know . . . and perhaps she did it on purpose."

"Did what on purpose?"

"The accident. She was driving, Ralph. She was the one at the wheel."

He shook his head. "I don't know where you heard that, but Ottoline wasn't well enough to drive. Hector did all the driving."

He went on. "I didn't hear about the accident for some time. And yet, bizarrely, it happened not far from me. It was . . . perhaps a month or so later when I heard about it—from Marie Therese. Then, when I learned Ottoline had left the cottage and land to me, and discovered that she'd left this place to you and your—to Lila," he quickly corrected himself, "I was angry with her. It seemed to me beyond cruel . . . to place us as neighbors." He raised his eyes to me. "It's why I didn't come back at first. But it all makes more sense now. So perhaps you're right. Perhaps Ottoline knew she had only months to live, and knew what she was doing when she revised her last will and—"

He stopped abruptly, winced and moved his hand over his knee, down his shin.

"Is it very painful?"

"Only at night—and in this damp weather. But at least I still have it," he said. "And quite a bit of shrapnel as a souvenir."

We sat in silence for a while. Each of us turned toward the angry darkness pounding at the glass. Then he asked, "Have you worn it all this time?"

At first I wasn't sure what he meant, but then I saw that he was staring at my hands in my lap—where I fiddled with his ring. "Yes."

He closed his eyes.

"Ralph . . ."

"No, don't," he said.

"*Don't?* But you don't know what I was going to say."

"My name—my name's enough," he said, his voice trembling; and with his eyes still closed, barely discernibly, he whispered, "I've imagined hearing you say it for so long . . . so long."

And finally I moved over to him, wrapped my arms around him and held him. And he placed his head on my shoulder and wept.

I never let go. I held on to him for hours in that room. He didn't want to talk about himself—or the war—he said. But he did.

I heard how his map-reading skills and knowledge of France and its language had kept him away from active service. For almost two years he had served with the Artists Rifles as a map-reading instructor in the safety of an Essex training camp. But in the summer of 1916, after the Somme, everything changed. He spoke about his quick promotion—to second lieutenant and then to captain—and about his training for warfare: a sixty-minute talk from his CO and a copy of the *Field Service Pocket Book*. Twenty-four hours later, he'd found himself the only officer in a new company of the Seventh Division and therefore the company commander.

"The most rapidly trained, poorly equipped company commander in the history of the British army," he said.

He mentioned Ypres, the battle of Passchendaele and other places vaguely familiar to me. Places I must have read about. And in a quiet, steady voice, one devoid of any emotion, he told me how killing men had sickened his soul, how his mind had blocked out everything other than the moment-to-moment instinct for survival, and how his body had fallen apart through dysentery. When I said the word *brave*, he flinched. "No, there were others far braver than I." Then, slowly at first, he began counting on his fingers and listing names—surnames that meant nothing to me but something to him.

I didn't say anything. I watched his fingers and listened to his voice as I held him, and I continued to stroke his once golden hair. But as he gathered pace, as the names began to run one into another, I realized there was some masochism in the activity of his hands, some self-cruelty in the reciting of names. I had no wish to know how many men he had seen killed, or how agile his memory was in recalling them. And eventually I said, "No. That's enough. Stop."

And he did.

I had no idea, then, that Ralph had been awarded the Victoria Cross. No idea that *his* war would rarely if ever be mentioned again, and would instead, like the medal, be locked away. What I did know—and all that mattered in that instant—was that he was there, and alive, and with me.

So when he said, "I should go," I said, "No, you can't." And I think I said something about it being too late, or too stormy, or both. Then I turned out the lamps, took his hand and led him upstairs to Ottoline's bedroom. I wrapped him in an eiderdown and lay down next to him, listening to the rain falling from an invisible sky to an invisible dark earth.

"Who gave you the white heather?" he asked.

"Billy."

He pulled me to him. "What are we going to do?"

"I'm not sure . . . But I have to explain to Lila."

"And then?"

"Then . . . I really don't know."

"What about this place? Will you stay here?"

"Only if you're here with me."

"I'm not sure it's to my tastes," he said. "But I have the land."

"How many acres?"

"Ten."

It seemed a paltry amount from an estate of some ten thousand acres, and all the more paltry considering Ralph had been Ottoline's cousin. I said, "Well, I suppose ten acres is ten more than most have."

"No, ten thousand," he replied. And as his grip tightened, I felt his mouth on my hair, and then his voice, heavy and laden with sleep, said, "I'll die if this is just another dream."

Within seconds his breathing deepened and slowed. But I did not close my eyes, nor did I want to. Instead, I continued to hold on to him, my golden boy—battered, scarred and gray, lying beneath an eiderdown on his lost cousin's bed, in his newfound daughter's house. And as the rain continued to pound against the windowpane, my mind bounced back and forth, spewing out random images and words.

I saw Billy Campbell leaping down a hillside with a knapsack on his back, singing a song about good luck and *another time*. I saw a filled-out Harry Rankin polishing up buttons on a uniform; and Mrs. Bart, in her usual chair, peeling a boiled egg and telling me to pace myself because *life is a very long road and one never quite knows where it may lead*; I saw Kitty, her blue eyes as bright as ever, assuring me that my life would be different to her own, and different to my mother's; and then I saw Ottoline, motoring south, toward the sun . . .

And then the rain stopped, and all was still and calm. And as darkness gave way to a flickering light, I unwrapped myself, climbed from the bed and went to the window. Beyond the glass, the earth exhaled in a long sigh, and so sweet was the mist rising, I could almost taste it on my tongue. And so new was the rippling in my heart, I wanted to go outside and dance; dance, just as I had one other dawn so many years before.

I looked down to the grass, and picturing myself, my younger self, and remembering the loneliness beneath the bravado, the optimism despite the odds, I smiled. Kitty would have been proud of *her*, I thought; not because it took a superior sort of girl to be a lady's maid, and certainly not for an illicit affair, but simply because she had not drowned.

When I heard Lila calling for me from the landing, I quickly moved over to the door. She stood in her nightgown. "What are you doing in—"

I put a finger to my lips. She peered past me, into the room, rising up onto her tiptoes to see the bed. I pulled the door shut and took her hand.

"Why is Mr. Stedman asleep?" she whispered, her finger still to her lips, his lack of consciousness more surprising than his presence in a bedroom.

It wasn't yet six, and I had had no sleep. But as I led Lila back toward her bedroom, and amidst more whispered questions—*Is he not very well? . . . Did you put him to bed, Mummy?*—I decided there was no better time.

I pulled the bedcovers over her, sat down and took hold of her hand. I said, "Darling, you know I said I'd tell you about Daddy and Mr. Stedman?"

With her thumb in her mouth, she nodded.

"Well, you see . . . your daddy *is* Mr. Stedman."

The strange thing about delivering what to an adult might be earth-shattering, is that to a child the world can reorder itself in the blink of an eye. Matters deemed sensitive are only so if a grown-up has determined them as such. And Lila, whose father had been a void filled with a name that meant little to her, was that morning offered something tangible and real. A man she had met, talked to and liked; a man who was alive.

And so her reaction was not one of shock, dismay, recrimination or anger. She pondered on what I had said for only a few seconds, and then she said, "Did you know he was going to be here?"

"No. I thought . . . Well, I thought he had died in the war."

"Oh, poor Mummy," she said, sitting up and wrapping her arms around my waist.

And it was then that I finally cried. As though I had been holding my breath for her, holding my breath for six years. She got out of her bed, riffled in her yet-to-be-unpacked bag for a handkerchief, and as she handed it to me, I saw the embroidered initials, RSS. She stroked my brow, showered my face in sweet kisses.

A little while later, after she had led me down to the kitchen, and whispering once more in soothing tones, she asked me about Henry Gibson. And I told her. I sat at the kitchen table and told her about her grandfather.

Together we made tea. And then, clutching a teapot, I followed her back upstairs as she slowly—very slowly and very carefully—carried the tray with three cups and a jug of milk. I sat down in the armchair by the window, as instructed, and watched her pour the tea, her hand struggling with the weight of the pot. She perched herself on the edge of the bed, staring, watching, waiting. And when this man—*her daddy*—eventually stirred and stretched out,

I saw him open his eyes and turn to her, and I saw him smile as he said her name.

He sat up, glanced at me briefly and then turned back to Lila. And having waited patiently, and for far longer than the minutes it had taken him to stir, and dying—positively dying—to say one word, she said, "Here you are, Daddy. We made you a cup of tea."

Ralph kept his eyes fixed on her—frowning, smiling, mesmerized, his mouth from time to time trembling as he listened. "You haven't got any jamas, have you? . . . Not everyone has jamas . . . Mummy thought you were dead . . . I had a funny feeling in my tummy when I saw you . . ."

Only once, as Lila took his cup and poured him more tea, did he look at me. Then he stared at me with a half smile and raised eyebrows, as if to say, *How?*

Later that day, before my body finally succumbed to exhaustion, I stood at the bedroom window once more. I watched Ralph and Lila walk out from the house and down the driveway hand in hand. And I could've sworn I heard Ottoline's voice: "There. There, now . . . What did I say? Didn't I tell you?"

She had.

Epilogue

Delnasay
June 28, 1925

Dear Theodore,

Thank you for your letter, and for the book & card you sent
for Lila—whose thank-you note I enclose. Luckily the fine
weather held out and she had a splendid birthday party in the
garden. Ralph led the singing—a baritone, decidedly operatic
version of "Happy Birthday"—and took photographs, including
one of her as she raised her eyes to him and blew out ten candles
(which I also enclose). He managed a spectacular fall in the egg
& spoon race, and another—even more spectacular—in the
sack race. It caused his children & their friends great hilarity
until sympathy overcame them and they all rushed to console
the giant, clumsy-footed but nevertheless gallant loser.

Rodney is with us once again for the summer. Lila adores him, and he is particularly good with Billy, and of course I have Mrs. Lister—now universally known as Granny Lister—to help with baby Kitty. She is completely besotted and has abandoned all efforts in the kitchen in favor of what she calls her "grandmother's duties." (Ralph is convinced she actually believes she is the children's grandmother, and in the absence of any other, she does an excellent job. I really can't imagine she will ever return south.) And Amy arrives next week with her new beau, a man she claims quite different to the others. We shall see!

I must say, you did make me laugh with your reference to our "antique perambulator," but it does the job fine and as you already know, Ralph is not one for unnecessary expense or luxury, and I quite like the fact that it is old, served the Campbell boys and has now served Lila, Billy & Kitty. And yes, we have finally finished the hallway—and you are most welcome to your pick of stags' heads & weaponry! It is now pink—a darkish pink—and it was a family effort with all of us, bar Kitty (who looked on from that fine baby carriage), having a hand in its transformation. Ralph has hung what he calls the Stedman Portraits: the one of me he finished last summer when you were here, which was in fact produced from a sketch he made of me in 1914 at King's Cross station, along with his rather brooding self-portrait, and his latest—of Lila. Billy & Kitty will no doubt be added one day, though I'm not sure Ralph will ever again have time for family portraits as he is struggling to keep up with the demand for his paintings and is working all hours in preparation for his forthcoming exhibition in London. His latest dilemma is whether to continue with the figurative bucolic landscapes of his prewar days, which seem to sell so well, or go in a new direction—one he prefers—and produce more abstract work.

As regards our marriage, it was quick and quiet and without any fuss. There has been no announcement, of course. (No one knew, apart from you & Rodney, and we are both extremely grateful to you for handling Marie Therese so well—and for seeing to the documentation & paperwork, particularly the children's birth certificates.) From the moment I told Lila, almost exactly four years ago, she never doubted that we were married, and to her and everyone else in the locality, I have been Mrs. Stedman for all of this time, so there has been no change, nothing new for me to get used to, and it is very queer for me to think of myself as a "newlywed"! And no, Ralph is no longer bitter about Marie Therese, that she held out for so long despite Lila—and Billy & Kitty's births. He says it is time to look forward and not back.

Rodney accompanied us to the registry office at Elgin and acted as a witness, along with one of the clerks there. As for "a celebration" . . . there was none, as such. But Ralph took a hip flask, and on the way back here we stopped at a particular place overlooking Delnasay & the glen. We left Rodney in the car while we walked up the hillside—to the cairn at the top. We each placed a stone, took a nip or two from the flask, and Ralph said some words I will treasure until the day I die. But perhaps most poignantly—when we looked down, we could see the

*shapes of Lila, Billy, Mrs. L. & the "antique perambulator"
moving along the road by the river.*

*Finally, I am touched by & grateful for your words. How-
ever, I thought we agreed last summer that there would be no
more guilt or recrimination? It was, after all, thirty-five years
ago, and you did not know, so how could you have done anything differently? I realize now that life is never how we plan,
and that judgment is the luxury of inexperience. Rest assured, I
am happy—immeasurably happy. I consider myself blessed to
be living amidst such beauty with the man I love and our three
children. I could want for nothing more. And I try to live by
Ottoline's motto—to seize every moment and make each one
count.*

Yours,
Pearl

*PS: I forgot to say, Ralph and I are to have a honeymoon of
sorts. A holiday (our first) at Biarritz in October—along with
Mrs. Lister, two dogs & three children!*

Dear Mr. Godley,

*I hope you are well. Thank you for the book of poems. It
was very kind of you and a bit of a coincidence as well because
I write poetry. I had my birthday party in the garden and seventeen friends not including Billy because he wasn't actually
invited and Kitty doesn't count anyway. Kitty is our new baby*

but you won't remember her because she wasn't here the last time you came. She doesn't do much but Granny Lister who is not really our Granny loves her to pieces and calls her the Queen of Babies!!! Daddy is taking me camping next week and says we will be able to stay up all night to look for shooting stars. I have already seen three. We are not taking Billy as he would only cry for Mummy and Kitty is just a baby.

Yours Faithfully,
Ottoline Stedman
(Aged 10)

Acknowledgments

This novel is set in the landscapes of my childhood and early life, and much of my inspiration came from people who once inhabited those places. They seemed to be waiting in the wings to be given their cue, and I am grateful to all of them.

I am grateful to my father, to whom this book is dedicated and whose boyhood memories of the interwar years are inexorably woven into my writing, not least this novel. I am also indebted to my brother, Geoff Sample, for his help and expert advice on birds and birdsong, and the natural history of Northumberland and Scotland.

Once again, I would like to thank my mother, Elizabeth, for being my first reader, and for her enthusiastic support; and my husband, Jeremy, for his love and unwavering kindness.

Finally, thanks to my agent, Deborah Schneider, and to my editor, Jenn Fisher, and the team at Berkley and Penguin Random House USA.

JK

HAMPSHIRE, ENGLAND

MARCH 2016

The

ECHO *of* TWILIGHT

JUDITH KINGHORN

QUESTIONS FOR DISCUSSION

1. The relationship between Pearl and Ottoline is central to the novel and, at times, complex. Was this relationship convincingly developed, and who do you think was more loyal—Pearl or Ottoline?

2. Discuss the ways in which a failure to tell the truth caused misunderstanding and altered Pearl's path. Who do you think was the most honest character in the novel?

3. Ottoline's perception of marriage and her attitude to fidelity are clouded. Can infidelity be excused in an arranged marriage or in one in which there is mental instability?

4. Women's attitudes to their roles at home and at work changed during the First World War. How is this depicted in the novel, and

why was being in domestic service "no longer something to be proud of"?

5. Discuss the novel's depiction of early twentieth-century morality, including attitudes concerning sex and pregnancy outside marriage. How did the men's behavior contrast with the women's?

6. Were you surprised by Hector Campbell's attitude concerning his wife's unfaithfulness? Why do you think he tolerated her behavior?

7. Loneliness, mental illness, and depression are recurrent themes in the novel. Discuss how the author handled them, and which characters suffer and why.

8. Part three of the novel takes place after the end of the war. Discuss the ways in which its effects continued to be seen and felt by the characters.

9. Apart from Pearl, which character do you feel undergoes the most dramatic transformation in the novel?

10. Were you shocked by Ottoline's and Hector's deaths? Who do you think was driving the car, and do you believe it was an accident?

11. Was Kitty's lie to Theodore Godley about the baby (Pearl) dying understandable and forgivable? How did you feel about this revelation, and did it alter your view of Kitty?

12. Is Ralph Stedman a convincing romantic hero, despite his absence for most of the story? What was it about him that Pearl fell in love with? Did you believe he survived the war?

13. Lila innocently and inadvertently reveals to Ralph that she is his daughter. How realistic is this exchange, and how do you foresee Ralph's future relationship with Lila?

14. Which of Pearl's relationships had the greatest influence on her—her relationship with Kitty, Ottoline, Lila, or Ralph?

15. At the end of the novel, Pearl hears Ottoline say, "Didn't I tell you?" Why do you think Pearl hears Ottoline's voice at that moment, and what does this question allude to?